Of Black Holes and Prophets

Jack Gerard

TABLE OF CONTENTS

Prologue, 850 BC

In the ancient days when offerings were made to false gods, a man known as Epsilon-Giga came to the offering place and said "Please hear me, god of the Federation: I have done everything you have asked me to do. Now answer me, god of the Federation, that all those who have come today to watch, that you would convince this crowd to come back to you, Oh god of the Federation!"

Then the god of the Federation sent a missile from space, that upon entering the atmosphere, became a fiery projectile, and it fell on the offering that Epsilon-Giga offered, and both the offering and even the water that had been poured on the offering by the priest of the false gods was consumed by fire.

The crowd that witnessed this became fearful of the god of the Federation, laid on the ground, and said, "The god of the Federation, He is truly god and our leader."

Stories of the past, as told by Jack Gerard, Oracle of the Federation

Prologue, 2192

The fact that you are reading this indicates that this book made it back to the 21st century. So, you can think of this book as a prophet. Sort of.

Do you believe in time travel? You know, where you can go back in time or race ahead to the future. If you are like most people in the 21st century, you would be unsure of your answer. You might first turn to a physicist friend and ask them how time travel could be managed. They would crush your time-travel aspirations with the following statement:

"I'm sorry. You would need to go faster than the speed of light, which is not possible."

"Why can't I go faster than the speed of light?" you may ask.

"Because of Einstein's formula:

$E = mc^2$."

A derivation of this formula shows that as you approach the speed of light, designated 'c' in the formula, your mass, designated as 'm,' would become infinitely massive. There is not enough energy, designated 'E,' to push you any faster."

If you were feeling puckish, you might retort to your physicist friend, "Can't I go on a diet to reduce my mass?"

Your physicist friend would simply shake their head and mumble something, then walk away. If you were listening to the mumbling carefully, you might make out the word "idiot."

I am not an idiot, and I believe in time travel for two reasons. The first reason is somewhat philosophical. It embodies thoughts that we have every day that have a huge influence on how we live.

These thoughts are called memories and dreams. I am not kidding. Memory is simply remembering the past. We all have memories. Sometimes we relive these memories in vivid color, over and over again. Memories play an important part in life. They provide us with information that is vital. For instance, I remember making vows to my fiancée at our wedding ceremony. Based on this remembrance of my vows, I remain committed to my wife. It is also important that I remember my children, who were born many years ago. A group of people should remember that, many years before, their group became a city, state, or country.

Then there are dreams. These are not as precise as memories, but they drive us to do things to fulfill them. You may dream that someday you will become a physicist. Based on this dream, you will work hard in your math classes in elementary school, take high school physics, then attend a college to get a PhD in physics, do a postdoc at a prestigious lab, etc. You would rearrange a significant part of your life to achieve your dream.

Memories and dreams have set the course of history. For example, Black Americans, when they were enslaved in America, dreamed of freedom. A number of white people in America also dreamed of setting the Blacks free. This dream, in one form or another, was the basis for the Civil War. Later, people would remember that the Civil War had been fought to end slavery, although I know that some folks think the Civil War happened because the federal government trampled on southern states' rights. Whatever. I digress.

Whole cultures, nations, and empires have dreams and memories as their basis. There is another thing that has its basis in memories and dreams: religion.

It is part of my job as Oracle of the Federation to know something about religions. I am not an expert on all world religions, but I do know something about Judaism and Christianity. In my library are many books and sacred texts from all major world religions. Of these books, the Christian Bible is my favorite. One reason it is my favorite is that it contains a large amount of the text for Judaism in the Old Testament, and Christianity in the New Testament.

In this Bible, Jews and Christians alike are commanded to remember the past. The reason for this is twofold: one is to keep people from making the same mistakes as their forefathers; the second is to show how their God takes care of His people.

There are also large portions of this sacred text that talk about what their God is going to do in the future. Christians and Jews alike call this 'prophecy.'

So, as you can see, memories and dreams have played a major role in the affairs of nations, cultures, and religions. Without memories and dreams, humanity would be a hollow shell.

One can think of memories and dreams (or prophecies) as a form of time travel. All you need to do is remember or dream, and you can avoid the messiness of letting the forward progress of time take its course. By exercising dreams and memories, we are able to effectively plan and act in the present.

Now for the second reason that you might want to consider time travel as possible: black holes. Some of you know something about black holes. Black holes are super-massive bodies in our universe that are endowed with tremendous forces of gravity. The force of gravity is so huge that even light cannot escape. Because of this, black holes are sometimes referred to as infinitely deep gravity wells.

What does your science in the 21st century know about black holes? Not as much as they would like to know. Your scientists have their best minds working on the enigma we call black holes. They have theorized that there may be a black hole at the center of every large galaxy. They have even found one that exists at the center of the Milky Way Galaxy, known as Sagittarius A*. They know that the black hole is surrounded by an accretion disk. The material and radiation in this disk come from space around the black hole and have been captured by the black hole's gravity. Most of the matter and radiation come from stars that orbit close to the black hole. This material and radiation orbit around the black hole and spiral into it. Eventually, the material in the accretion disk reaches a point referred to as the 'event horizon.'

You are probably wondering what happens at the event horizon. I can safely tell you that the laws of Newtonian physics largely no longer apply. Even the laws of Einstein, Bohr, Heisenberg, Hubble, and Chandra are stretched to their limits—and at times, broken.

That is what this book is about: time travel in the 22nd century. However, there is more. There are the people who are involved. And wherever people are involved, there are memories and dreams, compassion and abuse, love and hate, hopelessness and hope, faith and uncertainty, corruption and redemption, and above all: love. It is also about war and peace—and, strangely enough, aliens that are vaguely familiar to us. There are monsters, dragons, and a multi-headed beast.

By the way, I am adding lyrics from popular music from the 1960s and 1970s to this narrative that may resonate with some of the readers. I have one of the largest vinyl collections on the planet Beyond, and I find these lyrics add another dimension to the story. I find that poetry is a powerful advocate between the dry facts of a narrative and an engaging story for the reader.

So, if this book is in your possession, sit back and enjoy. However, be aware that this is a cautionary tale. We have one Earth—let's not mess it up. Also, keep in mind that there is something much larger than humanity: a powerful, sovereign God. We may think we are in total control of history, but we are not.

One last thing: I would like to thank Federation Admirals Kathryn Henderson, Ming Chu, and General Jackson for their recollections concerning the Rebellion of 2170 and their personal memoirs. I am grateful to Dr. Hays, who passed away last year, for his technical assistance.

I dedicate this book to the late Dr. Myron Abbot, whose memoirs show how one man can make a difference—especially when that man is guided by God.

Jack Gerard,

December 1, 2192

Oracle of the Federation

Admiralty, the Planet Beyond

Chapter 1

The Voice of One Crying in the Wilderness
Mohave Dessert, July, 2010

The wall on which the prophets wrote

Is cracking at the seams

Upon the instruments of death

The sunlight brightly gleams

When every man is torn apart

With nightmares and with dreams

Will no one lay the laurel wreath

When silence drowns the screams

Greg Lake, Ian McDonald, Michael Rex Giles, Peter John Sinfield, Robert Fripp

King Crimson Band

It was the end of a long shift. Alex Hays was driving down Highway 58 on a merciless day, with temperatures hovering around 115 degrees Fahrenheit. His mind wandered into thoughts of what it would be like to sit by his apartment pool, drinking one of his craft beers. He still had an hour to drive, looking for trouble. More daydreaming. He listened to rock band U2 on the radio. Then the two-way radio destroyed his reverie with a call.

"Officer Hays, are you west of Barstow?" the radio croaked.

"Affirmative. What do you have?"

"A motorist reported a loony in pajamas walking along Highway 58, just west of Barstow. We request that you pick him up and bring him home to the asylum."

"Roger and out."

This wasn't the first time he had to round up a loony. Over the past year, he had caught and returned about a half-dozen. Today was especially dangerous with the elevated temperature. An escaped loony could die of heatstroke or heat exhaustion in a matter of minutes. Alex made a U-turn to reach the loony. He flipped on his siren in hot pursuit. After about five minutes, he saw the escapee from the loony bin. Alex pulled in front of him and stepped out of his car. What he saw really confused him. The loony was dressed in pajama-like garb, but not the kind issued at the insane asylum. They looked more like something out of a *Buck Rogers* science fiction movie.

He walked toward the loony cautiously, held out his hands, and spoke in a calming voice. "I am Officer Alex Hays. It's okay, I'm here to help you and get you back home. You must be hot and thirsty. I have some ice water in my car to help you cool down."

The loony replied, "I don't belong here! You can't take me home because I'm not from here."

"Where are you from?" asked Alex Hays.

"It's not just where I am from, but *when* and where I am from."

"Okay, where and when are you from?" Alex was beginning to lose patience.

"I'm from the center of the galaxy, 160 years in the future!"

This confirmed to Officer Hays that this was a certified loony. "Let's get you in the car and get you home," said Alex.

"But your car is not capable of time travel!" the loony protested.

"Get in the car so I can get you out of this heat and get you some ice water." Alex was beginning to feel disturbed by this guy. Once in the car, he turned on the radio to the tunes of *Pink Floyd – Dark Side of the Moon*.

Once at the asylum, Alex escorted the loony to the front desk. Sally Moreno, whom Alex had met before, was working at the desk. He was attracted to her, but it was obvious she was much smarter than Alex. In other words, Alex was too chicken to ask her out on a date.

"I brought a friend of yours back," said Alex.

"I don't recognize him. He's wearing an interesting outfit," responded Sally.

"A real Buck Rogers. Well, he's clearly touched in the head. We can't turn him loose in this heat."

"Okay, we'll take him and have him evaluated tomorrow." Then Sally turned to an orderly and had him escort Mr. Buck Rogers to the annex.

Alex finally found the courage he needed and asked, "Are you available tonight? We could watch the new movie *Werewolf*."

"I'm working the night shift, so I'm not available. Thanks for asking."

"How about tomorrow night?" asked Alex.

"Sounds good. What time?"

* * *

That night, a real thumper came in—the kind of thunderstorm that holds some in awe, others in terror, and for most, it's just another desert thunderstorm. The lightning came fast and furious, and the wind blew with such ferocity that it shook the windows of the asylum. Some present at the asylum reported a strange glow over the asylum annex that was transient in nature.

As the storm began, the nurses and orderlies herded the residents into the storm shelter. This always turned into a comedy of errors, since the residents sometimes ascribed biblical meaning to the weather pattern. Many of them thought the world was coming to an end and began to pontificate to the nurses and orderlies that they needed to get right with God because His judgment was upon them. Then the storm ended as quickly as it began.

The newest resident, Mr. Buck Rogers, was in the one-story annex, which served as a padded cell until a psychiatrist could properly diagnose the patient's condition. After the thunderstorm, this was the last area to be searched by the asylum staff. When Sally reached the patient's room, she discovered that it had been destroyed. The only thing left was the foundation. And there was no patient.

The only thing Sally could say was, "I guess you went the way of Dorothy and Toto."

***

"What did you think of the movie?" asked Alex.

"I thought it was pretty stupid," responded Sally. "Let's talk about something more important."

"Like what?" inquired Alex.

"Like what you are going to be doing in the future," said Sally.

Alex thought for a minute. He did have plans. He was saving up his money so he could attend Stanford University. But he was afraid that Sally would laugh at him.

"I'm sorry to put you on the spot. Go ahead and tell me your dreams," persisted Sally.

Finally, Alex found the courage—or maybe Sally found it for him. Then he blurted out, "I would like to go to college and get a degree in engineering."

There was silence for what seemed like hours—or was it seconds? Then Sally smiled and said, "That is a marvelous idea. What grades did you get in high school?"

"I got A's in math and physics."

"You did better than me in those subjects. But I made up for it in biology and sociology. That's why I went to college to be a nurse in a psychiatric hospital. How will you pay for college?"

"I've been saving up my money from being a highway patrolman, and my father passed away last year and left me an inheritance."

"I'm sorry to hear about your father. Were you close to him?" asked Sally.

"Yes." Then Alex fell silent. He had been quite close to his father—a great man from the 'Greatest Generation.' Finally, Alex broke the silence. "He was a great man. He was a machinist. I know it might seem strange, but he grew up during the Depression, and his parents couldn't afford to send him to college. He was somewhat of a hero in World War II. He was a platoon sergeant in the 2nd Armored Division—a platoon of machinists. His platoon kept the

Sherman tanks going, even after getting blown apart by the German Tiger and Panther tanks. The guy was a genius. He could make anything. After the war, he ran a machine shop for a large manufacturing company. The plant manager finally recognized his genius and promoted him to engineer."

Alex paused. Why did he tell Sally so much about his father—especially on their first date?

"I'm sorry for telling you so much about my father."

Sally broke the silence. "I think you told me about your father because there's a lot of your father in you. You are a fascinating person, Alex. I hope to get to know you better."

***

Six months later, Alex was in crisis. The source of the crisis lay on his kitchen table in the form of a letter—an unopened letter from Stanford University. It might contain good news, but if that were true, it also meant that he and Sally might have to part ways.

He finally opened the letter. It began with this paragraph:

Alex Hays,

We are pleased to extend your acceptance into the Stanford Engineering Program. We are also pleased to offer you a full-ride scholarship, which includes covering expenses related to tuition, housing, books, and other incidentals related to the completion of your degree…

The next paragraph read:

We were especially pleased with your proposal on modifications to the Stanford Linear Accelerator that would enable more precise capture of subatomic particles. Some of our researchers would like you to work with them on Stanford's linear accelerator to assist in bringing your proposed improvements to life. The amount of time you spend on this project will need to be worked out between you, your professors, and the researchers.

Alex stared at this paragraph for a very long time. He was utterly dumbstruck. The idea for the improvements wasn't his—it was his father's. Alex and his father had talked about the concept during a fishing trip in the Sierra Nevada Mountains.

Then the doorbell rang. It was Sally.

"Hi, Sally! I have something important to discuss with you. Please sit down. Can I get you a beer?"

"Sure—but I have something to say first!"

Alex cocked his head. "Go ahead."

"I've been offered a new position at Agnew State Hospital near Santa Clara, California."

At hearing this, Alex broke out in uncontrolled laughter. He laughed so hard he fell to the floor and couldn't get up.

Finally, Sally asked, "What's so funny?"

"I've been accepted to Stanford University with a full-ride scholarship! My schooling and your job are only twenty miles apart!"

"I *knew*—I *dreamed*—that you would be accepted!" exclaimed Sally.

She fell into a chair and started laughing uncontrollably. The two of them were so loud that the neighbor in the downstairs apartment began banging on the ceiling with a broom handle, yelling, "Would the two of you keep it down? My wife is trying to take a nap!"

Sally and Alex stopped laughing and looked at each other.

Alex said, "Let's go to Las Vegas and get married!"

Chapter 2

A Physicist is Born
Palo Alto, California, February, 2020

Sally got off work early because of her contractions. The birth of her son was near. The first thing she did was call Alex on the telephone.

"Alex, come home now. What? I don't care if you're on the verge of getting a Nobel Prize in Physics—get your butt home now! Yes, I'm in labor. Okay, I love you, too."

Thirty minutes later, the screeching of tires could be heard coming around the corner. A car door opened and slammed shut. Then Alex burst through the door.

"Okay, don't panic, I've got everything covered. Let's see, what do I need to bring?"

"Settle down, Alex. Just take me to the hospital—they'll take it from there," replied Sally, a grin on her face.

***

Lamaze training had not prepared Alex for what he was about to witness: back labor. There was a lot of blood and gore. Alex thought that his normally gentle wife had turned into Godzilla during the transition phase of labor.

Then the doctor said, "Relax now!"

Screech! There was the baby's big, misshapen head sticking out of the birth canal, his body still inside Sally. The baby's head was screaming. This was the most barbaric thing Alex had ever seen—and it was happening to Sally. Yet she remained in control, gave one final push, and out popped the baby.

While the hospital staff cleaned up the carnage, the doctor said, "I don't give out too many 10s on the Apgar score, but this is one healthy baby."

The only thing Alex could think was: *This is one ugly baby.* It looked like Winston Churchill in miniature. Then something clicked inside of him—a sense of love for the baby that was only exceeded by his love for his wife.

"His name is Robert!" declared Alex. The doctor and nurses in the room began to clap…

***

Robert was a precocious child. He didn't learn to walk until he was 13 months old, but he started talking at 10 months—speaking in full sentences. He learned to read proficiently at age three, and by four he not only knew how to add and subtract, but had also memorized his multiplication tables from one to ten. At age ten, he read Sir Isaac Newton's *Philosophiœ Naturalis Principia Mathematica*… in Latin.

But Robert was an awkward boy. He didn't participate in sports unless he had to. And when he did play in his Physical Education class, he was always the last one picked for a team.

He had few friends. His only real friend in early childhood was Brad. Brad had Trisomy 23 Syndrome and was profoundly mentally handicapped—but Brad loved Robert, and Robert took to tutoring Brad to help increase his intellect. At first, Robert did this as a challenge. But then Brad began to learn—so much so that the school was eventually able to move him out of the special needs program and into regular classroom studies.

Brad and Robert remained close friends until high school, when Brad died from heart complications associated with his condition. Robert was devastated. He neglected his studies and was held back in his junior year. As tragic as this seemed, it turned out to be a blessing. Because he flunked his junior year, he met Betsy.

Betsy was the smartest student in her class. She was also the homecoming queen. She could do anything she set her mind to. And all the boys were scared to death of her.

Betsy had one small quirk—she was very religious. Not just religious, but she claimed to be a disciple of Jesus Christ. She tried to convert everyone to Christianity. She was so zealous in her mission that when she walked down the hall, students would part like the Red Sea to avoid her proselytizing.

Betsy and Robert met in Trigonometry class. Despite her intelligence, Betsy struggled in Trig. She had heard of Robert's genius—and also of his fall from it—so she sat next to him on the first day of class.

Robert took no notice. It had only been a year since he'd lost his only friend.

So Betsy took the initiative. "Can you help me with my homework?"

"Are you talking to me?" asked Robert.

Now, Betsy was the homecoming queen: beautiful, smart, articulate. Robert was short, awkward, and had pimples all over his face. The only person he usually spoke to was himself.

"I'm talking to you!" said Betsy. Her smile was as warm as a July afternoon breeze that could melt any ice cream cone.

"Um, sure, I guess," muttered Robert.

"Okay, after school you can come over to my house. My mom always bakes peanut butter cookies for me and my friends."

That small incident started a love affair that would span decades—and would change the world.

First, there was a change in Robert. His pimples went away. Then his grades shot up to straight A's. He grew six inches in one year. He started working out and became quite muscular. He joined the high school cross-country team (he was too uncoordinated to compete in other sports). He earned his varsity letter in that sport, and the left sleeve of his letterman sweater was covered with medals. He became president of the High School Science Club, and his project—*The Theoretical Probability of Time Travel: Potential Exceedances of the Speed of Light Near Black Holes*—won first place at the National Science Fair.

Some said Robert's hormonal system simply corrected itself, and that accounted for the dramatic change. But they were wrong.

Some said it was Betsy. They were partly right. It's true that Robert and Betsy were in love. And Betsy did much to help Robert grow and mature. She taught him how to behave in social situations. She encouraged him to stretch himself academically and physically.

This does not tell the whole story, however. It really had to do with Betsy's quirky religion.

Before Robert met Betsy, he had no meaning in life. He was chronically depressed and, at times, suicidal. Betsy introduced him to Christianity—not the kind that most people practice on Sundays, but she introduced Robert to *Jesus*. And that Jesus died for Robert. And that Jesus had a plan for Robert.

This was new for Robert. His parents had never gone to church, so he was a blank slate when it came to religious matters. He started reading his Bible every day, participated in Bible studies after school, and eventually began leading them—especially before cross-country meets.

Chapter 3

A Married Physicist Goes Missing
Palo Alto, California, March 2050

Robert Hays and Betsy ended up going to the same college. Since Robert's father, Alex, had gone to Stanford University, that was Robert's first choice. Also, Robert's SAT scores were off the charts. It didn't hurt that his father had graduated *cum laude* from Stanford and continued to work at the Stanford Linear Accelerator.

Betsy had no trouble getting into the Psychology program at Stanford. After all, she'd earned straight A's in high school. But she was on a mission too: she had a vision to help people with psychological problems. Part of her drive came from watching Robert tutor Brad. If Robert could help Brad—who had Trisomy 23—then she wanted to help people with disabling mental illness, for the glory of God.

After seven years of hard work and sacrifice, Robert and Betsy received their PhDs, got married, and pursued their respective careers. Everything was going well between them—until Betsy noticed some strange behaviors in Robert.

At first, it seemed rather benign. Robert seemed to drift into daydreams, as if he wasn't really present. One day, while on a picnic, she asked him about it.

"Robert, you don't seem to be yourself. You seem to be daydreaming about something. Can you tell me about it?"

"Uh, sure." Robert paused for about a minute before continuing. "I was thinking about a new theory that could revolutionize physics. But I need to visualize it."

"Visualize what?" asked Betsy.

"Visualize what time looks like in the space-time continuum."

"Say again?" asked Betsy, with a quizzical look on her face.

"Seeing time in the context of the space-time continuum. You know—Albert Einstein's general theory of relativity."

"Why do you need to visualize time?"

"To see what's happening near black holes, especially when matter and radiation fall into the black hole's event horizon."

Betsy pondered a minute. She and Robert had talked about black holes before—how they're super-massive and have exceedingly high densities. The gravitational forces associated with this 'gravity well' were so strong that all matter and even light couldn't escape once they crossed the event horizon. She then said, "I have a question. You've explained black holes to me before. I understand that they are super-massive objects that draw everything in—but you've never really explained what the event horizon is."

"It's a special place where the laws of classical physics no longer apply. Time becomes frozen at the event horizon. Physicists don't really know what happens there, especially as matter and light approach it."

"How do you visualize time?" asked Betsy.

"The simplest way is to start with the three dimensions of space—length, height, and depth. Now, take one of those dimensions—say height—and replace it with the dimension of time."

"Now you've lost me!" interrupted Betsy.

"Let me show you with the help of our picnic blanket. Here, you hold two corners and I'll hold the other two. Stretch it tight. What do we have now?"

"A stretched-out blanket!"

"No, we have a model of a flat plane."

"It sags a bit in the center."

"Ignore the sag for now, Betsy. Now I need something spherical that has some weight to it," said Robert, looking around.

"How about this orange?" replied Betsy.

"That'll work. Put the orange on the blanket."

"I can't—I'm holding two corners."

"Oh, yeah. Let's put the blanket down and place the orange on it. Then grab the corners again and stretch it out," said Robert.

So there stood Robert and Betsy, holding a stretched-out blanket with an orange in the middle. People around them began to notice the strange demonstration and wandered over to watch. Some thought it was a religious rite, or maybe some kind of paranormal behavior.

Robert noticed the growing audience. He turned to one of the young men nearby and asked, "Could you take the orange and roll it across this stretched-out blanket?"

The young man rolled the orange.

"Did it go straight, or did it curve in its trajectory?" asked Robert.

"It went straight—more or less," responded the young man.

Robert then turned to the crowd. "Could someone bring me that rock by the tree? Yeah, the round white one." One of the young women fetched it and brought it over.

Robert told her, "Place the rock in the middle of the blanket."

Once it was placed, Robert asked, "What effect is the rock having on the blanket?"

"The blanket is really sagging in the middle," she replied.

"In other words, the blanket's flatness is being distorted by the presence of the heavy rock. Could someone roll the orange across the blanket now?"

A young man rolled the orange onto the blanket. It curved and rolled directly into the rock.

"What does this represent?" asked Robert.

"That oranges like white rocks?" someone joked.

"No!" said Robert. "It represents how massive objects in space deform the space-time continuum, creating what we call gravity. In extreme cases, this is what happens to matter and light near a black hole. They can't escape. The point at which this happens is called the event horizon."

One of the young women in the crowd said, "This is what they're trying to teach me in my physics class, but after your demonstration, I finally get it! Thank you so much. I do have one question: What happens to matter and light *at* the event horizon?"

"That's what I'm investigating at Lawrence Livermore Lab," responded Robert.

At this, the audience began to clap. Robert gave a slight bow, but when he raised his head, he found himself facing two military men. One of them motioned for him to follow.

"Excuse me, everyone. Duty calls. Honey, I should be home before dinner. I'll call you if anything comes up."

That was the last Betsy saw of him for two weeks.

When he finally came home, he was sullen and quiet. He looked exhausted.

Betsy asked, "Where have you been? Our family and the police have been looking everywhere for you."

"I can't tell you. It's top secret," was all he said.

Interlude

Journal of Betsy Hays

Betsy Hay's played a central role in Robert Hays's conversion to Christianity and his maturation into manhood. She was a brilliant woman who had a special ability in seeing the potential in other people. After her untimely death from ovarian cancer, her personal journal was discovered by members of her church after Robert mysteriously disappearance in the Great Blizzard of 2061. This Journal was donated to Library of Congress, and has made its way to the Library of the Federation. I have taken some of her journal entries that I believe are essential to understanding her faith, and her point of view on the decent of Robert into Schizophrenia, and his alleged delusions.

Jack Gerard,

Oracle of the Federation

September 10, 2036: Today I met with Robert Hays, who helped me with my Trigonometry. He is not much to look at. However, he is absolutely brilliant! It is so refreshing talking to a boy who is so smart. I have grown weary of boys who are stupid and have no interest in learning. Robert is different. Really different. He seems lost in his thoughts, but occasionally, he comes back to reality with some very profound things to say.

Unfortunately, he is not a Christian. This is one area where he has no understanding at all. I asked him about God and Jesus, but he had no clue! When I told him that God created the universe, he just gave me a blank stare. So, I told him about how God created the earth and the heavens, and he became very interested in what I was saying. I could see the "light turning on" in his head. We talked about God for about an hour, then returned to our trig assignment.

September 24, 2036: I met with Robert again after school. Before we started our trig study, Robert asked me an interesting question:

"Why did God make humans?"

His question threw me off for a minute before I responded, "God made humans so that they could glorify God and have fellowship with Him."

Then he asked, "How can we glorify God?"

I thought about this, then replied, "We glorify God by acknowledging Him as God, and by the way we live."

"How can I glorify God if I become a scientist?" he asked.

"A good way is to study God's creation and to stand in awe of God's creative power," I replied. Then I added, "But before you can do this, you need to have a personal relationship with God. Do you want to have a personal relationship with God?"

"How do I have a personal relationship with God?" he asked.

"By believing that Jesus Christ is the Son of God, and that Jesus died for your sins, and that He rose from the dead three days later," I replied. I then told him to read the Gospel of John in the Bible, and we could talk about it next time we met.

October 1, 2036: Robert has accepted Jesus as his Lord and Savior! I can't believe it. God has answered my prayers! I told Mom and Dad the good news, and they are rejoicing.

March 30, 2037: Robert has asked me to go to the prom! Who would have thought? Robert has come a long way since our first meeting to discuss high school trig. He has grown six inches this year, and—I'm almost ashamed to admit it—he is really good-looking, articulate, and a joy to be around. I know we're young, but I feel like I'm falling in love with him.

March 2, 2042: Robert asked me to marry him! I said yes, but we need to talk about whether this is the right time. We are both still in college. I'm not working, and Robert's teaching aide job doesn't pay a living wage for two people. I suggested we wait until we are financially stable.

January 21, 2045: Robert was offered a permanent position at Lawrence Livermore Lab. He just finished his postdoc at LLL. The lead scientist over his group went to the National Academy of Sciences and secured funding for Robert's project on black holes and wormholes.

By the way, my paper on novel techniques for the diagnosis and treatment of schizophrenia was accepted by the *New England Journal of Medicine*. A real red-letter day!

June 15, 2045: Robert and I are now husband and wife. The wedding was perfect! We're now in our room at the Ahwahnee Hotel in Yosemite Park. Please forgive me if I don't write in my journal for a while. I think you understand.

January 12, 2050: Last night I awoke to find I was alone in bed. I looked around the house, but Robert was nowhere to be found. Finally, I heard his voice coming from the patio. I looked out the window and saw him standing there. I thought he might be praying out loud, stargazing, or talking to himself. But something seemed strange—he appeared to be in conversation with someone. Someone he referred to as "the General."

I listened carefully and heard him asking about going to the moon. I thought he might be sleepwalking and having a vivid dream. But he didn't seem asleep. Strange.

Later in the day, I asked him about what he was doing last night. Robert gave me a strange look and said it was top secret and that he wasn't allowed to talk to anyone about it.

February 2, 2050: Today, shortly after Robert and I finished our Bible devotional, I found him in his office talking to himself. He seemed agitated and started yelling. He was shouting that NASA should not be exploring the potential for time travel. He sounded like he was losing his mind. I was really frightened, but I found the courage to open his office door and look inside.

What I saw shocked me.

There was Robert, standing on his desk, wearing sunglasses, shaking his fist at the wall. He would yell for a few seconds, then pause, as if listening to someone speak to him.

I called to him, asking what was wrong. He turned, looked at me, and said I wasn't allowed to be in his office while he was speaking with his Army general.

I told him there was no one in the room but the two of us.

He looked around, blushed a deep crimson, and fell into his chair.

I asked him what was happening to him. He told me he was terrified. He said he was hearing voices. Sometimes he knew the voices were delusional. But other times, he said, he couldn't tell whether they were real or fantasy.

I prayed with Robert, which seemed to settle him down. Then he gave me a big hug and said that he was losing his mind! I told him that he had the classic symptoms of schizophrenia. I also tried to convince him to seek help. I told him that my director at the psychiatric clinic was a leading expert in treating people with schizophrenia—and that there was hope.

He asked me if I could take him on as a patient. I told him that it wouldn't be a good idea, since I loved him too much and might become co-dependent in his psychosis. He responded that he trusted no one but me. If I wouldn't treat him, then he would seek no treatment at all.

February 9, 2050: Another bad day for Robert. He has missed work all week. He's received daily calls from Lawrence Livermore Laboratory questioning his absence. Today, he hung up on his boss. Before he slammed the phone down, he started screaming at someone in the room—but there was no one there.

Fortunately, his employer was aware of Robert's strange behavior and called an ambulance. When the paramedics arrived, they tackled Robert to the ground, administered a heroic dose of tranquilizer, strapped him into a gurney, and took him away.

I followed Robert to the ambulance. All our neighbors were watching, and I felt unbelievable shame. Martha, from across the street, came running over and gave me a bear hug. She told me that Robert needed our prayers. I will never forget her prayer:

"Father God, King of the universe and the Great Physician, I ask You to destroy the evil spirit within Robert and heal him spiritually. I adjure You to bind Satan and his demons and bring Robert back to himself."

I couldn't even say *Amen*. All I could do was weep uncontrollably.

February 28, 2050: A good day. Robert came home, and he seemed like himself again. His managing psychiatrist—who happens to be my boss—pulled out all the stops in his treatment. Robert will need to take Risperidone for the rest of his life, but I don't care. I love him for everything he is, and everything he isn't. God can still use him for His glory as Robert unlocks the secrets of God's universe.

March 4, 2050: A good day—and a bad one. Robert went back to work today. His fellow scientists even threw him a party in his honor. Robert is fortunate to have such loving colleagues.

He came home excited! He has a hypothesis he wants to test regarding black holes and wormholes. He told me he's already begun designing an experiment.

I asked how he developed the hypothesis so quickly. He told me he began working on it over the last two months—*while he was having his delusions.*

This terrifies me. Oh, please, God! Rescue my Robert from this illness. *Amen.*

March 11, 2050: Robert did not come home tonight. I have no idea where he is. The last time I saw him, we were having a picnic in the park. Two men in military uniforms approached us and beckoned for Robert. He told me he'd be home for dinner.

It's now midnight.

My friend Martha came over and prayed with me. After she left, I called my boss at the clinic and asked for advice. She told me to call the police. They arrived quickly. After we spoke, they told me they would issue an all-points bulletin to find him.

March 25, 2050: *Praise God!* Robert came home this morning. He was unshaven, dirty, and smelled bad. He was so exhausted that he collapsed into bed and immediately fell asleep.

When he woke up this afternoon, I asked him where he had been. He told me it was top secret and he wasn't at liberty to say.

I asked if he had been taking his Risperidone. He admitted he hadn't taken it in three weeks.

I grabbed him by the arm, took him to the bathroom, and confirmed the pill bottles were full. I made him take a dose, then marched him to the car and drove him to the hospital. They're keeping him for a few days under observation and testing.

I *hope* this is the last of it. I cannot take much more. Oh, Lord, please intercede. *Amen.*

March 29, 2050: Robert came home today, looking like his old self. The discharge nurse told me to ensure he takes his daily meds. She assured me that Robert would be fine. My friends and I are praying that this is true.

April 1, 2050: Robert went back to work today and came home excited. He thinks he's unlocked the secret of the universe.

I asked if he had tested his hypothesis. He said he came across astronomy data that supports it.

I asked when he had accessed these data—considering he'd been missing for two weeks, followed by a three-day hospital stay.

He said he found the data *during the two weeks he was missing.*

This terrifies me. He is falling into the rabbit hole again.

Please God, heal my husband. Amen.

September 14, 2051: A red-letter day for Robert. The National Academy of Sciences has accepted his paper entitled:

The Role of Antiquarks Near Black Holes Concerning Disturbances in the Space-Time Continuum: Implications for the Existence of Wormholes and Time Travel.

I know I should be excited, and I am proud of him—but I would trade everything in the world to have Robert truly cured of his schizophrenia. He still has bad days. The good news is that he has more good days than bad.

Lord God, please heal my husband. *Amen.*

November 15, 2058: Robert received a letter today—from the King of Sweden.

When we opened it, we found that Robert had been awarded the Nobel Prize in Physics! We were both astounded.

Robert gave me a big hug and read the letter further. It noted that airline tickets and hotel accommodations would be covered by the Nobel Foundation.

We could use a vacation. Maybe this is what Robert needs to finally turn the corner in his illness. Robert also mentioned that the cash prize was badly needed by his lab for purchasing some state-of-the-art equipment.

December 14, 2058: Robert had a bad day—but I *think* he's back on track.

We're in Stockholm, Sweden, for Robert to receive the Nobel Prize. Everything was going well. He seemed like his old self. Maybe the meds and therapy are finally working.

While riding in a cab to the venue, we were met by a large protest—mostly regarding global climate change. After we were dropped off, we were accosted by a group protesting Robert's work on black holes, wormholes, and time travel. One of the protesters was an old colleague of Robert's. He was especially verbally abusive.

It really shook Robert.

Later, during the award ceremony, Robert gave a very strange acceptance speech—then ran out of the concert hall.

I talked him down a bit during the cab ride back to the hotel.

Robert is still a very sick man.

Oh, Lord, please heal my beloved husband. Amen.

January 8, 2060: A very bad day for both Robert and me. Today I was diagnosed with Stage 4 ovarian cancer. I have, at most, a year to live.

Death does not scare me—because to be absent from the body is to be present with the Lord. Although death does not scare me, the process of dying is frightening. Will there be unbearable pain? Will the treatments give me a somewhat normal life while I live? Who will take care of me—and who will take care of Robert?

That last question concerns me the most. Since Robert is so mentally ill, what effect will my cancer have on his already unstable condition?

Back to today. After Robert and I received my diagnosis, he had a complete and total nervous breakdown. When the doctor gave us the news, Robert bowed his head as if in prayer. He was quiet for a few minutes—then suddenly, he leapt to his feet and began pounding violently on my oncologist and his nurse with his fists. He was screaming at the top of his lungs:

"Oh, God, save my bride!"

Two large security guards and Robert's managing psychiatrist rushed into the room. They pinned Robert to the floor and administered a massive dose of Thorazine to knock him out.

Oh, Lord Jesus, our world is coming apart. You are the Great Physician—heal us so we may have peace and be enabled to serve You. *Amen.*

March 2, 2060: I haven't written in my journal for some time. I'm getting sicker—and so is Robert.

Robert is in the process of shutting down his laboratory. He's too unwell to publish scientific papers, and his grant funding has dried up. He's laid off all his technicians and post-docs. Our only source of income now is Robert's disability checks and the proceeds from selling off his state-of-the-art lab equipment.

Robert is horribly depressed and tends to skip his medications in favor of drinking straight bourbon. He says he prefers bourbon to his meds because it makes the pain easier to bear—and the side effects of bourbon are more pleasant than the side effects of his prescriptions.

We're moving to Milwaukee, Wisconsin. We received a great price for our home in Palo Alto, and the cost of housing in Milwaukee is much more reasonable. We'll be living near Froedtert Hospital. The university medical center there has some promising clinical trials for ovarian cancer.

Maybe—just maybe—if I can get my health back, I can help Robert with his mental illness.

September 30, 2060: This may be my last entry. I'm too sick to write, and I can't think clearly.

Robert is still sick, but at least he's going to church. The people at our church are very loving. They bring us meals, pray with us, and walk with us through this journey.

I am at peace, Lord.

I know my suffering will end soon, and I will pass through the door of death and into Your loving arms, Lord Jesus. Take care of Robert. Give him joy, and hope, and purpose.

Into Your arms I commit my spirit.

Amen.

Chapter 4

The Dreamer-Physicist Receives His Prize and His Criticism
Stockholm, Sweden, December, 2058

Two years later, after Robert disappeared for two weeks, Robert and Betsy Hays were on their way to Stockholm, Sweden. They had visited several European countries before—attending conferences and vacationing—but this was their first trip to Sweden.

"Where do you want to go after the ceremonies?" asked Robert.

Betsy responded, "I don't know. I know you want to see the wooden naval vessel *Vasa*. I looked into it, and we can get there quickly on public transit. I know how much you love historic ships. Let's start there. After all, this trip is on the King of Sweden's dime—we can be spontaneous."

"That sounds good to me. That lunch they served us on this flight was incredible. I could get used to flying first class," Robert said, gazing out the window at the ocean expanse below.

The flight had been smooth so far. He leaned forward to look out ahead and noticed a large land mass on the horizon.

"Hey Betsy, look out my window. Greenland is coming up."

As Betsy leaned over, she asked, "Hey, where's all the snow and glaciers? Shouldn't Greenland be covered in white?"

"There's still plenty in northern Greenland," Robert replied, "but with rising temperatures, most of the southern glaciers are gone. Look at that long fjord over there—it used to be a glacier."

"Wow. How long did it take that glacier to melt?"

"Not long. I've been flying to Brussels every year for the European Physics Conference, and I've watched the glacial retreat over the past decade. Ten years ago, that fjord was filled with ice."

"Is there anything we can do to reduce climate change?" asked Betsy.

"Well, we've made great strides in reducing our carbon footprint. This airplane we're on is using carbon-neutral fuel for propulsion."

"How does that work?" asked Betsy.

"The turbofans—or jets, if you prefer—are powered by a mix of electricity and methane. The electricity comes mostly from wind and nuclear power. Plus, the wings and fuselage are covered in photovoltaic cells that convert sunlight into electricity. The methane is harvested from sewage treatment plants and food waste facilities."

"Can we reverse the climate change?" asked Betsy.

"Probably not. At least not with current technology. But there's an emerging field called geoengineering. One idea involves increasing carbon dioxide absorption in the oceans using genetically modified photosynthetic microorganisms—without increasing ocean acidity."

At that, Betsy let out a big yawn. "If you don't mind, I'm going to take a nap."

"You and me both. We've been up since 3:30 this morning to catch this flight."

***

When Betsy and Robert landed in Stockholm, they picked up their bags and grabbed a cab to their hotel. After freshening up, they dressed to the nines and headed to the Stockholm Concert Hall.

As Robert held Betsy's hand, he whispered, "It means so much to me that you're here. You've been my rock. My lover. You've dealt with all my strange behavior, my long hours in the lab, and most importantly, you've been my confidante. You deserve this award as much as I do."

"Robert, you're so sweet," Betsy replied.

As they neared the concert hall, they ran into a massive traffic jam. The cab driver slammed on his brakes and muttered, "Those bozos are back."

"Bozos?" Robert asked.

"Protesters. They were blockading the concert hall last night."

"What are they protesting?" Betsy asked.

"Science. They say science should be banned."

"Why?"

"They think science and technology caused all the world's problems—especially climate change. But there was something else too. Something weirder—I forget what it was."

"Is there another way to the concert hall?" asked Robert anxiously. "We need to be there in 30 minutes."

"I know a back way. I'll drop you off nearby. You'll have to walk to the front door from there. But just a heads-up—the protesters are gathered at the front."

"Thanks," Robert said.

The cab dropped them off around the corner. As they turned toward the entrance, they found themselves in a sea of angry protesters. Most were holding signs protesting fossil fuels. But a small, more hostile group held up signs that read:

BAN RESEARCH ON WORMHOLES AND TIME TRAVEL

Dr. Hays couldn't believe his eyes. Why would anyone protest research on wormholes and time travel?

Then one protester locked eyes with Robert and shouted, "There's the devil himself—it's Dr. Robert Hays!"

Immediately, the crowd swarmed them. One protester got in Robert's face, screaming:

"What gives you the right to control time? Only God controls time! What do you think you are—God? Think about the risks! You could change history! You could destroy the future!"

"What are you talking about, Dr. Lunquist?" Robert asked, recognizing the voice.

"*Time travel paradox,* Dr. Hays!"

At that moment, riot police moved in, dispersing the crowd. They formed a protective ring around Robert and Betsy, escorting them into the concert hall.

The Nobel Prize ceremony in the Stockholm Concert Hall proceeded as planned—until it was Dr. Robert Hays's turn to receive the Nobel Prize in Physics for his research on wormholes and time travel.

He approached the podium and gave a short speech. History would later record it as the moment the world began to question whether the brilliant physicist had fully returned from the brink:

"Thank you for honoring me with this prodigious award. I know that some of you think I don't deserve it. That's okay. It's okay. It really is. In science—and in new technologies—there are always risks. Like Pandora's Box. I'm not sure what to say next. Please excuse me."

And with that, Dr. Hays left the stage and ran out of the concert hall.

He was followed by his wife, Betsy.

***

Once they were in the cab heading back to their hotel, it was utterly silent.

Then Betsy began to cry.

Finally, she blurted out, "Robert, what is wrong with you? Have you lost your mind? You should've been gracious, accepted the Nobel Prize, and sat down. What was that speech all about?"

"I'm sorry! I'm sorry! I'm sorry! I don't deserve you. I don't deserve to live!" screamed Robert.

"Get a hold of yourself and talk to me. What's going on?"

"That man in the protest—the one screaming at me. His name is Dr. Lunquist."

"Who is he? Do you know him?" asked Betsy.

"He was a postdoc in my lab a few years ago. We had a falling out, as they say," Robert muttered, looking out the cab window.

"You seemed really upset. What's the deal with him? He seemed like a crackpot."

"He's a brilliant statistician. He did Monte Carlo risk assessments—modeling with multiple data ranges and calculating the probability of those data to predict possible future outcomes."

"Okay, I get it. He's a math nerd," said Betsy.

"When our lab discovered that time travel was a real possibility, we thought it would be wise to bring in someone like Dr. Lunquist to determine if there was any risk involved. You know, assess the probability of unintended consequences."

"Unintended consequences? Like what?" asked Betsy.

"Time travel paradox," Robert replied.

"What's that?"

"It's best described by example. Say I go back in time to visit my father before he was married—before I was born. We're driving, and we come to a fork in the road. I say, 'Let's go right,' but my father says, 'Let's go left.' I insist, and we go right—even though my father knows that road is dangerous. Five minutes later, he crashes. He dies. I survive.

That's a time travel paradox—because if my father dies before I'm conceived, then I would never have been born. And if I were never born, I couldn't have gone back in time to cause the accident. The logic collapses."

"That's... complicated," Betsy said, slowly. "But I get how Monte Carlo models could be used to evaluate that. We sometimes use them in psych research."

"So, where did Dr. Lunquist fit in?" she asked.

"Hey—we're at the hotel. Let's grab a cup of coffee and continue this."

***

Once inside the hotel restaurant, they sat in a quiet corner. Robert picked up where he left off.

"Okay, so Dr. Lunquist used Monte Carlo simulations to predict a range of possible outcomes if someone traveled back in time. The models accounted for multiple variables: what the time traveler did in the past, how long they stayed, how many people they interacted with, and how much time passed after they returned."

"Sounds like a complex system," Betsy said.

"It was. But here's what he found: If a traveler went back just a few years, did nothing, and returned immediately, the chance of unintended consequences was less than one in ten trillion."

"Okay, that's practically zero."

"Right. But if someone stayed a week and interacted with about twenty people, the risk climbed—to anywhere between one in a thousand and one in ten trillion."

"That's a huge range."

"It gets worse. Apply the same scenario to a trip 100 years into the past—the probability of unintended consequences jumped to as high as 50 in 100. That's a 50% chance of disturbing the timeline."

"How severe are these consequences?" Betsy asked quietly.

"Some are minor—like a house being painted blue instead of pink. Others are more significant—like different people winning elections. And then there are the catastrophic outcomes—genocide, world wars. It all depends on the variables in the simulation."

"That sounds too risky for me," she said. "So, what happened after Dr. Lunquist shared his findings?"

"We argued. Badly. I told him his models were flawed. He accused me of playing God. When his postdoc contract ended, I let him go. I didn't expect to see him again."

There was a long pause before Betsy asked, "If we do develop the technology for time travel... should we use it?"

Robert thought for a long moment.

"I don't know," he said finally. "Maybe we shouldn't even develop the technology. But I can't stop others from doing it."

Chapter 5

The Gates of Heaven
January, 2060

The lunatic is in my head.
The lunatic is in my head.

You raise the blade; you make the change
You re-arrange me 'til I'm sane.

You lock the door
And throw away the key:
There's someone in my head but it's not me.

And if the cloud bursts, thunder in your ear
You shout and no one seems to hear.

And if the band you're in starts playing different tunes
I'll see you on the dark side of the moon.

Roger Waters,

Pink Floyd Band

The alarm pierced the darkness. Where was it coming from? There was a pause while Dr. Robert Hays lay suspended between sleep and wakefulness. He chose wakefulness by default as he shut the alarm off. But the darkness persisted.

It's a funny place to be—between sleep and wakefulness. Dr. Hays wanted to choose to live in his dream. A good dream. A dream about his wife, Betsy. The light of his life.

In his dream, she was alive and well. They were walking through an alpine meadow in the John Muir Wilderness. She was utterly beautiful, and he was in love. The sky was a piercing blue, and the mountains stood close at hand. Then, a flock of ravens flew in. Dr. Hays had always liked ravens and their problem-solving ability.

But the dream ended with the alarm, and he had to come to terms with the fact that this was not his current reality.

Things had changed.

First, there was his wife—a casualty of ovarian cancer. It killed her slowly. In bits and pieces. Like some cruel torture. He thought on this, piecing the timeline together.

When was it? he wondered.

It was sometime after he had received the Nobel Prize in Physics.

He could still remember the day. The weather. The doctor's office painted in sterile white. The smell of antiseptic in the air. The doctor's sad face as he said:

"The test results have come in. You have Stage Four ovarian cancer."

"What does this mean?" Betsy asked.

"It means we can make you comfortable. You'll need supportive care, including a full-time nurse. I can recommend a good hospice team. There's a promising clinical trial at University Hospital, but I'm afraid the cancer has progressed too far for it to be efficacious."

Then there was silence.

Dr. Hays didn't know how long it lasted. Time felt suspended—hours, perhaps—though it was likely just a few minutes.

"I suggest you go home and discuss this," the sympathetic doctor said.

Another silence. And in that silence, Dr. Hays prayed.

Then something strange happened.

He was no longer in the doctor's office, but standing at the Gates of Heaven. The gates were high and made of iron. They were locked. He was pounding on them, screaming at the top of his lungs:

"God, save my bride!"

He pounded until his arms were reduced to bloody stumps. God did not answer. He continued screaming.

Until hospital security tackled him to the floor.

A different doctor and a nurse stood over him. The doctor had a syringe, which she used to inject something into his arm.

Then the room went dark.

***

When Dr. Hays awoke, he was in a white room with barred windows. There were pictures on the wall of flowers and peaceful landscapes. The room smelled faintly of lilacs. Outside, the PA system occasionally blared announcements.

He tried to sit up, but found he was restrained.

As he stared at the ceiling, his mind drifted back to the Gates of Heaven.

Then the door creaked open. The same doctor he'd seen before stood there, flanked by two burly security guards.

"Hello, Dr. Hays. I'm Dr. Williams. I'm sorry to restrain you like this, but you really gave quite a pounding to Dr. Winstead and his nurse. You were a danger to both yourself and to others."

"Who are those two big guys with you? My wife…"

Robert tried to speak, but his tongue felt heavy and paralyzed.

"She's really worried about you. She told us about your condition. Have you ever experienced intense thoughts or fantasies—ones you later realized weren't true?"

"Yes… but I'm not sure," Robert said.

"Would you be willing to tell me about one of those episodes?"

Dr. Hays lay quietly for a moment, then began.

"It was ten years ago, give or take. I either dreamed it or imagined it. It was too fantastic to be true. Two military men approached me and took me to a facility on the Florida coast. They brought me into a conference room and locked the door.

"I remember the room smelled like roses. The air was loud and cold—the ventilation system, I think.

"After some time, a one-star general entered. He asked about my work on wormholes and time travel. Then he told me something had been discovered on the far side of the moon."

Dr. Hays paused. "You must think I'm nuts."

Dr. Williams calmly pulled a pill bottle from her pocket. "Take one of these—it'll help you relax."

After a moment, she said, "Please continue."

"Where was I? Oh, yes. I asked the general what had been discovered.

"He told me, 'A possible wormhole.'

"Then he took me to a tall building with no windows. He opened the door, and inside was a Saturn V rocket, with an Apollo space capsule on top."

He hesitated.

"I wanted to make sure it was real, so I walked up to the rocket and touched it. It felt real.

"Then I turned to the general and asked, 'Why are you showing this to me?'

"He said, 'Because *you're* going to the far side of the moon.'"

Robert paused a long moment. Then he turned and looked Dr. Williams in the eye.

"Do you think I'm schizophrenic?"

Dr. Williams paused. "We have a treatment here that can get you back on track. But answer this: Did you *actually* fly in that Saturn V rocket to the far side of the moon?"

"Yes," said Robert.

"So why do you think that's a fantasy?" she asked.

Robert looked away. "Because it's too fantastic to be true."

***

The next day Dr. Hays was taken to a room and was hooked up to an IV drip. Dr. Williams was in the room calibrating some equipment, when she turned and said, "Good morning! I hope that you had a good night sleep."

"I slept like a rock. But that is to be expected with all the sedatives you gave me."

"Today I would like to continue the conversation we had yesterday. I will be administering an I.V. dose of pentothal. This will assist us in determining whether you believe that you went to the moon, and what you perceived that you did there. This will allow us to determine the depth of your schizophrenia, and will assist us in determining the proper treatment."

"Do I have a choice?" asked Dr, Hays.

"Your wife has the power of attorney for your medical treatment. You are a sick man, Dr. Hays. Please let us try to help you."

Dr. Hays acquiesced. The pentothal was administered, and he was soon in a dream state.

I was back at the Saturn V rocket. I turned to the one star general and asked him, "Why are you showing me this rocket?"

"Because we want you to go to the far side of the moon and determine if the phenomenon is a wormhole for yourself. What we know is that there is a significant distortion of stars when the moon's

far side points to a particular point in the sky: Which is in the direction of the constellation Sagittarius."

"But I am not an astronaut!"

"Don't worry. We will have a pair of astronauts accompany you on your journey."

Chapter 6

Did I really go to the far side of the moon?

Patients Name: *Dr. Robert Hays*

Date: *January 12, 2060*

Managing Psychiatrist: *Dr. E. Williams*

Exam Notes: *Patient admitted to psychiatric ward after becoming violent in the oncology offices at the hospital. After being restrained and sedated, he was moved to isolation room 2C. While the patient was sedated, his spouse, Elizabeth Hays, was interviewed. Apparently, the patient has a history of bipolar behavior and paranoia. His spouse also gave several accounts of the patient relaying stories to her that could not be verified, and that she felt the stories may be delusional.*

When the patient regained consciousness, he was interviewed to verify past delusions and hallucination. The patient gave a very detailed account of his supposed abduction and incarceration in a military facility. Then patient claimed, he was flown to the moon in a Saturn V rocket to investigate a newly discovered wormhole.

One last thing. Dr. Hays has an IQ of nearly 200. He recently received a Nobel Prize in Physics for his work on wormholes and the potential of time-travel. I believe that his immersion in these topics may be one of the causes of his psychosis.

Diagnosis: *Severe Schizophrenia.*

Proposed Treatment: *Shock treatment, followed by a regimen of Risperidone (dose dependent on efficacy of shock treatment).*

From: Dr. Williams Psychiatric report regarding Robert Hays

Robert Hays slept until almost noon the next day. He was awakened by an orderly delivering his lunch.

"Well, Robert, I hope you had a good night's sleep!"

Robert could not speak. His mind was in a fog. *Where am I? Oh, that's right, I am in the psychiatric ward.*

"We have a surprise lunch for you: macaroni and cheese with lima beans. Yum-yum!"

"The only thing I hate more than macaroni and cheese is lima beans," responded Robert in anger.

"Well, bon appétit!"

Even though Robert hated his lunch, he was so hungry that he devoured it in a matter of minutes. After finishing, Dr. Williams came into his room and asked,

"How are you doing today?"

"Fabulous! I got to sleep in, and I was brought some fine French cuisine."

"You are being sarcastic," smiled Dr. Williams. "Do you mind telling me the rest of the story you started yesterday?"

"Sure. Let's see… Oh yeah, the Saturn V Rocket."

"Do proceed."

When the general told me I was going to the moon, I thought he was joking.

"I am not joking. We will give you a few days of training and a crash physical fitness regimen to get you ready. We are scheduling you for launch in three days."

"What if I don't want to go to the moon? You can't make me go."

The general looked off to the side for a moment and then said,

"I would expect that you'd jump at the opportunity to see a wormhole for yourself. But I think I can provide some additional incentives. Your physics lab operates on grant money from NASA. The Administrator for NASA is a friend of mine. She personally recommended you for this mission. She would be personally offended if you declined. She might even redline your research grant out of her budget for next year. How much were you expecting in grant money?"

"Fifty million dollars."

"Well, you may not get a red cent next year. The Administrator is a reasonable woman, and you could count on $100,000,000 if you cooperate. And think of all the things you would learn when you see the wormhole. I'm sure the data you gather on this little trip would lead to additional hypotheses that you'd like to explore. In fact, I'm sensing that the work from this trip may even earn you the Nobel Prize in Physics. What do you say?"

"Okay, I see your point. Can I call my wife and let her know that I won't be home for two weeks?"

"No, we can't let you do that. This project has the highest top-security classification. Don't worry, we have developed a perfect alibi."

It took a few minutes for me to take this in. Then I asked,

"What's my alibi?"

"That you had a nervous breakdown. The breakdown was so complete that you became schizophrenic. You had to be institutionalized for two weeks. We even have two psychiatrists who will vouch for this."

"So, I don't have a choice."

"That's correct."

At this point, Dr. Williams shut off her recorder.

"Robert, is this what you believe, or are you trying to mock me?"

"I believe it is true. Check my medical records. You'll find that two psychiatrists, Dr. Rashid and Dr. Shah, diagnosed me as being schizophrenic."

Dr. Williams quickly typed the search parameters onto her electronic tablet. There was silence for five minutes. Then Dr. Williams spoke.

"I can't believe this. This is true—or I mean, it is not true. I'm confused. I'll deal with Dr. Shah and Dr. Rashid later. Let's get back to your story," said Dr. Williams.

"Certainly."

I won't give you all the details, but suffice it to say that after some very intense training, I was put into a space suit, loaded into an Apollo space capsule, and launched to the moon. They did the launch after the area in Florida was evacuated due to an approaching hurricane, which I recall never made landfall near the launch site. I think it was Hurricane Amos. At any rate, no one was in the area when we launched, so there were no witnesses.

It took us four days to get to the far side of the moon. The far side of the moon always faces away from Earth. At that time, the far side was facing the constellation Sagittarius.

When we arrived, I was still really sore from the intensive training, so it felt good to weigh less on the moon. We landed in Mare Moscoviense. There was a base there—just a few buildings. No humans were present when we arrived. The buildings were filled with state-of-the-art equipment. Another building about a kilometer away housed a nuclear reactor that provided power.

Most of the equipment was familiar to me; I had the same equipment in my lab back on Earth. One piece, however, was unfamiliar. It was a device that measured the space-time continuum. This device was powered by the nuclear reactor. Midway between the reactor and the instrument building was a cyclotron used to smash atoms into quarks.

Fortunately, somebody had written excellent instructions for operating the instrument. The device used certain quarks produced by the cyclotron to probe for wormholes. It took me a full day to familiarize myself with the operation. The next day, I used the device to locate a wormhole.

At this point, Dr. Williams paused the recorder and asked,

"What does a wormhole look like?"

"You can't see a wormhole, Dr. Williams. You look *through* a wormhole."

"What did you see?" asked Dr. Williams.

"I saw Sagittarius A*, the massive black hole at the center of the Milky Way Galaxy."

"What does it look like?"

"You can't see it," said Robert. "You can only see the space it occupies and the effect it has on starlight."

"Dr. Hays, my recorder is not running right now. I need to verify your story. The two astronauts who accompanied you to the far side of the moon—may I contact them?"

"No."

"Why not?"

"Because they were killed in a helicopter accident shortly after we returned to Earth," said Robert.

Chapter 7

Two Psychiatrists Become Sleuths

"Betsy, thank you for coming. How are you feeling?"

"I am feeling fine today. Yesterday I was not feeling well at all."

"I have an information release form for you to sign," said Dr. Williams as she slide the forms over to Betsy.

"I've already signed a HIPAA form for Robert. Why do I need to sign this form now?"

There was a pause for a minute or so, then Dr. Elaine Williams answered Betsy Hays' question. "I need to meet with two psychiatrists who previously treated Robert."

"I don't understand, Elaine. You're the only psychiatrist who has treated Robert."

The two psychiatrists stared at each other quizzically. Dr. Williams was Betsy Hays' manager at the psychiatric clinic, and yet, they were friends. Betsy decided to hold back her questions and let Dr. Williams set the pace of the conversation.

Finally, Dr. Williams replied, "There are parts of Robert's story about going to the moon that don't make sense to me. I cannot untangle his delusions from facts. In therapy yesterday, he told me that an army general created an alibi for his two-week absence. The alibi was that he had a major schizophrenic episode and had to be treated by two doctors."

"Who were the doctors?"

"Dr. Shah and Dr. Rashid," replied Dr. Williams. "Robert gave me their names while under Pentothal. I checked out what Robert told me and found that these two doctors work for the military and are based at Walter Reed Hospital in Maryland. I want to interview them to verify Robert's story."

"Do you have a pen I can borrow? Thank you. There, the form is signed. Let me know what you find out, Elaine," Betsy paused for a moment, then asked, "Can I come with you when you meet with Dr. Shah and Dr. Rashid?"

"Yes, of course!" replied Dr. Williams.

Then the two women gave each other a hug.

***

Dr. Williams and Betsy waited about an hour at Walter Reed Hospital before they were called in to meet with Dr. Shah and Dr. Rashid. They were brought to a conference room where both doctors were seated.

"I am Dr. Williams. I am a board-certified psychiatrist. With me is Dr. Elizabeth Hays, who is also a board-certified psychiatrist. One of my patients, Dr. Robert Hays, believes that you treated him for schizophrenia here at Walter Reed Hospital. I would like to know the circumstances and the treatment regimen. My associate here— who happens to be Robert Hays' wife—signed a protective information release. Let me show you the release." She took out an official-looking sheath of papers and pushed them toward Dr. Shah and Dr. Rashid.

Dr. Shah and Dr. Rashid looked at each other nervously. Finally, Dr. Rashid spoke.

"Dr. Hays was in Washington, D.C., meeting with NASA officials when he had a massive schizophrenic breakdown. We found that he wasn't taking any medication. We administered shock treatment and followed up with Risperidone and cognitive therapy."

"That is very interesting," replied Dr. Williams. "I found no documentation of your diagnosis and treatment in Robert Hays' medical records. Was this an oversight?"

Dr. Shah and Dr. Rashid began to squirm. Then Dr. Rashid spoke up.

"I am very sorry that this oversight happened..."

"I also found no documentation that Robert Hays was even admitted to Walter Reed Hospital. There is no record in your drug dispensary that he was ever given Risperidone," replied Dr. Williams, who felt her blood pressure rising.

Dr. Shah began to reply, "Let's not let this get blown out of proportion..."

"Don't patronize us!" shouted Betsy Hays. "I could report you to the medical board and have your licenses revoked on the grounds of malpractice!" When Betsy finished shouting, she doubled over in pain.

Dr. Williams looked over at Betsy, and place her hand gently on Betsy and asked, "Are you okay?"

"I'll be fine. Just give me a minute, Elaine."

Dr. Shah and Dr. Rashid looked at each other. Finally, Dr. Shah wrote a note on a piece of paper and slid it across the table. The note read: *Can we meet somewhere else to discuss this? This conference room may be bugged.*

Twenty minutes later, the four MDs took a short walk to a local coffee shop. Since it was the middle of the day, there were only a few customers inside. Dr. Shah selected a table that was fairly private. He looked around at the customers and out the coffee shop's window, checking for anyone who might have followed them from the hospital.

Then he spoke. "I'm really sorry about what has happened. Both Dr. Rashid and I are looking for a way to get out of this mess. We were misled by General Hancock. He told us that Robert Hays was on the way to Walter Reed Hospital. The problem was—Robert never showed up."

"Did you follow up with General Hancock about Robert Hays?" asked Betsy.

"We did," replied Dr. Rashid. "He told us that Robert was sent to a different hospital for treatment at the request of his wife."

Betsy Hays recoiled at this statement. "I was never contacted by anyone about the whereabouts of my husband!"

Silence reigned for a minute, then Dr. Rashid continued. "Dr. Shah and I thought this was the end of our involvement with your husband. However, this was not the end of it. Suddenly, a host of appointments to see Robert Hays appeared on our electronic calendars. Robert Hays never appeared at these appointments. We tried to find out who was scheduling them, but we couldn't determine who did it. Even our I.S. people couldn't trace the source."

"So, what did you do?" asked Betsy.

"We tried to reach out to General Hancock, but the military would not give us his address or phone number. We even went so far as to contact the Pentagon, but no one would tell us how to reach him," replied Dr. Rashid.

Then Dr. Shah spoke up. "We started to get threatening calls and emails, saying that we needed to stand by the story that Robert Hays was sent to Walter Reed Hospital. When we asked who was calling, they hung up."

The four of them sat there staring at each other, then Betsy broke the silence.

"Is there any chance that General Hancock retired recently?"

"Hold on!" Dr. Shah exclaimed. "My e-tablet is connected to a database of all retired military personnel. All MDs at Walter Reed Hospital have access to this database, since we provide medical care to retired military personnel. Hold on… I'm pulling it up now. Here he is: Brigadier General Robert A. Hancock, retired. He has a local address in Arlington, Virginia."

"Let me see that!" exclaimed Dr. Williams. After a minute or so, she continued, "I just put his address into my Apple Maps. It's a 30-minute drive from here. Betsy, let's pay a visit to General Hancock."

"Can we come too?" asked Dr. Shah.

"It would be better if you and Dr. Rashid did not come. Thank you for the offer, though," replied Dr. Williams.

***

"Elaine, do you believe what Dr. Rashid and Dr. Shah said to us? Do you think they told us everything?" asked Betsy.

"No, I don't. But I don't need to know everything they know. I just need to know enough to follow a lead to General Hancock," replied Dr. Williams.

When Betsy and Dr. Williams turned down the street where Gen. Hancock lived, they noted a large black car in his driveway. They drove by his house slowly and saw a middle-aged man on the front porch shouting at a younger man wearing a three-piece suit. They parked their car three houses down from Gen. Hancock's house and waited until his visitor left. Betsy was curious about the visitor and asked Dr. Williams what she thought of him.

"I have no idea who he was, but the car he drove was really fancy, and he was all dressed up. The middle-aged guy was shouting at the younger guy, but I couldn't make out what they were arguing about," replied Dr. Williams.

"He looked to me like he was an attorney or some government official," added Betsy. "Well, let's go over to Gen. Hancock's house and see what we can learn."

"Are you scared, Betsy. Do you feel okay?" inquired Dr. Williams.

"I feel okay. I am a little scared though. How about you, Elaine?"

"I'm more outraged than scared. Let's go!" exclaimed Dr. Williams.

The two women stepped out of the car and walked toward the general's house. It was a quiet neighborhood with colonial-style houses. There were neighbors outside talking to each other. Some of them waved to Betsy and Dr. Williams.

"At least this is a peaceful neighborhood. I don't think anything bad is going to happen to us," said Betsy.

They rang the doorbell and waited. They heard footsteps that stopped just on the other side of the door. A male voice from within asked, "Did you forget something? I thought this was a done deal. Go away and leave me alone!"

"Excuse me, General Hancock, we want to talk to you about Dr. Robert Hays," said Dr. Williams.

The door opened, and they were greeted by a middle-aged man who was powerfully built. He looked over Betsy and Dr. Williams for a few seconds, smiled, and said, "Please come in!"

Both Betsy and Dr. Williams were taken aback by the warm greeting. They walked through the entryway into the living room, past a glass case that held numerous military decorations and pictures. One of the decorations looked like the Congressional Medal of Honor. Then they were led to the outdoor patio by their host. The three of them sat at a table that was richly decorated and scented by a wisteria vine in full bloom.

Once they were seated, General Hancock stared off into space for a minute or so, then said, "I am very upset with our new president. He is in the process of gutting the federal agencies. He really went after NASA. Since I was NASA's military attaché, I was sacked. Did you see my visitor who just left? He was an attorney from the Justice Department who was sent here to tell me what I could and could not say or do in retirement. Some way to treat a loyal veteran after 40 years of service! This country is really going to the dogs!"

The general went silent for a few minutes, then he changed the subject. "I'm sorry to drag you into my problems. Can I get you anything? Lemonade? A beer?"

"I'll have a lemonade."

"I would like one too."

A minute later, their host returned with the lemonade. Dr. Williams took the opportunity to introduce herself and Betsy.

The general smiled and said, "Elizabeth Hays, you must be Robert Hays' wife. A pleasure meeting you! How is Robert doing?"

"He is schizophrenic and has been committed to a psychiatric ward. You knew he was schizophrenic, didn't you? You tried to fool everyone by allegedly sending him to Walter Reed Hospital," replied Betsy.

"I didn't know he was schizophrenic! I really didn't. He seemed perfectly normal to me. We just used that story as an alibi for his two-week absence. I'm really sorry for what I've put you through," said Gen. Hancock, looking at the ground. "How can I make this right?"

"By telling us the truth," replied Betsy.

"What is truth? Where do I start?" said the general, fumbling for words.

"Where was Robert for two weeks?" asked Betsy.

"You won't believe me! You'll think that I'm crazy," replied the general.

"Try me," said Betsy, as she stared him down.

"NASA sent Robert Hays to the Moon," replied Gen. Hancock. "It was a top-secret mission. Robert was the best scientific candidate for this mission. His discoveries will revolutionize space travel. I can't tell you anymore. I've already said too much. Please do not speak to anyone about this mission. I am ashamed of my part in this whole affair. Please forgive me."

"What about the two astronauts who went to the Moon with Robert? I understand that they died in a helicopter crash shortly after the mission was completed," asked Dr. Williams.

"I had nothing to do with that. I heard that the CIA was involved, but I can't prove anything," responded the general. Then Gen. Hancock continued, "Is there anything I can do for Robert?"

"You could visit him in the psychiatric ward and thank him for his service to his country. Confirm to him that he really went to the Moon," replied Dr. Williams. "That might help anchor Robert to the reality of his mission. Robert believes that his recollection of the event was actually a schizophrenic delusion."

"Give me the address for your clinic and I'll get the first flight I can. It's the least I can do for him! He is a hero in my book!" replied Gen. Hancock.

After Betsy and Dr. Williams left, the retired general sat in his easy chair, smiled to himself, and thought: *It was a good thing they did not ask me more questions about my meeting with Robert Hays. That might have caused a lot of trouble for me.*

Chapter 8

Ending it all, but Thwarted
February 2061

The lunatic is on the grass

The lunatic is on the grass

Remembering games

And daisy chains and laughs

Got to keep the loonies on the path...

And if the dam breaks open many years too soon

And if there is no room upon the hill

And if your head explodes with dark forebodings too

I'll see you on the dark side of the moon

Roger Waters

Pink Floyd Band

Eventually, Dr. Hays was discharged from the psychiatric ward. He was able to go back to work in his physics laboratory, but the meds he was prescribed compromised his previous intellectual brilliance. On top of this, he had to take care of his sick wife.

Because of all of this, his publications in scientific literature diminished to zero.

Since he had his own laboratory that depended on grant money, he needed to have his grants renewed annually to pay his staff and buy expensive instruments. After a year or so, he found that his grants were not renewed, so he had to lay off his assistants and start selling off his scientifically valuable instrumentation. Finally, he had to close his laboratory.

At this point, he could not afford to live in the San Francisco Bay Area anymore. After talking it over with his wife, they decided to move to the Milwaukee, Wisconsin area, so they could be close to Froedtert Hospital, where some cutting-edge ovarian cancer treatment trials were being conducted.

At this time, his wife of 20 years continued her downward health spiral, despite the excellent care she was receiving. Every day, she died a little more. Dr. Hays did all he could, but soon, this took a toll on him. He stopped teaching adult Sunday school at his church, he resigned from the elder board, and he started drinking.

The worst part was his disillusionment with God, which soon became active hatred of God. Dr. Hays began to think, then speak aloud, then start screaming, "Where are you, God? Come out so I can see you and tell you how bad this is. I want you to feel my pain. STOP HIDING FROM ME!"

Then his wife passed away after dodging in and out of a coma for a week. The last person Dr. Hays cherished was gone. The people in his church tried to help him through prayer and meals. Many came over to his house simply to cry with him. The pain Dr. Hays felt was unbearable, and soon darkness enveloped him. And the darkness was great.

He stopped going to church and chased off any of his Christian friends with cussing and threats. Then he was alone in his darkness. To complete his isolation, he moved to a small cabin off the grid in the Northwoods of Wisconsin. His only contact with humanity was his weekly trips to the grocery and liquor stores.

He started to drink more. First at night, to help him forget his situation and fall asleep. Soon, he was drinking from noon until bedtime. Then he simply drank all his waking hours. This went on for six months.

Finally, he hatched a plan: to end it all. He wanted to make it look like an accident so his estranged son would receive his life insurance payout.

He went into his kitchen and turned on the radio. The weather report was on: "Today Northern Wisconsin is under a Blizzard Warning. All residents are encouraged to stay indoors. DO NOT DRIVE. Visibility may diminish to zero. Winds will exceed 60 mph. Snowfalls will be 4 inches or more an hour. Temperatures are expected to drop to -5°F. The wind chill will make it feel like -40°F."

Dr. Hays pondered this for a moment. "I have the perfect accident," he said. He looked outside. "A bit windy and no snowfall yet."

He jumped in his compact SUV and drove to a spot on a secluded road where it crossed a small creek on a wooden bridge. Very few people ever drove to this spot. "This looks like a great place to die. Wolves frequent this area, and when they find me, it will look like I went off the road, tried to walk out, died of hypothermia, and was consumed by wolves."

So, Dr. Hays put his SUV in neutral and pushed it down the slope into the creek. To his delight, the SUV rolled over onto its roof. He walked off about 100 yards to a meadow and sat on a rock. The snow started to fall, gently at first, then in buckets. It was snowing so hard that he could not see more than 20 feet in front of him.

Perfect, he thought.

But something strange happened. He sensed that someone was nearby. He couldn't see them, but he thought he could hear them. He thought he heard someone calling his name. There it was again. Someone was looking for him.

Then something inside welled up in him—something he had not experienced in a long time: the desire to live. He listened for the voice again. Silence.

Dr. Hays began to scream, "I am here! I am in the meadow! Come help me, please!"

It was then that a great torus of light, like a ring of fire, formed directly overhead. Dr. Hays looked up and stared at the phenomenon.

What was that? he thought.

Suddenly, something black came out of the ring of fire. A cylindrical object about 3 meters long and 1 meter in diameter. It landed just a few feet from Dr. Hays. A door opened on the cylinder, exposing a cockpit and seat.

Dr. Hays thought he was having schizophrenic hallucinations. But then something weird happened: the cylinder talked to Dr. Hays.

"Dr. Hays, please get into this craft. We have important business to discuss with you."

Interlude

World War III and its Aftermath
2105-2109

At this point, I need to interrupt the narrative and inform the reader about the impact of World War III, which was declared on March 4, 2105. This war was instigated by two coalitions: first, the coalition of the Russian Federation, India, and China. The second coalition was comprised of the United States of America, the European Union, and the countries that made up the Organization of the Petroleum Exporting Countries (OPEC). The two major causes of this war were economic: trade imbalances and the growing shortage of petroleum.

I will not spend any time explaining the details of the causes of the war, but I think it would be beneficial to discuss the aftermath of this conflict. This war involved the tactical use of nuclear warheads. Neither side wanted to use nuclear warheads indiscriminately. However, catastrophic mistakes were made, and large civilian populations were annihilated along with military targets.

The main impact of this unfortunate business was more than 100,000,000 dead within the first two days of the conflict, and approximately 200,000,000 condemned to die prematurely from cancer and other radiation-related illnesses. Another untold number of people died during the nuclear winter and famine that lasted for five years after the initial nuclear holocaust.

Fortunately, humans are a persistent species, and the vast majority survived to rebuild society. This was a difficult process that required rebuilding infrastructure that, for the most part, had been destroyed. This included the records stored at vast data centers worldwide, which were destroyed in the first two days of the conflict. The loss of this knowledge resource prevented the rapid rebuilding of technology for nine years. In addition, there was not an accurate reckoning of those who perished in the first two days of the nuclear holocaust.

One point worth mentioning is the presumed deaths of those who died in rural areas, distant from the nuclear blasts. No one has developed a credible explanation for these rural casualties. However, some have put forth a theory that these rural people, along with others, were simply removed from the scene by their Christian God before the nuclear warheads were detonated. This theory has been largely discredited.

The second area of reconstruction was nation-building. The independent countries of the European Union consolidated into one country and merged with what was left of the Russian Federation to form the European Federation. Mexico, Canada, the United States, and Central America merged to form the Federation of North America. South American countries not part of OPEC merged to form the Federation of South America. China, India, Korea, Australia, New Zealand, and Japan were absorbed into the Federation of Asia Pacific. All African nations that were not part of OPEC consolidated to form the Federation of Africa. Finally, OPEC became the Free State of Petroleum Producers, which, by the Treaty of 2105, was protected from invasion by the mutual consent of the five Federation Nations.

One of the benefits of having only six nations was the technical cooperation within each Federation that followed. From 2109 on, technology quickly advanced, especially aerospace technology. Once nation consolidation was completed in 2105 and economic recovery was underway, all nations joined together in space exploration with the formation of the super-agency, the Space Federation. The reason for creating this super-agency was to exploit Dr. Hays' wormhole discovery to expedite space exploration with the intent of colonizing planets within and beyond our solar system. A large and well-funded division within the Space Federation Agency was the Terra-Forming Technologies and Strategies Division. These technologies developed rapidly and would be used on distant planets to make them inhabitable by humans.

All this changed when the planet *Beyond* was discovered. Then the Space Federation became much more than an agency.

More on this later. For now, let's continue with the story.

Jack Gerard

Oracle of the Federation

Chapter 9

Big Sur River Gorge, California
July, 2170

Take a walk down by, take a walk down by the river

There's a lot that you, there's a lot that you can learn

If you've got a mind that's open, if you've got a heart that yearns

If you listen to, if you listen to the water

You will hear the sound, you will hear the sound of life

There's a million different voices, there is happiness and strife

Message in the deep, from a strange eternal sleep

That is waiting there, that is waiting there for you

Like hidden treasure

Steve Winwood

Traffic Band

Dr. Leslie Jones was running for her life. It was a difficult run above the Big Sur River. The river flowed out of a gorge where the canyon walls were nearly vertical. So, the only way to cross this difficult terrain was to go up a series of switchbacks, which had a southern exposure in the hot July sun. No trees grew in this arid climate. Ironically enough, 700 meters below, there was a lush redwood forest.

The temperature was a stifling 50 degrees Celsius in the shade—and there was no shade. Dr. Leslie Jones was running *from* something *to* something. She was running from the two men who were in hot pursuit. If they caught her, she would certainly be raped—and probably killed. She looked down the trail and saw her pursuers about 150 meters below.

She was also running toward something. That something was a band of rebels that occupied the interior of the Big Sur River basin. Rumor had it the band was led by a charismatic leader. His followers in the Ventana Wilderness—once central California—numbered somewhere between a few hundred to several thousand, depending on whom you believed. The rebel group had thousands of cells in all the big cities, so their numbers were probably in the tens of thousands or more.

Leslie had done some research on this rebel group. They fascinated her. It seemed that the rebels wanted to solve the problems of Earth and the environment by living in harmony with it.

Leslie had grown discontented with the Federation. Although the Federation was a unifying force that gave political stability, their wanton disregard for Earth's environment and their fixation with the 'Beyond' was troubling. Their tendency to ignore problems on Earth and flee to distant parts of the galaxy was irresponsible.

Leslie loved the Earth. If she had not studied physics, she would have studied environmental science. Nature meant everything to her. She studied the religions of the Aboriginal Americans. She spent all her spare time immersing herself in nature. So, it made perfect sense for her to seek out this rebel group in the Big Sur River basin, on North America's west coast, 150 kilometers south of San Francisco.

Dr. Jones was driven toward this group and their leader by an idea. The idea was somewhat complicated, but the short version was that Dr. Jones had something she could bargain with—a technology that could give the rebels an edge against the Federation. But what really drove her was something that logic could not figure out: a cause worth fighting for. She knew that the continued use of fossil fuels, fertilizers, and cement production had greatly increased greenhouse gas emissions.

As she ran up the switchbacks on the Pine Ridge Trail, she remembered from her college days that the temperature on this exposed mountain rarely exceeded 35°C. This climate change was conspiring against her immediate quest for safety and purpose.

She turned to look for her pursuers. Leslie was quite athletic. She had run in two marathon races. However, running up this trail was different than running in San Francisco. The hills were much higher here. She finally spied her pursuers about 100 meters below her.

They were catching up.

The top of the gorge was still 100 meters above her, if her memory served her well. As a college student at the University of San Francisco, she would backpack this trail to the hot spring at Sykes Camp. The rebel fortification, according to rumor, was about kilometer above Sykes at the confluence of the North and South Forks of the Big Sur River. She had about 20 kilometers to reach this fortification.

Her legs began to cramp, and her mouth was parched. She was becoming light-headed. She needed water, and she needed it soon in this heat. Then Leslie remembered that there was a spring about a kilometer ahead. *That's it,* she thought, *I can make it to the spring and get rehydrated. After that, the trail is wooded, so I can hide from my pursuers.* Changing her immediate goal from 20 kilometers to one kilometer gave her some hope.

Finally, Leslie crested the top of the trail. The trail veered to the right into a small ravine. The spring would be just inside that ravine. Her legs began to pump harder, despite the cramps. Her breathing was harsh with dryness, but she fell into a rhythm that was almost musical.

She made it to the spring. The water was cold and delicious. She savored it for a minute while she caught her breath. She breathed the air in deeply with her eyes closed. The smell of live oaks and bay trees was rich.

Suddenly, she was knocked down. Her assailant pinned her to the ground. She broke one hand free and jammed her thumb into his left eye. He fell backward with his hands covering his face in agony.

"You bitch, wait until I catch you. It's not going down good for you!"

Meanwhile, the other assailant ran past him and after Leslie. She ran with all her might down the trail and soon outdistanced the man.

"So, this is the benefit of running marathons. I think I can make it to the forks." Then, suddenly, her foot caught on a root on the trail, and down she went.

The man caught her and started ripping at her clothes. She closed her eyes, as if trying to hide. But then she had the courage to look her attacker in the eyes.

That's it. Stare him in the eyes. Maybe he has some moral compass.

As she opened her eyes to look at him, she heard a *whoosh,* followed by a *thud.* What she saw was incredible.

An arrow sticking through her assailant's neck.

He made a ghastly gurgling sound as blood gushed into his throat. Leslie instinctively rolled to one side as her assailant fell to the ground, desperately trying to remove the arrow. But soon, he choked to death on his own blood.

She looked down the trail and saw her other assailant standing with a look of horror on his face, staring at something past Leslie. Then Leslie turned around and looked up the trail.

To her surprise, she saw a man on a horse, with his bow still in his hands. The horseman dug his heels into the horse's side, and at a full gallop, the horseman was heading for Leslie—and perhaps her other assailant.

She quickly rolled off the trail to avoid being trampled by the horse. As the horseman passed her, she saw him pull out a sword, and with one sweep, the head of her other assailant was lifted off his body. It bounced twice on the trail, then rolled down the ravine to the Big Sur River, 700 meters below.

The horseman paused at the body, thoughtfully inspecting it. At first, Leslie thought he was checking to see if the man was dead— but that was absurd. Then she realized it was something deeper, almost a lament over the loss of life.

The horseman, sword still in hand, reined his horse over to Leslie. The look on his face was one of anger and sadness combined. He pointed the tip of his sword at Leslie's throat and said, "You have violated this holy place by coming here. Tell me why I should not remove your head."

Leslie blurted out, "This place, holy? I don't understand. Why is it holy?"

"It is the temple of The Tree. No one is permitted to drink the water from this spring. The water is for The Tree."

There was a moment of silence—or was it an hour? Then he said, "Look behind you!" Leslie turned and gazed. Why hadn't she seen this before on her previous backpacking trips? Was it real?

There, about 500 meters in front of her, was a mass of red color. It was cylindrical in shape, about six meters wide, with deep furrows in it. She looked down into the ravine from which it arose. There, the base of the cylinder anchored to the stream, at least 70 meters below her. Her gaze followed the trunk of this massive tree until she saw its lowest branches, 50 meters above her head. The top of the tree was obscured by its own foliage.

Sequoia sempervirens. A Coast Redwood. She pondered the sight for a moment. She had seen many redwoods in the Coast Range but never one as massive as this.

"This tree is holy," the rider repeated. Then she paused to take in the sight again. The tree was indeed magnificent. How old was it? It must be at least 2,000 years old. The thought of the tree being holy made sense to her pantheistic sensibilities.

"It is holy, and you are a trespasser. Tell me why I shouldn't kill you now?"

"Because I need to see Aristides on important business," replied Leslie.

"Why would he want to see you?" asked the horseman.

"Because he needs the last teleporter."

A pause then ensued for a few seconds—or maybe an hour; it was hard to judge the passage of time.

"It is true that Aristides wants the last teleporter, but you have no authority to give him something that is so precious to the Federation," responded the horseman.

"I am Dr. Leslie Jones, and I am the lead scientist at the teleporter in San Francisco."

The horseman pondered this for a minute and then said, "Get on the back of my horse, and I will take you to Aristides."

***

It was about a 20-kilometer ride to the Citadel, which Leslie had discerned from rumors was called *Forks*. This citadel was located at the confluence of the North and South forks of the Big Sur River. Back in her college years, Leslie remembered backpacking in the Ventana Wilderness area along the Big Sur River to the overlook above the forks. It was 150 meters straight down to the river at that point—way too steep to climb. But she remembered the large flat area around the forks. Just big enough for a citadel.

The rider's horse turned off the main trail and began its descent into the river gorge, following a set of switchbacks on a recently made trail. The heat was intense here, and the smell of bay trees was rich. Horned toad lizards ran off the path as the horse approached, avoiding being crushed.

When they had descended halfway down, horns began to blare their rich baritone melodies. When they reached the gate of the citadel, the guards yelled, "Open the gates for Aristides!"

Suddenly, Leslie felt faint. The horseman taking her to the citadel was Aristides! What was going to happen to her in the citadel? Would she be tried and executed, or would she be granted an audience with Aristides where she could explain her plan?

She was brought to a large wooden structure that reminded her of lodges she had seen in national parks. The structure was made from Ponderosa pines—but no redwood. Strange. But then Leslie remembered that the large redwood where she was rescued and captured by Aristides was considered holy.

Two sentries in buckskins guarded the door to the lodge. As Aristides approached, he turned to Leslie and said, "You wait here until I discuss this matter with my counsel."

She did not need to wait long before she was beckoned inside.

Inside, it was twilight-dark, with the only light coming from a large fireplace at the other end of the room and a few small windows. The smell of pine fragranced the air. At the far end of the lodge sat six men and six women. In front of these people—presumably the Counsel—stood Aristides. He beckoned her forward.

"Tell us about the last teleporter and how we might capture it," asked Aristides.

Interlude:

The Rise of the Ecological Rebellion
2015-2171

Before I continue with this story, I need to give the reader some background on the origin of the Ecological Rebellion.

The origin of this rebellion has its roots in the early 21st century. At that time, nine Planetary Boundaries were established by the Stockholm Resilience Centre. The research organization found several of these boundaries being exceeded in areas related to declining biodiversity, freshwater, soil, and climate change.

Some people chose to ignore these boundaries for the sake of making and maintaining wealth. Many became indifferent or remained ignorant of the consequences of these exceedances. Some took the boundaries seriously and sought political means to reverse these trends, especially in the area of climate change.

In the first half of the 21st century, a group of people concerned with the wanton disregard for exceeding these planetary boundaries sought to form a new society outside the existing norms. Their primary means of doing this was to remove themselves from existing societies and form new communities that sought to live in harmony with Earth's ecosystems. Also important was the indoctrination of members in ecological principles and the effort to bring their beliefs to bear on societies that chose not to live in harmony with Earth's planetary boundaries.

These early pioneer eco-rebels settled in pristine areas that had not been significantly degraded by humans. In what was known as the United States of America, these groups tended to form communal communities in designated wilderness areas. The largest of these communes was found in the Ventana Wilderness on the west coast of North America.

After the Third World War and the rise of Federation states, Earth's population could be seen as three distinct groups: wealthy persons within Federation states, poor people within Federation states, and the eco-rebels. As time went on, the amount of arable land declined drastically, which resulted in global famine. Global climate change refugees, displaced by high temperatures and rising sea levels, also increased drastically. Rich people, who had the resources, simply disappeared to a place called The Beyond. These ecological catastrophes and global migrations led to increasing political instability. Poor Federation people began to invade the lands of the eco-rebels. In response, the eco-rebels developed militias to protect their lands and communes from these marauding bands of poor people.

It was at this point that the eco-rebels began to infiltrate Federation lands and teach their doctrines of ecologically sustainable living to poor people. These were referred to as eco-cells. The ultimate goal of these cells was to rebel against the Federation and take over the Earth. Once this was accomplished, the eco-rebels would establish societies that would live in harmony with Earth's planetary boundaries.

Jack Gerard,

Oracle of the Federation

Chapter 10

Love Is Friendship Put to Music

(Old Laotian Proverb)

Several days later, Leslie took a hike to Logwood Ridge. As strange as it seemed, Aristides gave her a remarkable amount of freedom. He didn't seem to be worried that Leslie would wander off. The ridge was located between the Big Sur River and Logwood Creek. The smell of bay trees filled the air, and the air was deliciously warm after the morning fog had burned off. Leslie closed her eyes and inhaled the air. The warmth penetrated her inner being.

Then she heard something—the sound of a loud snort. She opened her eyes and saw a large wild boar. It had an arrow in its side, but the arrow must have encountered a rib, because the boar didn't look very injured. But it did look mad!

The boar pawed the ground and snorted again. Then it charged Leslie. She started to run, but the boar was closing in fast. Leslie then tripped and fell. She turned her head only to see the boar drop to the ground. A second arrow now penetrated its chest, just behind its front legs.

Leslie did not move, afraid that the boar would resurrect itself and rip her to pieces. Finally, a voice cried out, "What are you doing here, all by yourself? It's a good thing I showed up."

Leslie looked up and saw Aristides. The two of them stared at each other for about a minute. It was hard for Leslie to tell if she had again violated some sacred place and would be an object of wrath—or something worse. Aristides did seem a little unpredictable. Then Aristides smiled, and all was well with the world.

Leslie picked herself up off the ground and sat on a fallen tree. Aristides sat down next to her. There was silence for a few minutes before Leslie spoke.

"I just wanted to be alone for a while and enjoy this afternoon. I am quite familiar with Big Sur. I spent much of my free time here when I was a graduate student. Logwood Ridge is one of my favorite places."

Aristides changed the subject. "I appreciate your willingness to help us in the rebellion. However, there is more at stake here than just gaining technological superiority over the Federation." Aristides paused for a minute, then continued. "We are attempting to achieve a proper balance with the natural world, where man is just a part of nature, not the dominant force. Under the Federation, global climate change has progressed to a point where the global temperatures are now 8 degrees C hotter. The Arctic Sea ice is gone, and the ice fields of Greenland and Antarctica are fast disappearing. The rise in sea level has inundated the Eastern Seaboard in North America, Amazonia, Central Africa, and the low countries in Europe. The areas around the equator are no longer inhabited by humans because of the high temperatures and the collapse of the tropical ecosystem. And what is the Federation's response to all this?"

"Reduce carbon emissions?" responded Leslie, timidly.

"No!" exclaimed Aristides. "Their solution to the climate problem is to teleport their people to the far side of the galaxy and let Earth burn."

"Why do you need the last teleporter then? When everyone who uses fossil fuels has gone to the Beyond, won't the temperature drop back to normal?"

"Even if all greenhouse gas emissions ceased today," Aristides continued, "it would take at least 500 years for temperatures to return to normal, and the temperature will continue to climb over the next 200 years. Man will not be able to survive anywhere on Earth. All ecosystems will collapse. Food production will decline to zero."

When Aristides finished saying this, he looked at the ground and started drawing a picture of the Earth in the soil and said, "Those of us left behind will suffer the consequences. Without food, we will starve, and even if we could migrate to areas that would support food production, there will simply not be enough of this land to produce enough food to feed those left behind. Why are the privileged allowed to migrate to another suitable world, and 15 billion people consigned to a slow death from heat and starvation?"

Aristides then said, "We also need the scientists of the Federation to come back to Earth—especially those who are currently involved with terraforming the planet Beyond. We need their geoengineering skills to reverse global climate change. Our group here in Big Sur lacks the skills to complete this work. Your teleporter will enable us to reach out to them and bring them back. It is our goal to save the Earth." After saying this, Aristides became very quiet. The only sound was the warm wind blowing in the trees.

Leslie pondered the words that Aristides had said. She was aware of the terraforming effort that the Federation environmental scientists were performing on the far side of the galaxy. Fifty percent of one planet had already been terraformed by first inoculating the sterile ocean with blue-green algae, then brown and green algae. Once these algae filled the oceans and streams, enough oxygen was liberated to support human respiration. Then fish were introduced to the waters. The sterile terrestrial soils were made fertile by the introduction of man-made fertilizer and genetically modified soil organisms. Terrestrial crops were planted to feed the 20,000,000 people that had relocated to this planet. Hunger was a problem, so food had to be rationed until the terraforming was completed.

"I see what you are saying. The skills involved in terraforming distant planets could be used to geoengineer the situation on Earth, and maybe, just maybe, reverse the effects of global climate change," said Leslie. This was all new to her. She was a physicist, not an environmental scientist. Then she asked, "What if the Federation will not let the scientists come back, or worse yet, keeps those left behind from migrating to the Beyond? Will your passionate appeal convince them? I don't think so. As I understand it, the terraforming work that the environmental scientists are doing on the planet Beyond is critical."

"If they will not come back on their own, or the Federation will not let them come back, we will resort to the old way of convincing," said Aristides.

"What way is that?" asked Leslie.

"War," responded Aristides.

"I hope not!" cried Leslie.

Then there was silence. The scent of the bay trees was still there. The warm wind was still there. The Earth beneath their feet was still there. Something inside Leslie was beginning to grow. She always thought men were weak and inconclusive in their thinking. But here was a man—an intelligent man—a leader of a movement. A movement much bigger than the man, and yet, the two were inseparable. She wanted to believe. But more than that, she wanted him. Not because he was strong, intelligent, and a leader. It was more than that. It was a shared vision. She felt a light touch to her chin. It was Aristides, gently turning her face to his. They both closed their eyes and kissed.

Chapter 11

Dr. Tempus's Laboratory
Federation Space Fortress *Sagittarius A**
July, 2170

Take me on a trip upon your magic swirling ship

My senses have been stripped

My hands can't feel to grip

My toes too numb to step

Wait only for my boot heels to be wandering

I'm ready to go anywhere, I'm ready for to fade

Into my own parade

Cast your dancing spell my way,

I promise to go under it

Bob Dylan: Mr. Tambourine Man

He always liked looking at new data the best. Old data was from the past, and the past had no place in his mind. The data he was reviewing was from the most recent star pass near the black hole, Sagittarius A*. The amount of data before him was voluminous, but that did not trouble him. In fact, nothing seemed to trouble Dr.

Tempus. He lived in the present, making hypotheses about the future work he would do. In fact, as hard as he tried, he could not remember the past. He could remember everything from the time he started his work on the space station, but nothing before. What was strange: that lack of memory never troubled him.

So, he lost himself in data. The supercomputer was Dr. Tempus's best friend. It never made demands, never held an account of right or wrong—it only examined the millions of terabytes of data coming in. It took all this data and transformed it into something that Dr. Tempus could relate to.

There were others in the lab with Dr. Tempus, but they could have been lab rats for all Dr. Tempus cared. He needed no one, only the supercomputer.

An attractive lab technician came up to him and said, "Dr. Tempus, you have been reviewing these data for the last 16 hours. It's time for you to go out and enjoy yourself."

He only grunted, "I am enjoying myself. I am looking at the secrets of the universe here. I am developing an understanding of a power that will improve the lives of all those who live in the Beyond."

"But you need your rest. You could relax and read a book, or watch a movie, or go out and enjoy the company of others," replied the technician.

"No thank you," responded Dr. Tempus.

"Well, remember to turn off the lights when you leave."

Dr. Tempus was relieved to hear her steps going out of the lab. Now he could concentrate. When he was sure that all the lab technicians were gone, he went back to his data. But his mind was distracted. Something was trying to well up inside his thoughts. Something about that lab technician reminded him of something. He couldn't put his finger on it. It was like déjà vu. He went back to his data, his grand purpose in life. However, the incomplete thought remained. He pushed the incomplete thought aside and soldiered on.

Then he saw it: the data he had been looking for. Yes, there it was. The velocities of the accretion disk were approaching relativistic speed, and then—the numbers looked all wrong. They were right, but wrong. Hydrogen and other elements were being torn into quarks. The velocities in some of the quarks exceeded relativistic speed, and by several orders of magnitude. He had found the Holy Grail in physics!

He ran the data through the supercomputer three more times to be sure, and he found perfect agreement. Dr. Tempus threw his head back and laughed. Then the incomplete thought came back to him— to haunt him. It lodged there in defiance. Immovable.

He paused. He took a deep breath and wrote down a few notes on his discovery. He closed his eyes and tried to remember. What was it about that lab technician that churned up the mud in the river of his mind? Then something compelled him. A feeling. A feeling that he should go out and socialize. It was a totally irrational thought.

Dr. Tempus found himself walking down the corridors of the space station with no destination in mind, but a thought kept haunting him: *Where was she...* Not the lab technician, but the memory of something. He was pursuing the memory, but it seemed to be part of a distant time. The faces that he passed in the hall belonged to now, and not to his memories. Something was lodged there, like a splinter in his brain.

Walking in the space fortress was different than walking on Earth. As was true of all Federation ships, space stations, and fortresses, this space fortress had artificial gravity. This gravity was created through centrifugal force. In other words, all naval ships and fortresses rotated radially. This meant that the floor, where people walked, stood, and slept, was on the walls furthest from the hub of rotation. If you were walking down the corridor, it looked like you were walking uphill. If you looked behind you, it looked like you were walking downhill.

Dr. Tempus was walking about halfway around the naval fortress, which was about one kilometer's walking distance. Eventually, he came to one of the station canteens. He stopped and pondered: not exactly a wormhole to another time, but it would do.

Stepping inside the canteen, he spotted the lab technician sitting alone at a table nursing a neat bourbon.

"Mind if I join you?" he asked. It was then that he realized he didn't know her name. "I know this is awkward, but what's your name?"

"Let me understand. I have been working in your lab for six months, and you don't know my name? What are you, some kind of creep?" responded the technician, angrily.

"I—I'm sorry, I didn't mean to offend. I got off on the wrong foot. I am so immersed in my work that I seem to be missing some important parts of my humanity," responded Dr. Tempus, defensively.

"Is that the only thing you are missing? Do your scientific endeavors take precedence over your humanity? I don't think I want to be part of the discovery of your humanity."

At this, the lab tech rose from the table and walked off. Dr. Tempus just sat there for a few minutes until a waiter came to the table.

"Can I get you anything, sir?" asked the waiter.

"Yes. Get me a shot of humanity."

Chapter 12

Sickbay, Federation Naval Fortress *Sagittarius A**
August, 2170

And Epsilon Nochis was 65 years old when he became the father of Majoris Theta. Epsilon Nochis had a special relationship with the god of the Federation after he became the father of Majoris Theta. Epsilon Nochis had more sons and daughters. And all the days of Epsilon Nochis were three hundred sixty and five years in the ancient times.

Epsilon Nochis continued his special relationship with the god of the Federation. One day he simply disappeared: for the god of the Federation took him in a fiery vehicle.

Stories of the past, as told by the Oracle of the Federation

Lieutenant Kathryn Henderson was just coming on shift when her coworker called her over.

"We have a real crazy guy in Room 5. He keeps jabbering away, and no one can understand a word he says."

"Is he a crew member?" asked Kat.

"No, I've never seen him before. I think he may have been teleported in from somewhere else."

"What is his physical condition? What does he look like?" inquired Kat.

"He appears to be quite old, maybe 80 or so. All his vitals are quite normal. There's another strange part: health-wise, he seems to be incredibly healthy, more like a 30-year-old."

"How is he mentally, other than jabbering incoherently?"

"He is in restraints. But other than him babbling, I'm not sure there are any signs of mental illness. Oh, one other thing: he gets excited when Dr. Rosenstein comes into his room."

"Does Dr. Rosenstein know him?" asked Kat.

"Not as far as I can tell. Well, I'm off now. The mystery patient is now your problem."

"Uh, thank you," replied Kat.

Kat sat at her station and looked over the orders for the patients.

Room 1 was Marine Sergeant Willis, who was in sickbay with a broken hand from a fight he'd picked with a naval midshipman.

Room 2 was Midshipman Chu, who was being treated for a concussion he received from Sergeant Willis.

"Hmmm," thought Kat, "Ming Chu is new to the station and kind of cute. No, this is not the time and place to develop a relationship. Maybe we could get together over coffee after he is discharged from sickbay. Maybe he could relieve the boredom on this God-forsaken station."

Kat read the other orders—mostly naval personnel and Marines who did something dumb, and now had to heal from their stupidity in sickbay.

Then she read the orders for the patient in Room 5:

Name: John Doe "Not very helpful," she muttered.

Sex: Male

Age: About 80

Height: 125 cm. *A short guy,* she thought.

Weight: 60 kg

Race: Uncertain, but thought to be Middle Eastern

Vitals: BP: 110/70, Pulse: 60, Temperature: 37.0°C. *Looks normal to me!*

Diagnosis: Severe mental dislocation due to excessive teleporting.

Kat closed her eyes and rubbed the bridge of her nose and thought, *I've seen this syndrome before in Marines who teleported several times in one week. They're literally a nervous wreck. Why would an old man be teleporting in the first place? It doesn't make sense!*

About this time, Commander Rosenstein, M.D., poked his head into Kat's station and said,

"Kat, I need your assistance with John Doe in Room 5. Bring the electroencephalogram with you."

Five minutes later, Kat was in Room 5 with the EEG. Dr. Rosenstein was holding the patient's hand and speaking calming words. Kat could tell from John Doe's expression that he had no idea what was going on. That said, John Doe did have a strange look of peace, and if anything, he was mildly amused by the doctor's words.

Kat asked Mr. Doe, "I need to prep your scalp for the electrodes."

John just cocked his head.

Kat thought to herself: *He's a cute old man, but look at those muscles. It looks like he's been working out at the gym every day. And his skin is like leather—he obviously has been out in the sun his entire life. And something else: John Doe has a look of peace on his face—not consistent with severe mental dislocations from excessive teleporting.*

The patient was compliant with Kat's prep work. He even winked at her at one point. Dr. Rosenstein just laughed, and Kat turned a bright crimson. Kat knew she was an attractive woman, but she always hated the unsolicited attention of men.

Dr. Rosenstein started up the EEG and did all the usual things to try to elicit abnormal brain waves, such as strobe lights and sudden loud sounds. Kat looked at the printout: all brain activity was totally normal. This was not consistent with severe mental dislocation syndrome.

Strange, she thought.

After finishing her shift, Kat went to the space fortress's library. Kat was a curious sort of person, and when something didn't make sense, she would go to the library and do a computer search to get answers.

After she was assigned a computer terminal by the librarian, she entered the following keywords:

Middle Eastern

Teleporting dislocation

This search brought up over 1,000 hits.

I need to refine this search and get the number of hits down, she thought. She next typed in:

Refine search /

Teleported to space fortress

Number of hits: *356. Display list?*

No.

Refine search/

Sagittarius

Enter/

0 hits.

Delete Sagittarius/

Refine search/

Ethnicity Rosenstein, MD

Number of hits for Middle Eastern, Sagittarius, Rosenstein: *4. Display list?*

Yes

> 1. Dr. Abraham Rosenstein: Naval Surgeon on Space Fortress *Sagittarius A**. Previous employment: Emergency Room doctor at Jerusalem General Hospital…

Refine search/

Ethnicity

Jewish. Display list?

No.

Refine search/

Second languages

Number of hits: 2. *Display list?*

Yes

Yiddish

Hebrew

Refine search/

Hebrew greeting

Number of hits: 1. *Display list?*

Yes

Shalom: A greeting in Hebrew, which means peace.

With her new knowledge, Kat made her way back to sickbay. When she reached sickbay, she went to Room 5 and peeked in the door. John Doe seemed to be asleep. She walked into the room and said,

"Shalom!"

John Doe's eyes popped open, and he replied,

"Shalom!" Then he began to speak rapidly in some language that Kat could not understand.

"Sorry, I need to go." Then, without thinking, she said,

"Shalom!"

"Shalom," replied John Doe.

***

After Kat left sickbay, she walked down the main corridor of the space fortress until she ran into Midshipman Ming Chu.

"I thought you were in sickbay."

"I was discharged an hour ago," responded Ming.

"Welcome to our naval fortress," said Kat with a smile on her face.

"Thank you. Hey, I'm starving. No one has told me where I can get food in this place."

"I'll take you there. Do you mind if I join you?" asked Kat.

"Not at all!"

When they reached one of the canteens, they ordered their dinners and sat at a table in the corner of the canteen.

"Thank you for showing me around. I just got assigned to this fortress last week," said Ming.

"What were you doing in sickbay?" asked Kat.

"I got into a fight with a Marine, and he got the best of me," responded Ming.

"That was pretty stupid to pick a fight with a Marine. They're a pretty tough bunch of guys."

"He was harassing a female midshipman. I stepped in and told him to bug off. Then he hit me. The next thing I know, I'm in sickbay."

"You're still stupid—but a nice kind of stupid," said Kat with a smile on her face.

"Hey, when I was in sickbay, I heard that old guy in Room 5 yammering away in some exotic language. What's the deal with him?"

"You know, I'm not supposed to talk about my patients. Confidentiality," responded Kat.

"Oh, okay. I understand. Well, I better get some sleep. I'm on watch in 3 hours. Hope to see you again."

Chapter 13

Los Angeles Rabbinical School
West Coast, North America
September, 2170

Mad men and prophets are very similar. The only difference between them is that mad men are made into mad men by people, and prophets are made mad by God.

Jack Gerard

Oracle of the Federation

Myron Abbot was stumped. One of his adolescent students had asked him why there are no prophets today. The silence in the room hung in the air, looking for someplace to land. Myron then started to speak, "There may still be prophets today; we just don't hear them like the people heard them in ancient Israel." The answer he gave made him feel inadequate to be a teacher. In fact, it made his whole life feel like a charade. Myron couldn't even remember the student's name. Frustration.

He looked at his watch and saw that it was 3:00 PM. Time to dismiss the students for the day. Saved by the bell! After dismissing the class, one student stayed behind—the student who had asked the question. Unfortunately, Myron still could not remember the student's name.

"Dr. Abbot, if you believe that there are still prophets today, why can't we hear them?"

"I think that we cannot hear Jehovah's prophets today because there are so few who believe in God. Technology has given them everything they need. There is no room to hear and believe God," responded Myron Abbot.

"But why can't *we* hear the prophets? We who believe in God and read the Torah," responded the nameless student.

Myron pondered for a minute, then continued. "What is a prophet?" asked Myron.

"A prophet is one who speaks on behalf of God to the culture that the prophet lives in," responded the nameless student.

"True. But a prophet is compelled by God to speak. Perhaps God may call you to speak on His behalf."

"How would I know?" asked the student.

"As I said, you would be compelled by God to speak."

The student thought for a moment and asked, "What about miracles and foretelling the future?"

Myron pondered for a moment, then said, "A prophet tells the future regarding God's judgment and His everlasting love. It's part of the message from God. Miracles are there to show that God is Master over His creation, and to show His everlasting love. Here, let me give you a paper that I wrote on this subject many years ago." Dr. Abbot reached into a dusty old filing cabinet and pulled out an eight-page paper regarding prophets. It smelled moldy, like your grandparents' house.

After the student left, Myron pondered about nothing in particular, and his mind drifted back to Oslo, Norway, ten years ago—to the time he received the Nobel Peace Prize for his work on forging peace between those of faith and the atheistic Federation. It was a confusing time. For many years, the Federation had tried to stamp out all forms of religion. Churches and synagogues were burned. Believers were tried and forced to deny their faith—or suffer the consequences.

Then something strange happened. The Federation Council elected a new president. William Nelson had been an unknown entity two years before, but suddenly, there he was. And he wanted peace between those of faith and the atheists. Myron, at the time, was a college professor, teaching ancient Hebrew. For some reason, he was able to speak freely. Perhaps this was because he did not attack the atheistic government but spoke of showing God's love to all men.

He was hated by both the Jews and atheists, but he was not hated enough to be arrested or kicked out of his professorship. Then President Nelson reached out to him. He needed his help in uniting a fractured world.

This all occurred when humanity began a mass migration to a place called the Beyond. Why did they call it "the Beyond"? Beyond what? This lack of memory caused Myron to become confused and agitated. The migration to the Beyond also occurred at the same time that Myron began to forget names and places.

Overall, these memories made Myron smile. He did not think as fast as he once did. He was 70 years old, and he had been diagnosed with incipient Alzheimer's disease. He resigned his professorship and became a lowly rabbi to adolescent boys.

His memories still made him smile. He remembered his wife of 45 years. He called her Tilly. Not sure why he called her Tilly, but he did. Then Myron started talking to himself. "It is good to balance productive work with my good memories!"

His reverie was interrupted by a knock at his classroom door. At his door was the school principal, flanked by two Federation Marines.

"I'm sorry, Dr. Abbot, but these men insisted on seeing you now. They would not leave!"

One of the marines stepped forward and said, "I am Major Singh. I have been ordered to take you to the teleporter in San Francisco."

"Am I under arrest? What are the charges?" asked Myron.

"This is not an arrest, but an appeal for help," responded the Marine major.

"Do I have a choice, Major?" responded Myron, who was becoming agitated.

"No, sir. You are to come with me immediately."

"Ah! A *de facto* arrest!" exclaimed Myron.

Chapter 14

Defending The Last Teleporter
San Francisco
West Coast of North American
September, 2170

Lieutenant Jackson stared out over the carnage. Bloated bodies stacked in heaps provided food for feral dogs, rats, and a plague of flies. The scene was totally different from that of a naval space fortress, where Lt. Jackson was typically posted. He turned to the ranking sergeant and said, "Sergeant, do you think they will come again today?"

"Sir, you know they will come again, and again, and again. They are animals. No minds." The sergeant flicked his cigarette away and stared out into the street.

"Going to be another hot one today," said Lt. Jackson.

"Sir?" replied the sergeant.

"The weather, of course. I wish our high command would allow us to bulldoze the bodies away from us. The stench is unbearable," responded Lt. Jackson.

"They have their reasons, Sir, and we have our orders. I imagine this is quite different for you, being assigned to a naval space fortress."

"That is true, Sergeant. Being assigned to a space fortress is very antiseptic. If a ship or fortress is hit by gunfire, the hull is breached and the bodies are simply sucked into space. No odor."

Lieutenant Jackson pondered these orders again in his mind: *Deliver the goods and hold the last teleporter at all costs.* He wanted to look confident in this sergeant's eyes, but he was sure that this seasoned warrior saw his fear and lack of confidence. He was new to command, only commissioned two months ago. How could he keep his superior's orders against such staggering odds?

Two months. It seemed like an eternity. In that time, he had seen the pride of the Federation Marines reduced to a band of cornered animals. What moves this Rebellion against the Federation? What force is there in the universe that propels men to die in such vast numbers to achieve final victory? Who was this man, Aristides, who leads them? What can he promise them that would make them charge Federation troops armed with only machetes, garbage can lids, and a few antique guns?

"Sir, the men tell me that their laser power packs are almost empty," whispered Sergeant Becker in Lt. Jackson's ear.

How he wished that they had more men and weapons to hold the teleporter...

"Sir! Did you hear me?" screamed Sergeant Becker.

"We can expect no further power packs—or men, for that matter. I understand that our troops in this city are entirely cut off from Federation supplies and reinforcements. You have your orders: protect the last teleporter at all costs," said Lt. Jackson.

"Sir, we can't hold back another attack!"

"I don't give a damn! Do the best you can. Scavenge power packs from the dead. Use bayonets, fists, whatever. If the rebels gain possession of the teleporter, they will have access to all those we are trying to protect—our homes and families who live in the Beyond. The whole order of things that we hold dear will be destroyed!"

Sergeant Becker simply cocked his head in dismay. "Sir, you know that my men are willing to fight to the last man. But how long does the Federation expect us to hold on? All the other teleporters have been destroyed. Why are we defending this teleporter? Why can't we return to the Beyond and destroy this last teleporter?"

"I don't know!" responded Lieutenant Jackson. He did not want to share what he had heard from the other officers. Rumors. Rumors of trying to locate one last person to teleport. An enigma. An old man who held to a long-dead religion. A Jewish scholar, some say—and he did not want to be found.

Lieutenant Jackson's mind began to wander: *Time is a strange thing. When living in pleasure, time is fleeting. When faced with an impossible task, time is a long, slow torture. There is no standard passage of time. The passage of time is related to whatever business we find ourselves in. This religious scholar: Who was he, and what was his import? Why the loss of Federation troops who die for this scholar? Why the waste of time? We could close off the Rebellion to this part of the space-time continuum—like amputating a gangrenous arm...*

A hover vehicle suddenly appeared and stopped before the lieutenant. A marine major stepped out, looked around, and said, "Man, the stench is bad!"

When the major looked around, he could feel the stares from the men—men more like rats on a sinking ship. No time for morale-boosting, though...

"I have orders for Lieutenant Jackson."

"You found him," responded Lt. Jackson.

"You are to report to the teleporter immediately. Sergeant, your men are to provide a delaying action if the rebels should attack. After Lt. Jackson and his human cargo teleport, you and your men are to teleport to the Beyond and destroy the teleporter with timed explosives. Do you understand?"

"Major, where am I and my cargo teleporting to?" asked Lt. Jackson.

"You are to take your cargo to the Federation Naval Fortress *Sagittarius A**. The teleporter must not be destroyed until you and your cargo have passed through the wormhole. Now come with me. I think the rebels are coming," commanded the major.

Off in the distance, one could hear the roar coming. It sounded like a great tsunami, destroying everything in its path.

Lieutenant Jackson entered the hovercraft and was spirited off to the teleporter.

The marines, commanded by Sergeant Becker, looked down the long street. Mobs filled the street from the side streets—thousands of them. There would be no way that the Federation troops would be able to hold them off. However, duty, love of family, and the Beyond dictated that the supreme sacrifice needed to be made.

The rebel mob charged the Federation barricades. The marines mowed down the first dozen or so rows of rebels until their power packs were empty. This created a small mountain range of mangled corpses. But the rebels scaled the mountain and, in a human tsunami, crashed into the Federation troops. Most of the rebels were armed only with machetes, but the troops, after their laser power packs were empty, were armed only with bayonets.

On an armament basis, the odds were even.

On a numeric basis, the odds were in favor of the rebels: 1,000 to 1.

The Federation troops committed themselves to an orderly retreat, but many men were lost. They finally ended up at a large high-rise building. Barricades had already been erected by the few troops protecting this building. The retreating troops dove behind the barricades. A few laser power packs had been left for them, which they immediately deployed.

Suddenly, a great humming noise filled the air. Marines and rebels alike stopped their fighting and turned to look at the high-rise building. The hum started low but soon rose to a scream, like that of a siren's song. The building and sky around the building began to warp grotesquely. Suddenly, a giant flaming vortex appeared above the building. A dark tunnel issued from the vortex to the top of the building. The teleporter was being activated. Lieutenant Jackson and his cargo were being teleported to the space fortress.

Suddenly, the vortex and tunnel snapped closed. The visual disturbances stopped. The siren's song was silenced. Now it was the Federation troops' turn to teleport to the Beyond.

However, some of the troops behind the barricades suddenly opened fire on the defending marines. Rebels in Federation uniforms!

In the fight, Sergeant Becker was mortally wounded. As he lay in his own pool of blood, he saw the last of his men slaughtered. In his telecom, he messaged the Beyond:

"Lieutenant Jackson and his cargo teleported. Mission to destroy the last teleporter has failed. The teleporter is now in rebel hands."

Chapter 15

Teleporting from Here to There:
Alpha Wormhole
September, 2170

Myron sat on a couch opposite Lt. Jackson on the teleporter ship. It was quite comfortable, if not a bit cramped. The distant hum and comfort of the couch caused Myron to drift off to sleep. Then he remembered where he was. He remembered being led to a ship of some kind. Really quite small, about the size of his bedroom at the rabbinical school. These thoughts in Myron's mind crowded out his desire to sleep.

Lt. Jackson then asked, "Do you need anything, Dr. Abbot?"

"Where are we going?" asked a groggy Myron.

"Federation Naval Fortress *Sagittarius A*.*"

"Where's that?" inquired Myron.

"At the center of the Milky Way Galaxy."

Myron pondered what Lt. Jackson said. He had no idea where Earth was in the Milky Way Galaxy, let alone where the center of it lay. Funny. He did not know where he had come from or where he was going. Worse yet, he had no idea why he was going there. It was hard for him to grasp this journey. He could speak Hebrew, English, and Russian fluently, and a half-dozen other languages passably.

Yet the concept of traveling outside of Earth was indeed baffling. He felt like he was in a fog.

He finally broke the silence. "Why am I being sent to this space station?" asked Myron.

"I'm sorry, sir. I am only following orders to deliver you safely to the space station," replied Lt. Jackson.

"Safely? I am deeply concerned about this trip to who knows where," said Myron.

Lt. Jackson pinched the bridge of his nose as he closed his eyes. He wondered why on Earth he had to transport this senile idiot to the best-kept secret in the Federation. He opened his eyes and looked across at Myron. What he saw was an old man dressed in black, with a black hat on his head. He had long sideburns. The look in Myron's eyes was dazed—like nobody was home. He wondered why the entire platoon of marines had been slaughtered trying to deliver him to the teleporter. When he could not answer his own questions, he fell back on his default answer for everything that didn't make sense: *I am just following orders.*

Suddenly the sound of snoring distracted his thoughts. Myron was sound asleep with a big, goofy grin on his face. Suddenly, Myron's snoring got so loud that it actually woke him up.

"Why are you taking me to Space Station Sagittarius whatever? I think I deserve an answer!" Myron was beginning to display anger that did not seem consistent with a nice old man.

"I don't know. I'm just following orders," replied Lt. Jackson.

Myron was starting to become fearful. He had heard this phrase before. Let's see, back in the 1930s and '40s in Nazi Germany, according to the history books he had read. Then Myron began to remember all his Jewish friends who had been recently arrested and never seen again. Was history repeating itself again and again?

"I'm sorry for lashing out at you, young man. It's just that so many of my friends…" As soon as these words left his lips, Myron began to weep.

At this point, Lt. Jackson began to understand Myron. Even though he was not involved in the last pogrom against the Jews, Christians, Muslims, Buddhists, and Hindus, he had heard stories at the Marine Academy. He distinctly remembered an incident in the Academy's lunchroom when he sat next to a table of commissioned officers. He remembered their laughter as they shared stories about being involved in rounding up one particular group of religious fanatics—how they abused them and even how they killed them in what they thought were innovative ways.

Lt. Jackson felt somehow responsible for Myron's fear and anger. He felt a need to reassure him. "Sir, I think no one means you any harm. Times are different now. I know that President Nelson has proclaimed an amnesty to all people of faith. May I ask you a question? Why would people believe in a God they have never seen or met, and be willing to die for a Deity that may not exist at all?"

"Young man, if you have to ask that question, you probably would not understand the answer," replied Myron.

At this point, Myron changed the subject. "Can you explain how I am being teleported from Earth to this, this, this… ah, space fortress that you speak about?" Myron ended this question rather embarrassed, since he could not remember the space fortress's name.

"Oh, do you want to know how we are being teleported? I'm a soldier, not a physicist, but I will try. Ever hear of wormholes?" asked Lt. Jackson.

"What do holes that worms make have anything to do with travel?" asked Myron.

Lt. Jackson pondered this. *Try not to use jargon. Make it simple.* "Well, sir, it works like this, as I understand it. The universe has more than three dimensions—you know, height, length, and depth. There is also the dimension of time. But there are other dimensions that cause the universe to actually be fluid, and folded, and twisted. Wormholes are simply portals, or shortcuts, that allow quick travel across the vast expanse of space. Ever hear of Dr. Robert Hays? The physicist who won the Nobel Prize in Physics in the 21st century?"

Myron thought and tried to remember. *Hmmm.* He remembered taking bonehead physics in college—a class designed for non-science majors. *Think, think, think,* and suddenly a pathway in Myron's mind began to take shape. Robert Hays... oh yes, wormholes and the theory of time travel by means of black holes. This made Myron smile. Not because he knew who Robert Hays was, but because Myron's mind still worked well enough to remember.

"Yes, I remember reading about Dr. Robert Hays many, many years ago. I do recall something about his research on the existence of wormholes, black holes, and the possibility of time travel," said Myron.

Lt. Jackson smiled and leaned toward Myron. This little old man seemed to be transformed, and any dementia seemed to have passed.

"Okay," said Lt. Jackson, "I will try to explain the way it was explained to me. Wormholes just exist in the fabric of the space-time continuum. We can't see them because the wormholes are very, very small. We are creatures who live in the present and live in a three-dimensional world. But there are ways of locating wormholes. One hundred years ago, government scientists developed the technology to locate wormholes and manipulate the locations of these holes closer to us through the use of anti-matter quarks. They found two such wormholes: one that was located on the far side of

Earth's moon that produced a shortcut to the center of our galaxy, and one from the center of the galaxy to the far side of the galaxy."

"What are Auntie Matter quacks? Who is Auntie Matter? Does she have ducks?" asked a puzzled Myron.

"No, no! Not *Auntie*, but *anti*. Physical substances are made out of matter. Matter is made of atoms. Atoms are made out of protons, neutrons, and electrons. These subatomic particles are made out of quarks. Antimatter quarks are quarks with the opposite properties of regular quarks. For instance, the antimatter quark of an electron is a positron. These do not exist by themselves in our normal environment. However, near black holes, quarks and anti-quarks exist and can be produced for short periods of time during fusion reactions. This exotic matter can be harvested and used to make wormholes much larger for short periods of time," explained Lt. Jackson.

Myron pondered this. It took him some time to understand what was being said. Then suddenly, it hit him.

"The wormhole to the far side of the galaxy: That is the one that goes to the Beyond. The place where people are migrating to. An unspoiled planet. Yes, now it makes sense to me."

The look on Myron's face was transformed. Lt. Jackson smiled back.

***

Myron must have drifted off to sleep, because he woke up with a start. The teleporter spacecraft was bucking like a wild mustang.

"What's happening?"

Lt. Jackson was sound asleep. Myron shook the lieutenant to get his attention. When Lt. Jackson awoke, he said,

"Oh, what's the problem? Oh, the turbulence. We must be getting close to the space station. We always get turbulence when we approach the station during teleporting. Gravitational waves, I think they are called."

After trying to explain this, Lt. Jackson gave a big yawn.

"Gravitational waves from the space station?" asked Myron.

"No. The gravitational waves from the black hole, Sagittarius A*. The mass of the black hole is huge. As we draw near to it, the lines of gravity are crossed, changing the trajectory of our teleporting spacecraft and producing the turbulence we are experiencing. I am not sure of all the details, but that is what I have been told," said Lt. Jackson.

"But I thought we were in a wormhole."

"We were. But we left the wormhole some time ago. Don't worry. When we get off the teleporter craft at the space fortress, it will be nice and calm. The space station is in a stable orbit around the black hole," explained the lieutenant. "The station has the world's most advanced supercomputer and retro-jets to keep it that way. Except when a massive star orbits in close to the black hole— then things get a bit wild. Would you like to see the black hole?" asked Lt. Jackson.

"Yes, I would!" responded Myron.

"Let me open this shade. Look over there," said the lieutenant as he pointed out the window.

When Myron Abbot looked out the window, he was treated to a marvelous sight. The number of stars and nebulae visible to him was amazing, being this near the center of the galactic core. However, there was a small, round area where no stars could be seen. This area was blacker than anything Myron had seen. Around this black hole was a ring of blinding light. Just outside this ring, the concentration of stars seemed much higher than in other areas of the galactic core.

"Why does it look that way?" asked Myron.

"I don't know, Myron. You will have to ask Dr. Tempus when you meet him."

"Who is Dr. Tempus?" asked Myron.

"I'll introduce you when the time comes," replied Lt. Jackson.

Myron Abbot was so enthralled with the sight of the black hole, he did not even notice that the turbulence had settled.

"What happened to the turbulence?" asked Myron.

"We have synced up our motion with the space station. Look over here—it is coming into view."

When Myron looked out the window again, he was treated to a new spectacle. At first, it appeared as a curtain, moving from left to right in the window. Hundreds of pinpoints of light moved with the curtain.

"Let me turn off the lights in the cabin so you can see better, Myron."

With the lights turned off in the cabin, Myron's eyes could see much more detail. The station was a dark grey color. The pinpoints of light resolved into square and round portholes. There were at least 100 plasma guns of various configurations, as well as scores of missile launchers.

Myron pondered, "This looks more like a fortress than a space station, Lieutenant."

"It is. Welcome to the Federation Naval Fortress, *Sagittarius A**. The purpose of the fortress is mainly scientific, Myron," replied Lt. Jackson.

"Then why all the weaponry? What are you trying to protect?"

"The most important secret in the universe, Dr. Abbot."

"Protect it from whom, Lieutenant? With all those weapons you could stop just about any threat!" exclaimed Myron.

Chapter 16

Federation Mothballed Fleet
September, 2170

The mothballed fleet floated 100,000,000 from the black hole, Sagittarius A*, and about 150,000,000 kilometers from the FNF *Sagittarius A**. It was the place where outdated vessels and discredited naval officers and crews were sent to die. These were the wrecks of the last war—the war that united all the nations on Earth and colonies throughout the solar system under one government. In reality, one side destroyed the other, and the losing side was simply absorbed by the victors. The loss of life was estimated to be in the billions. The actual number of casualties will never be known, since whole nations and planetary colonies were annihilated, and no body count could be done.

It was a large fleet of 96 vessels. Ten of these were 74-gun ships-of-the-line, the largest ships with an array of 74 missile launchers and plasma guns. Twenty-two were frigates, with 28 to 50 missiles and guns. Twenty were sloops with 12 to 26 guns and missiles. The remaining ships were marine transports and support vessels.

The administrator of this derelict fleet was Rear Admiral Torres. His job was to administer what he called *Purgatory*. During the war, he rose to the rank of Admiral of the Fleet, a 5-star job, until his debacle in the Battle of Phobos, where the enemy trounced his fleet in an ambush, with the loss of five 74-gun ships-of-the-line and a dozen or so frigates. In recognition of this debacle and his previous service—which was mostly sitting behind a desk—the Admiralty removed three stars from his rank and gave him command of the now obsolete and useless mothballed fleet. Hence, he was sent to *Purgatory* to pay for his sins and to wait for his redemption, which never came.

Each ship had its own captain, usually a discredited officer or some other lackluster post-rank individual. They, in turn, commanded a useless ship with no orders other than to keep them in working trim and to await their reactivation to active service. Then these discredited officers would be replaced by eager, younger men who would use the ship for its combat capabilities.

Each ship had a skeleton crew of a few dozen low-lives. It was said in the Navy, "If your crime was such that death was too easy a sentence, you would be sent to *Purgatory*." *Purgatory*. Ninety-six decaying ships and a couple of thousand men and women, paying for their sins until the day of their redemption.

Admiral Torres sat at his desk on his flagship, the 74-gun Federation Naval Ship *Brazil*. The nameplate on his desk had his old rank of Admiral of the Fleet. Some speculated that the Admiralty ordered him to keep his old nameplate as a reminder of how far he had fallen, but some said that Admiral Torres kept the old nameplate as a sign of hope.

He had his laptop open to his messages. He was reading a message from the Admiralty.

"Something is going on," he thought to himself. He quickly scanned the message for anything that might be an opportunity for him but found none. Most of the message pertained to an incident on Earth—something to the effect that the last teleporter was captured by the Rebellion. He didn't see anything that concerned him, and yet…

There was a knock on his cabin door. The admiral yelled, "Who's there?"

"Captain Decadorsky."

Admiral Torres hated Decadorsky, the captain of his flagship FNS *Brazil*—the most incompetent sailor in the service. Before being sent to *Purgatory*, he served as the quartermaster for the fleet. He could count beans, but in terms of his commanding abilities, he couldn't command a paddleboard.

"Come in. Please be seated," said the admiral in a patronizing tone. Admiral Torres hoped that this visit would be short.

"Have you read the message from the Admiralty?" asked Capt. Decadorsky.

"I have," responded Admiral Torres, who was hoping that this pest would soon go away.

"What do you think? Do you think our fleet will be reactivated?"

"You are an eager fool, Captain. We are halfway between Earth and the Beyond. The probability of the Admiralty reactivating this fleet is somewhere between nil and zero."

"But sir, the Rebellion has captured the last teleporter on Earth!"

"Has it ever occurred to you that a bunch of rebel savages have no idea how to operate a teleporter? This news has about as much meaning as a string of pearls to an ape."

"But…"

"But what, you idiot! Where would they teleport to? To the Beyond? They would be cut down as they came through the wormhole by the Federation Fleet near the Beyond. You know how heavily guarded wormholes are. And even if they got through, they have no ships and no weaponry to fight the military might of the Federation. Dismissed, Captain."

"But sir!"

"I said you are dismissed."

After Captain Decadorsky had left Admiral Torres's cabin, the admiral reached into his desk and pulled out a cigar. He struck a match and took three puffs, leaned back in his chair, closed his eyes, smiled, and said to himself,

"Decadorsky, you are right, and yet a fool. This Rebellion will cause this fleet to be reactivated."

***

Captain Decadorsky was making his rounds on the FNS *Brazil* to ensure that everything was in working order and that none of his crew was slacking off. As he walked the circular decks that took advantage of the spinning ship's centrifugal force, he also had to pull himself up or down the central ladders that connected the decks where this force was not in operation.

He started at the top deck that manned 12 plasma guns (six forward and six radial) and two nuclear missile launchers. This deck also had the equipment for controlling the ship, which included the AP3000 computer that controlled all the functions of the ship. Since this is where the captain, helmsman, weapons officer, and communication officer resided, it was referred to as *The Bridge*.

The next deck had six radial plasma guns and the shuttlecrafts that, during times of war, would ferry Marine boarding parties to enemy ships. This deck also served as the Marine barracks. A typical

'74-gunner' would carry a company of 120 marines. However, on a mothballed ship-of-the-line, there were few stationed marines.

Below these decks were the Space-Time Deck, Sickbay, Navigation Deck, and Engineering Deck. Below the Engineering Deck were the deuterium and tritium fuel tanks and the fusion engines. Each of these decks had plasma guns and missile launchers, bringing the total number of guns and missiles to 74.

Now Captain Decadorsky was on the third deck, which was the Space-Time Deck. This deck contained the instrumentation that would measure the distance to stars and planets and would be used to monitor the space-time continuum. It could also be used to detect unusual massive objects, like enemy ships. Typically, this deck housed about 75 Scientific Officers and technicians. On the FNS *Brazil*, there were only a couple of ancient SOs who were too old to be of use on a ship with active status. The two scientists on duty were Charles Wood and Davonte Richards.

When Captain Decadorsky came down to the Third Deck, both Dr. Richards and Dr. Wood were having a heated discussion.

"And what makes you think that there is a large influx from Alpha Wormhole? Something like this has not happened before. It would imply that there is a large herd of buffalo coming through. I am sure that this is simply instrumentation failure," said Dr. Richards.

"Look at the amount of antimatter being discharged from the torus. It's way off the scale. It could only mean that either something very large is coming through, or there is a very large number of packages coming through," replied Dr. Wood.

At this point, Captain Decadorsky cleared his throat. There was silence, disturbed only by the hum of ventilation fans.

Now Dr. Wood and Dr. Richards were on the opposite side of the Third Deck from the captain, so they and the captain were looking straight up across the deck to see each other.

"Richards and Wood, what are you discussing? Report!" ordered Capt. Decadorsky.

"We are seeing a huge anomaly in the space-time continuum near the Alpha Wormhole, Captain. We haven't determined what it is, but it is coming from Earth," said Dr. Wood.

"Where is it heading?" asked Capt. Decadorsky.

"Straight for us! More precisely, to the second deck of our ship, Captain."

"Hold on, Captain. Another anomaly is coming through the wormhole torus. This one is targeting the FNS *Russia*. We have several more anomalies, all targeting mothballed ships-of-the-line."

"What does this mean?" asked the captain.

"It appears that we are being boarded, Captain."

"Robots or sentients?"

There was a pause as the two scientific officers pondered the data.

"All sentients, Captain," the scientists said in unison.

***

Admiral Torres was still pondering his conversation with Captain Decadorsky. The part about the capture of the last teleporter on Earth was disturbing—or maybe this was an opportunity. What would the Rebellion do with the teleporter? Did they have the expertise to operate it? Could they access ships to come through the wormhole torus and attack FN Fortress *Sagittarius A**, or even the planet Beyond? He had the ships to thwart such an attack, but he did not have the crews to operate them. He would need almost 40,000 sailors and officers, and almost 6,000 marines. He had only two thousand men and women—and they were the worst of the worst.

At this point, his cabin hatch was kicked open, and he was faced by a tall, powerfully built man in a buckskin costume. Very strange. He was also holding a high-powered laser weapon, like the ones marines used—the kind that could cut him in half or cause his brains to explode.

Behind the buckskin man stood a muscular woman, also clothed in buckskin. In her hand was an AP3000 computer. This was the same kind of computer that captains and admirals carried with them. All the logic for commanding a ship-of-the-line was contained in this 15 kg package.

"In the name of the Rebellion, I am taking command of this ship and your fleet, Admiral Torres. You are relieved of your command. Hold your hands in the air where I can see them and step away from your desk," said the man in buckskins.

"Who do you think you are? This is high piracy! I can have you spaced through an airlock for your insolence!" At this, Admiral Torres pressed the intercom button on his desk and said, "Captain Decadorsky, please come to my cabin with a security detachment."

A voice came over the intercom. It wasn't the voice of the captain, but Dr. Richards.

"I'm afraid the captain cannot come to the intercom right now, Admiral."

"Why not!" yelled the admiral.

"Because he's unconscious. We have been boarded by the Rebellion. They came through the Alpha Wormhole just a few minutes ago."

The buckskin man resumed his declaration. "We have control of this ship and all of your ships in this fleet as we speak, Admiral. I will make you a deal: join our Rebellion and become the High Admiral of our fleet, or refuse—and I will blow your brains out now."

At this point, the woman standing behind the buckskin man said, "Aristides, I will go to the bridge and plug in our AP3000 computer to take us on a course to FNF *Sagittarius A*.*"

"Make it so, Dr. Jones," replied the man in buckskins.

Chapter 17

An interview Between John Doe and a Jewish Rabbi
September 2170

Between the iron gates of fate

The seeds of time were sown

And watered by the deeds of those

Who know and who are known

Well, knowledge is a deadly friend

When no one sets the rules

The fate of all mankind I fear

Is in the hands of fools

Greg Lake, Ian McDonald, Michael Rex Giles, Peter John Sinfield, Robert Fripp

King Crimson Band

Myron Abbot must have drifted off to sleep in the teleporter craft because he was violently awakened. There was a sudden jolt of the craft as it came to rest at the space station. Myron looked out the window of the craft and saw a dizzying array of equipment.

"Are we at the space station?" he inquired.

"We are now at the teleporter docking station of the naval fortress. This is not just a space station, but a space fortress. The fortress has over 50 missile launchers and 100 plasma guns," replied Lt. Jackson.

Myron and the lieutenant were met by Kat Henderson and Midshipman Chu. Lt. Jackson took a special interest in Kat, which made the midshipman look ill at ease.

"I bring you Myron Abbot, per the request of Dr. Rosenstein," said Lt. Jackson.

On hearing this, Myron asked, "Is Dr. Rosenstein Jewish?"

"I don't know if he is Jewish, but he is our naval surgeon. Come this way, please. He is waiting for us in sickbay," replied Midshipman Chu.

The four of them took the long walk to sickbay. The walk was quite disorienting to Myron because of the rotation of the fortress to produce artificial gravity. To the walker, it looked like you were walking uphill, even though no extra energy was required. If you looked behind you, it looked like you were walking downhill. They finally arrived at sickbay, which was on the opposite side of the fortress. Kat slipped a keycard into the hatch, which was in the hall ceiling, to let them in. This was also very disorienting to Myron because he had to climb a ladder to get into the reception area.

Once in sickbay, the foursome walked down a short, upwardly curving hall to Room 5. To get into this room, they had to climb yet another ladder in the ceiling. The room was quite small. To one side of the room was a small bed occupied by an elderly man who looked Middle Eastern. There wasn't much room, so everyone had to stand shoulder to shoulder. Once in the room, they were greeted by Dr. Rosenstein and two other men.

"Permit me to introduce to you our Chief Scientific Officer, Dr. Tempus, and the space fortress naval commandant, Captain Son Ri."

Dr. Rosenstein turned to Myron.

"Shalom to you, Dr. Abbot. I am a great admirer of yours. Congratulations on your Nobel Prize. You have done much to bring peace to the Federation."

"So, you are Jewish!" exclaimed Myron.

"Let me get to the point—John Doe here may be Jewish also. When he talks, I can make out a few Hebrew words. He seems to speak some dialect related to the Hebrew language," explained Dr. Rosenstein.

Myron moved over to the bedside of John Doe and said, "Shalom."

John Doe responded with a dialogue with Myron that lasted 15 minutes and might as well have been Martian to the others in the room. Finally, there was a pause.

Dr. Tempus asked Myron, "What language are you speaking?"

"Ancient precursor to the Hebrew language that predates the time of Abraham."

The wheels inside of Kat's brain began to turn. She wondered how this old man could speak a long-dead language. Where was he from?

Dr. Tempus stepped forward and asked, "Ask him his name, please."

"He already told me. His name is Enoch."

Dr. Tempus gave a meaningful look toward Captain Son Ri and said, "See Captain, I told you so!"

Then the captain said, "Leave us—all of you except Dr. Abbot!"

As everyone climbed the ladder down to the hallway, Kat began to wonder: *Enoch. Where have I heard that name before?* As she walked down the hall, she could hear Myron Abbot screaming incoherently.

***

About an hour later, two older men were seen in the space fortress canteen. Myron and Dr. Tempus decided to have a "little chat." This was in response to an outburst from Myron during the interview with Enoch in sickbay. After the passage of a few minutes, which seemed to be an eternity, Dr. Tempus said,

"You really didn't need to scream at me. I am a rational person. Why are you so angry?"

"Don't patronize me! I know who you have in sickbay. And yet, you and Captain Son Ri are just using him as a failed experiment!" Myron screamed.

"Don't worry. We will take good care of Enoch," said Dr. Tempus in a soothing voice.

"That's the problem with you scientists: your sense of power comes from the technology you create. You use it without the slightest thought of whether you should. It's like a kid finding his father's loaded pistol and firing off a shot at his mother! I want to go back to Earth now! I don't want anything to do with your experiment!" screamed Myron Abbot.

"We can't let you go back to Earth now. You know too much. We will give you freedom on this space fortress. At some point, we will send you to the planet Beyond. However, we can't let you go home," replied Dr. Tempus.

At this point, two marines appeared in the canteen. One of them walked over to Dr. Tempus and Myron and asked,

"Is there a problem here?"

"No, we are just having an adult conversation," replied Dr. Tempus.

"Can you keep it down, please?" said the marine.

After the two marines left, there was a pregnant pause in the conversation between Myron and Dr. Tempus. During the silence, Myron noted that Dr. Tempus had a long scar behind his ear. Normally, Dr. Tempus's long hair covered the scar. However, during their heated argument, Dr. Tempus's ponytail had come apart and his hair had started to fly around.

Finally, Myron broke the silence. "Maybe we got off on the wrong foot. Let me tell you something about myself, then you can tell me something about you. I am Myron Abbot. I am 70 years old and I teach at a rabbinical school in Los Angeles. I am recently widowed."

Myron's last comment about being recently widowed lodged in Dr. Tempus's mind. Some primordial thought was trying to express itself in his mind. The thought would appear like the sun on a cloudy day and quickly disappear behind another dark cloud. Dr. Tempus felt like he was trapped in the prison of his incomplete memories.

Myron saw the confusion on Dr. Tempus's face. For a moment, Dr. Tempus looked almost human. At this point, Myron said something that was very disarming: "I have Alzheimer's disease."

"I'm sorry to hear that. Is that why you have outbursts of anger?"

"It's the result of my frustration. When I can't understand what is happening around me, or when I can't remember something, I become frustrated and angry. Most of the time, I can't even remember what day it is. I can remember things perfectly that happened 10 or 20 years ago, but I cannot remember what happened 5 minutes ago. Please tell me something about you."

"I am Dr. Tempus, Chief Scientific Officer on the FNF *Sagittarius A*.*"

"Do you have a first name?" asked Myron in amazement.

"I don't need one," responded Dr. Tempus.

"Everyone needs to have a first name. It is part of who we are."

"I don't have one."

"Do you have a family?" asked Myron in a sympathetic voice.

"I don't know," said Dr. Tempus, who looked quite confused and seemed like he was going into a mental crisis.

"Where did you come from before coming to the space station?" Myron asked.

"I don't know. I do know two things well, though. I know a lot about physics and the Bible," replied Dr. Tempus.

"That is strange—that you would know a lot about two subjects that have little to do with each other—and that you cannot remember your past. Very strange. I can remember things from 10 or 20 years ago perfectly, but you cannot remember who you are or where you came from," said Myron.

At this point, Dr. Tempus rose, looked at his electronic tablet, and said, "If you will excuse me, I have an important matter that I must attend to in my laboratory. You may come along, if you like."

Chapter 18

Inside a Problem of Time

And as they still went on and talked,

behold, a ring of fire and a fiery vessel separated the two of them.

And Epsilon-Giga went up by the fiery vessel into space.

And his assistant saw it and he cried, "Epsilon-Giga!

The fiery probe of the Federation and its ring of fire!"

And he saw him no more.

Stories of the past, as told by the Oracle of the Federation

Myron Abbot and Dr. Tempus entered the darkly lit Space-Time Laboratory. On the far wall was a large monitor that showed the expanse of space outside the station. The view was like nothing Myron had ever seen. The velocities of the stars were so high that their movement could be perceived in a matter of minutes. The stars were orbiting around an object that was blacker than black. Around this black object was a circle of blinding light. Farther out from this circle, the sky resolved into individual stars. A disk of light circled around the equator of the black object.

Dr. Tempus pointed at the screen and explained, "The blackness in space that you see is a deep gravitational well in the space-time continuum. The well in the space-time matrix is so deep that all matter and even light that ventures too close is drawn into the well, never to return. This well in the space-time continuum is also known as a black hole. Massive stars rotate around the black hole at velocities approaching 1% of the speed of light. The circle of light around the black hole is the light from 10,000 stars being bent around the hole to create a ring of light. In effect, the gravitational field of the black hole serves as a lens to create this ring of light. The Saturn-like disk around the middle of the black hole is an accretion disk, composed of matter and radiation captured from surrounding space."

"I don't understand. How can we see this black hole and not be drawn in?" asked Myron. Myron seemed much more aware than he was a few minutes ago.

"The FNF *Sagittarius A** orbits a safe distance away. Also, we have a state-of-the-art supercomputer and thrusters that make instantaneous orbital corrections if the gravitational field changes. The mission of this space station is maintained as the Federation's most highly kept secret."

Dr. Tempus stepped over to the control panel. When he seated himself, a group of scientists and technicians sat down around him, like stars orbiting a black hole. One thing that Myron noticed right away was that Dr. Tempus treated his colleagues like cogs in a wheel. Even though he was the Chief Scientific Officer, no one spoke to him. They didn't even look at him. Finally, one of the scientists, the oldest amongst them, spoke, "Portal Finder, what data do you need?"

"I need the mass of that Blue Giant O-class star that is making its close pass to the black hole. I need the mass and the precise temperature of the star's photosphere, and its orbital and rotational velocity. I also need to know the mass of the residual matter in the accretion disk from the last star that made a close approach to the black hole," said Dr. Tempus.

Myron listened to this verbal exchange and thought: *Very strange. The scientific staff refers to Dr. Tempus as the 'Portal Finder.' I wonder why?*

The look on Dr. Tempus's face seemed to be that of someone who was lost. In fact, Dr. Tempus *was* lost. He was lost inside a problem in time. He knew how to follow the movement of the stars that orbited around the black hole: this was merely Newtonian and Relativity Physics. What the Portal Finder was looking for were stars orbiting closer to the black hole, especially the ones that had elliptical orbits. When one of these elliptical-orbiting stars came close to the black hole, matter and energy were stripped off the star at relativistic velocities and torn apart into quarks and anti-quarks. At times, these quarks exceeded the speed of light. When this occurred, a portal in time would open for a matter of minutes.

In other words, a time machine.

Dr. Tempus was lost inside a problem of time. He was tracking a Blue Giant O-class star that had a highly elliptical orbit, like a leopard tracks an elephant. The star was closing in on its near pass to the black hole. As the Blue Giant entered the vicinity of the black hole, the gravitational field began to warp, causing the space station to buck like a bronco. The space fortress itself began to creak loudly, like an ancient sailing ship. The loudspeakers across the space station blared a warning for all personnel to brace themselves. Engineers aboard the space station worked with the supercomputer to make corrections for the perturbations in the orbit of the space station to prevent them from falling into the black hole's event horizon.

Dr. Tempus was lost inside a problem of time. He knew the implications of reaching back into time. Others before him *had* done this once but miscalculated the time portal by thousands of years. The result of this miscalculation was the 'capture' of the wrong subject.

One of the scientists in the control room shouted across the room, "Dr. Tempus, the Blue Giant photosphere is making first contact with the gravitational field of the black hole!"

On the wide-field monitor was a highly filtered image of the Blue O-class star and, presumably, the invisible image of the black hole. The shape of the star was tear-dropped, with the pointed end oriented toward the black hole. One could barely make out a thin filament of matter and radiation that bridged between the Blue Giant and the black hole. Dr. Tempus had this filament greatly magnified. The thread became a large river of light and plasma that spiraled in toward the black hole and formed an accretion disk that orbited and spiraled into the black hole. More matter poured from the Blue Giant, which fed the accretion disk around the black hole. Brilliant jets appeared, emanating from the north and south poles of the black hole. Within the accretion disk were smaller spirals that looked like whirlpools.

The Portal Finder moved his computer cursor to select from the monitor a dozen or so whirlpools that developed in the spiraling mass. These were wormholes with time-machine potential. The Portal Finder had to find the right wormhole that had an abundance of quarks and anti-quarks, along with the correct whirlpool velocity to get to the correct time and place. He was looking for the right time portal. One of these wormholes caught Dr. Tempus's attention. He quickly initiated an analysis of this maelstrom.

Lost inside a problem of time… Dr. Tempus began to mutter a countdown to himself, barely audible. When he reached zero, he raised his voice to be heard above the bedlam, "Prepare the probe to launch… coordinates x: 180.806, y: 15.675, z: 0.00; launch at my command."

Then the room in the space station became so silent that Myron could hear his own breathing and heartbeat, but no one else was breathing. All that could be heard was the creaking of the space fortress. They were waiting for the right time and command to send the probe. The Portal Finder's mind was now racing: he knew that he had the power to issue the command, he knew the great power he wielded, but a thought crossed his mind: Was his decision and action right?

Was it right from a moral standpoint—to take a man out of his context of space and time and transport him, against his will, to a totally different space and time? To bring the prisoner to their space and time to exploit his abilities? There were theological implications: what if the power he wielded was against the sovereign will of God? Then there was the risk of causing a paradox in time that would change history, and change the present. Many things to consider, thought Dr. Tempus.

However, the Portal Finder had an opportunity that could save the present. His window of time would close soon, so the probe needed to be launched now! Dr. Tempus issued the command, "Launch the probe!"

There was a barely perceptible shudder in the Space Station as the probe launched. The scientists in the control room watched the trajectory of the probe disappear into the maelstrom of the wormhole. The probe had now left Dr. Tempus's space and time.

***

Dr. Tempus and the other scientists gathered at the airlock to the docking station of FNF *Sagittarius A**, waiting for the probe to arrive. Standing before them was a squad of heavily armed marines, commanded by Lieutenant Jackson. Myron Abbot stood behind the scientists and marines. Behind all of them stood Lt. Kat Henderson.

Everyone there was silent. Kat had no idea why she was ordered to report to the shuttle bay. Maybe some casualties were being shuttled in. The hair on the back of her head stood up in anticipation of who knows what kind of wounds she would need to treat.

The inside of the shuttle bay was brightly lit. The floor was metallic and smelled of hydraulic fluid. *One of the shuttles that came in this week must have had a leak—or maybe the hydraulic lifts for the shuttle bay doors needed maintenance,* wondered Lt. Jackson.

Myron Abbot broke the silence. "What are we waiting for?"

No one answered at first. Only the sound of air recyclers kept the silence at bay. Finally, Dr. Tempus spoke, "We are awaiting the salvation of the Federation."

The silence reigned until the alarm sounded. Lieutenant Jackson spoke in a hushed voice, "Okay men, keep your anti-riot stun guns on the probe at all times, but nobody fires unless I give the order. Keep your laser rifles behind your back so you do not provoke the subject. We will use our anti-riot stun guns to subdue the subject. We will only use lethal force from our laser rifles if our personal safety is at risk."

The large door on the other side of the airlock began to open silently. Myron found the silence to be strange, like a scene out of a silent movie.

A dark shadow appeared, its presence only revealed by the absence of stars that it was blocking. The shadow danced back and forth, then became larger. Almost like magic, the shadow developed more defined shape and color as the shuttle bay lights reflected off the probe's metallic surface. The probe moved into the bay, lowered its insect-like legs, and settled on the shuttle bay floor.

Dr. Tempus told one of his techs to close the shuttle bay doors and to begin pressurizing the bay. This process took about 10 minutes. A green light went on the control panel. Then Dr. Tempus, in his soft voice, said, "Open the airlock door, then the probe doors."

When the probe door opened, the subject in the probe appeared to be a small old man, looking somewhat like John Doe in sickbay. His eyes first took in the scene before him. He shook his head and rubbed his eyes with the palms of his hands. He then looked up, yelling something that was incomprehensible.

Myron then tapped Dr. Tempus with one hand, and Kat with the other, and whispered, "Get down on the floor. Now!"

Kat and Dr. Tempus responded in unison, "Huh?"

"Now!" screamed Myron. Although Myron was a gentle old man, he grabbed both Dr. Tempus and Kat by their collars and pulled them to the floor.

This caused the marines to turn and look at the scene behind them—an old rabbi lying on top of Dr. Tempus and Lt. Henderson. They started to laugh. Until it happened.

What happened was a force emanating from the subject in the probe. It at first whistled around them like a siren from Greek mythology. It felt like wind, smelled like roses, and seemed to communicate something. Lt. Jackson looked worried. He knew he shouldn't be, but something in the air told him that something large and powerful had come through the shuttle bay door. Something terrible, and yet, beautiful.

"Men, keep your eyes on the probe and the subject."

At this point, Kat was looking up from the floor. She too felt the presence of something huge, powerful, and yet benevolent.

Myron said to Dr. Tempus and Kat, "Don't look. Whatever you do, don't look!"

Without warning, the subject in the probe looked from the ceiling to the floor. His eyes grew large. He moved his head back, like a cobra getting ready to strike.

The marines, in unison, clicked off the safeties on their electric anti-riot weapons. There was a dread in the air. Something was about to happen. Then it happened.

The subject suddenly lunged forward. The cobra had struck.

All of the marines were knocked to the floor. Lieutenant Jackson gave the order to fire their anti-riot guns. Each gun shot two small, conductive darts. The guns produced little reports as all of the marines fired the darts.

The darts never made it to the subject. He simply raised his right hand, and the darts just stopped. The subject studied the darts like an entomologist would study a rare beetle in the wild. Then the subject collected the darts in his right hand, and with lightning speed, hurled the darts back at the marines.

Lt. Jackson shouted, "Disable the electric pulse before we get shocked!" But it was too late: somehow, the subject was able to remotely charge the darts, and all of the marines writhed in agony on the floor. Then the subject ran out of the shuttle bay.

Dr. Tempus pushed Myron to the side and ran to the comm. He hit the microphone button and shouted, "All hell has broken loose. The subject has neutralized all of the marines in the shuttle bay and is free in the station. Request that all personnel lock down all means of egress, and all available marines to seek out the subject and subdue him at all cost. Do not—I repeat—do not kill the subject.

The subject has taken on the appearance of a bearded old man dressed in a burlap tunic, wearing sandals on his feet."

Chapter 19

Who was that alien?

The marines were still writhing when Kat got off the floor. "Who was that man? He was old, but he took off like an Olympic sprinter! How did he stop the anti-riot electrode darts like that?"

Myron stood and brushed himself off. "I'm not sure, but he spoke ancient Hebrew." Kat and Dr. Tempus only stared at Myron.

Finally, Dr. Tempus spoke. "It is an alien."

Myron blurted out, "This is blasphemous! He is not an alien. You are playing God when you removed him from his context of time and space. What evil has befallen you, Dr. Tempus?" At this point, Myron began to shake. His anger was palpable. He was breathing deeply. Myron's physician had warned him to avoid stressful situations. His physician told him that stress could trigger delusions. Myron then began to wonder—was this really happening, or was it the Alzheimer's taking over his thoughts and his ability to interpret reality? Myron then simply collapsed to the floor.

Kat quickly took Myron's pulse and other vital signs. "He has only fainted, Dr. Tempus. Help me get Myron to sickbay. I think his delusions have hit a crisis level!"

In the station, there was a detachment of marines under the command of Lt. Jackson. The strength of the detachment was 40 men. One squad, or 10 men, was on the floor of the shuttle bay, writing in pain. Somehow, Lt. Jackson drew the lucky straw and did not get hit with one of the ten anti-riot darts. This left 30 men to find the elusive subject. They broke up into three squads and began to comb through the space station. But the subject could not be found.

After about an hour of this random search, Lt. Jackson recovered his composure. He got on the comm and ordered his men to meet in the shuttle bay to devise a strategy to find and subdue the subject. While the marines were trickling into the shuttle bay, Lt. Jackson got on the comm to find and query Dr. Tempus and Myron to get more details on the subject. He finally found them in sickbay. Myron was given a sedative and was blissfully drifting off to dreamland.

"Dr. Tempus, my detachment of marines has been unable to locate the subject. Can you tell me anything about him?"

"It is an alien taken from the Rigel Sector. It is typically in a reptilian form that can change color and form like a chameleon. It has taken on human form to elude us."

"How can we subdue him?" asked Lt. Jackson.

"I don't know. Whatever you do, don't kill him. Try using a taser or tranquilizer darts. Use the riot ammo," responded Dr. Tempus.

"This is not helpful," replied Lt. Jackson. "Sir, we have a madman, or an alien, or who knows what, running around here with the ability to change its appearance and the power to take out my whole detachment of marines. You need to be more helpful."

"Look, the alien can manipulate the laws of physics to bend to its liking. It also has extraordinary strength. You will have to catch it unaware. Otherwise… it will not go down well for you," said Dr. Tempus.

At this point, Midshipman Chu got on the comm. "Lt. Jackson, I think you need to see something… I will meet you at the hatch to the space fortress nuclear reactor." Midshipman Chu was on his first tour of duty. He was green and frequently clueless. Some thought that he was on the Asperger's–Autism spectrum. Some people thought he was not the brightest bulb in the box.

Lt. Jackson was in the outer 'wheel' of the space fortress and needed to get to the hub. This required him to climb "up" a ladder to the hub, since he had to climb against the centrifugal force that gave the main decks in the wheel of the fortress its artificial gravity. When he reached the hub, he was nearly weightless, since the centrifugal force was much less there.

The midshipman was floating at the hub, near the hatch to the reactor. Well, it *was* the hatch. The hatch to the reactor was made of lead to shield the space station occupants from radiation if the reactor were to malfunction. The hatch was one meter thick and had to weigh at least 15 tons. The hatch had been ripped from its titanium hinges and bent in half.

Lt. Jackson was the first to meet Midshipman Chu. The lieutenant simply stared at the damaged hatch. "The alien has done this," muttered Lt. Jackson.

At this point, Dr. Tempus arrived. He too, stopped and stared at the damaged hatch.

"Is the reactor still operating normally? Are we being exposed to radiation?" asked Dr. Tempus.

"Well, that's just the thing. My shift assignment was to monitor the reactor. I am new here, so Captain Son Ri assigned me to reactor duty since these types of reactors rarely fail," said Ming Chu.

"What's your point?" asked Dr. Tempus in an irritated tone.

"Well, it's just this," answered Midshipman Chu. "The reactor power has dropped to 10% of baseline power. At this power level, we can only maintain life support, and electricity to the supercomputer and lights and things like that. Fortunately, we are not receiving dangerous levels of radiation."

Dr. Tempus closed his eyes and rubbed his temples, then asked, "Do we still have power for the thrusters?"

"No, sir," replied Ming Chu.

"Mr. Chu, do you realize that we are orbiting the most massive object in the Milky Way Galaxy? Do you have any idea what will happen if we cannot maintain our orbit?"

"No, sir," replied Ming, meekly.

"We will fall into a massive gravity well, where even light cannot escape. Do you know what will happen then?"

"No, sir."

"All molecular, atomic, and subatomic space in our bodies will be crushed to a point of singularity," said Dr. Tempus, as he clapped his hands together for effect.

"That doesn't sound pleasant."

"It's not," replied Dr. Tempus.

At this point, the chief engineer for the station arrived with her diagnostic equipment. She plugged it into the reactor computer.

"This is very strange—90% of the plutonium fuel rods are missing. There is no record in the computer of the removal of the reactor fuel. It just vanished."

Dr. Tempus closed his eyes again and rubbed his temples. Then he opened his eyes and said, "I think I know what took it."

***

The hub was poorly lit and jam-packed with air recycling equipment, plumbing, wiring, and fiber-optic transmission lines. It had a hum like a hornet's nest. Angry hornets. It smelled of ozone and dust. Off in a corner, something was stacked like cordwood. The ozone smell was emanating from the cordwood. Sitting near the cordwood was the alien. It looked forlorn and perplexed. It was talking to itself in a language that few understood.

"Why am I here? Why did I steal the wood for the furnace? Who are these creatures that pursue me?"

It sat in silence for a few moments. The sense of dread it was experiencing was awful.

"Where am I? I thought the fiery vehicle was taking me to you. Please tell me what to do next?" muttered the alien.

It brooded for a few moments. The confusion in its mind was starting to make the situation look fuzzy, like it was in a fog bank.

At this point, the alien began to weep.

Midshipman Chu and Lt. Jackson were about to ask Dr. Tempus what he meant about knowing who stole the reactor cores when they were interrupted by the intercom.

"Midshipman Chu, this is Captain Son Ri. I am going to pipe down to you a message that we received a minute ago from the reactor room. It's a bunch of jabbering that no one can make heads or tails out of."

"Pipe it through." As Midshipman Chu and Lt. Jackson listened, they heard a language that was incomprehensible. The jabbering ended, and something strange was heard: it almost sounded like weeping.

"Can you pinpoint the exact location?" requested Ming Chu.

"I am transmitting the coordinates to you now," responded Capt. Son Ri.

Lt. Jackson turned to his fellow marines and said, "Let's go and catch our reactor fuel-rod thief. Midshipman Chu: have radiation suits brought for my men."

The entrance to the hub was a ladder that went up through one of the spokes of the space fortress wheel. The reactor was in the hub of the rotating space station. This made it disorienting to navigate: the space fortress rotated, which gave the illusion of gravity to the arms and ring of the space station; gravity was lowest at the hub, where the reactor was located.

"Midshipman, is there another access point to the other side of the hub?" asked Lt. Jackson.

"Yes sir. About 600 meters to your right," responded Ming Chu.

"Is the hub lit?" asked Lt. Jackson.

"Yes sir," replied Ming Chu.

"Can we cut the lights from here?"

"Yes sir."

Lt. Jackson then turned to the marines and said, "Okay, so here is the plan. Sergeant Bernowski, you take your men to the other access point. When I give you the signal, turn off the lights in the hub, and activate your infrared detectors in your goggles. Get as close to the alien as you can without being seen. Take up good sniper positions at your discretion. When I give you the second signal, open fire with your anti-riot ammo. This will deceive the alien into thinking that our primary attack is from you. Then Sergeant Xing will attack the alien from this access point."

Dr. Tempus, who was standing in the background, suddenly spoke up, "Do not use deadly force. We want to subdue the alien. After that, we will take the alien to sickbay."

"Why sickbay?" asked Lt. Jackson.

"The alien may harbor pathogens that are new to humans. We will have no immunity to the pathogens. We need to keep the alien heavily sedated and in isolation," replied Dr. Tempus.

"Okay men, you heard what Dr. Tempus said," replied Lt. Jackson as he turned to face them.

Lt. Jackson took Sergeant Xing and half of his detachment and had them guard the ladder to the hub. He took the other half of the platoon under Sgt. Bernowski's command and sent them about a quarter of the space fortress's radius away. Lt. Jackson muttered to himself, "Now we have the alien where we want it."

At this, Dr. Tempus turned away and smiled.

After donning their radiation suits, Sergeant Bernowski and his marines worked their way through the main part of the station to one of the four spokes. Here, they ascended a ladder to the hub of the station. They carefully opened the hatch to the core. This room in the mezzanine was a storeroom, where communications cables and routers were kept. They quietly floated (there is very little centrifugal force in the core) to a hatch across from where they entered. Passing through this door, they saw the reactor fuel rods stacked on the far wall. The alien could not be seen from this vantage point, which was good, since it also meant that the alien could not see them. Using the myriads of cables, pipes, and equipment, Bernowski signaled to his squad to take up various sniper positions in the hub where they waited for Lt. Jackson's first signal.

Lieutenant Jackson and Sergeant Xing readied themselves in their radiation suits at the spoke access point. The lieutenant whispered instructions to them,

"Sergeant Xing, you take half of your squad through the spoke to the hub access and wait for my first signal to shut off the lights in the hub. Make sure that your squad dons their infrared goggles, because it's going to get really dark. When you hear the second signal for Bernowski to open fire on the alien, enter the hub and subdue the alien. If for some reason the alien gets past you, I will use the other half of your squad to subdue the alien as it makes its escape through this spoke. Make sure your guns are on stun, and make sure that you and your squad do not come into physical contact with the alien. Any questions?"

The marines affirmed their understanding with a nod.

"Good. Go!"

Bernowski's squad waited in their sniper positions. Then the first signal came through Bernowski's headset. The lights went out and there was silence at first, then his squad could hear the alien moving about. Since the alien was warm-blooded, they could see its movements in their infrared goggles. Then the second signal came through, and they opened fire. Their fire was rather ineffective, since the alien easily caught their rifle darts with its hands. Nevertheless, the squad kept up their diversionary fire.

Meanwhile, Sergeant Xing's squad quickly and silently moved from the spoke into the hub. After the first signal, they extinguished the lights. When the second signal was given, they entered the hub. When they entered the hub, they saw the alien moving towards them and moving its hands very quickly, as if it were fending off darts from Bernowski's squad. However, the alien's head was facing Bernowski's squad, so it did not see Xing's squad. Xing signaled to his troops, and all of them fired their stun darts simultaneously. All the darts found their mark, and the alien fell into a comatose state.

Lt. Jackson pulled out his comm and said,

"Engineering Deck, the missing reactor fuel rods have been found in the service core of the fortress hub. Please recover the fuel rods and reinsert them into the reactor after the reactor room hatch has been repaired."

Outside the hub in the spoke, a medical team garbed in isolation gear, headed by Lt. Kat Henderson, waited for their signal to retrieve the alien from the hub of the station. The signal was given, and the team placed the alien in an isolation stretcher and sent it to sickbay.

However, Kat was not to be fooled. This wasn't an alien, but the same species as her. Also, she could tell that the "alien" had the same ethnicity as "John Doe," who was also still in sickbay.

A few hours later, Kat received a copy of the microbiology report. In the summary of the report, it read:

The patient's microflora and viruses are not extraordinary, and are commonly found on human skin, in the respiratory tract, and in the gastrointestinal tract. No exotic extraterrestrial microflora or viruses were found.

Kat began to think: *The subject is definitely not an alien from another world. I need to get to the bottom of this.*

Chapter 20

When A Demented Theologian and A Broken Physicist Talk...

Dr. Tempus was waiting in sickbay when the alien was brought in on an isolation gurney. The alien was aseptically removed from the gurney into an isolation room. Dr. Rosenstein took Dr. Tempus to the side and spoke in a low voice, "Given the nature of the subject's extraordinary powers, I suggest that we keep the subject heavily sedated until we stabilize his functions and get a better idea of what we are dealing with. This will also give the Microbiology lab some time to check out any microbes that came with the alien."

"Make sure you use restraints on the alien, and contact me when he regains consciousness," whispered Dr. Tempus. "By the way, how is Myron Abbot doing?"

"He's doing fine. In fact, we are releasing him as we speak," responded Dr. Rosenstein. "But be careful what you say to him—he is still a little disoriented."

"Of course," responded Dr. Tempus, as he looked over Dr. Rosenstein's shoulder. There behind him was Myron.

"Myron, may I escort you to your quarters?" inquired Dr. Tempus.

"Do you promise not to quarrel, Dr. Tempus?" replied Myron.

"I promise, if you promise, Myron."

Myron's cabin was on the outer deck of the space station. They gave him a cabin on this deck because the centrifugal force was greatest, and therefore the artificial gravity was like that found on Earth. This cabin was assigned to him out of deference to Myron's age and Alzheimer's disease.

Dr. Tempus showed Myron how to open his cabin door with the key card, and said, "This is your key card to lock and unlock your cabin. You can also use this card to get food at the mess hall and, if you choose, to access the gym, which is also on the outer deck."

"I don't think I'll be using the gym. I am an old man and a little past all that," replied Myron.

Once inside the cabin, they sat there for a few minutes and stared at each other. Finally, Myron broke the ice, "What made you decide to come to this space fortress, Dr. Tempus?"

"I don't recall," responded Dr. Tempus. There again was a pause of about a minute. "Strange that I don't remember how I even arrived here."

Myron pondered for a moment, then asked, "May I check something on your head?"

"Go ahead," responded Dr. Tempus.

Myron stood up and walked over to Dr. Tempus. He undid Dr. Tempus's ponytail and pulled back some of his hair behind his ear.

"Oh my goodness, Dr. Tempus! Where did you get this 4-inch scar behind your ear? Was it an injury?"

"Scar? What scar?" exclaimed Dr. Tempus.

"Come into the bathroom and let me show you."

The two of them went into the bathroom and looked in the mirror. It took a few moments to get Dr. Tempus in position so Myron could get him to see his scalp behind his ear. And there it was: a four-inch scar.

"I don't recall how I received this scar, Myron."

Dr. Tempus took his index finger and ran it over the scar for about a minute. He closed his eyes, then tried to remember. Vaguely, at first, he began to see a bright light come out of the darkness. There was a jumble of voices, speaking softly at first, and then more understandably. There was a female and male speaking. The male was asking the female for a scalpel, then for a Striker saw. The vibrating sound of the Striker filled Dr. Tempus's vision. The repugnant smell of bone dust filled his vision of the past. He felt the vibrations on his head, behind his ear. Then the Striker saw was silent, but he could still hear the voices in his vision of the past. The voices were familiar. Suddenly, Dr. Tempus opened his eyes and shouted, "Dr. Rosenstein and one of his nurses! What were they doing to me?"

"Please lie down, Dr. Tempus," said Myron as his kind face stared into Dr. Tempus's eyes. "You were remembering something that must have been terrifying."

After Myron helped Dr. Tempus to the bed, he noticed a very small bottle of bourbon in the cabin. He opened the bottle and poured about half of it into a glass, offering it to Dr. Tempus. Dr. Tempus took a small sip and shook his head.

"The last time I had bourbon was in Northern Wisconsin!" exclaimed Dr. Tempus.

"Northern Wisconsin? I thought you didn't know where you came from!" exclaimed Myron.

When Myron heard this, he brought a second glass to the night table and poured the rest of the bourbon. He picked up the glass and examined the contents. He brought the glass to his lips, tilted his head back, and consumed the entire contents in one motion.

"Take it easy, Myron! Should you be drinking this stuff? I mean, with your Alzheimer's and all?"

Myron waved off Dr. Tempus and said, "So, Dr. Tempus, you are from Northern Wisconsin. Why were you drinking bourbon there?"

"I was trying to forget something. Something real terrible. I wanted to kill the pain."

There was silence in Myron's cabin for about five minutes. Then Dr. Tempus broke the silence, "I was trying to forget my wife. She had passed away from ovarian cancer."

"I know how you must have felt. I lost my wife about five years ago. What was your wife's name?"

"Betsy. She was beautiful in form and spirit. When she died, my whole world came apart, Myron. What was your wife's name?"

"Tilly. We were married for 40 years. She was killed during 'The Persecution' by a group of marines." At this, Myron became silent and crestfallen. "They were beasts, you know. They killed her slowly before my eyes. When did your wife die?"

"Back in 2061."

"Oh, you must mean 2161."

"No! I mean 2061. I remember the date well. It was one year before…"

"Before what, Dr. Tempus?"

"Before I committed suicide, Myron."

"How is this possible? You are not dead!" exclaimed Myron.

"I don't know," replied a confused Dr. Tempus.

"Dr. Tempus, are you sure about the date when all this happened?"

"Definitely 2061," confirmed Dr. Tempus.

"It's 2170. You have been dead for 110 years!" exclaimed Myron.

At this point, the effects of the bourbon began to set in. Both Myron and Dr. Tempus became a bit tipsy. Then Dr. Tempus made an interesting observation: "Myron, you don't seem to be so disoriented. You have changed. What happened?"

"You happened! I have just witnessed a miracle. Not only do you remember, you have changed. You have changed from a computational machine to a human. But I am still confused. How can you be dead for over one hundred years? This is not possible. Is your real name Dr. Tempus?" asked Myron.

"My name is Dr. Robert Hays. I won the Nobel Prize in Physics in 2058. Wait, there is something else. Something really important. It's coming. I. Am. A. Disciple. Of. Jesus. Christ. Myron, I am a Christian!"

"And I am an Orthodox Hasidic Jew!" exclaimed Myron. "We need to talk about the alien on this space station. We need to talk now because he is not an alien!"

"Why do we need to talk now, Myron? The alien is safely sedated in sickbay."

"That's the point. The alien is not an alien, Dr. Hays."

"What is the alien, then?" asked Dr. Hays with a confused look on his face.

"It is not what, but who."

"Who is the alien?" inquired Dr. Hays.

"He is the Prophet Elijah! This space station has ripped Elijah out of the context of his time!" shouted Myron.

Dr. Hays thought about this for a minute or so, then replied, "Oh, no! Time paradox! All history—past, present, and future—is balancing on a knife's edge. What can we do to correct this, Myron?"

"You need to send him back to his time, as soon as possible. Can you do this?" asked Myron.

"It may be difficult, but not impossible… There is another large star coming in close to the black hole in three days. It all depends on how the star's material is stripped off by the black hole… We might be able to pull this off. I will need your help, Myron."

"You have it!" shouted Myron.

Chapter 21

Space Fortress is Under Attack!

Grand Admiral Torres of the rebel fleet was back in command. He was standing on the bridge of his flagship *Brazil*, and he was in his glory. Next to him was Captain Hung Ching. One of the first things Admiral Torres did after being selected by Aristides was to *space* Captain Decadorsky. He even televised the spacing event to the entire fleet. He did this for two reasons. The first reason was that he hated the idiot Decadorsky. The second reason was that he wanted to set an example to all other crew members and officers in the fleet that incompetence would not be tolerated.

Besides, Admiral Torres was fond of Hung. Hung was one of the few officers who had been unjustly condemned to the mothballed fleet, also known as Purgatory. He was quite competent. Admiral Torres wanted the best officers on the *Brazil* to show the rest of the fleet how a ship-of-the-line should be handled.

Currently, the rebel fleet was using the black hole to shield its movements from the FNF *Sagittarius A**. The admiral did not want to announce his intentions to the enemy. Quite literally, he was keeping the enemy in the dark.

"Helmsman, keep your course set to 270.367, 0.000, and 11.423. Maintain speed at 0.02% relativistic. Space-Time Deck, keep a watch out for gravitational waves near the black hole. I don't want any surprises that cause us to be sucked into the black hole," commanded Torres.

At that moment, the central hatch to the bridge opened, and in floated Aristides. He grabbed the lateral ladder and stepped down to the circular deck, where the centrifugal force of the spinning ship held him to the floor.

Aristides turned to the admiral and said, "Admiral Torres, was it really necessary to space Captain Decadorsky and make the entire fleet watch? My rebel fleet will not be operated like a fleet of pirates!"

"You are wrong on two points, Aristides. First, this is not *your* fleet—it's *my* fleet. Second, the integrity of any space fleet is based on discipline. My officers are not a bunch of toadies who kiss up to their admiral. This fleet operates because of fear and absolute loyalty to the chain of command. And besides, how many in your army, if it can be called that, were senselessly sacrificed in suicide charges on Earth? I have heard that the number exceeds 100,000…"

"Enough!" cried Aristides. "Why haven't we engaged the enemy yet?"

"Now see here, Aristides. We are not engaging a squad of marines here. We are engaging the largest space fortresses in the Federation. We are masking our movements behind the black hole. We also need time to train your men and women. When you captured our fleet, we had skeleton crews on board—not nearly enough men and women to get underway. And how shall I say it? Your people are not the fastest learners."

"Admiral Torres, I get what you are saying. When do you think you will make your move on the fortress and capture it?" asked Aristides.

"The capturing of the fortress in its entirety will be much more difficult than destroying it. When we emerge from the shadow of the black hole, the fortress will seek to understand what our intentions are. They have the equipment to identify every ship in the fleet. They will know that we are the mothballed fleet. The deployment of the entire fleet will raise questions. If we shoot a warning shot, they will most certainly open fire on us with everything they've got. I know Captain Son Ri, who commands the naval fortress—tough as nails. His primary orders are to defend the space fortress and the Beta Wormhole to the planet *Beyond* at all costs," said Admiral Torres.

"Maybe you, Dr. Jones, and I should meet to put together a strategy to capture the space fortress. Can we meet in your cabin after dinner?" inquired Aristides.

***

After dinner, the Admiral, Dr. Leslie Jones, and Aristides met in the admiral's quarters. One of the advantages of being a fleet admiral was that the cabins were quite luxurious and large. There were two rooms: one was his private cabin, and the other was a large meeting room that could accommodate 20 or more officers.

At the door of the cabin and meeting room stood a very large Marine with a vicious-looking laser rifle. When the three of them approached, the guard shouted, "Halt: What is your intention?"

"1X34B00.004," replied Admiral Torres.

"You may pass."

Once in the room, the admiral turned and said to Aristides and Dr. Jones, "Don't try to use that code again. All of our ships have an enigma code machine that generates new codes every five minutes.

If you give the wrong code, the Marine guard has orders to liquidate you."

"Very convenient, Admiral," replied Aristides.

"It keeps mutinies down to zero. The Federation Navy is a tight operation with strict discipline. In other words: don't try anything funny. I am the Lord of this fleet," said Admiral Torres in a patronizing tone.

Aristides then asked, "You know Captain Son Ri. Did he serve under you in the past?"

"Yes," replied the admiral.

"Yes, what! Let's not hide anything from each other. We are all friends here," said Aristides in an irritated tone.

"You are wrong there. You are not my friend. But you are my ally. To answer your question: Captain Son Ri served under me in the last war. The fleet I was commanding was ambushed in the Battle of Phobos. Captain Son Ri commanded one of my ships, the 74-gun *Ukraine*. When a court-martial hearing was held, Captain Son Ri testified against me to save his own skin," explained Admiral Torres.

"Okay, I get it. So, you are not exactly on speaking terms with each other. May I offer an alternative to bringing out the entire fleet from the shadow of the black hole?" asked Aristides.

"Sure. Go ahead, Aristides."

"Actually, this was Dr. Leslie Jones' idea. I'll let her speak for herself."

At this point, Leslie jumped into the discussion. "Why not bring out just three ships instead of the entire fleet? Say, bring out the *Brazil* and two escort frigates. And Admiral, with all due respect, you need to not be seen or heard during the negotiations. Just the sight of you would cause Son Ri to fire all his guns and missiles at you. Why not have Captain Hung Ching of the *Brazil* contact Captain Son Ri? I understand that Son Ri and Hung Ching were roommates at the naval academy."

At this, Admiral Torres turned to Aristides and said, "Smart woman! Where did you meet her?"

Aristides answered, "Dr. Leslie Jones was the lead scientist at the last teleporter on Earth. She was the mastermind who orchestrated the use of the San Francisco teleporter to take over the mothballed fleet."

"Ah, *my* fleet," corrected Admiral Torres.

"Okay, your fleet," conceded Leslie. "Is there anything the space fortress has that we need? For example, supplies or fuel?"

"There is only one thing that the fortress has that we need: permission to enter the Beta Wormhole to get to the planet Beyond. Wait a minute! That's it! Capt. Ching and Capt. Son Ri are buddies that go way back. Why didn't I think of this! We can have our Captain Ching contact Son Ri to tell him that we are on a special mission to the planet Beyond, and he is asking permission to enter the wormhole. Once permission is granted, Capt. Hung Ching would request to come over to the space fortress to reminisce with Capt. Son Ri. Then we could have a company of Marines shuttle over to the space fortress in a shuttlecraft and take over the space station. It would all have to be well-coordinated and fast for this to work," said Admiral Torres.

"What are the risks?" asked Leslie.

"We will be under all 100 of the fortress's plasma guns. If they open fire on us, we will be blown to atoms. If they start shooting, we will need to fire back," said the Admiral.

"Try not to!" answered Aristides and Dr. Jones in unison.

"One more thing. They will want to know the disposition of the rest of the mothballed fleet. They are expecting that the last of the teleporters has been destroyed. If that command was carried out, then the space fortress will be expecting some naval force to come through with the last of the evacuees from Earth and the mothballed fleet. But they will also need to know that the rest of the mothballed fleet has been scuttled," said the admiral.

***

"FNS *Brazil*, please state your enigma code," Captain Son Ri ordered.

"44X!!34AZ00.04," replied Captain Ching.

Both captains were smiling at each other. They had been roommates at the Naval Academy and had maintained a friendship throughout the years.

"State your intentions," ordered Captain Son Ri.

"Our intentions are to enter Beta Wormhole and to deliver four regiments of Marines from Earth and 2,000 officers and crew from the mothballed fleet to the planet Beyond. All of the teleporters have been destroyed, and all mothballed naval vessels—except the flagship Brazil and the frigates *Daisy May* and *Hercules*—have been scuttled," responded Captain Ching.

"Permission granted."

"I do have one more request, Captain Son Ri. Ah, you know how Marines are—these guys are getting under my skin. They keep asking me for whiskey, and we have no alcohol on board except Naval-Issued Rum, and they hate the stuff. I've heard that you have some primo whiskey on board. Could you spare some with us? I'll send over a detachment of Marines to pick it up. You know, you still owe me a favor from our escapade at Callisto three years ago."

"Sure, with my compliments, Captain Ching. Please come over with the detachment and we'll uncork a bottle or two between us."

***

As the three naval ships came in close to the space fortress, a shuttle craft containing not 10 but 120 Marines shuttled across the gulf. The captain of the FNF *Sagittarius A** was looking forward to getting drunk with his friend, while the 120 Marines on the shuttle craft had their laser rifles set to kill.

The shuttle carrying the rebel Marines came into the FNF *Sagittarius A**'s shuttle bay. Since it was assumed that this would be a friendly visit involving whiskey, a minimal amount of security was in the bay. When the shuttle door opened, the first 20 that exited had their laser guns blazing. The Security Division didn't even have enough time to notify the Communication Division about the attack.

From there, the rebel Marines fanned out to all three decks of the space fortress and quickly crushed all resistance. Any Federation naval forces and Marines who surrendered were promptly placed in an airlock and 'spaced.' The last place to look for Federation personnel was the Space-Time Laboratory.

The boarding party from the *Brazil* thought they had killed or captured all the Marines, naval personnel, and civilians on the space fortress. But seven escaped.

Chapter 22

Sent To the Wrong Adress

Just before the rebel marine boarding party came on board the space station, Dr. Hays and Myron Abbot burst into sickbay, armed with a laser rifle.

"Everyone cooperate and no one will get hurt," cried out Dr. Hays.

At this point, Dr. Rosenstein lunged toward Dr. Hays. However, before he could get to him, Dr. Hays blasted Dr. Rosenstein and created a rather large hole in his chest. This sent blood all over sickbay, producing a sickening metallic scent.

Lt. Henderson stepped out of Enoch's room. "Oh, my goodness," she screamed. "What is going on, Dr. Tempus?"

"We are taking Enoch and the alien to the Space-Time Laboratory," said Dr. Hays.

"He is not an alien, Dr. Tempus. He is Epsilon-Giga, the Federation prophet!" exclaimed Lt. Henderson.

"How did you know that, Lt. Henderson?" asked Dr. Hays.

"I knew Enoch and the alien were the same ethnicity, and they seemed to speak the same language. So, I looked up Enoch on the space station computer and found a reference in the Old Testament about Enoch. According to the Bible, Enoch did not die but was translated to heaven by the Jewish God. I did a further search and found in the Federation Bible that the prophet Epsilon-Giga was transported to heaven in a fiery vehicle. So, I checked the Old Testament again and found that the prophet Elijah was transported to God in a whirlwind. I surmised that the alien must either be Epsilon-Giga or Elijah."

On hearing this, Dr. Hays and Myron became quiet. Then Myron spoke, "His name is not Epsilon-Giga, but Elijah, the Hebrew prophet. Please help us get Enoch and Elijah to the Space-Time Laboratory."

"Both men are heavily sedated. It would be best to transport them on their gurneys," said Lt. Henderson.

***

When the five of them approached the Space-Time Laboratory, they found Lt. Jackson guarding the hatch. He and Midshipman Chu were having an argument.

"Then explain to me, Lieutenant: How on earth did the alien tear the hatch off the reactor room?" asked Ming Chu.

"I think you have been drinking too much Navy rum. What makes you think the alien is really an Old Testament prophet? That is fantasy. Who told you this?" countered Lt. Jackson.

"I was talking to Lt. Henderson this morning, and she showed me the results of a data search on the ship's computer that…"

At this point, Dr. Hays and company appeared at the hatch.

"Stand aside, Lt. Jackson. We need to get into the Space-Time Laboratory. It's urgent!" ordered Dr. Hays.

"Captain Son Ri has ordered that no one is allowed in the laboratory. Hey, what are you doing with the aliens? They should be in sickbay!" exclaimed Lt. Jackson.

Lt. Henderson spoke up, "They are not aliens. As Midshipman Chu was trying to explain to you, one of them is Enoch, and the other is Elijah. They are both humans from the distant past."

"Now I am totally confused! How did they get here?" asked Lt. Jackson.

At this point, there was the sound of a click. Dr. Hays noticed the big, threatening laser rifle in the marine lieutenant's hands. He saw that Lt. Jackson had taken the safety off his laser gun. Dr. Hays followed suit, and a second click was heard. The two pointed their laser guns at each other. The only sound that followed was heavy breathing, and the air was rich with the smell of perspiration.

"Excuse me, may I say something?" All eyes turned to Myron. He didn't look confused, and he looked ten years younger than before. His face seemed to glow, and his eyes sparkled.

"Lt. Jackson, remember our discussion on the portal craft on our way to this space station?"

"Of course, I remember. What part are you referring to?"

"The part about the wormholes and the ability to travel vast distances of space in little time. There is something at work here that is very similar," replied Myron.

"I don't get your meaning," said a confused Lt. Jackson.

At this point, Dr. Hays joined in. "You know that this space station is orbiting a gigantic black hole. The space-time continuum is very distorted here. The same black hole responsible for the wormhole from Earth to here—and the wormhole from here to the planet Beyond—has distorted the space-time continuum and created a supermassive gravity well.

"There are a dozen or so supermassive stars orbiting the black hole in elliptical orbits. When a star's elliptical orbit has a close approach to the black hole, an accretion disk of matter and energy from the star spirals into the black hole. This matter is shredded to quarks and anti-quarks, and these quarks can achieve velocities faster than the speed of light. I don't have time to explain all the details of what happens when quarks exceed the speed of light, but these transient situations make it possible to go back in time. Both Enoch and Elijah were brought here through this phenomenon."

"Now my head hurts, Dr. Tempus," said Lt. Jackson as he rubbed his forehead.

"I am not Dr. Tempus; I am Dr. Hays. I came from the 21st century."

There was a pause of silence for about a minute, then Myron spoke up.

"Let me cut to the chase, Lieutenant. Having Enoch and Elijah here is an extremely dangerous situation. According to Dr. Hays, the presence of Enoch and Elijah here may produce a time-paradox. I can't explain it right now, but we need to send them back to their proper times as soon as possible."

"What happens if we don't send them back?" asked Lt. Jackson.

Myron became very animated and seemed to sparkle as he answered, "History will be rewritten—especially if we don't send Elijah back. He was a real mover and shaker 3,000 years ago. If history is rewritten, then our present history may also be changed. There is even a chance that we will not exist anymore."

Myron looked over at Dr. Hays, who picked up the conversation from there.

"We need to get into the Space-Time Laboratory now. There is a large star that will be passing close to the black hole, and there is a good chance that I can find a place in the black hole's accretion disk where we can send Enoch back to his time—and Elijah to his."

On hearing this, Lt. Jackson lowered his laser gun.

"Okay, go inside and send these two guys back to where they came from. I'll guard the door, but I am letting just Myron and Dr. Tempus into the lab. Midshipman Chu and Kat will stay with me."

"Thank you, Lieutenant!" said Dr. Hays. "Here, Midshipman, take my laser rifle. Godspeed!"

Myron and Dr. Hays climbed through the hatch to the Space-Time Laboratory and locked the hatch behind them.

Then, the alert was heard: "The space fortress is under attack!"

***

Once inside the Space-Time Lab, Dr. Hays took command of the controls. On the screen, the location of the black hole was obtained. There it was: a blacker-than-black sphere surrounded by a ring of bright light. Off to the right, a large red giant star was approaching. Already, the sphere of the red giant was being distorted by the massive gravity of the black hole.

Dr. Hays gave the Space-Time computer the command, "Move space fortress to location $X = 151.752$; $Y = 307.986$; $Z = 0.000$." Almost immediately, the entire space fortress started to buck like a

Brahma bull at a rodeo. Then the fortress calmed down when the new orbit was established.

"We are not a minute too soon, Myron. Help me load Enoch in probe A over there, and help me load Elijah in probe B on the other side of the control room."

Once Elijah and Enoch were loaded, Dr. Hays returned to the controls. He gave the command to the ship's computer, "Load probe A into probe launcher one, and load probe B into probe launcher two. Await my coordinates."

By the time the probe launchers were loaded with their cargo, the black hole was beginning to strip off matter and radiation from the giant red star. This formed a plate-shaped accretion disk around the black hole. Countless whirlpools and eddies were forming all around the accretion disk.

Dr. Hays's hands were moving at lightning speed, as if he were a concert pianist playing Rachmaninoff's 2nd Piano Concerto. Then he gave coordinates for each of the probes. "Coordinates for probe A: $X = 92.726$; $Y = 327.908$; $Z = 0.000$. Coordinates for probe B: $X = 124.312$; $Y = 13.494$; $Z = 0.000$. Launch on my command."

At this point, Myron could see that Dr. Hays was counting down silently.

"Launch both probes," he ordered the computer. The space fortress shuddered mildly when both probes were launched.

On the screen in the control room, the two probes could be seen moving toward their targets until they disappeared into the accretion disk. Dr. Hays magnified the accretion disk 1000X and had the two targeted whirlpools on split screens. Even at this magnification, the probes could not be seen, but Dr. Hays knew that the probes were quickly approaching their targets.

Then something very strange happened.

Both the targeted whirlpools slowed their rotation down, stopped, and then reversed their direction of rotation.

"Computer, recall the probes, now!" screamed Dr. Hays.

The computer responded, "The space fortress can no longer recall the probes, since the probes have already entered the time wormholes."

"Rats, we lost the probes!" cried Dr. Hays.

"Where did they go, Dr. Hays?"

"I have no idea. Computer, where did the two probes go?" requested Dr. Hays.

The computer responded, "The probes have gone to Earth, two-sol years in the future, coordinates 31°46′41″ North, 35°14′9″ East. This area is known as the Temple Mount in Jerusalem."

"Oh no! What have we done?" cried Dr. Hays.

"Now what do we do?" asked Myron.

Chapter 23

Condemned!

When the alarm sounded that the space fortress was being boarded, Kat Henderson, Midshipman Chu, and Lt. Jackson looked at each other.

"What should we do, Lieutenant?" asked Ming Chu.

Lt. Jackson reached into his pocket and pulled out a small electronic device. "Let me look at my communicator to see what is going on. Oh no! The space station is being boarded by rebel marines! Cripes! We need to get out of here. I've dealt with the rebels before, and they are a bunch of barbarians who will space us if they capture us. We need to get out of here, now!"

At this point, Midshipman Chu pulled out his communicator. "Lieutenant, we can't go down to the shuttle launch area, because that's where the rebels boarded the space fortress. However, I know where there's another shuttle. It's in the maintenance center. Maintenance uses the shuttle to repair the outside of the space station when there's damage from micrometeors. If we go up one of the fortress's spokes through this hatch right on the ceiling over there, then go down the opposite spoke, we can enter the maintenance bay by means of the service core. Chances are, we won't be captured. Follow me!"

"What about Myron and Dr. Hays? We can't just leave them here to be captured and spaced!" screamed Kat. "We need to take them with us."

"We can't get into the Space-Time Lab. Dr. Hays locked the hatch, and his security clearance is much higher than mine," replied Ming Chu. "Let me see if I can get him on his communicator. Oh, oh! His communicator is off."

"Let's get out of here now! I can hear the rebels coming," cried out Lt. Jackson.

Both Midshipman Chu and Lt. Jackson grabbed Kat's hands and dragged her up through the ceiling into the spoke of the space fortress. Once in the spoke, they climbed a ladder toward the hub of the station. The farther up the ladder, the easier it got, since the centrifugal force decreased to almost zero in the hub.

They worked their way through the storage areas in the hub until they reached a hatch in the floor on the other side. Then they climbed down the ladder to the maintenance center. When they reached it, Chu opened the hatch and looked inside. No rebels. Good.

On the other side of the room was another hatch with a sign that read:

"Authorized Personnel Only."

Midshipman Chu took his security card and held it up to the reader, and the hatch opened to reveal the shuttlecraft inside.

"Good thing I have clearance for this area. These guys are in my division. Unfortunately, it looks like all my maintenance friends have been killed," said Ming Chu, as he turned his head to see his dead comrades in the corner.

Ming Chu then opened the hatch and they all climbed into the shuttle. He turned the light on—and what a mess. Tools were all over the floor, and several bottles of lubricant were spilled. It smelled like a frying pan.

Lt. Jackson slipped on the lubricant and almost fell, but Kat caught him before his head slammed into the bulwark.

"Oh, thanks," he said sheepishly.

"Oh, shut up and sit in the chair before you get hurt," replied Kat.

Midshipman Chu sat in the pilot chair at the front of the shuttle. Kat sat next to him in the navigator/manipulator chair. Lt. Jackson sat behind them.

"Fasten your seatbelts, fold up your tray tables, and make sure the aisles are clear for takeoff," said Midshipman Chu. Then he said to the onboard computer, "Close the airlock door and open the space door. Check all systems for takeoff."

The onboard computer replied, "Space door is open and all systems are green. Please initiate thrust and enter destination coordinates."

This question resulted in dead silence. Finally, Midshipman Chu asked Lt. Jackson and Kat, "Where are we going?"

"I haven't the foggiest," responded Lt. Jackson.

Finally, Kat spoke up. "There is a small station just this side of Alpha Wormhole—on this side of the black hole. It's really a small orbiting hospital used to treat injuries that happen in Purgatory."

"Purgatory?" asked Lt. Jackson.

Midshipman Chu was about to answer the lieutenant when Kat broke in, "I can explain Purgatory later. Here are the coordinates."

The midshipman entered the coordinates. There was a gentle bump in recoil, then a steady acceleration. They were underway.

On the ship-of-the-line *Brazil*, there was so much activity—and several shuttles were going back and forth from the *Brazil* to the space station—that no one noticed the maintenance shuttle launching from the Space Fortress *Sagittarius A**.

***

The last place in the space fortress to be taken over by the rebels was the Space-Time Laboratory. This was the same room where Myron and Dr. Tempus, now Dr. Hays, attempted to send Enoch and Elijah back to ancient Israel. The room had the highest level of security, so the rebel marines were having some trouble getting inside.

Inside the Space-Time Laboratory, another rebellion was being squashed by Captain Son Ri, commandant of the space fortress. The only one on the space fortress with a higher security clearance than Dr. Hays was Capt. Son Ri. In the corner were two men—one in a scientific officer's uniform, the other in black attire.

"Where are the two aliens? Answer now!" growled Captain Son Ri.

"What aliens?" said Dr. Hays.

"You know who I am talking about. Where are they?" Then the captain moved over to the control panel. "You didn't cover your tracks well, Dr. Tempus. You left the probe computer program up and going. Hmm, I can even see the accretion disk whirlpools on the screen. I could just 'space' the two of you, but that would be too quick. You look surprised, Dr. Tempus. You didn't know that I am very well-versed in your little science fair project. I run this fortress, and I make it my aim to know something about everything that goes on here. So, I have decided what to do with you two. Hmm, let me see… there are still two probes in the control room. Let's say that you get into one of the probes, and you, senile old man, get in the other probe. We'll just send you two to wherever you sent the aliens."

Myron and Dr. Hays gave a meaningful look at each other. Captain Son Ri did not see Dr. Hays and Myron winking at each other.

"Whatever you say," responded Myron as he and Dr. Robert Hays strapped themselves into the space-time probes.

After the probes were launched, the probe carrying Myron Abbot entered the same wormhole as Elijah. The rotation direction and speed remained the same as when Elijah's probe entered the wormhole. This sent Myron to the Temple Mount in Jerusalem two years into the future. Unfortunately, the wormhole that Dr. Hays' probe entered reversed its rotation again, and it was not possible to figure out when and where he was sent.

***

The shuttle carrying Lt. Henderson, Lt. Jackson, and Ming Chu meanwhile slid from view of the space fortress toward the Alpha Wormhole. When they came near the Alpha Wormhole, Ming Chu exclaimed, "Oh my God! Purgatory has been reactivated!"

"You mean the mothballed fleet?" cried Lt. Jackson. "That's where the FNS Brazil just came from. There is power behind the Brazil. Do you think that the rebels took over the entire fleet? How would that be possible?"

Then Lt. Jackson answered his own question, "Oh no! The last teleporter was not destroyed! The rebels must have gained possession of it. But how can they operate the teleporter? There are only a few people who have the technical know-how."

"What should we do?" asked Kat.

Ming Chu began to flip several switches on the shuttle control panel. He was humming to himself, then finally said, "I have just made the shuttle invisible."

"How did you do that?" asked Kat.

"This is a maintenance shuttle used to repair the outside of Naval Fortress *Sagittarius A**. The space fortress is doing scientific surveys of the black hole continuously. In order to not interfere with the delicate instrumentation on the fortress, this shuttle has an electromagnetic shield. In effect, it makes us invisible to the sensors on the fortress, and fortunately for us, the sensors aboard any Federation naval vessels. I just turned it on."

After this, there was silence on the shuttle for a minute or so— or was it much longer? Finally, Kat spoke up, "Ming, you are full of surprises." She leaned over and kissed him on his cheek.

***

The FNS *Lockford* was the fastest ship in the Federation fleet. The captain of the Lockford, Enrico Alvarez, had been given orders to investigate space-time anomalies in the area of the mothballed fleet. This anomaly caused enough concern to have the Federation Admiralty order all naval vessels to a defensive posture on the far side of the Beta Wormhole, near the planet Beyond. So, while the rest of the Federation fleet passed through the Beta Wormhole to the Beyond system, this very fast frigate was sent to find out what was going on.

"Captain, the Space-Time Deck has reported that much of the mothballed fleet has been deployed. It seems that the deployed mothballed ships are heading in the direction of the space fortress," reported First Officer Ikram Shah.

"I don't see how that is possible, Mr. Shah. All the ships in the mothballed fleet had skeleton crews—not nearly enough men and women to deploy most of the fleet. Get me the Space-Time Deck," said Capt. Alvarez.

"This is Space-Time Deck," reported the scientific officer.

"What speed is the mothballed fleet moving toward the space fortress?" asked Capt. Alvarez.

"They are moving at 0.02% relativistic. Wait. One of their 74-gun ships-of-the-line has split off and is heading toward the space fortress at 0.05% relativistic. Captain, we are also picking up movement of a 48-gun heavy frigate. It is heading in our direction. We think it may be the FNS *Wingate*."

"FNS *Wingate*, this is Capt. Alvarez of the FNS *Lockford*. Please declare your intentions."

"Sir, the *Wingate* has armed her nuclear missiles," said the Weapons Officer.

"Engineering, give me full power," commanded Capt. Alvarez.

"You have it, Captain. We should reach 2% relativistic speed in 20 minutes."

"Helmsman, institute evasive action and export them to the ship's computer," said the captain.

"Evasive actions are loaded into the ship's computer. Computer AI is activated," responded the helmsman.

"Mr. Shah, see to it that all missiles are armed and ready."

"They are armed and ready," replied Cmdr. Shah.

"Prepare to fire on the *Wingate* at my command," shouted Capt. Alvarez.

"Sir, the *Wingate* has fired four of her nuclear missiles at us. Impact in 10 seconds," shouted Ikram Shaw.

Capt. Alvarez then shouted, "Helmsman, order computer AI to initiate evasive actions NOW! Prepare for impact! Mr. Shah, fire when—"

The missiles from the *Wingate* missed the *Lockford*, but still exploded within 10 kilometers. The energy from the blast threw the entire crew of the *Lockford* around like rag dolls. When Captain Alvarez recovered his senses, he cried, "Damage control, has our hull been breached?"

"Negative, sir, but half of my men and women are down."

"Captain, this is Space-Time Deck, we have two light mothballed frigates on our port beam. We are surrounded and outgunned."

"Commander Shah, I am ready to give the command to surrender. Please give me your recommendation."

"I concur, Captain. We have no other choice," said Ikram Shah, as he began to weep.

Chapter 24

I'm lost

Confusion will be my epitaph

As I crawl, a cracked and broken path

If we make it, we can all sit back and laugh

But I fear tomorrow I'll be crying

Yes, I fear tomorrow I'll be crying

Greg Lake, Ian McDonald, Michael Rex Giles, Peter John Sinfield, Robert Fripp

King Crimson Band

The trip in a space-time wormhole is quite disorienting. As you enter the wormhole, there is blinding light followed by profound darkness. The strangest part is that there is no sense of time. Time becomes inconsistent and irrelevant. But this did not trouble Dr. Hays. He expected this.

Three things, however, that did trouble him were the paradox of being both heavy and light at the same time, not knowing where he was going, and finally, what was happening to his friend, Myron. He knew that Enoch and Elijah were accidentally sent to Jerusalem two years into the future, but something about this wormhole he was in did not feel right in terms of where he was going and when he would get there.

After a time that seemed like forever and instantaneous, he saw a circular opening rimmed by a blinding torus. He was exiting the wormhole. Suddenly, he popped through the hole and was descending through the atmosphere of the destination planet. At first, he could not see much in front of him, but then he saw the planet's surface. It looked like a desert with a few scattered bushes. The rest of the landscape was occupied by sand and rock. Off in the distance, several chocolate-colored mountain ranges punctuated the landscape. Near the horizon was a large mountain range that was snowcapped at the highest elevations.

Good, he thought, *there is at least water on this planet.* If there is water on the planet, it is likely that there is an atmosphere at this destination planet. Perhaps the conditions were favorable for human life, which meant that Dr. Hays would have a good chance of survival. Then Dr. Hays remembered that the time travel probe had instrumentation for evaluating the atmospheric composition. He had the onboard computer run an analysis: 78.08 percent nitrogen, 20.95 percent oxygen, and the rest trace gases. *Good news,* thought Dr. Hays.

Then he saw something that made his heart skip a beat: there below him was a straight black line that bisected the landscape from horizon to horizon. It looked like his time-traveling probe was going to be landing there.

When his probe did land, about 100 meters from the black line in the desert, Dr. Hays still wondered when and where he was. He opened the hatch on the probe and was immediately greeted by a blast of 50°C air. The heat almost instantly desiccated his eyes and respiratory tract. At least the atmosphere didn't seem to be poisonous.

He started walking toward the black line. When he reached it, he found the line was about 20 feet wide, and a white dashed line ran down the length of the blackness. In both directions, the black line ran all the way to the horizon.

He reached this conclusion: *I have been sent to Earth!* The black line was a highway in the desert. But where was he? In the Gobi, Sahara, Mojave, or the Kalahari Desert?

Then he saw something approaching him on the highway. One car drove past him but did not stop. Dr. Hays started walking down the highway for about 15 minutes when a second car appeared. The car drove past him and came to a stop. A black car with white doors. There was a red blinking light on top. A young man, quite a bit younger than Dr. Hays, stepped out of the car. He was wearing a uniform. Dr. Hays knew the man. It was his father.

***

Myron Abbot was completely disoriented. He felt nauseous as the time-traveling probe entered the wormhole. He felt that he was traveling into a deep well. The darkness was complete. He closed his eyes to keep his nausea at bay. He felt himself descending, almost like he was falling into Sheol.

"Oh, God of my fathers! The God of Abraham, Isaac, and Jacob. Jehovah Jireh! Please rescue me!" he prayed out loud.

Then suddenly, he felt that he was in the presence of Abraham, Isaac, and Jacob. The thousands of years between Myron and the patriarchs collapsed into the well he was falling into. Then he felt the presence of his deceased wife, Tilly. Also, all the times of the Jews seemed to be melded together. Time, which was once a linear string, became a ball of string.

Myron felt the probe decelerating. He opened his eyes and looked out of the probe's portal. What he saw amazed him. He was looking at the Great Pyramids of Egypt. The probe he was in flew past these relics, and then flew over a large river, then a narrow sea inlet, before banking to the left. The probe followed a rift valley until it reached a salt flat. The probe banked a bit more to the left and followed a low mountain range that ran parallel to the rift valley.

Suddenly, a large city built on one of the mountains appeared. In the middle of the city was a large domed temple.

Myron had come home!

***

The maintenance shuttle containing Kat, Midshipman Chu, and Lt. Jackson moved stealthily through the mothballed fleet. Thanks to the midshipman, they were effectively invisible to the fleet. All of the fleet was on the move toward the Sagittarius A* black hole. There was, however, a small group of ships that seemed to be staying behind. The maintenance shuttle moved closer to the group of sedentary ships.

"Is there anyone on board those ships?" asked Lt. Jackson.

"Let me see. Oh, there it is. I'll flip this switch to turn on the life scanner. All of these ships seem to have no one on board except for those three light frigates close to us, and the heavy frigate way over there. Let's see—there seem to be 104 aboard one of the light frigates. This is interesting…"

"What's interesting?" asked Kat.

"Hmm. About 98 of them are on the Space-Time Deck. Very strange. I think I will go in to have a closer look. By the way, the shuttle's computer identifies that frigate as the FNS *Lockford*, 28 laser guns and missiles. It is not part of the mothballed fleet. I can't figure out what it is doing here. Look at the top speed of that frigate," said Midshipman Chu, pointing to the light frigate's specifications on the screen display. "This one has been clocked at 2% of the speed of light. I don't think there is any ship in the Federation fleet that is faster than the *Lockford*."

"Why do you think 98 people are on the Space-Time Deck?" asked Kat.

"Hold on. I am receiving a signal. Strange frequency. This is not a Federation naval frequency. It's similar to the frequency used on asteroid ore barges. An SOS of sorts. Let me route this through the shuttle cabin speakers."

"Mayday… We are being held captive by the rebel navy… They are planning to space us… Please come to our aid."

"This is Midshipman Ming Chu of the FN Fortress *Sagittarius A**. We are on board the maintenance shuttle from the space fortress. To whom am I speaking?"

"This is Captain Alvarez of the FNS *Lockford*. There are three marines and three rebels holding us captive. We believe they are on the bridge. How close are you?"

"We are three kilometers away."

"You remained undetected?" asked a surprised Capt. Alvarez.

"Yes. We are using an electromagnetic shield to cloak our craft, Captain. We are invisible to Federation detectors. Is anyone on the Marine Deck?"

"No," replied Capt. Alvarez.

"Good. We will dock on the Marine Deck. One of us will attack the rebels on the bridge, while the rest of us will attempt to rescue you."

"How many are you?" asked Capt. Alvarez.

"Three. However, one of us is a marine lieutenant."

"We also have seven casualties, Ming. Three of them are in bad shape and need immediate medical care," said Captain Alvarez.

"No problem. One of us is a naval nurse."

"Are you a Boy Scout?"

"Why do you ask?"

"You came prepared!" replied Captain Alvarez.

Ming maneuvered the shuttle in closer. As he approached, Lt. Jackson checked his laser rifle to make sure it was fully charged and good to go. The lieutenant also examined the *Lockford*'s schematic that the shuttle computer provided. The *Lockford*'s bridge, where the rebel captors were, was on the anterior end of the frigate. The deck below this was the marines' barracks where the shuttle was docked. The next level down was the Space-Time Deck, where the Federation prisoners were being held.

There was a cylindrical utility core that passed through each deck's centerline and housed electrical and communication cables, water, oxygen, and climate control. The core had maintenance portals on each deck to allow access for servicing these utilities. There were two passageways between the decks, located on the perimeter of the ship, for crew movement.

Since the rotation of the frigate provided artificial gravity, the rebels would be standing or sitting on the perimeter of the bridge. Lt. Jackson surmised that the rebels would be watching the perimeter passageways, since that would be the most likely route the prisoners would take to gain their freedom. Instead, he would float through the service core from the marine barracks to the bridge, entering and exiting through the core's service portals. Then he would neutralize the rebels with his silenced laser rifle. If he was fast and accurate enough, he could neutralize the rebels before they became aware of his attack.

While the midshipman and the marine lieutenant planned and maneuvered, Kat spent her time examining the few medical supplies she had quickly gathered from the FNF *Sagittarius A**—which pretty much added up to a first-aid kit. Not enough to treat the seriously wounded on the *Lockford*.

"Ming, could you ask the shuttle computer for the size of sickbay and the inventory of the medical supplies aboard the *Lockford*?"

Soon a graphic display popped up on the shuttle's display screen. Unless the rebels had trashed sickbay or sent the medical supplies off with the mobilized fleet, there should be adequate supplies to treat the wounded on board the *Lockford*.

Ming carefully maneuvered the shuttle into position at the *Lockford*'s shuttle port. He had to be careful; any clanging or vibration from the shuttle docking with the frigate would alert the rebels to their presence. It was not enough to be invisible to the frigate's sensors.

"Ming, how are we going to activate the airlock door?" asked Kat. "Won't their computer alert the rebels of our presence?"

"Not if I enter the maintenance code," replied Ming. "The same airlock code for maintenance shuttles is used across all Federation vessels. I know, it seems like a stupid idea to have the same codes. However, because of the continual maintenance that these vessels and fortresses require, and the fact that maintenance personnel may forget the code, the Admiralty decided to use a universal maintenance code that does not set off an alarm."

Once docked, Ming quickly entered the maintenance security code to open the airlock. Then they had to wait 10 minutes while the airlock pressurized. When the airlock was fully pressurized, the interior airlock door opened.

Once in the marine barracks, they opened the utility portal. First Kat and Ming entered the portal and floated 'down' to the Space-Time Deck, where the captured Federation crew was being held. As Ming emerged from the core into the Space-Time Deck, he was startled to find a crewman threatening him with a very large pipe wrench.

"Don't hit me! I'm Ming Chu, midshipman from the FNF *Sagittarius A**."

"Sorry. I thought you were one of the rebels," responded the crew member with the wrench.

When Kat emerged, you would think the *Lockford*'s crew had seen an angel.

"Where are the wounded? I can give limited first-aid treatment to those who need it the most. Once we have control of the Bridge Deck, we can transport the wounded down to sickbay."

***

Meanwhile, Lt. Jackson was working his way up the utility core to the bridge. He had to move stealthily to prevent any noises that would betray his presence to the rebels. When he reached the portal access hatch to the bridge, he found that he could not open the portal. After thinking about it a bit, he decided to use his laser rifle. He positioned himself in the utility core so he would not be exposed to specular reflection from metal surfaces. He slowly turned the power up on his laser rifle until the metal portal latch glowed a dull red. After about five minutes, he was able to push the portal open gently and silently.

When he looked through the crack in the portal, he could see three rebel marines sound asleep. He could not see the three rebels on the other side of the deck, but he could hear their muted voices.

"Are those three marines still asleep? I guess that they drank too much of that naval-issued rum," said one of the rebels to his two comrades.

"Just as well, they give me the creeps. Did you hear the fat one threaten me? All I did was beat him in poker," responded one of the other rebels.

"How much did you win? It looked to me like you took his entire paycheck. No wonder he wanted to hurt you."

After this, the deck went silent. Lt. Jackson wondered which body part of each marine he should shoot. He wanted the neutralization of the marines to be as quiet as possible. He decided that he should shoot them at the bases of their brains. That would initially paralyze them and sever the nerves to their vocal cords. He aimed carefully and dispatched the first and second marine.

Dispatching the third marine did not go according to plan. Lt. Jackson's aim must have been off a bit. The marine woke up with a start and began making a gurgling noise.

"Can you please do your vomiting in the head, you Neanderthal?" yelled one of the rebels.

Lt. Jackson could hear one of the rebels walking around the perimeter of the Navigation Deck toward the sleeping (and by now, dead) marines. By this time, Lt. Jackson had finished off the third marine. As the rebel came into the lieutenant's view, he gave him a short laser burst into the base of his brain.

"What is going on over there? Is there something wrong?" shouted one of the two remaining rebels.

Lt. Jackson could hear another set of footsteps coming over to investigate. The lieutenant squeezed off another shot. Five down, one to go. This time, however, he could not hear the footsteps of the last surviving rebel. *This guy was being quiet and sneaky*, he thought.

Assuming that the sixth rebel was coming around the other way, Jackson opened the portal all the way and moved in the other direction. Then he encountered the last rebel. The rebel drew his laser pistol, but too slowly. The lieutenant already had him in his sights, and the last rebel was history.

Lt. Jackson then walked over to the com-box and hit the transmit button. "This is Lt. Jackson. The bridge is secured and the rebels have been neutralized. I am opening all passageways so the crew can take full possession of the ship. Inform Captain Alvarez that the FNS *Lockford* is now his command. Tell him that I have no idea how to operate a frigate."

Chapter 25

Deja Vu

If I had ever been here before

I would probably know just what to do

Don't you?

If I had ever been here before on another time around the wheel

I would probably know just how to deal

With all of you

David Crosby

Crosby, Stills, Nash, and Young

The black car with white doors slowed down and stopped just in front of Dr. Hays. A young man in a highway patrolman's uniform stepped out and approached him. Dr. Hays could not believe his eyes: the highway patrolman was his father! Dr. Hays began to wonder: *Is my schizophrenia returning? Was this a bad dream?*

His father, the highway patrolman, said, "I am Officer Alex Hays. It's okay. I am here to help you and get you back home. You must be hot and thirsty. I have some ice water in my car to help you cool down."

"I don't belong here! You can't take me home because I am not from here!" cried out Robert Hays. Robert was beginning to feel faint from the extreme heat and dehydration.

"Where are you from?" asked Alex Hays.

"It's not just where I am from, but *when* and where I am from."

"Okay, where and when are you from?" asked Alex.

"I am from the center of the galaxy, 150 years in the future," responded Robert.

"Let's get you in the car and get you home."

"But your car is not capable of time travel!" Robert cried out.

"Get in the car so I can get you out of this heat and get you some ice water."

Dr. Hays had an epiphany: *I have had this dream or these delusions many, many times before. It was only when I was teleported to the space fortress that the dreams and delusions stopped. Must have had something to do with my 4-inch scar behind my ear. Dr. Rosenstein must have surgically altered me so my memories could not haunt me. Maybe these are not delusions and dreams. I need to take it at face value: the Space-Time Lab had inadvertently sent me to California in the early 21st century. I must think. What should I do?*

Then the second epiphany came to Dr. Hays: *I am involved in a potential time paradox. If I say or do the wrong thing, my history could be forever changed. I know my future story, at least from a 22nd-century point of view. I need to play dumb. Take my cues from my father and play along with this present scenario. It would be best if I play the part of the lunatic. I need to be passive. I need to remember what comes next in this dream or delusion. Oh yes. My father is going to take me to the insane asylum. Play along with this as best I can.*

Dr. Hays got into the patrol car in the back seat. His father pulled an ice-cold bottle of water out of his ice chest and handed it to Robert. Once Robert Hays was hydrated, his thoughts became clearer, and he said, "I'm sorry for the fuss out there. This heat got to me, and I became light-headed. I haven't had my meds since this morning."

Then a thought came to Robert: *I need to remember the name of the meds. I can't think of them. What music is playing on the patrol car radio?*

The lunatic is in my head.

The lunatic is in my head.

You raise the blade; you make the change

You re-arrange me 'til I'm sane.

You lock the door

And throw away the key:

There's someone in my head but it's not me.

And if the cloud bursts, thunder in your ear

You shout and no one seems to hear.

And if the band you're in starts playing different tunes

I'll see you on the dark side of the moon.

Now I remember, thought Robert. *The drug they had me take when I was diagnosed with schizophrenia: Risperidone.*

Officer Hays didn't say much as they drove down the road. Then he suddenly asked Dr. Hays, "Do you have a favorite band?"

"Pink Floyd," answered Robert.

"Oh yeah, the band who just played the last song—*Brain Damage* from *Dark Side of the Moon*. Did that last song bother you?"

I need to be careful here. I am walking in a minefield. Say the wrong thing to change Officer Hays' thinking, and I might not be part of his history. He may not take a liking to Sally, his future wife, and then I wouldn't be born. Then I couldn't be sent from the future to get here. This is making my brain hurt!

"No, this song does not bother me. I know that I am sick in my head. Where are you taking me?" asked Robert.

"To a place where you can be helped," responded Alex.

"I need to be helped," said Robert Hays. *That's it, play along with this. Go with the flow.*

The patrol car pulled up to a large institutional-like building. Officer Hays parked his car in a loading zone and helped Dr. Hays out of the back seat. They went through a set of double doors and came to the lobby.

There at the lobby desk is my mother! Just like the many, many dreams and delusions before, thought Robert.

"I brought a friend of yours back," said Officer Hays.

"I don't recognize him. Interesting outfit," responded Sally.

"A real Buck Rogers. He is clearly touched in the head. We can't turn him loose in this heat," replied Alex.

"Okay, we will take him and have him evaluated tomorrow." Then Sally, his mother, paged an orderly to escort Dr. Hays.

"What's your name?" asked his mother, Sally.

"My name is Robert."

"Do you have a last name?" asked Sally.

Robert Hays began to panic. *What kind of answer should I give to my mother?* Then he responded, "I don't have a last name," declared Dr. Hays. *I figure I can get away with this answer, since I am crazy.*

"Well, you just make yourself comfortable until the orderly can see you to your room."

Uh-oh! The last time I had this dream or delusion, the orderly was waiting at the desk when I arrived. I'm seeing some slippage in space-time. I need to be more careful.

At this point, the orderly arrived and took Dr. Hays to the annex, which was not part of the main building. The annex was located across the parking lot.

Man, is it hot outside. I sure hope that it is air-conditioned in that trailer. Wait a minute. It's not supposed to be a trailer, but more of a Quonset hut! Be careful, play the crazy, but be realistic at the same time.

"Here we are, Robert. You just make yourself at home. Just push this button if you need anything. Don't try anything crazy. Ha-ha! We can see your every move at our desk," said the orderly.

***

That night, a real thumper came in. The kind of thunderstorm that holds some in awe, others in terror, and for most, just another desert thunderstorm. The lightning came fast and furious, and the wind blew with such ferocity that it shook the windows of the asylum. Some present at the asylum reported a strange glow over the asylum annex trailer that was transient in nature.

As the storm began, the nurses and orderlies herded the residents into the storm shelter. This was always a comedy of errors, since the residents sometimes ascribed biblical meaning to the weather pattern. Many of them thought the world was coming to an end and began to pontificate to the nurses and orderlies that they needed to get right with God because His judgment was upon them. Then the storm ended as quickly as it began.

The newest resident, Mr. Buck Rogers (also known in the future as Dr. Tempus or Dr. Robert Hays), was in the trailer annex, which served as a padded cell until a psychiatrist could properly diagnose the patient's condition. This was the last area to be searched by the asylum staff.

When Sally reached the patient's trailer, they discovered that it had been destroyed. The only thing left was the cement blocks on which the annex trailer rested. And there was no patient. The only thing Sally could say was, "I guess he went to Munchkin Land."

***

However, Buck Rogers, also known as Dr. Hays, did not go to Munchkin Land. He was sitting in a space-time probe heading back to FNS *Sagittarius A** in the future. He was cajoled into the pod against his better judgment. The robot that helped capture him said something about Dr. Leslie Jones. Who was she? Dr. Hays had no idea.

Chapter 26

A Black hole Saves the Day

Captain Alvarez came to the bridge of the frigate *Lockford* first thing. He found the bridge to be a bit of a mess because of the work that Lt. Jackson had done on the rebel captors. Once the bridge was cleaned up, the captain had his officers meet him on the bridge to plot an escape from the rebel fleet.

Once his officers were assembled, the captain said, "We need to leave the mothballed fleet as stealthily as possible. Speed is not important until we are out of range of the fleet's plasma guns and missiles. Any recommendations on how to give the fleet the slip?"

His executive officer, Ikram Shah, replied, "We could reduce our orbital speed by about 10%. This will cause us to orbit closer to the black hole. Once we are near the fleet's perimeter, we can fire up our fusion engines and give the *Lockford* everything we've got. The *Lockford* is, after all, the fastest frigate in the fleet."

"Make it so, Mr. Shah," replied Capt. Alvarez. "Keep in mind we are outgunned by almost every frigate in the mothballed fleet. We will have to rely on stealth and speed."

***

The rebel heavy frigate *Wingate*, 48 guns, was a powerhouse on guard duty. While most of the fleet, which included all the ships-of-the-line, had moved out of the mothballed fleet area, the *Wingate* had the duty of making sure that all the remaining ships maintained proper orbits around the black hole—and to keep an eye on the captured FNS *Lockford*. The *Wingate* also had to watch for any other Federation ships that might be prowling about in their sector.

The post captain on the *Wingate* was Rhonda Ashe. She had been in command of the *Wingate* for just under a solar year. Previously, she had commanded a few light frigates. Her record was clean, if not a bit ordinary. When the mothballed *Wingate* lost its previous captain to an accident involving high voltages, Captain Ashe was reassigned to Purgatory to command the heavy frigate. Her sin that needed purging was her lack of imagination.

Captain Ashe was on the bridge when one of the science officers in the Space-Time Deck came on the comm.

"Captain Ashe, we have determined that the light frigate *Lockford* has moved out of its stable orbit due to degradation of its orbital speed. The frigate may be in danger of crossing the event horizon."

"That's what happens when you turn over the command of a frigate to a group of marines and rebels. They have no idea how to maintain station. Let's move in a little closer and tap into their navigational computer to step up their speed and get them back into a reasonable orbit," said Capt. Ashe, who was a bit annoyed about the whole situation.

As the *Wingate* moved in closer to establish a strong communication link with the *Lockford*, the communication officer on the heavy frigate reported, "Captain Ashe, we are unable to establish a link with the *Lockford*'s navigational computer."

"Have you tried all frequencies?" asked Capt. Ashe.

"Affirmative."

"Give me the comm. I'll find out what's wrong. Maybe they are having problems with their prisoners," responded Capt. Ashe.

When Capt. Ashe was given the comm, she inquired, "*Lockford*, your orbit has degraded significantly. You have less than an hour to correct the situation before your orbit degrades to the point that we will not be able to keep you from falling into the black hole."

Suddenly, the fusion thrusters on the *Lockford* came to life with a blaze of light. When this happened, Captain Ashe got on the comm and tried to reach the *Lockford*.

"*Lockford*, please turn your ship around. If you fail to do so, I will be forced to fire my guns on you. Please respond!"

There was no reply.

Captain Ashe called down to the Engineering Deck on the *Wingate*. "This is the captain. Please start the fusion thrusters and give me full power as soon as possible."

Then she called down to the Weapons Control Deck. "Get a fix on the *Lockford*'s position and fire at her Space-Time Deck."

She then contacted Fleet Command. "This is Captain Ashe of the heavy frigate *Wingate*. The frigate *Lockford* has gone rogue and is attempting to escape. The *Wingate* is preparing to pursue and disable the *Lockford*. Please give confirmation."

"Captain Ashe, this is Admiral Torres. My orders are for you to destroy the *Lockford*. Do not let the *Lockford* escape. Failure to do so will carry extreme consequences."

After about five minutes, the *Wingate* got underway and was in pursuit of the *Lockford*. Even though the *Wingate* was heavily armed, she was a bit slower than the *Lockford*. Knowing that there was no way the *Wingate* could catch her, Captain Ashe gave the order to open fire on the *Lockford*.

***

On the *Lockford* there was considerable panic. Captain Alvarez and his crew had hoped to sneak away quietly, but now they were being pursued by a heavy frigate with twice the firepower of the *Lockford*. The only hope they had was that they would be able to outrun the heavy frigate. Captain Alvarez knew, however, that there was no way they could outrun the plasma guns. Captain Alvarez got onto the comm and gave the following order:

"We are being pursued by a heavy frigate believed to be the *Wingate*. I anticipate that we will be fired on at any moment. Please seal all hatches between decks. If the *Wingate* scores a hit on your deck and breaches your hull, do not open your hatches to escape. If you open your hatch, you may kill the entire crew from the loss of atmosphere."

Suddenly, the *Lockford* lurched to port and began to spin uncontrollably. The crew on the *Lockford* held onto anything they could to avoid being thrown into the bulkhead.

"Damage control: Report!" shouted the captain.

"The Navigation Deck has been hit and breached, Captain. No one on the deck responds and are presumed dead."

"Is there anyone who can take over navigation?"

"Negative. Wait a minute!" responded Damage Control. "Midshipman Chu. He was stationed on the space fortress and was able to navigate the maintenance shuttle through the mothballed fleet without being detected."

Captain Alvarez looked to the left, and there was the midshipman working at a computer station.

"Great, you are already here. You heard the woman in Damage Control. Can you get us out of this mess?"

"Sir, we need to get the *Lockford* out of this uncontrolled spin first," said Ming Chu. "We need to use the navigational thruster to act antagonistically to the rotation of the spin. Can we bypass the circuitry to the Engineering Deck?"

The captain got on the comm to the Engineering Deck.

"Can you do what Midshipman Chu is suggesting?"

"I can do better than that. I can control the navigational thrusters from here."

"Make it so!" shouted Capt. Alvarez.

Within a minute, the *Lockford*'s uncontrolled spin ceased.

Once the spinning stopped, Ming Chu asked, "How much mass does the *Wingate* have, relative to our mass?"

"The *Wingate* has at least twice our mass," responded Capt. Alvarez.

"We can use this difference in mass to our benefit. Plot an oblique course toward the black hole. Move ahead at top speed. Then, when we are as close as we can get without falling into the black hole, establish a new orbit around the black hole. We will need to be very close. The ship's navigational computer should be able to provide the details on the parameters."

"I see your plan, Mister Chu. If the *Wingate* tries to pursue us on this tight orbit…"

"The greater mass and slower speed of the *Wingate* will cause them to fall into the black hole," replied Ming Chu.

"Engineering, make this so. NOW!" ordered the captain.

The *Lockford* ran like a thoroughbred horse through its paces. As they approached the black hole, the light frigate began to shudder violently.

"What's that, Engineering?" asked Capt. Alvarez.

"We don't know. I am talking to the Space-Time Deck right now. I will connect you to their scientific officer," replied the engineering officer.

"Capt. Alvarez, this is the Space-Time Deck. Gravitational waves from the black hole are causing disturbances. If this keeps up long, the waves will shake the *Lockford* to pieces!"

"This will not take long," said Ming Chu. "Is the *Wingate* still on our tail?"

"Affirmative. No. Wait. Where did *Wingate* go?" said the scientific officer on the Space-Time Deck.

"The *Wingate* has passed through the event horizon. The *Wingate* has been crushed to a point of singularity!" shouted Midshipman Chu.

"Captain, where do you want us to go?"

"Through the Beta Wormhole. We need to report to the Admiralty that the Rebellion has taken over the mothballed fleet," replied Capt. Alvarez.

"How will we get through the rebel fleet and the space fortress?" asked the engineering officer.

"How fast are we moving now?" asked Ming Chu.

"Our velocity is off scale! We must be approaching 10% relativistic velocity," reported Engineering. "There is no way that the rebel fleet can capture us!"

"The acceleration toward the black hole gave us this speed," said Ming Chu.

"Engineering, plot a course to the Beta Wormhole," said Capt. Alvarez.

***

The rebels on the ship-of-the-line *Brazil* and the captured space fortress, *Sagittarius A**, saw something moving incredibly fast on their sensors that seemed to come from the direction of the black hole. Whatever it was, it slingshotted through the zone of FNF *Sagittarius A**, toward the gate of the Beta Wormhole.

Chapter 27

The Rebellion Now Controls the People of Earth.
Who Controls Earth's Climate?

It was time for Aristides to return to Earth and consolidate his authority, and to give the people on Earth a report of the progress that was being made against the Federation. Leslie Jones accompanied him from the front lines near the entrance to the Beta Wormhole to the FNF *Sagittarius A**. Along the way, Leslie asked, "So, what do you want me to do while you are back on Earth?"

"I want you to take charge of the space fortress and get the Space-Time Lab on the space fortress back in operation. Then I need you to find Dr. Tempus. That idiot, Captain Son Ri, sent Dr. Tempus off to some strange place and time. We need him back so we can utilize the time-travel capabilities of the lab," said Aristides in a grumpy voice.

"Is Captain Son Ri still on board the space fortress, or did you 'space' him?" asked Leslie.

"I'm not that stupid. The good captain is in the space fortress brig. He is the key to finding Dr. Tempus. Under interrogation, he confessed that he knows almost as much as Dr. Tempus about the Space-Time Lab," responded Aristides.

"What means of persuasion should I use to get him to talk, Aristides?" asked Leslie.

"Whatever means you deem fit. If necessary, you may use your female charms," answered Aristides in a somewhat sarcastic tone.

At this point, Leslie Jones gave Aristides a dirty look.

"I'm just kidding. But feel free to use any other methods to get him to talk. Once you have Dr. Tempus back on the space fortress, you are to space Captain Son Ri."

"That seems extreme, Aristides. Captain Son Ri might be of some use when it comes to operating the space fortress," replied Leslie.

"Captain Son Ri is a loose cannon. Get rid of him the moment Dr. Tempus is back on the fortress," said Aristides.

The real reason Leslie wanted to keep Capt. Son Ri around had to do with the rebels' lack of technical skills to keep the space fortress in operation. Most of the space fortress's original crew had been 'spaced' once they divulged important information regarding the operations of the space fortress. The rest of the staff on the space fortress were rebels brought from Earth based on their technical skills.

Once Aristides and Leslie were on the fortress, they had a warm embrace and parted ways. Aristides reported to the teleporter room, which was his means of transportation back to Earth. Aristides entered the teleporter room and asked, "Is the teleporter ready to take me back to San Francisco?"

"Everything is ready, Aristides. We sent a message through the Alpha Wormhole notifying them of your visit," replied the rebel technician.

"Have all security arrangements been made?"

"Yes, sir. You will have a rebel marine company escort you to all your Earth-bound destinations."

"Have the rebel commanders been informed of my itinerary?" asked Aristides.

"Yes, sir. All have acknowledged, except the commanders in Europe."

"No problem. I'll take care of our European friends when I get there," said Aristides.

***

When Aristides' teleporter vessel came through the Alpha Wormhole in San Francisco, there was a crowd awaiting him. When Aristides stepped from the teleporter building, there was a tumultuous cheer. Aristides took advantage of the opportunity to say a few words:

"Thank you, friends, for the warm welcome. I have good news! The Rebellion has taken control of the Alpha Wormhole, the mothballed fleet, and Naval Space Fortress, *Sagittarius A**. We are on the verge of taking possession of the Beta Wormhole. After that, we will move forward to take the planet *Beyond*. Once victory is ours, we will bring environmental scientists and geoengineers back to Earth to reverse the effects of climate change that have befallen our home. We will make Earth a paradise again!"

Before the crowd could cheer, someone in the audience screamed, "And we will hang the Federation fascist pigs!"

To this, Aristides responded, "We are not barbarians. The people of the Federation are our misguided brothers and sisters. We will give all of them the opportunity to join our righteous cause."

Aristides and his entourage then boarded an aerial transport to go and meet with the various leaders, starting with the commanders from South, Central, and North America. The meeting was held in Panama City. When their transport plane approached Panama City, Aristides was shocked to see most of the city underwater.

"What happened to Panama City? What caused this flood?"

Aristides' host responded, "Sir, the Greenland ice cap has collapsed, and most of the Antarctic ice cap has disappeared. This subject will be covered in our meeting with the American commanders."

The transport craft landed on a small airstrip located on a low ridge overlooking the Culebra Cut of the Panama Canal. When Aristides stepped off the aircraft, he was blasted with extreme heat and humidity.

"Is it always this hot and humid here? This is oppressive!" said Aristides as he wiped the sweat from his forehead.

Unlike the reception that Aristides received in San Francisco, there were only a few rebels, armed with laser guns, to meet him.

"We are here to escort you to the meeting with the American commanders. It will be a short Jeep ride up that hill over there," pointed one of the rebels.

Once at the building, Aristides was escorted to a meeting room with about a dozen or so rebel commanders. One commander, Benjamin Ngo, rose to meet Aristides, showed him to his seat, and then kicked off the meeting.

"Aristides, we will give you time later in the meeting to update us on your victories at the center of the galaxy," said Benjamin Ngo. "However, we have urgent matters to discuss with you. Let me get straight to the point. Global climate change has displaced over a billion people in coastal areas. In the Americas alone, over 200 million have been displaced. Another crisis is the increasing temperature in the tropics. We agreed to hold the meeting here near the equator to show how hot it has become. The average temperature here is 40 degrees Celsius, or 105 degrees Fahrenheit—and that includes nighttime temperatures! Today's temperature outside this building is almost 50°C, which is 120°F. The relative humidity is typically over 70%.

"The reason there was no crowd to greet you is that there is almost no one living here. They have all migrated north seeking cooler climates. It is estimated that almost 250 million people have been displaced by these temperatures in the Americas alone. In short: we are facing a humanitarian crisis that is taxing food production and housing on an unprecedented scale."

Aristides pondered this for a few minutes, then asked, "Why didn't I see flooding in San Francisco when I landed?"

"North America has the resources to dam up the Golden Gate to prevent the Pacific Ocean from flooding the San Francisco Bay Area."

Then Aristides asked, "Have you asked for help from the Europeans?"

The panel of commanders was quiet and looked at each other anxiously. Finally, Benjamin Ngo spoke. "There will be no help coming from Europe. The Gulf Stream that gave Europe its mild climate has failed due to the rapid melting of the Greenland ice cap. Europe has entered an ice age. All agriculture in Europe has failed. Over half the population has starved, and the rest are facing starvation."

"Can things get much worse?" shouted Aristides.

"There is one more thing," replied Benjamin Ngo.

"What's that?"

"Something strange has happened to 130,000 people. They just… vanished into thin air."

"Who were these people?" asked Aristides.

"From what we can tell, they were all people of faith. It's hard to get specifics on them. After the persecution of people of faith, many of them worshipped in secret. Those that were open about their faith were killed before President William Nelson of the Federation reached out to Myron Abbot. You remember: the Jewish rabbi who helped to forge peace between the Federation and people of faith. At any rate, most people of faith registered with the Federation as Jewish, Muslim, Hindu, Buddhist, or Christian. However, many Jewish Christians did not register. We had no way of tracking them. It is believed—but we are not certain—that 130,000 of these Jewish Christians simply went off the grid. We have no idea where they are," explained Benjamin.

"Benjamin, do you think they are planning a counter-revolution? One hundred and thirty thousand guerrillas who have a grudge against anyone who might persecute their people group could cause us problems. Have any of these rogue Christians been captured? What have we learned about them?" asked Aristides.

"That's the problem, Aristides. Since these Christians went off the grid, we have never captured a single rogue Christian," responded Benjamin Ngo.

***

Captain Son Ri sat in his cell in the brig. He was one not to worry about his fate but rather concerned himself with his sense of duty. Duty had called on him to send Dr. Hays and Dr. Abbot to unknown locations and times. Duty had compelled him to defend the FNS

*Sagittarius A**. Now, duty compelled him to sit in this cell. He could only hope that his family had made it safely to the Beta Wormhole, which would take them to the planet Beyond.

Suddenly, he heard the clank of the brig hatch open and close. He looked above his cell to the aisle that was above him and saw a woman looking down at him. Before he could say anything, she spoke.

"Captain Son Ri, I need to talk to you."

"Why should I talk to you? You're probably one of those idealistic rebels who thinks they know everything. Go away," said Capt. Son Ri.

Still, she wouldn't leave. Finally, she said, "I am Dr. Leslie Jones. I need to find Dr. Tempus. Can you help me?"

"Why should I care? What's in it for me?" asked Capt. Son Ri. "I know that as long as I remain silent regarding the whereabouts of Dr. Tempus, the Rebellion will not space me. Silence is my cloak of safety."

"How would you like to have your old command back?" asked Dr. Jones. "I'm sure you would want to command this space fortress again."

"And work for you and your rebel friends? No way!" shouted Capt. Son Ri.

"Do you want to save the rest of your crew?" asked Dr. Jones.

"The rest of my crew? The crew that was loyal to the Federation have been 'spaced' by you and your band of barbarians. No deal," said Capt. Son Ri.

"What about your wife and two children?"

"What about them?" asked Capt. Son Ri.

"You thought they were safe, didn't you," said Leslie Jones. "You put them on a fast frigate and sent them to safety. Well, I have just been told that we captured that frigate just this side of the Beta Wormhole. They are now in our custody. It would be a shame to space them without you knowing about it. So, we thought we would show you on your monitor in your cell."

"You really are a barbarian. I'll see you eviscerated if the Federation ever captures you."

The screen in Captain Son Ri's cell blinked to life. There on the screen was his wife being held by two burly rebels. His two small children cowered in the corner. The scene was in the space fortress shuttle bay.

"Henry, please cooperate for the sake of our two children! Tell them whatever they want." After she said this, the rebels turned off the monitor.

"I'll cooperate," said Capt. Son Ri, as he looked at the floor.

"Good. I'll have the guards escort you to the Space-Time Laboratory. I'll meet you there," said Leslie Jones, with a smile on her face.

***

Leslie was already in the laboratory when Captain Son Ri entered with the two rebel guards. Leslie turned to the guards and said, "We won't be needing guards now. I'll call on you if I need anything."

Once they were alone, Dr. Jones asked Son Ri, "Can you give me a tour of the control panel to show me where you sent Dr. Tempus? I have already looked at the interface and found it to be like the teleporter that I operated in San Francisco. There is some similarity between these two systems."

Son Ri responded, "We need to access the memory buffer in the computer. Here we go: here is the last time the Space-Time Lab was used. Here is the file on Dr. Tempus… Let's see, he was sent to Barstow, California… a small town in the Mojave Desert. He was sent back in time to July 14, 2010."

"How can we capture Dr. Tempus and have him returned to this space fortress?" asked Dr. Jones.

Captain Son Ri replied, "I am quite familiar with the teleporter system and this system, so we can get straight to the point. First, we need to have a large star on an elliptical orbit around the black hole to make a close pass. When matter and light get drawn off the star to form an accretion disk around the black hole, we need to have this system… here on the control panel… activated. This will enable the system to isolate all the vortices that have time-travel potential. Then you enter the desired physical coordinates and time parameters. After this, we need to select this function… here… that will give the best matches for potential vortices. Then all you need to do is launch the time-travel probe, and let the computer do the rest. If you are going to 'capture' Dr. Tempus, you will need to supply a recording that will give him convincing reasons to enter the probe and return to the fortress."

"When is the next close pass of a star to the black hole?" asked Dr. Jones.

"There is one due to happen in eight days," replied Capt. Son Ri.

"Captain, can you assist me then in capturing Dr. Tempus?"

"Certainly. Can you assure the safe passage for me and my family to the Beta Wormhole?"

"Certainly. I shouldn't be telling you this, but Aristides told me to space you after Dr. Tempus is captured."

"Why are you telling me this?" asked Capt. Son Ri.

"You have something that I can't have: a family," replied Leslie Jones, with tears in her eyes.

***

Eight days later, Captain Son Ri and his family found themselves on a fast frigate heading to the Beta Wormhole. While all of this was happening, Aristides reported to San Francisco to be teleported back to FNF *Sagittarius A**. From there, he joined the rebel fleet at the gate of the Beta Wormhole. His main concern was to get the invasion of the planet *Beyond* started.

Chapter 28

Jerusalem

And did those feet in ancient time

Walk upon England's mountains green?

And was the holy lamb of God

On England's pleasant pastures seen?

And did the countenance divine

Shine forth upon our clouded hills?

And was Jerusalem built here

Amongst these dark satanic mills?

Bring me my bow of burning gold

Bring me my arrows of desire

Bring me my spear, o clouds unfold!

Bring me my chariot of fire.

I will not cease from mental fight

Nor shall my sword sleep in my hand

Till we have built Jerusalem

In England's green and pleasant land.

Hubert Parry and William Blake

Myron Abbot felt like a tourist as he walked the myriads of narrow streets and alleys in Jerusalem. Jerusalem is a city built in the hills of Judea, so it's not just about navigating streets, but hills as well. The aromas from exotic foods from street vendors added another dimension. The sounds of exotic music and the calls to prayer from the city's mosques added yet another dimension. Myron fit into this scenario seamlessly. There was a myriad of other Orthodox Jews, just like him and dressed like him.

One thing Myron was not prepared for was the extreme heat. Many of the trees were quite dead and had been dead for some time. He also noted that many people were carrying buckets of water. Apparently, the water system in Jerusalem had failed—another casualty of climate change.

Myron was lost in his thoughts, and was quite literally lost. He wanted to find out what happened to Elijah and Enoch. Was he in the right time period? It felt like the year 2170, but did the Space-Time Continuum Lab on the Space Fortress *Sagittarius A** have that level of precision? He didn't know, nor did he want to know. He wanted to find them.

Then he came to an intersection with a main street. Suddenly, there was a rush of people running down this street. The talk among them was excited, and the meaning impossible to discern. Myron stopped a young Jewish woman and asked, "What is all the commotion about?"

The young woman responded, "Where have you been? Everyone in Jerusalem has been talking about this since last week. You haven't heard of the two guys that showed up last week? One of them can do miracles, and the other one talks to us about what it means to walk with God."

"Can you take me with you? I would like to see them," asked Myron.

"Okay, but you will have to hurry. They appear and disappear suddenly. By the way, what's your name?" said the Jewish woman as she took his hand and led him through the crowd.

"My name is Myron Abbot…"

"*The* Myron Abbot? The one who forged the peace accord between the people of faith and the Federation?" exclaimed the young Jewish woman.

It then occurred to him that the name 'Myron Abbot' might have some notoriety in Jerusalem. He responded with a simple, "Yes," and hoped that he did not get involved in a brutal argument.

"Hey, I would like you to meet some friends of mine after you see the two guys at the Temple Mount," said the excited young woman.

"Sure! What's your name, young lady?" asked Myron.

"Keziah."

The two of them raced up the steps to the Temple Mount. As they approached the top steps, they could see thousands of people gathered in the open plaza. At the other end of the plaza, standing in front of the Temple of the Rock, were Elijah and Enoch. Elijah was speaking:

"… and those who are the children of Israel, repent, for the Kingdom of Heaven is at hand. Make straight in the desert a highway for your God. For those of you who persecute Jews and Christians, beware and repent, for you will be cast down in the fiery furnace to condemnation with the false prophet and the dragon."

Then someone from the crowd shouted, "What has happened to the 130,000 Jewish Christians who have disappeared? I had a brother who was a Christian, and one day he just disappeared."

"They have not disappeared. They have been transported to God, who will sanctify them for a great work. They will return!" replied Elijah.

"You mean that the Federation has transported them to the planet Beyond. That's the story we are getting from the Revolutionary Council," replied another man in the audience.

"Believe what you will," cried Enoch. "You will see that the truth will prevail."

Myron, when he heard this, wished that his friend, Dr. Hays, was here. At thinking this thought, Myron suddenly panicked and thought, *Where is Robert Hays now?* He set this thought aside for now and continued to listen to Elijah and Enoch.

"… if you walk in my ways, I will give you rest from your enemies. You who follow the beast and the false messiah, your doom is sure. Repent…"

At hearing Elijah and Enoch, Myron thought, *Neither Enoch nor Elijah spoke modern Hebrew on the space fortress, but ancient dialects of Hebrew. But here in Jerusalem, they were speaking perfect modern Hebrew. Strange.*

After about an hour or so, Elijah and Enoch disappeared rather suddenly. The crowd dispersed, and Myron and Keziah left the Temple Mount. They wove their way down the twisted streets and alleys until they reached a set of stairs that took them to a second-story apartment.

When they reached the apartment door, Keziah rapped with her knuckles a code on the door, which sounded like a tune from a popular band from the 1960s. The door then opened a bit, and an eye peeked out to see who was there. Then the person in the apartment said, "Oh, it's you, Keziah. Before you come in, can you tell me who is with you?"

"This is Myron Abbot. You know, the Orthodox Jew who won the Nobel Peace Prize a few years back," responded Keziah.

"Come in. I am Joseph. Let's go to the kitchen and talk."

When Myron entered the room, it took a couple of minutes for his eyes to adjust to the darkness in the apartment. He was led into the kitchen and was seated at the table. There were two other gentlemen at the table. One was an Orthodox Jew, and the other was dressed like a Palestinian.

"Let me introduce you. This is Abraham Hecker, and our Palestinian friend over there is George Mustafa."

"I am surprised to see an Orthodox Jew seated next to a Palestinian," responded Myron.

"George is no ordinary Palestinian—he attends the Maronite Christian Church," responded Joseph.

"Myron and I just got back from the Temple Mount. The two 'Witnesses' were there. They were pronouncing some dire predictions. When Myron introduced himself to me, I thought to bring him here. Perhaps he can answer some of our questions."

All eyes in the room turned to Myron. This made Myron very uncomfortable.

Joseph asked the first question, "Do you know who the men are that you saw at the Temple Mount?"

Myron had to think for a minute. The answer to Joseph's question was easy, but the way to deliver the answer was not so easy. After pondering a moment, he said in a soft voice, "They are Enoch and Elijah. They were sent here from the past."

At this point, Myron's mind became a muddled mess.

"That's not possible!" exclaimed George. "They have been dead for thousands of years."

"George, neither Enoch nor Elijah saw death. God took them to Himself. Here, let me show you in the Torah," said Abraham.

"Okay, but how did they get here?" asked George.

All eyes were fixed on Myron. "I know how they were sent here, but I'm afraid you won't believe me. They got here the same way I did."

"Okay, Myron. How did *you* get here?" asked George.

"I was sent here by the FNF *Sagittarius A**." All eyes were locked on him. He could tell that everyone in the room thought he was crazy.

"Where is this Naval Fortress located?" asked Abraham, in a sarcastic tone.

"It is at the center of our galaxy," answered Myron.

"You're crazy! Let's get him out of here. He is no use to us," said George.

"No, wait. I can show you the craft that brought me here. I have it hidden under some tree branches. Please let me take you there."

They were about to follow Myron to the Space-Time probe when George spoke up.

"Hold on a moment. There is something in the New Testament about two witnesses. Yeah, here it is… the 11th chapter in the book of Revelation. Let me read it to you."

"Then I was given a reed like a measuring rod. And the angel stood, saying, 'Rise and measure the temple of God, the altar, and those who worship there. But leave out the court which is outside the temple, and do not measure it, for it has been given to the

Gentiles. And they will tread the holy city underfoot for forty-two months.

And I will give power to my two witnesses, and they will prophesy one thousand two hundred and sixty days, clothed in sackcloth.'

These are the two olive trees and the two lampstands standing before the God of the Earth. And if anyone wants to harm them, fire proceeds from their mouth and devours their enemies. And if anyone wants to harm them, he must be killed in this manner.

These have power to shut heaven, so that no rain falls in the days of their prophecy; and they have power over waters to turn them to blood, and to strike the Earth with all plagues, as often as they desire.

When they finish their testimony, the beast that ascends out of the bottomless pit will make war against them, overcome them, and kill them. And their dead bodies will lie in the street of the great city which spiritually is called Sodom and Egypt, where also our Lord was crucified.

Then those from the peoples, tribes, tongues, and nations will see their dead bodies three-and-a-half days, and not allow their dead bodies to be put into graves.

And those who dwell on the Earth will rejoice over them, make merry, and send gifts to one another, because these two prophets tormented those who dwell on the Earth.

Now after the three-and-a-half days, the breath of life from God entered them, and they stood on their feet, and great fear fell on those who saw them. And they heard a loud voice from heaven saying to them, 'Come up here.' And they ascended to heaven in a cloud, and their enemies saw them.

In the same hour there was a great earthquake, and a tenth of the city fell. In the earthquake seven thousand people were killed, and the rest were afraid and gave glory to the God of heaven."

After this was read, there was a pause in the room for a minute or two. Then Myron spoke.

"I wish that my friend, Robert Hays, was here. He might be able to speak about this. Since I do not hold to the opinion that the New Testament is inspired by God, I cannot speak of this."

Keziah then spoke. "What if Myron is not crazy and is speaking the truth? Do you think one of us could arrange a meeting with these two 'Witnesses'?"

"I have met with the two men in question this morning. I know where they are staying. Keziah, can you go with me and keep a lookout for rebel and Federation troops? You know that Palestine and Israel are about to erupt in open warfare," said Abraham.

"Even though the Rebellion has taken control of Earth, how can there be war between Israel and Palestine?" asked Myron.

"The Revolution was good at defeating the armies of Earth. But remember, most of the Federation government has already teleported to the planet Beyond. The Revolution is utterly incompetent when it comes to governing the peoples of Earth. Things have become chaotic," answered George.

"What about the question I heard from the crowd? Keziah, do you remember the question about what has happened to the 130,000 Christians who simply vanished?" asked Myron.

"Wait a minute!" exclaimed George. "We had a couple of people from our church disappear. These two people, who were ethnically Jewish, were fanatical followers of Jesus. Do you think they were part of the 130,000 that disappeared?"

Everyone looked at each other in the room. No one spoke for a couple of minutes. Finally, Abraham spoke up.

"We can ask Elijah and Enoch when we meet with them."

"May I come, too? After all, they can corroborate everything that I have said," shouted George.

"Myron, it would be great to have you along. I think you may help the conversation go more smoothly."

"Good, so we have a plan! Please be careful—these are dangerous times," said Joseph.

Chapter 29

Where Am I Now

As stated previously, Robert Hays was being held at the insane asylum in a trailer called the annex. He was in the annex when a tremendous thunderstorm broke. He had never experienced a thunderstorm in the desert before, except in his schizophrenic delusions.

He was sitting on the bed, watching television, when suddenly the roof of the annex was ripped off the trailer. There above him was a flaming torus. Then a probe came through the torus and landed just outside the asylum annex.

Dr. Hays immediately realized that this was a Space-Time Continuum probe from FNS *Sagittarius A**. He went outside to the probe. Although the door to his room was locked, he was able to climb over the wall of his room, since there was no ceiling anymore.

So, there was Dr. Hays, standing in the pouring rain, looking at the time-traveling probe. Suddenly, a hatch on the probe opened and a very small robot came out. The robot spoke to him in a tinny, high-frequency voice, "Are you Dr. Tempus?"

"No, I am Dr. Robert Hays."

The small robot thought for a few seconds, then said, "Were you the Chief Scientific Officer on the FNF *Sagittarius A**?"

"You found him," answered Dr. Hays.

"Please get into the probe. Your services are required by the Rebellion."

"What if I do not wish to give my services to the Rebellion? The last time I heeded the call, I got into a world of hurt. I think this is a bad idea, Mr. Robot!" responded Dr. Hays, with a scowl on his face.

"That would be unwise of you," continued the small robot. "You may not know, but the Rebellion has taken over the space fortress. It was an officer of the Federation who sent you here. You are now *persona non grata* to the Federation. The Federation is a godless entity that has largely destroyed the planet Earth by greenhouse gas emissions, which have caused the collapse of a significant number of ecosystems. They have left Earth to go to another world and have abandoned most humans to perish. This is a crime against humanity," said the robot in its tinny voice.

"My, you do have a moral compass, my little robot friend. I do not have any strong feelings about the Federation or the Rebellion. I am quite content to stay on Earth in the 21st century. When this asylum figures out that I am not insane, they will let me go free," responded Dr. Hays, with a half-smile on his face.

"Your reasoning is illogical," answered the robot. "They will see the scar on your head and will run a series of tests. They will determine that your brain has been greatly compromised, and you will become a ward of the state. Freedom will be elusive. On the other hand, if you join the Rebellion, you will be reinstated to your previous position as Chief Scientific Officer on the Space Fortress *Sagittarius A**. You will become a part of man's struggle to undo the damage to Earth's ecosystems. The potential impact you have may save billions of lives."

"Let me think on this," said Dr. Hays.

"One other thing that I was programmed to say: On board the space fortress is Dr. Leslie Jones. She is now the commander of the space fortress. Dr. Jones believes in the tenets of the Rebellion. She is also becoming disillusioned with Aristides, the leader of the Rebellion. She now sees him as an arrogant tyrant who lusts for power. Dr. Jones has studied your background and has concluded that you are a good man who can bring the Rebellion back to its tenets for saving Earth. She has confidence that you can bring balance back to the Rebellion, and by extension, to Earth itself."

"I don't know about this. How does Dr. Jones know this?" asked Dr. Hays.

"Does not compute," replied the robot.

"What do you mean: *Does not compute*? You are nothing but a useless piece of—"

"Dr. Jones did not provide adequate detail to answer your question. Just get into the probe now, before the Space-Time Continuum Wormhole closes."

With that, Dr. Robert Hays stepped into the probe and disappeared from the insane asylum in July 2010, to return to Space Fortress *Sagittarius A**.

***

It did not take long for Dr. Hays to return to the space fortress. In only a matter of seconds, the probe popped out of the wormhole. Within seconds of leaving the Space-Time Continuum Wormhole, he could see the space fortress dead ahead. When they approached the fortress, the airlock hatch opened, and in flew the probe.

It took about 10 minutes for the air pressure to equilibrate. Then the hatch to the Space-Time Continuum Lab opened, and there in the lab stood Dr. Jones. Unfortunately, she was not alone. With her was a squad of rebel marines with their laser rifles aimed right at Dr. Hays.

"Dr. Tempus, I presume. I am Dr. Leslie Jones, commander of this space fortress," said Dr. Jones.

Dr. Hays pondered this situation for a moment, then said, "I am not Dr. Tempus, I am Dr. Hays. Why are the marines here?"

"We are not sure which side you are on. We can never be too careful," responded Dr. Jones. Then she turned to the rebel marines and said, "You are dismissed. We won't be needing you now."

Once the marines left, Dr. Jones escorted Dr. Hays to his quarters.

On the way, he asked, "Dr. Jones, about the small robot in the probe. What was the meaning of the last thing it said to me regarding the leader of the Rebellion?"

"Oh, that!" said Dr. Jones. "Let's discuss this when you get to your cabin. It's a bit touchy, and I don't want to be overheard. By the way, please call me Leslie. We are not real formal around here. You go by Robert or Bob?"

"Robert. How did you know my first name?"

"From our little robot friend in the space probe," replied Leslie.

When they reached Robert's cabin, Leslie used her key card to open the door. Inside, the cabin had not changed a bit. In fact, the empty bottle of bourbon and the two glasses were still on the table.

"It looks like you and someone else were having a small party here. Was it with Myron Abbot?" asked Leslie.

"Yes, and I am very worried about him. I believe that he was sent into the future. He has incipient Alzheimer's disease, and I fear for his health and safety."

"You are friends with Myron?" asked Leslie.

"Yes, and I owe him a lot," replied Robert.

"Tell me why."

"He helped me recover my memory. You probably know that I was known as Dr. Tempus. At any rate, Myron located the scar on my scalp and walked me through my past events. It finally came back to me that my real name is Robert Hays, and I came from the 21st century."

"You are a fascinating man, Robert," replied Leslie. "I have run a complete search on you. You were way ahead of your time. I tried to find the background on Dr. Tempus, but I couldn't find a thing. So, I looked in the archive for a scientist who knew how black holes interact with the time-space continuum, and your name kept cropping up."

There was a pregnant pause in their dialogue for about a minute, then Leslie asked, "What did Myron get out of this?"

"Why are you asking this question?" asked Robert.

"Everyone does something to get something back in return. It's the way people operate," said Leslie.

Robert just stared at Leslie for a minute, then said, "I helped Myron with his Alzheimer's disease, but the reason for helping him—and Myron helping me—has nothing to do with reciprocity. It has to do with friendship. Do you believe in friendship?"

There was a long silence in the cabin. Leslie seemed genuinely perplexed by Robert's question. Finally, she answered, "I have no friends. I have collaborators, and in rare times I even have romantic relationships, but I have no friends."

"This is very strange that you have no friends!" exclaimed Robert. "I thought you were buddies with the rebel leader. What's his name?"

"Aristides," responded Leslie. "He is a brute. Real slick and seems sincere at first. Professed to have high moral standards, but he would sell his own mother into slavery if it served his purposes. I fell in love with him, but the closer I got to him, the more I was repelled by his lust for power. He claims to be an environmentalist, but he uses that title as a foil to get others to follow him."

"Life does not need to be like this, Leslie. God made people to be in relationship with Him and each other. Friendship is important," responded Robert Hays.

"I read in your history, Robert, that you are a Christian, correct? I understand that in your time back in the 21st century there were quite a few Christians around, but I have never known any Christian in the 22nd century. Is Myron a Christian?"

"No. Myron is an Orthodox Jew," replied Robert. "He is rather famous, you know. He won the Nobel Peace Prize a few years ago. What about you? Do you believe in God?"

Leslie began to feel quite uncomfortable with this line of conversation. Robert kept coming back to God and religion. She sought to change the topic.

"May we continue this conversation sometime in the future? I need to talk to you about getting the Space-Time Lab back up and running."

"Why do you want the lab back up and running?" asked Robert.

"There are some interesting targets that we want to capture," replied Leslie. "The skills they possess will aid the rebel cause."

"Is that what you think of people who lived in the past or the future—as interesting targets?" shouted Robert.

"What if one of those targets is Myron Abbot?" asked Leslie. "We can use him for a training exercise. We would both win. You would get your friend back, and the Rebellion would learn how to operate the lab."

"Let me think on this for a while. First, though, you need to consider the risk of a 'time paradox.' This is the risk of changing history by messing with the past. For instance, what would happen if you went back in time and killed your mother before you were born?"

"I have never thought about that," replied Leslie.

"Well, give it some thought," said Robert.

Chapter 30

The *Lockford* Finds Safe Harbor

After the battle with the *Wingate*, the light frigate *Lockford* needed repairs badly—and quickly. Captain Alvarez knew that flying the frigate in this condition, and at its current high speed, could cause the ship to break apart.

"All officers and midshipmen are to report to the bridge at once," the captain announced on the comm.

Once his officers had gathered, the captain said, "Our ship has lost its Navigation Deck, and it was only because of Lieutenant Chu and the Engineering Deck, and of course, our friend, the black hole Sagittarius A*, that we were able to give the *Wingate* the slip. To attempt to jump through the Beta Wormhole would be suicide at our current disposition. I will give the order to decelerate. This will make us vulnerable to any ships of the rebel fleet that might be lurking in the area."

"Sir," said Ming Chu, "we could use the maintenance shuttle that I used to cross from the space fortress to the *Lockford*. It has all the equipment and material to repair the breaches in the Navigation Deck. The space fortress maintenance crew was in my division, and they taught me how to repair breaches from meteoroids."

"Lieutenant Chu, that is an excellent idea," replied the captain.

"Sir, I also need to point out to you that I am not a lieutenant, but a midshipman," responded Ming Chu.

"Not anymore, Lieutenant. Once we have decelerated, I want you to take two of my maintenance men and my Chief Petty Officer Hicks to effect repairs."

Captain Alvarez then issued the following order: "All hands, prepare for deceleration. All crew members are to be strapped in securely. Make sure that all gear and instrumentation is secured. Deceleration to occur in two hours."

***

The deceleration of the *Lockford* was somewhat brutal. Many of the crew were confused that their previous acceleration to 10% the speed of light did not cause much in the way of g-force effects.

"How did the crew of the *Lockford* survive the massive amount of force from the acceleration as we approached the black hole?" asked Petty Officer Laura Hicks.

"I am not sure. It might have something to do with our close approach to the black hole. Maybe when the gravitational field of the black hole accelerated the *Lockford*, our bodies and organs were accelerated at the same rate, as well. That's the only thing I can think of," answered Lt. Chu.

"Well, I am really feeling the effects of this deceleration. I feel like I weigh a ton," replied Laura Hicks.

"Well, Ms. Hicks, maybe you weigh a ton right now. Just kidding! How long is this going to take?" asked Lt. Chu.

"My estimate is about six more hours. Why do you ask?"

"Uh oh. I need to use the washroom," said a sheepish Ming.

At hearing this, Laura Hicks just laughed and said, "Didn't you hook up your catheter? You know, for a smart guy, you are really an idiot."

Laura Hicks was very accurate in her estimation of how long it would take to get the *Lockford* down to standard cruising speed. Once the *Lockford* was down to standard cruising speed, Lt. Chu was released to do his business. After cleaning himself up, he met Laura Hicks outside the shuttle bay.

"Thank you for waiting for me."

"No problem," said Laura Hicks. "I need you to pilot the maintenance shuttle. None of us has a clue how to pilot this thing. While we were waiting for you, we cleaned up the inside of the shuttle. What a mess!"

Lt. Chu piloted the maintenance shuttle with two maintenance men and Laura Hicks. Once outside the shuttle bay, it took only a couple of minutes to see the worst damage.

"Look at the size of that breach to the Navigation Deck. How many crew members were on the Navigation Deck when we took the hit from the *Wingate*?" asked Ming.

"Twenty-one," said Laura Hicks, as she turned away. "One of them, Lt. Olson, was my fiancé."

Silence reigned in the shuttle for five minutes.

"I am sorry for your loss," Ming finally replied.

"There are risks to life," said Laura Hicks. "One takes risks in picking a career. One takes risks in forming relationships. Once I made those choices, the deck of cards was reshuffled, and I was dealt a hand that was not of my choosing. The result from this reshuffling is loss. There is nothing I can do to prevent the loss. However, if I am brave, I can move forward and make new choices, which, of course, have risks associated with them. For now, survival of the crew is the most important thing. I will be brave and assist in that goal. Then I can grieve."

"Let's get this hull breach repaired and get through the Beta Wormhole," responded Lt. Chu after a thoughtful pause.

Then Ming did something that is out of character for a person with autism: he gave Laura Hicks a long hug.

After about eight hours, the repair to the hull was completed and tested for vacuum leaks. Lt. Chu and Laura Hicks worked well together, in spite of the circumstances.

"Looks like we are good to go. Let's get back into the *Lockford* and get through the Beta Wormhole," said Lt. Chu.

Once the shuttle was back in the shuttle bay, the captain gave the order: "Prepare to enter the Beta Wormhole. It's time to go home."

At first, the wormhole could not be seen. The hole was too small to be seen. The instruments on board the *Lockford* could detect the wormhole, but it needed to be enlarged to be big enough to let the light frigate through. This required that the space-time continuum be manipulated in the area of the wormhole. This was the job of the science officers on the Space-Time Deck.

"We have located the wormhole at sector 18.373, 10.403, and 124.496. Ready for gravitational torus to be deployed."

"Gravitational torus is ready," shouted the officer on the Space-Time Deck.

"Helmsman, steady as you go. All ahead slow," said Commander Shah.

"Launch gravitational torus." At this command, a ring of anti-quarks with the appearance of a brilliant ring appeared in space at the location of the wormhole.

"Increase gravitation of torus to 1.245 mega-newtons."

When this order was carried out, the Beta Wormhole appeared. Then the gravitational torus moved down the wormhole.

"Helmsman, move forward at minimum impulse speed. Lock on to the center of the gravitational torus for coordinates. Maintain distance of one kilometer behind torus," said the space-time scientist.

From the outside of the *Lockford*, a truly magnificent sight: the ship entered the wormhole as it was forced open one kilometer ahead of the *Lockford*. Then, one kilometer behind the *Lockford*, the wormhole snapped shut. It all had the appearance of a rat being swallowed by a rattlesnake.

Chapter 31

Solar System G4014E1J1A2 and the Planet *Beyond*

As the FNS *Lockford* exited the wormhole, Ming Chu, Kat Henderson, and Lt. Henry Jackson were having a cup of coffee in the *Lockford*'s canteen. Lt. Jackson had some time to think, and he wanted to expand his knowledge horizons. The three of them were trying to figure out how wormholes could be used to travel great distances.

As they were trying to figure this out, one of the scientific officers from the Space-Time Deck came to join them.

"I couldn't help but hear what the three of you were discussing. So, what do you want to know about traveling through wormholes?" asked the scientific officer.

"What is a wormhole?" asked Lt. Jackson. "I had an old Jewish Rabbi ask me once, and I had a hard time answering him."

The scientist pondered a moment, then answered, "We perceive space in three dimensions: height, length, and depth. However, in space-time, there are actually four dimensions—the fourth being time. We think that the shortest distance between two points is a straight line. This is true the vast majority of the time, no pun intended. There are cases, however, when space-time folds on itself. If the fold in space-time brings distant parts of our galaxy together, small touchpoints can and do occur. A penetration may occur at these touchpoints. We call these wormholes."

"Why travel by wormholes?" asked Kat.

"There are advantages to traveling great distances through a wormhole. First, you can avoid the need for crazy fast speeds and the resulting huge use of fuel. Even with fusion propulsion, the amount of tritium and deuterium required for such speeds would easily exceed the gross weight of the vessel. You can also avoid all the massive acceleration and deceleration g-forces. For a craft to reach relativistic speed, the acceleration could potentially kill an entire spaceship crew. Then there is the time factor issue. To travel from one end of the Milky Way Galaxy to the other at the speed of light would take about 100,000 years—not counting the time to accelerate to the speed of light and decelerate before reaching your destination."

"Are there any disadvantages to traveling by wormholes?" asked Lt. Chu.

"There is just one major drawback to using wormholes to travel great distances in our galaxy: the lack of known wormholes. Presently, there are only two known wormholes. The first wormhole was discovered back in the mid-21st century by NASA and Dr. Robert Hays," stated the scientific officer. "The second wormhole was discovered more recently."

Kat thought about this for a minute or so and raised another disadvantage.

"When I was stationed on the FNF *Sagittarius A**," she said, "we would see another problem with marines who teleported through the wormholes several times in a week—a medical condition called Teleporting Mental Dislocation. We noted that these marines would be very confused and would become agitated by the littlest of things, like someone slamming a hatch too hard. We found that we would have to put them on tranquilizers for a week or so, then they seemed to recover."

"I have heard of this, too. I know that there is a team of Naval M.D.s working on this at the Admiralty," replied the scientific officer.

Ming then asked, "Tell us something about Dr. Hays' work on wormholes."

The scientist pondered for a minute, then responded to Ming's question.

"Let me give you a little history. The United States had built a research station on the far side of Earth's moon. The reason for building the station there was that that side of the moon always faces away from Earth. This enabled researchers to probe much further into the galaxy and allowed them to receive faint radio signals without interference from man-made sources of radio frequencies. It was hoped that they might locate intelligent extraterrestrial life. At any rate, this research failed to find intelligent life. But it did find one thing. The position of the stars became distorted whenever the far side of the moon pointed in the direction of the constellation Sagittarius. It was like a lensing effect that made objects at the center of our galaxy seem much closer. That's when NASA and the military brought Dr. Hays into the equation.

Dr. Hays was the leading expert in wormholes, so he seemed to be the best person to bring to the moon station to study this phenomenon. When Dr. Hays was brought to the station on the far side of the moon, he identified the anomaly as a wormhole. Dr. Hays developed a method for enlarging the wormhole to a diameter that allowed a small probe to be launched through it.

What they found was astounding. In a matter of a few hours, the probe started sending data back that indicated it was near the black hole at the center of the galaxy, also known as Sagittarius A*. What was also amazing is that the probe could transmit these data back to the far side of the moon in a few hours. After a few days, the data transmission stopped. It is believed that the probe fell into the black hole. I'm sorry! I am running off at the mouth!"

"Please continue! I am fascinated by this!" said Kat.

"Okay, most of the time people aren't interested in this. I will continue," replied the scientist. "So where was I? Oh yeah. So they sent a small manned spacecraft into the enlarged wormhole. The spacecraft made it through, but the wormhole snapped down to its original small size when they exited the wormhole near the black hole. They were able to transmit their observations for a time, until their air ran out. The lesson learned from this tragedy was that spaceships needed to be equipped with Dr. Hays' wormhole enlarger so they could enter and exit both sides of the wormhole."

"Is this the wormhole that we refer to as Alpha Wormhole?" asked Lt. Chu.

"Yes," responded the scientist. "Once we discovered how to travel to the center of the galaxy, a question arose: were there other wormholes in the vicinity of the black hole? After years of exploring, only one other wormhole has been discovered. That's what we call Beta Wormhole—the one that takes you from the area of space near the black hole to the planet Beyond," answered the scientist.

***

Exiting the Beta Wormhole was a much more pleasant experience than exiting the Alpha Wormhole near the black hole. There were no gravitational waves to negotiate—just smooth space-time. The Beta Wormhole exited in a small solar system. The star in this system was very similar to the sun which the Earth orbits.

Lt. Jackson, Lt. Chu, and Kat Henderson were on the bridge with Captain Alvarez.

"Welcome to Solar System G4014E1J1A2," said the captain.

"What does G4014E1J1A2 stand for?" asked Kat.

"The G stands for the star type. Both Earth's sun and Beyond's sun are G-class stars that are a bit on the small side and derive their energy from the fusion of hydrogen to form helium. The number 4014 is shorthand for the location of the solar system in the Milky Way Galaxy. The term E1 tells how many Earth-like planets orbit around the sun, and J1 indicates the number of Jupiter-like planets. A2 is the number of asteroid belts," responded Capt. Alvarez.

Even though the bridge on the *Lockford* had the best display screen for viewing the scene outside the ship, they couldn't see a thing.

"Why can't we see anything on the display?" asked Kat.

"Because the moon that orbits around the planet Beyond is in front of us. Just as the Alpha Wormhole entrance is on the far side of the Earth's moon, the Beta Wormhole exit terminates on the far side of this moon. This must be your first trip to the planet Beyond, Lt. Henderson," answered the captain.

"Yes, it is."

Then they saw the planet Beyond rise above the limb of the moon. Like Earth, the planet was predominantly blue in color, with accents of white where clouds resided. There was also white at the poles of the planet. Near the equator was a landmass that was peeking out of the clouds. This landmass was a verdant green.

"That landmass there," pointed Kat, "is that where we are heading?"

"No. We are heading to the other side of the planet. That landmass is not inhabited by humans yet. It is quite tropical, and some of the faunae are extremely dangerous. Most of the predators are reptilian-like. They are ectothermic, lay eggs, and can be quite large. Some of the fauna can fly. The largest flying reptiles are called dragons. They are very intelligent and very dangerous," replied Captain Alvarez. "We will be heading to a temperate landmass that has been almost fully terraformed. We call it *Paradisus*, which is Latin for Paradise."

Kat pondered this for a minute, then asked, "What terraforming actions have been taken to make the planet Beyond more livable?"

"First, the atmospheric composition needed to be modified. The atmosphere at the time of the planet's discovery had 10% oxygen and 10% carbon dioxide. The rest of the atmosphere was largely nitrogen, with a small amount of other gases, such as argon. The terraforming engineers and environmental scientists introduced phytoplankton and algae from Earth to the oceans on the planet Beyond to convert carbon dioxide to oxygen through the process of photosynthesis," replied Capt. Alvarez.

"What is that bright star off in the distance? Is this a double star system?" asked Lt. Henderson.

"No. That is the planet Zeus. It is almost identical to Jupiter in its size, composition, and orbit. This solar system has only two planets: Beyond and Zeus. There are two asteroid belts: one between Beyond and Zeus, and a second belt beyond Zeus. The composition of these asteroid belts is quite different. The near asteroids are composed of silicates, iron, and other metals and orbit this sun along the ecliptic. The far asteroids are composed of water and silicates and orbit above and below the ecliptic," explained Captain Alvarez.

"Captain, we are being hailed by the Federation. They are asking the reason for our delayed return," said the communication officer.

"They must not know about the Rebellion taking command of the mothballed fleet. Tell them that we were detained by the Rebellion, but we managed to break away from their confinement. More details to follow when we shuttle to the Admiralty. Request permission to enter geosynchronous orbit around the planet Beyond and to shuttle a small party to the Admiralty," responded Captain Alvarez.

"They are sending the heavy frigates *Luisa* and *Einstein* to escort us in," said the communication officer.

"Tell them that will be satisfactory," replied Capt. Alvarez.

Then Captain Alvarez turned to Lt. Jackson, Lt. Chu, and Kat Henderson.

"We will be escorted by two heavy frigates. They obviously don't trust us. Otherwise, they wouldn't be so kind as to provide an escort of two heavy frigates. Helmsman, steady as you go and do not provide any excuse to have those two frigates open fire on us."

***

Once the *Lockford* came into geosynchronous orbit, Captain Alvarez, Kat Henderson, and Lieutenants Chu and Jackson took a shuttle to the surface of the planet. They were met by Henry Ord, a Federation Admiral, and a detachment of marines. The weather was quite pleasant under partly cloudy skies and a light breeze. The only two things that were different from Earth were that the gravity was slightly less, and there was a terrible odor.

"What's that terrible smell!" cried Kat Henderson.

"Ah yes, the smell," responded Admiral Ord. "The flowering plants here produce scents that differ from flowering plants on Earth. Don't be too concerned. In a few days, you will not notice the smell," responded their escort. "If it wasn't for the plants and algae on the planet, there would be no oxygen for us to breathe. I would offer you a ride, but the Admiralty building is only about half a kilometer from here."

It was a pleasant walk to the Admiralty. The native flowers were gorgeous, if not a bit odiferous. There were also swarms of insect-like flying animals alighting on the flowers. One of these landed on Kat's hand. Upon closer examination, the flying animal at first looked like a hummingbird and was the size of a honeybee. However, instead of feathers, the animal was covered with small, iridescent scales.

The escort stopped and told Kat, "All of the native animals on *Beyond* are reptile-like. They are ectotherms with scales, and they lay what we would call eggs. However, their organs are totally different from that of reptiles."

Kat responded, "Is there someone I can meet with to find out more about the flora and fauna of this planet?"

"We will set you up with an exobiologist after we have met with the Admiralty."

***

Once they were in the Admiralty building, they were brought to a meeting room. There were three admirals and one marine general. Their escort, Admiral Ord, introduced them:

"This is Admiral Vlad Bernowski, Chief of Staff. To his left is Admiral Frederick Wenz, Head of the 1st Fleet near Earth. To his left is Ursula Beeman, Head of the 2nd Fleet near the planet Beyond. Last but not least is Ibrahim Shah, Head of Marine Operations."

Then Admiral Ord turned to the Chiefs of Staff. "This is Lieutenant Kathryn Henderson, Naval Nurse, FNF *Sagittarius A**. Next to her is Acting Lt. Ming Chu, also of the FNF *Sagittarius A**. Next to him is Post Captain Enrico Alvarez, Commander of the FNS Lockford. Last but not least is Marine Lt. Henry Jackson, recently assigned to FNF *Sagittarius A**."

"First, recognition to whom it is due: Acting Lieutenant Ming Chu, in recognition of your bravery and quick thinking in your escape from the FNF *Sagittarius A** and your actions that led to the escape of the FNS *Lockford* from the rebel heavy frigate *Wingate*, you are hereby awarded the Naval Silver Star. And before I forget, you are promoted to the full rank of lieutenant," said Admiral Bernowski.

"Next to be recognized is Naval Lieutenant Kathryn Henderson. For your actions in the escape from the *Sagittarius A** and your heroic efforts to save the lives of the wounded on the FNS *Lockford*—during both the *Lockford's* liberation from rebel hands and the action with the *Wingate*—you are hereby awarded the Naval Medical Star. I also have a question for you, Lt. Henderson: I have heard a rumor that you have completed correspondence courses toward your Medical Doctorate. Is that true?"

"Yes, sir," replied Lt. Henderson.

"And that all you have left to do before you are awarded the rank of ship surgeon is to take your board exams?" asked Admiral Bernowski.

"Yes, sir."

"Are you ready to take your Board Exam? We can arrange to have you sit for your exams tomorrow."

"Permission to have more time to study before I take the exam," requested Lt. Henderson.

"Permission denied. You are to report to the Admiralty Testing Center at 0800 tomorrow. We need good ship surgeons now more than ever," responded Admiral Bernowski.

Admiral Bernowski nodded in the direction of General Shah, who then turned to Lt. Jackson and said, "I heard that you were instrumental in the liberation of the frigate *Lockford*. Is that true?"

"I don't know what you are talking about," replied Lt. Jackson.

"Cut it out! Captain Alvarez tells me that you single-handedly neutralized six rebels on the *Lockford*. I also heard from reliable sources that you were instrumental in capturing the alien on the FNF *Sagittarius A**."

"Actually, the alien on the space fortress was not an alien, but a..."

"Cut the chatter! You are hereby awarded the Marine Bronze Star, Captain Jackson."

"I'm not a captain..."

"You are now! Congratulations to all of you for a job well done. It has been noted that amazing things happen when the three of you are together. I am no fool. To assign you to different ships would be a terrible mistake. Therefore, all three of you are assigned to the *Lockford*," responded Admiral Bernowski.

He then turned to Captain Alvarez. "Here are your orders, Captain. You are to open these the moment you enter the Beta Wormhole. But first, you all have one week's liberty on the planet Beyond."

Chapter 32

President William Nelson and Fiery Dragons

The president of the Federation was having a bad day. He woke up with a headache. If the truth be known, he didn't wake up, since he never fell asleep the night before. He was having chronic sleep deprivation: he only slept about 6 to 8 hours a week. William Nelson never asked for this job. Being president of the Federation was not on his bucket list. He would rather write poetry and songs, and sing songs to his beautiful wife, Marina. However, Marina was gone. She had just disappeared into thin air—her and about 14,000 other Federation loyalists.

He was the president, however. He took the job because he thought it was the right thing to do. The previous Federation administrations were incompetent and brutal. The incompetency issue was easy to explain. People are generally stupid and self-serving. That has been the story of human history since man came down from the trees and started walking on two legs—since the time that evolution gave the protohumans an opposable thumb. At least, that is what President Nelson believed. It was the brutality part that really bothered him. Why did humans commit atrocities against other people? he thought.

President Nelson sat on the side of his bed and rubbed his hands on his forehead and temples, even though he knew that doing this would not get rid of his headache. He then reached into his bedside drawer and pulled out a silver flask. He read the engraving on the flask, which read: *To President William Nelson: Our Greatest President. From the Federation Parliament.* He didn't care about the engraving, his job as president, or what the Parliament thought. What he cared about was what was inside the flask. He opened the flask and took a long swig of the amber-brown liquid inside. It burned his throat as it went down, but it tasted strangely pleasant. Then there was the rush to his brain, then quiet. Much better.

Then came a knock at his door. The president got up, put on his bathrobe, and asked, "Who is there?"

"It's Heinrich. There is someone here to see you."

"Tell them to go away," responded the president.

"It's your Chief of Staff, Admiral Bernowski. He says it's urgent."

"Tell him I'll be down in 15 minutes. Have some bagels and cream cheese at the conference table, along with a pot of Ethiopian coffee," replied President Nelson.

"We don't have Ethiopian coffee," said Heinrich.

"Then serve something hot with caffeine in it."

President Nelson dressed himself and shaved. He popped a breath mint in his mouth so the admiral couldn't detect the bourbon on his breath. When he exited his bedroom, he was met by Heinrich. Heinrich was more than the president's personal secretary. He was his friend.

"Did you sleep well last night?" asked Heinrich.

"Yes, I did. Thank you," responded the president.

"Breath mints really don't work well," said Heinrich in a patronizing voice. "You have time to use mouthwash."

"Good idea. Wait here, I'll be right back out."

The two walked slowly to the elevator that would take them to the conference room. Nelson felt a lecture coming on from Heinrich.

"Sir, I know that you must miss Marina in an awful way. She meant the world to you. However, you must move on. The Federation needs you more than ever. Your drinking is getting worse. I could arrange to have a psychiatrist see you. It might do you some good," said Heinrich.

"You're right," replied the president. "Go ahead and make the arrangements. Don't tell anyone about my stash of bourbon."

They came to the conference room and were met by Admiral Bernowski and a Post Captain.

"Mr. President, this is Captain Alvarez of the frigate *Lockford*. He has something urgent to tell you."

"Do tell."

"Sir, I was on a mission with my crew to investigate an anomaly associated with the Alpha Wormhole. Upon entering space in the vicinity of Naval Fortress *Sagittarius A**, we were captured by overwhelming forces. It appears that the Rebellion that has been going on for the last two years on the planet Earth has captured the entire mothballed fleet and has designs of laying siege to the planet *Beyond*."

"I appreciate the conciseness of your report," said President Nelson. Then turning to Admiral Bernowski, the president asked, "What do you recommend, Admiral? How do we get out of this mess?"

The admiral pondered the president's question for a few moments, then said, "Mr. President, if what the captain says is true—and I have no reason to doubt him—we can anticipate the rebel fleet coming through the Beta Wormhole sometime in the future. As I understand it, Admiral Torres is a turncoat and has thrown his lot in with the Rebellion. He knows if his ships come through the Beta Wormhole one at a time, each of his ships will be destroyed in detail. So, time is on our side. I recommend that we send Captain Alvarez through the Beta Wormhole to gather reconnaissance on the disposition of the rebel fleet. We run the same risk as the rebel fleet if we send the 2nd Fleet through the Beta Wormhole one ship at a time. The frigate *Lockford* is the fastest ship in our fleet and has a good chance of not being destroyed when it exits the Beta Wormhole."

"Make it so, Admiral!" commanded the president. "Godspeed, Capt. Alvarez. You have my prayers."

Admiral Bernowski cocked his head and said, "I didn't know you were a man of faith, Mr. President."

"I'm exploring all options open to me," replied the president. "Why not believe that there is a God? He is supposed to do miracles. Maybe He can get us out of this unfortunate business."

"We can use all the help we can get," replied Admiral Bernowski.

"May I ask, Mr. President—did Marina have anything to do with this recent interest in religion? Pardon me for being so forward," asked Heinrich.

"There are many things I am considering. I am a small man in a large job. I am in over my head. As President Abraham Lincoln said: 'We cannot escape destiny.' By the way, Admiral, have we located any of the 14,000 people of the Federation who vanished into thin air?"

"We do not know where they have gone, Mr. President. But one thing we know: they were all people of faith, and most of them were ethnically Jewish."

"If that is the case, then wherever the 14,000 people of faith are, Marina will be amongst them," said the president.

***

Kathryn was still recovering from the Medical Board exam. Her head hurt. Ming Chu tried to console her, but his efforts were not going very well.

"That is the worst exam I have ever taken!" screamed Kathryn.

"Don't worry, I am sure that you did well. You're just…" Ming started to say.

Then Kat interrupted, "It's not that I failed or anything like that. I knew all the answers, but I had to think fast to complete the exam. They only gave me 16 hours to complete the exam. I thought the multiple-choice section would be the easiest, but I was wrong. Every multiple-choice question had combination answers, like A, B, and D; A and D; or A and B. After a while, all the answers looked correct."

"How was the essay part of the exam?" asked Ming.

"That was much easier. The questions seemed more like real life," replied Kat.

Ming thought about this for a while and decided to change the subject. "Well, what do you want to do for the next 5 days of liberty?"

"I want to go to the continent that has not been fully terraformed. I want to see what the wildlife is like," answered Kat.

Ming thought for a minute, then said, "You remember what Capt. Alvarez said when we entered this solar system? He warned us that there is some dangerous wildlife there. Are you sure you want to go there?"

"I am sure. Do you want to come along?" asked Kat. "Don't worry. I met with Eric, the exobiologist, today after the exam. He agreed to give me a guided tour of the Forbidden Continent."

Ming had met the exobiologist the other day and was impressed with how muscular he was. A smooth talker. *Hmm. Maybe I should go along just to make sure that there's no monkey business,* thought Ming.

The next morning, Ming and Kathryn met with Eric, the exobiologist, at the shuttle station. Eric gave them an orientation lecture for their trip.

"We will be taking the shuttlecraft *Galileo* over there. It has a cruising speed of 2,000 kilometers per hour. When we land at the continent, stay close to me. There are some extremely large and dangerous carnivores there. There are no trails or roads on the Forbidden Continent, so we will need to bushwhack our way through the forest."

"What should we do if we see one of the large carnivores?" asked Ming.

"Run as fast as you can. However, these carnivores can fly very fast, and they can disable you with their fireballs," responded Eric.

"Fireballs?" responded Ming and Kat in unison.

"This particular carnivore has a gland in its mouth that produces a mixture of wax and sodium nitrate. The carnivore ignites this mixture with a high-voltage arc generated by its nervous system and spits it at its intended prey, disabling it," said Eric.

"This does not sound pleasant," said Ming.

"It is not. We lost several exobiologists to these carnivores last year. Hey, what's wrong with you? Are you chickening out? If you are, don't worry: I'll take care of your girlfriend," said Eric, with a devious smile on his face.

"I am not chickening out. If this carnivore can fly faster than we can run in the jungle, and spit fireballs at us, how will we defend ourselves?" asked Ming.

"With this," said Eric.

Eric walked over to a large case that must have weighed at least 50 kilograms. He opened the case and hefted out something that looked like a small cannon.

"This is a high-powered Neodymium YAG pulse laser. It puts out 50,000 watts of energy in infrared. This sucker can literally cut one of those large carnivores in half."

"Where do you get the power to drive this laser?" asked Kat.

"From this backpack," responded Eric. "Would you like to try it on?"

"Sure," responded Kat.

Eric picked up the backpack and put it on Kat. After he let go, Kat collapsed under its weight. Then Eric picked up the backpack and said, "Pretty heavy, isn't it? Would you like to carry the power pack, Ming?"

"No, that's okay. My back is a little sore today. Maybe next time."

The three of them climbed aboard the shuttle *Galileo* and began their journey to the Forbidden Continent. It didn't take them long to get there. During the journey, Kat did not speak much to Eric. In fact, Ming had the distinct impression that Kat was squeezing in closer to him.

"Look over there. That's our destination, straight ahead," said Eric.

Straight ahead lay a landmass with very high mountains in the distance. Smoke was issuing from several of the peaks. Below the shuttlecraft was a rocky coastline with several near-shore islands that were brilliant white in color. Between this coastline and the mountains extended a dark green forest that was punctuated with small swamps and meadows. Some of the forested areas had a purple tinge to them.

"What are those purple areas over there?" asked Kat.

"Those are the Carrion Trees. They are in blossom this time of year. We will stay away from them for two reasons: they smell like dead fish, and they are a favorite hangout for the large flying carnivores. There is some sort of mutualism between the two species where both the Carrion Trees and the large flying carnivores get something from each other. We are still investigating this."

"By the way, you have never told us the name of these carnivores," said Ming.

"They are called *Draconis ignei*, or Fiery Dragon," replied Eric.

The shuttlecraft set down in a small meadow near a swamp. The forest was about 200 meters away from the craft. The three of them exited down a ramp onto the meadow. Although the meadow looked like it was inhabited by grasses of some sort, upon closer inspection it looked like a primitive moss—but the moss was moving. With each step that the human adventurers took, the mosses moved out of the way.

"Are these moss-like living things plants or animals?" Kat asked Eric.

"They are actually photosynthetic animals. The closest thing on Earth would be arachnids. Of course, arachnids don't have chloroplasts like these critters do. These small photosynthetic animals have eight small legs that give them their mobility," answered Eric.

The three of them made their way to the forest. The trees were much larger than anything on Earth. The trunks of the trees were up to 20 meters in diameter and were 100 to 200 meters tall. At different levels of the forest canopy, there were whole, unique ecosystems. Near the forest floor, which was quite dark, small insect-like animals predominated and seemed to be consuming detritus. As Kat looked up higher in the canopy, epiphytes, similar to orchids, were rooted in the branches. Small flying animals were everywhere, in every shape and color.

Kat was just staring up at this amazing scene when a hurricane-force wind came down out of the trees. The sky suddenly darkened, and there was an unearthly sound that bellowed:

"VARUMP FRUGET INESTERINE CALLA!"

A short distance away, another unearthly sound bellowed back:

"INESTERINE LOGOM FIRSTHI UMP COM CALLA!"

Eric quickly turned to his two companions and said, "Quick, get into the hole at the base of that tree over there, and do be quiet."

Once inside the trunk of the tree, Kat asked, "What made those sounds?"

"*Draconis ignei*. They hunt in packs and communicate in some language that we have not been able to translate. We are being hunted. These carnivores are capable of problem-solving, communicating with each other, and remembering what they have learned."

Suddenly, the hollowed-out trunk that they were hiding in began to shake violently. All three of them looked up. Suddenly, they saw daylight above them.

"The dragon has torn the top of the tree off!" exclaimed Eric. "It's just a matter of time until they get to us. We need to run. You and Ming run out of the hole quietly and run as fast as you can. I'll stay here and cover you with the laser gun," said Eric.

Ming and Kat ran as fast as they could. When they made it to the meadow, they looked back. Kat almost screamed. There, back in the forest, they saw a winged creature. Its body was 20 meters long. It had two large bat-like wings with a wingspan of 60 meters, a long neck, and an alligator-like head. It looked straight at them and bellowed:

"INESTERINE CALLA!"

Suddenly, a second dragon appeared out of the forest and flew toward them. It landed between them and the shuttlecraft. Then the dragon near the shuttle bellowed:

"INESTERINE FRAGEL GOG!"

As the dragon made this sound, it pointed a single finger that protruded from one of its wings at Ming and Kat.

Kat turned to Ming and said, "These dragons call us 'inesterines,' and I think 'gog' means stay. I think this dragon wants us to stand still."

"I don't think we have a choice," responded Ming in terror.

Then they looked at the dragon that was tearing the giant tree trunk apart. The dragon looked down into the hollow tree and closed its mouth. Then suddenly, there was a sound like thunder, and the dragon spit out a fireball into the hollow tree trunk. They heard the awful cries of Eric as he was burned alive.

Then the dragon flew over to Ming and Kat and landed opposite the other dragon that was blocking their escape to the shuttlecraft. The dragon that had just torched Eric bellowed:

"INESTERINE FRAGEL GOG!"

Then the dragon nearest to Kat and Ming reached down one of its wings and, with its protruding wing finger, drew two circles in the meadow soil. One circle looked remarkably like Earth, showing the Western Hemisphere. The second circle looked like the planet Beyond, showing the Forbidden Continent.

Then the dragon drew what looked like a tube between the Earth and the planet Beyond. It then drew what looked like human stick figures walking through the tube from Earth to the Beyond. Next to the Beyond, the dragon drew a human stick figure with what looked like a laser gun pointing at a dead dragon.

When the dragon finished the drawing, it stomped its foot—which felt like an earthquake—and bellowed:

"INESTERINE GOGA RUNACA!"

And pointed its winged finger at the shuttlecraft.

"It is letting us go! I think the dragon wants us to take the shuttle back to the Federation and deliver a message," said Ming.

"Whatever it is telling us, let's do it before it changes its mind!" answered Kat.

Chapter 33

Let's talk about the Dragons…

Ming knew how to fly the maintenance shuttlecraft aboard the FNF *Sagittarius A**. He found the controls in the *Galileo* to be very similar to the space fortress shuttlecraft, so he was able to fly this shuttlecraft back to the continent Paradisus and landed it near the Admiralty complex.

They were met by President Nelson, who said, "I heard that you had some trouble on the Forbidden Continent. The Admiralty was concerned that you took an unauthorized journey there, so we sent a second shuttle to watch out for you and intervene if you had any trouble. I hate to admit it, but we decided not to intervene when the dragons captured you. It seems that you were able to communicate with them."

"That was very nice of you," responded Kat sarcastically. "So, let's see—you let Eric get fried by the dragon so your curiosity would be satisfied. Who are you, anyway? You kind of creep me out!"

The admiral standing next to President Nelson looked over at her, smiled, and responded, "This is William Nelson, the President of the Federation. I know that you must think our actions are uncaring, but we have been trying to establish contact with the dragons on the Forbidden Continent. It is unfortunate that the dragon killed Eric before we could save him. The dragons knew we were watching. They are quite intelligent. So, we didn't think you were in real danger…"

When Ming heard this, he stepped forward and started to scream, "If these are my leaders, who show no remorse for their actions, I hereby resign my commission."

"At ease, Lt. Chu," replied the admiral. "Regarding your resignation: request denied!"

President Nelson looked a bit nervous, but he finally regained his composure and said, "We would like to talk to you about your encounter with the dragons. You must be starving! I will be serving lunch in the Presidential Palace. Please come!"

"Do we have a choice, Mr. President?" asked Ming.

"No," replied President Nelson.

***

The Presidential Palace was not really a palace, but more like a mansion. In fact, it looked like the White House where presidents of the United States used to live. After going through security, they went into the West Wing, where a small man with a winning smile awaited them.

"I am Heinrich Steuben, President Nelson's Chief of Staff. The president needed to step away on an urgent matter. Please, help yourself to the sushi bar. It's made from aquatic life that was brought here from Earth and raised in the oceans on the planet Beyond. It's quite good."

"Can you tell us something about the president?" asked Kat. "I think I got off on the wrong foot with him."

There was a pause in the room. Heinrich looked at Ming and Kat carefully. This made them both very nervous. They felt as though Heinrich was reading their thoughts.

Finally, he spoke, "The president is a melancholy man. His wife, Marina, disappeared rather suddenly. No one knows where she is. He is also hard to get to know. I have been his Chief of Staff for three years, and I still don't know everything about the man. However, he did tell me he really wanted to talk to you, even before you had the encounter with the dragon on the Forbidden Continent. He seems to be searching for something. Oh, I hear him coming."

The president came in and smiled—first at Heinrich, then at Ming and Kat.

"Ever since you came to our planet, I wanted to talk to you. I am interested in extraordinary people. You are heroes, but there is something else—especially you, Kathryn. You seem to be on a journey, and you are fearless. But let us talk of this later. For now, let's talk about the dragons."

"The dragons seem to be very intelligent and can speak to each other. We were able to decipher three of their words: 'Inesterine' is a word they use to describe humans. 'Gog' means stay; 'goga' means leave. They were also able to communicate with us through pictures they drew on the ground," said Kathryn.

"What did they draw on the ground?" asked the president.

"I am going to let Ming answer this, since he seemed to understand this better than I did," responded Kathryn.

"May I have a piece of paper and a pencil?" asked Ming.

Ming took the paper and pencil and drew the picture that the dragon had drawn. First, he drew the Earth, and then humans walking through a tube from Earth to the planet Beyond.

"This part of the picture represents humans traveling from Earth to the planet Beyond through the Alpha and Beta Wormholes." Ming then drew the rest of the picture drawn by the dragon. "In this part of the picture, a man is killing a dragon with a laser gun. The dragons were trying to communicate to Kathryn and me that dragons have been killed by humans. I believe that is the reason the dragons killed our guide, Eric—because Eric had a laser gun. The dragons were acting out of self-defense. The reason they drew this picture was that they hoped we would take this message back to our leaders, and perhaps the dragon killing would stop."

The West Wing became very quiet. Finally, the president spoke up.

"Ming, do you really believe this?"

"How many dragons have been killed by humans?" asked Ming.

"Maybe a half dozen or so," responded the president.

Kathryn then spoke. "The dragons are apex predators, and they are very large. There can't be more than a few dozen on the Forbidden Continent."

"We estimate that there are less than 20 dragons," responded the president.

"You must stop killing them," said Ming. "I recommend that the Forbidden Continent be made a wildlife sanctuary."

"The dragons are dangerous. They have killed 23 of our exobiologists. We need to terraform the entire planet to allow for human population growth," responded the president.

Suddenly Ming erupted. "Is that all you can think about—terraforming the planet? You trashed Earth, and when Earth was trashed, you came here to repeat the process!" After saying this, Ming stormed out of the room.

"Heinrich, please chase Ming and calm him down," requested the president.

"Yes sir, Mr. President."

After Heinrich left, Kathryn and the president continued the conversation.

"Lt. Henderson, Ming Chu is a very astute man, but he seems to be troubled. You know him well, correct? What is going on with him?"

"Ming is very bright, but I think he may be on the Asperger–Autism spectrum. With that said, Ming does make a good point. The dragons were here long before humans arrived. But I also see your point about the dragons being dangerous and the need to terraform the entire planet."

"May I change the subject?" inquired the president.

"Sure, go ahead."

"I lost my wife some time ago. She and 14,000 others living on the planet Beyond just disappeared."

"I'm sorry to hear that. Any idea what happened to them?" asked Kathryn.

"The way I understand this is that those 14,000 souls were all people of faith. I believe that they were all Christians. I knew that Marina, who is ethnically Jewish, was a Christian, but I kept it a secret from my staff. Marina left behind her Bible. I have been reading it every day. I have a lot of questions. When you and your crew members came to the planet Beyond, I took the liberty to run a background check on you. I found out that while you were stationed on the FNF *Sagittarius A** that you ran many queries on the topics of Judaism and Christianity. Since all the Christians are gone, I thought I could ask you. Do you believe in the precepts of Christianity?" asked President Nelson.

"I originally searched the space fortress computer files because I was trying to determine if an alien in sickbay was an ancient Hebrew," said Kathryn. "Then I encountered a Jewish scholar. You know him—Myron Abbot. Myron told me that the alien was an ancient Jewish prophet. I went back into the computer files and confirmed what Myron told me. This put me on a journey to understand more about the Jewish faith, and by extension, the Christian faith."

"I had many long talks with Myron Abbot," said President Nelson. "He is a smart man, and a man of God. I reached out to him for his help to stop the senseless killing of peoples of faith. I also wanted to stop the killing because my wife was a Christian. The more I read her Bible, the more I have come to see that Jesus was the Son of God. But I am confused about His crucifixion. What was the point of that?"

Kathryn thought about that for some time, then responded, "I don't really know. When I was searching the computer files on the Jewish faith, there was a lot about sin—you know, doing the wrong thing. Every year, the Jews had to sacrifice animals to take their sins away."

"That's it!" cried the president. "Jesus died on the cross for sin. Now it makes sense to me. Yes! Jesus died for my sins. Like a sacrificial animal, Jesus was sacrificed."

Kathryn backed away from the president. She was afraid that he was becoming mentally unstable.

"Mr. President, get a hold of yourself. Jesus died on the cross, and that's the end of it."

"It is the end of it. The penalty of sin has been removed. That's what Marina kept telling me. Do you agree with this, Lt. Henderson?" asked the president.

"I need to think about this some more, Mr. President," responded Lt. Henderson.

Chapter 34

The FNS *Lockford* is Deployed

Ship's log: July 24, 2171

The Light Frigate Lockford is underway and preparing to enter the Beta Wormhole. The ship has been modified with much larger fusion engines. The crew is all here. No one reported to the Shuttle Deck to be transported to the planet Beyond. May good fortune bless each crew member and keep them safe and courageous.

Post Captain Alvarez

After Kat and Ming had their meeting with President Nelson, they reported to Captain Alvarez to prepare for their tour of duty on the other side of the Beta Wormhole. On their walk to Captain Alvarez's quarters, they stopped for a couple of beers.

"Man, that was some weird meeting with the president. I think he has a few loose screws in his brain. You missed the part about him coming to Jesus," said Kat.

"Coming to Jesus? You mean he had a God-moment when you were in the room? I am pretty ticked off at him. Imagine him and his admiral watching our guide, Eric, get fried by a dragon and doing nothing to save him," responded Ming.

"In spite of the President's religious moment, I felt sorry for him, Ming. His wife mysteriously disappeared with 14,000 others. All of them were people of faith. Very strange. And yet, there was something special about the president's simple statement of faith. Do you know that he ran a security check on us before we met with him?"

"I didn't know about the security check, Kat. Tell me more about this security check."

Kat pondered for a moment and continued, "When he did the security check on me, he found that I had done extensive searches on the space fortress computer regarding Jewish and Christian faith. I had done these searches to help me identify Enoch and Elijah when they were in sickbay. President Nelson wanted to know what I had learned about these two religious systems."

"What did you learn about the Jewish and Christian faiths, Kat?" asked Ming, with a curious look on his face.

"I learned that the Jewish faith has a detailed law that needs to be followed, and there was an intricate system of animal sacrifices that the Jews had to do when they did not keep the law. Christianity is said to be a fulfillment of the law and the sacrifices. It purports to teach that Jesus, a Jew, was actually the Son of God, and that he died on a Roman cross for our sins, once and for all," replied Kat.

"Sounds kind of weird. I remember that my grandmother used to talk about this stuff."

"I know it does, Ming. Yet I am somehow drawn to it. Well, I have finished my beer. Let's see Captain Alvarez," said Kat.

***

When Ming and Kathryn arrived at Captain Alvarez's quarters, he was not there. A Marine sergeant in the hall informed them that the captain had gone back to his ship to oversee repairs and modifications to the FNS *Lockford*. They walked over to the shuttlecraft port and were able to get a ride on a shuttle to the *Lockford*.

As their shuttle approached the *Lockford*, they noticed that most of the damage to the outside of the ship had been repaired. The thing that caught their eye, though, was the Engineering Deck—and that the fusion engines were twice the size of the ones previously on the *Lockford*.

"Would you look at that!" exclaimed Ming. "Those fusion engines are the same as the ones used on the ships-of-the-line. I have seen those on some of the faster 74-gunners. Those engines look strange on a 28-gun frigate. The *Lockford* was one of the fastest ships in the fleet before. Now it must be the fastest by far! It also must be dangerous to fly. That's probably why the Engineering Deck is twice as big. There must be a large contingency of engineers on board, along with a lot of safety interlocks."

"Ming, I wasn't supposed to tell you, but I heard that you have been assigned to the Engineering Deck. Well, we just entered the airlock. In a few minutes, we will report to Captain Alvarez."

After the airlock pressure equilibrated, the hatch to the Shuttle Deck opened, and there was Captain Alvarez waiting for them.

"Welcome aboard. You are just the officers I wanted to see. Come with me and I'll show you to your quarters. After that, I'll take our new ship surgeon to sickbay, and the Chief Engineer to the Engineering Deck."

"Oh, so our section officers are here to give us an orientation?" asked Lt. Chu.

Capt. Alvarez smiled and said, "Lt. Chu, you are the Chief Engineer. I have scrounged up the best technical petty officers in the fleet to give you a hand. Most of them have experience on the big ships-of-the-line. They will teach you everything you need to know about operating these huge fusion engines. You also have Chief Petty Officer Hicks as part of your crew. You remember her?"

"Yes, I do. She is one smart engineer! Thank you, sir!" exclaimed Lt. Chu.

Then Captain Alvarez turned to Kathryn Henderson and said, "I am pleased to tell you, Commander Henderson, that you passed your medical exams with flying colors. You are now the ship surgeon for the *Lockford*! You will have four naval nurses assigned to you. Come along, we have much to get done before we deploy."

***

Once the *Lockford* repairs and modifications were completed, and the crew came on board, Captain Alvarez got on the comm and addressed the crew:

"Welcome aboard the light frigate *Lockford*. Some of you are new crew members, and many of you have served on this ship for years. I am not at liberty to tell you the exact nature of our mission, since I have been commanded not to open our orders until we enter the Beta Wormhole.

"However, I can tell you what I already know. You all know that this frigate has been heavily modified. This is true. We have fusion engines that are typically found on 74-gun ships-of-the-line. This will enable this frigate to cruise at 10% of the speed of light. I must tell you that this vessel has not been tested at these speeds, and it remains uncertain if the hull and crew can withstand the stresses that will come at these speeds.

"I can also tell you that the entire rebel fleet will be awaiting us when we exit the Beta Wormhole. The rebel fleet is composed of the mothballed ships that orbited around the black hole, Sagittarius A*. Its current commander, Rear Admiral Torres, is a disgraced sailor and a traitor to the Federation. His crews are a sorry mixture of disgraced officers and rebels from planet Earth. What they lack in good seamanship is made up for by the fleet's immense firepower. We have only six nuclear missile launchers and twenty-two laser cannons; they will have hundreds of missile launchers and much larger plasma cannons.

"I need not tell you to do your duty. The seasoned crew of the *Lockford* has shown their mettle and demonstrated courage not found on any other vessel in the Federation. I trust that our new crew members possess these same qualities. The conflict that we are now involved in is deadly, and the consequences of our mission will determine the fate of the Federation, our ideals, and our loved ones.

"The odds are against us, but statistical odds do not take into account the character of humanity. I am fully confident that we possess all that is needed for victory. But there may be some on board who doubt this. It's fine to be afraid, for heroes are fearful people who do courageous things in spite of their fears. With that said, there may be some of you who would rather not embark on this great enterprise. For those of you who wish not to be part of the crew on the *Lockford*, you may report to the Shuttle Deck and be transported back to the planet *Beyond*. Nothing more will be said about you.

"For those of you that choose to stay and fight, you have my personal gratitude."

One hour later, no one reported to the Shuttle Deck to be sent back to the planet *Beyond*.

***

As the FNS *Lockford* entered the Beta Wormhole, Captain Alvarez was on the bridge. With him were First Officer Ikram Shah and Chief Engineering Officer Ming Chu.

Captain Alvarez opened his orders and read them aloud so his staff could hear them:

"Captain Alvarez, when you enter the Beta Wormhole, you are to increase speed to 8% relativistic. Have your Chief Navigational Officer plot an evasive course on exiting the wormhole. When exiting the wormhole, have your Chief Engineer increase speed to 10% relativistic. After evading the rebel fleet, reduce speed to 5% relativistic and set a course to Space Fortress *Sagittarius A** and take it as a prize, if feasible. Then plot a course beyond the weapon's range of the rebel fleet and perform reconnaissance as to the disposition of the rebel fleet. Then plot a course to the Beta Wormhole and increase speed to 10% relativistic. Re-enter the Beta Wormhole and close the hole down with a security lock. If the opportunity arises, you are to take the rebel flagship, *Brazil*, as a prize, along with Admiral Torres."

Chapter 35

The Grand Rebel Fleet of the Rebellion at the Beta Wormhole

"I will not give the order to go through the Beta Wormhole right now. If you attempt to override my command, I will have you spaced. Your haste to put my fleet through the wormhole will be putting my entire fleet at risk!" shouted Admiral Torres.

"If we don't pass through the Beta Wormhole as soon as possible, we will lose the element of surprise. By the way—this is not *your* fleet. This is the *Rebellion's* fleet."

"You are a real pompous moron, Aristides. You know what will happen when we enter the wormhole? We will have to go in one ship at a time. When we exit the hole, the entire Federation 2nd Fleet will be stacked up against us. Three or four 74-gun Federation ships are all they would need to destroy us. They would have the advantage of concentrated firepower. They don't even need to shoot at us. All they need to do is turn off the wormhole enlarger. Any ship in the wormhole will be crushed by the wormhole returning to its normal, tiny size."

Aristides and Grand Admiral Torres were screaming at each other. They were so close to each other that their noses were almost touching.

"What do you recommend, then, Admiral?"

"I recommend that we wait on this side of the wormhole. When the Federation fleet comes through, one ship at a time, we will have the advantage of concentrated firepower," replied Admiral Torres.

"I don't like this at all. How long should we wait?" asked Aristides.

Admiral Torres responded, "Long enough for the Federation to lose patience. We now know that the fast vessel that entered the wormhole was the FNS *Lockford.* We had captured this Federation frigate near the mothballed fleet. The Federation crew we held prisoner somehow regained control of the frigate and escaped by using the gravity of the black hole. We lost a heavy frigate to the black hole while it pursued the Federation frigate. I am sure that the Admiralty at the planet Beyond is well aware of our presence here. I can just see them with 20 ships-of-the-line waiting for us."

"What should we do in the meantime?" asked Aristides.

"Wait," responded Admiral Torres.

"If you are just going to sit here and wait, I'll take my leave and return to the space fortress," growled Aristides.

With that, Aristides came off the bridge of the *Brazil* and headed to the shuttle bay. On the way, he was seething as he thought about Admiral Torres: *I need to replace him as soon as possible. My question is, who should replace Admiral Torres?*

When he reached the teleporter room, Aristides was met by his aide, Jennifer Bo.

"Looks like you just had a friendly chat with our charming admiral," said Jennifer.

"You can tell? Yes, I met with the admiral. Let's shuttle back to the space fortress and meet with Leslie to discuss the future of our charming admiral."

Jennifer looked over at the shuttle bay officer and said, "We need a fast shuttle to get back to Space Fortress *Sagittarius A**."

"We have coordinates set. We are ready when you are."

Once in the shuttle, Jennifer spoke up, "I know what you are thinking. I am thinking the same thing. Admiral Torres needs to be replaced. I did a little research on potential replacements."

"There are no replacements!" exclaimed Aristides. "He was our best shot. No other admiral in the Federation will defect to our cause. They are a loyal bunch, you know."

"You're thinking too much in the present. We control *time* on the Naval Fortress *Sagittarius A**. We can go back in time to get you history's best admiral," responded Jennifer.

"Great idea! Let me think on this," replied Aristides.

***

Admiral Torres was glad to be rid of Aristides. Standing on the bridge of the *Brazil*, surrounded by his crew, gave him a feeling of control without the constant nagging from Aristides.

Suddenly, the quiet and calm was rudely interrupted by the notification from the Comm on the Space-Time Deck.

"Admiral, we are picking up a time-space disturbance from the direction of the Beta Wormhole. From the size of the disturbance, it appears to be a light frigate moving at high velocity."

"What is the estimated time for exiting the Beta Wormhole?" inquired Admiral Torres.

"Five minutes," replied the space-time scientist.

"I want all batteries on the *Brazil* to be ready to fire at the exit of the Beta Wormhole at my command," said Admiral Torres. He then turned to the communication officer and asked, "Connect me to the captain of the rebel frigate *Farragut*."

In a few seconds, the captain of the *Farragut* responded, "This is Captain Antonin Spinelli of the frigate *Farragut*, Admiral. What is your pleasure?"

"We have a Federation frigate about to exit the Beta Wormhole at high velocity. I was going to blast the frigate to atoms as it exited, but I think it may be better to capture the frigate instead. Do you have your fusion reactor up to 100% capacity?"

"Sir, we were at 70% when you contacted us." There was a pause, then Captain Spinelli came back on the comm. "Engineering is bringing the fusion reactor up to 100%. We should be up to 100% in 10 minutes."

"That's not fast enough!" shouted Admiral Torres. "I need you up to 100% in three and a half minutes. Override the safety interlocks on the reactor and dump 1.5 tonnes of deuterium and 1.5 tonnes of tritium into the reactor vessel. Compensate reactor containment by increasing the magnetic field on the fusion reactor by 200%. That should keep the reaction contained during the fusion spike."

"With all due respect, sir, I'm not sure that we can maintain a 200% increase in the magnetic field. I am not even sure that a 200% increase in the field will contain the—"

"You have my orders, Captain! Proceed with your preparation, and good hunting. Remember that I want that Federation frigate for a prize—with its entire crew," ordered the admiral.

Another message came through the comm. It was the space-time scientific officer.

"Admiral, the Federation light frigate has significantly increased its velocity and will exit the wormhole in 1.5 minutes."

At this news, the admiral let out a string of profanity. When he had finished, the communication officer broke in.

"Sir, Captain Spinelli is on the comm."

"Pipe him in," ordered Admiral Torres.

"Sir, we must discharge the deuterium and tritium from the magnetic containment. Temperature is rising too fast. If we don't—"

At that moment, the ship-of-the-line *Brazil* violently lurched. The jolt was so powerful that the crew on one side of the deck was hurled to the opposite side. Admiral Torres slammed his head into the bulkhead and was knocked unconscious.

On the visual display, there was a blinding white light. Then all the systems went down on board the *Brazil*.

Chapter 36

The Search for a Replacement Admiral

When Aristides and Jennifer Bo returned to the space fortress, they were met by Commander Ahern.

"Sir, I have some bad news for you. A fast Federation frigate made passage through the Beta Wormhole and eluded capture."

"Did Admiral Torres do anything to prevent this passage?" asked Aristides, who was trying to remain restrained.

"Admiral Torres sent the heavy frigate *Farragut* in pursuit, but the *Farragut* experienced an explosion from her fusion engines," responded Commander Ahern.

"How is this possible? I thought that all naval vessels had triplicate interlocks to prevent this from happening."

"Admiral Torres ordered Captain Spinelli to override the interlocks," replied Commander Ahern, with a grimace on his face.

Aristides paused for a moment and considered, *Admiral Torres needs to be replaced now before the whole fleet is destroyed.* Then Aristides simply responded, "Thank you for the update. As you were, Commander."

As Jennifer and Aristides walked to the conference room onboard the Space Fortress *Sagittarius A** there was a deadly silence between the two of them. This silence caused Jennifer to experience a high level of anxiety. After what seemed like a 10-kilometer walk, they met Leslie Jones at the conference center.

"Welcome back, Aristides," said Leslie as she gave him a kiss on the cheek. "How are things on Earth?"

"From a revolution standpoint, Leslie, the Rebellion has pretty much taken control of the government. The problem is that no one is in charge. We have leadership at the local and, in some cases, at the regional level. We need to establish a legislature and courts. All the previous Ministers of Parliament, judges, and executives have gone to the planet *Beyond*. To make matters much worse, there has been a catastrophic collapse of the Greenland and Antarctic ice fields. This has resulted in a massive rise in sea levels. Billions of people have been displaced from coastal areas. Much of Europe is freezing and entering an ice age due to the collapse of the Gulf Stream," said Aristides, who had a deeply concerned look on his face.

"Oh, my goodness. What are we going to do? We need to capture the environmental scientists and terra-form engineers from the planet *Beyond* now if we are going to save planet Earth!" cried Leslie.

"We can't win this fight with an admiral like Torres! We need to replace him now! Jennifer Bo has come up with a plan." When Aristides finished his diatribe, two sets of eyes turned on Jennifer. Jennifer became nervous and began to fidget.

"It's okay, Jenn, we really need your help now. It's okay to be nervous," said Leslie in a soothing tone. This did not soothe Jennifer—inside, she felt like a volcano about to explode. Her heart was racing at 150 beats a second. Her adrenal glands were working overtime. She needed to get away. She started for the door, but Aristides stopped her.

"What's the matter with you, Jennifer!" screamed Aristides.

"Back off her, Aristides!" said Leslie as she slammed Aristides to the ground.

"Jennifer, come sit next to me. I think I can help you. Now I want you to close your eyes and take an inventory of everything in this conference room. No fair peeking—do it from memory. I'll help you get started. What color is the room?"

"The room is a sky-blue color. There is a large computer screen. There is a large table in the middle of the room, and there is a computer on the table. I believe that there are ten or twelve chairs around the table. There is a blue carpet on the floor," responded Jennifer, as her nerves started to settle down.

"Are there any pictures on the wall?" asked Leslie.

"Yes," answered Jennifer. "Let me think. Yes, there is a picture of the space fortress, and there are pictures of spacecraft of various kinds."

"What kinds of spacecraft?" asked Leslie.

"Apollo, Voyager, a current 74-gun ship-of-the-line, a squadron of frigates. I almost forgot—a picture of Earth, and a picture of an astronaut on the moon."

"Feel better?" asked Leslie.

"Much better! Thank you, Leslie! You are a real friend," responded Jennifer, with a smile.

Aristides was still picking himself off the floor. "Leslie, you pack a punch," said Aristides, who was still recovering from Leslie's jujitsu move. "What did you do for Jennifer to get her to calm down?"

"Jennifer was having a panic attack. I had a college roommate who had panic attacks. A counselor friend of mine taught me this technique that would help my roommate." Then Leslie turned to Jennifer and said, "We are very interested in your plan, Jenn."

Jennifer walked over to the computer on the table and slid a memory card into it. On the screen there appeared a slide titled: **Proposal to Capture a Qualified Admiral to Command the Rebel Fleet.**

There were several slides that showed criteria for selecting a new rebel admiral. Then the next set of slides had bios on a dozen or so admirals from the past. The last slide was a table that provided a summary of characteristics for the top three admirals, whose names were redacted. There were about ten characteristics listed in the left-hand column. The headers for the other three columns were simply titled: **Admiral A; Admiral B; Admiral C.** The rest of the grid were Xs. Only the last row had one X and two 0s.

"This table was based on data for admirals in the past who demonstrated brilliance in battle and who died in action. I included the criterion that the top three admirals had to die in combat to reduce the risk of a time-paradox. As you can see, all three admirals met all the characteristics for leading the rebel fleet. You will note that the admirals were not rated on their potential understanding of our navy's technology."

"Why didn't you include that?" asked Aristides.

"We don't need that because we have Scientific Officers from the mothballed fleet who have that knowledge. We need an admiral who has skills in naval warfare and strategy. As you can see, all three of these admirals are qualified—except for the last criterion. We need the admiral to die in action to reduce the time-paradox risk. As you can see from this table, Admirals A, B, and C meet that criterion. However, look at the last row of the table. In the cases of

Admirals A and B, the bodies of the deceased admirals were recovered and given state funerals. Admiral C died when his flagship went down, and his body was never recovered," Jennifer paused, knowing this was the time for Leslie and Aristides to ponder what she had said.

Aristides broke the silence. "Can you tell us the admirals' identities?"

"No. To do so would bias your decisions."

"Okay. I vote for Admiral C," replied Aristides.

"I second that," said Leslie.

"That would be my choice, too," concluded Jennifer.

"Make it so!" cried out Aristides. "Can you tell us who the admirals were?"

"Yes. Admiral A was Horatio Nelson, whose British fleet defeated the combined French and Spanish fleets at Trafalgar in 1805. Admiral B was Michiel de Ruyter, the Dutch admiral who defeated the English fleets many times and who also sailed up the Thames River and captured the English flagship."

Aristides pondered this for a while and responded, "Very impressive résumés for both these admirals. Who is Admiral C?"

Chapter 37

The Witnesses

As Keziah, Myron, Abraham, and George walked the narrow streets of Jerusalem, there was a barrier of silence between them. Each one of them was lost in their own thoughts. Each tried to imagine what would happen when they got to the apartment where Elijah and Enoch were staying.

Finally, George broke the silence. "Are we almost there? The suspense is killing me."

"We just have half a kilometer before we get there," replied Abraham.

"Hey, Myron. Did you really come here from outer space?" joked Keziah.

"I really did," responded Myron.

This banter continued until they reached their destination. Strangely enough, they had to go down a flight of stairs to a basement door. It was a filthy area that accumulated all the flotsam and jetsam from the street above. Abraham knocked on the door in code, which sounded like something from *Fiddler on the Roof.*

The door opened, and there was Enoch, dressed in an outfit that looked like it was made of burlap. His eyes first met Abraham's, then when he saw Myron, he said, "Shalom. How did you get here, Myron?"

"Shalom. The same way you did!" responded Myron.

"So, God transported you here?" asked Enoch.

"No. I was sent here by the Space-Time Laboratory on board the Space Station *Sagittarius A**."

"What are you talking about, Myron? I think you have a few loose screws. Elijah and I were transported here by the chariots of God."

It then dawned on Myron that nobody ever took the time to explain time travel to Enoch and Elijah. He sought to change the subject.

"The last time I saw you, Enoch, you spoke an ancient dialect of Hebrew. Now you are speaking perfect, modern Hebrew. How is this possible?" asked Myron, with a puzzled look on his face.

"With Jehovah, all things are possible," said Enoch. "Please come in. Elijah and I have just reclined for dinner. Please join us. We do not have much—just some bread, terrible-tasting cheese, raw vegetables, and the worst wine we have ever drunk. Please come in and accept our hospitality, such as it is."

When the visitors entered, they found the basement apartment to be quite clean and spacious. They entered the dining area, where they found Elijah lying on his side at a very low table. There was sawdust on the floor around the table. In the corner of the dining area were the crudely cut-off legs of the table. Elijah and the visitors looked at each other, then over to the cut-off legs of the table.

Elijah then spoke. "Shalom! Please forgive the mess I made with this table. For some reason, people here eat at high tables. Enoch and I are used to reclining at table. So, I cut the legs off and made the table more useful for Enoch and me."

"Shalom. Did you use a saw to cut the legs off?" asked Myron.

"I didn't need a saw! I'm Elijah!"

"Oh, that's right! I forgot," said Myron, with a sheepish smile on his face.

After Enoch prayed, the six of them reclined at the short table and ate. Myron thought the cheese and wine tasted quite good. Then it occurred to him that the microbes used in the fermentation of cheese and wine were a bit different than those used back in Enoch and Elijah's time.

Then Abraham broke the silence. "So why are you here?"

"We are warning people of Jehovah's imminent judgment," replied Elijah. "We are also proclaiming the coming of the Messiah. Occasionally I must do a miracle or two to get the people's attention. My friend Enoch over here is teaching the people what it means to walk with God. It's been great getting to know Enoch. I knew about Enoch from the ancient scrolls, but I have come to appreciate his practical nature when it comes to walking with God. He is also much more level-headed than I am. I have a history of mental depression, and Enoch helps to steady me when I am having mood swings. But I digress."

"You're much too modest, Elijah. I just walk with God. You talk to God, and He answers you!" exclaimed Enoch.

"So, when is God's judgment coming?" asked Myron.

"In about three and a half years, give or take a week or so."

At this point, George, who had been keeping silent, spoke up. "What's going to happen in three and a half years?"

Elijah looked over at Enoch, then back to Myron. "The two of us will be killed. This is going to make the majority of people very happy. There will be a big celebration! But then," Elijah paused, "then we will be revived. Don't ask me how God will do this, but

Jehovah is God, and He does what He wills. We are just His servants."

"What happens when the Messiah comes? Will He place King David back on the throne of Israel?" asked Abraham.

"When the Messiah comes, He will have absolute authority. He will come and stand on the Temple Mount with 144,000 sealed from the twelve tribes of Israel. He will cast the False Prophet and the Beast into the Lake of Fire," answered Elijah.

"I know what a false prophet is, but what is the Beast? Is it a dragon? Also, I thought that dragons were for fairy tales," responded Abraham.

"The Dragon is a dragon. You will know it when you see it. The Beast is a beast, in a sense. He will have a mortal wound on his head, but the wound will be healed. Both the Beast and the False Prophet will be difficult to recognize. The False Prophet has been around for a few years and is gaining power as we speak. The Beast will be a partner of the False Prophet," answered Elijah.

Myron was listening intently to this exchange. He wasn't sure if what he was hearing was true or some sort of delusion he was having. He became confused but thought it might be helpful if he entered the discussion.

"Pardon me, you said that the False Prophet has been around for a while. Who is he?"

Elijah looked over to Enoch for a minute or so. It almost seemed that they were communicating with each other in their silence. Finally, Elijah answered. "The False Prophet will seem to have all the answers to humanity's problems. He will gain a huge following and lead many astray. At some point he will wage war with the redeemed, but in the end, he will be defeated. Those who have ears, let him hear!"

George, who had been silent all this time, asked a question. "Who are the redeemed? I have heard reference to the redeemed many times at my Maronite Church. Are the redeemed those who have placed their faith in Jesus Christ and His finished work on the cross?"

"You have said so," responded both Enoch and Elijah.

Abraham and Myron just stared at George and thought: *This was blasphemy.* In their minds, Jesus was a Messiah Pretender. It looked like Abraham was about to explode. Myron thought it would be best to speak first, peaceably, before this discussion became a brawl.

"I have a good friend by the name of Robert Hays. A physicist, who is also a Christian. He has not tried to proselytize me to his faith, but there is something about him that attracts me to his faith," said Myron.

At this time, Myron looked over at George, then to Abraham, and finally to Elijah and Enoch. Then he asked, "How can I be redeemed?"

Enoch answered this time, "I was once a Jew like you. I believed that by walking with God and by keeping His commandments, that I would be considered righteous by God. God took me before I died. He revealed to me that living a righteous life was well and good. However, God revealed to me that every thought and my private actions would bring me up short of the righteousness of God. I needed someone who could cancel out this judgment against me. In other words, a Savior. That Savior is Jesus."

Myron did not respond verbally to Enoch, but the words struck him to the heart. Since Myron began to experience his Alzheimer's disease, he found it difficult to live a righteous life. When he became confused, he would often become very angry and say mean-spirited things to people. He felt shame for this. He could just make excuses for this behavior and blame it on his Alzheimer's disease… Then it hit him: If even Enoch couldn't live a perfect life, God could still choose to take him to Himself.

Then Myron turned to Elijah and asked, "What about you, Elijah?"

Elijah looked at the floor for a minute or so, then spoke, "I had an up-and-down walk with God. When I was on my good behavior, I was hot, and God did great things through me. But I had a dark side. I had fear—fear of man. Do you remember the account of when Jezebel, Queen of Israel, wanted to kill me? What did I do?"

"You ran away," responded Myron.

"I forgot who God was and what He could do. I felt that God had abandoned me and His people, Israel. I felt alone, depressed. However, God sustained me and brought me to a cave. God created several events—wind, fire, and an earthquake. I looked for God in these supernatural events, but God was not there. Then God came to me in a small voice. God is not just the God of the spectacular, but He is the God of His Word. Later, when God took me in the whirlwind, He taught me that real righteousness is believing God and His promises. He made a promise to Eve in the Garden of Eden that someday, one of her offspring would defeat Satan. That person is Jesus," said Elijah as he stared deep into Myron's eyes.

Myron did not respond but pondered these things in his heart. He also pondered whether God spoke to Enoch and Elijah in the space-time probes that brought them here.

Finally, Keziah asked a question, "Yesterday, someone in the crowd asked a question about the 130,000 people who vanished into thin air. You said they were transported to God. Who were these people who were transported to God?"

"They are the 144,000 sealed by God from the 12 tribes of Israel. They are the Jews who have placed their faith in Jesus Christ, their Savior, in these last days," answered Elijah.

"Wait a minute! You said there would be 144,000 sealed by God that will return, but only 130,000 were taken up to God. Where are the other 14,000 people?" asked Keziah.

Chapter 38

An Unlikely Ally

"What is wrong with you, Aristides!" exclaimed Leslie.

"Look, Leslie, I'm under a lot of pressure. Why can't you understand that!" shouted Aristides.

"You struggled with saving the Earth, but you have no problem killing anyone who gets in your way!" cried out Leslie.

"What's the deal? You don't like Admiral Torres either. His incompetence is keeping us from launching an attack on the planet Beyond. His incompetence caused us to let that light frigate get back to the planet Beyond. That light frigate knows the disposition of the rebel fleet," growled Aristides.

"I get it that Admiral Torres is a bumbling buffoon, but that's no reason to kill him. Just fire the idiot and replace him with someone more competent," responded Leslie. "Remember, Jennifer has identified an ideal candidate to replace Admiral Torres. We just need to wait until Dr. Hays helps us use the Space-Time Laboratory to get the replacement for Torres."

Leslie Jones and Aristides were standing just inches from each other in their cabin on board the space fortress. Since Aristides had returned from Earth to the space fortress, they rarely had a peaceful moment with each other. In fact, Leslie tried to avoid being with Aristides at all.

"Look, Aristides, I am sorry to yell at you, but you are not the same person that I met in Big Sur. You used to hold to high ideals and you were charismatic. What has happened to you?"

"Things have changed," said Aristides. "I am under a lot of pressure. The global climate and ecosystems on Earth are degrading much faster than the computer models predicted. When much of the Antarctic and all of the Greenland ice mass just disappeared in two years, the ocean levels flooded the coastal plains around the world. Billions of people have been displaced. To make matters worse, the Gulf Stream in the Atlantic has failed, sending much of Europe into an ice age."

"I get it about the rising ocean levels, but I am not getting the part about Europe," said Leslie.

Aristides was glad that this argument had morphed into a discussion on global climate change. This was territory that he was familiar with, so he said, "The catastrophic loss of the Greenland ice mass, which was directly related to the rising temperature, released all that cold freshwater into the North Atlantic Ocean. That water was less dense than the ocean saltwater. Because this freshwater is less dense, it is flowing south on top of the Northern Atlantic Ocean and mixing with the warm Gulf Stream waters. This has stopped the thermohaline circulation in the Atlantic. Europe has the same latitude as Northern Canada. Without the warm Gulf Stream, Europe's climate is now like Northern Canada."

"Now you are making sense," replied Leslie. "What can we do about this?"

"I thought we had time to work through things with the Federation more diplomatically, but that opportunity has come and gone. We need to be more aggressive in our conflict with the Federation. Admiral Torres is more concerned with saving his fleet and keeping it intact. He has no idea of the urgency of the collapse of Earth's climate and ecosystems. The rebel fleet needs to attack now, go through the Beta Wormhole as soon as possible, and force a surrender of the Federation 2nd Fleet. Then, we can negotiate from a position of strength."

"Negotiate what?" asked Leslie.

"Conditions of their surrender will hinge on them making technology available to Earth that they are using to terraform the planet Beyond. This will enable the Rebellion to reverse the effects of global climate change on planet Earth. We would also need the technical expertise of the geoengineers and environmental scientists who know best how to use these technologies."

"Why would they be willing to give this up, Aristides? I thought that their long-term survival depended on using these technologies for terraforming the planet Beyond."

"It's simple math. How many people live on the planet Beyond?" asked Aristides.

"I have heard that there are about 20 million," responded Leslie.

"Okay. Now how many people live on the planet Earth'?" asked Aristides.

"Roughly 15 billion. I hear what you are saying, but it seems like your strategy is lopsided in favor of the Rebellion and Earth at the expense of the Federation and the planet Beyond. I still don't understand why you must kill Admiral Torres," said Leslie.

Aristides paused for a minute to gather what he would say next. Then he spoke, "His officer corps all came from the mothballed fleet. They are loyal to him. His strategy of sowing fear and praise amongst his officers has worked well, making his officers blindly obey his idiotic commands. The most recent example of this that I heard when I came back on board this space fortress: Captain Spinelli blindly obeyed Admiral Torres's command to ignore the nuclear reactor safety interlocks on the frigate *Farragut*, which resulted in the loss of this frigate and its entire crew. Admiral Torres needs to be killed. I think we can make it look like an accident."

At hearing this, Leslie closed her eyes and rubbed the bridge of her nose. "Can we talk about this some other time?"

"That works for me!" replied Aristides as he stormed out of the room.

***

Leslie made her way to the Space-Time Lab. She needed to get a second opinion from someone who had some sanity. For some reason that she didn't quite understand, this meant she had to talk to Dr. Hays. When she reached the hatchway to the lab, she looked both ways to make sure no one was watching her. Then she realized that she could not use her key card without Aristides finding out that she was meeting with Dr. Hays in the lab. She did not have to wait long for a solution, however, as Dr. Hays himself came through the hatchway.

"What are you doing here, Dr. Jones?" asked Robert Hays.

"Please call me Leslie. I need to talk with you, Robert. Can we meet in the lab?"

"Sure. I was just stepping out to get a cup of what passes as coffee on the fortress."

Once they were back inside the lab, Leslie came to the point. "Dr. Hays, do you understand what the Rebellion is all about? I mean, has anyone discussed the goals of the Rebellion with you?"

"I haven't a clue. I just want to find my friend Myron and bring him back. I have no interest in the Rebellion," responded Dr. Hays.

"You originally came from the 21st century. It is now the 22nd century. I know that people in the 21st century were experiencing global climate change," said Leslie.

"That information must have been erased from my memory when I was captured from the 21st century. There are a lot of things I don't remember, Leslie," replied Robert.

"You're a brilliant physicist. Let me refresh your memory. Rising levels of greenhouse gases, such as carbon dioxide, were causing heat to be trapped in the atmosphere. Robert, do you remember any of this?" asked Leslie urgently.

"Hold on, Leslie. It's coming back to me. Oh yeah, now I remember: rising temperatures, increasing atmospheric humidity, increasing desertification. I also remember that there were a lot of climate change skeptics back then."

"Robert, were you a skeptic?"

"No. With that said, I was not very vocal on this topic, either. My area of research was the space-time continuum and the potential for time travel," replied Robert.

"Okay, Robert: It is now over a hundred years later. Based on the science, do you think Global Climate Change has become worse on planet Earth?"

"Assuming the continued increase in greenhouse gas emissions, I would hazard a guess that climate change has become much worse," answered Robert.

At this point in the conversation, Leslie thought it would be a good idea to talk to Robert about the history of the Federation and the mass migration from Earth to the planet Beyond.

"Robert, that is what the Rebellion is all about. Once you discovered the wormhole on the far side of the moon, people began to develop technology to exploit the wormhole. The wealthy countries figured that planet Earth was not worth saving, and once probes were sent through the Alpha and Beta Wormholes, the planet Beyond was discovered. This was the point in time that the Federation government was formed. The Federation began terraforming efforts on the planet Beyond and began moving people to the new planet."

"Wow! I didn't know that. So, what does the Rebellion have to do with Global Climate Change?" asked Robert.

Leslie took a few moments to gather her thoughts, then she continued, "This is where Aristides came into the picture. He led a rebellion on Earth and founded a global government with the goal of returning greenhouse gas levels and the climate on Earth back to pre-industrial levels. The problem is: climate change has greatly accelerated over the past 100 years. In the last two years, it has accelerated even more. A significant portion of the Earth is now uninhabitable. The lives of 15 billion people are at stake. Are you familiar with the terraforming of the planet Beyond?"

"I actually know something about this, Leslie. When I was the chief scientific officer on this space fortress, some of my lab techs and fellow scientists talked to me about the terraforming effort of the planet Beyond. No one, however, told me about what was happening back on Earth. I just assumed that everyone had migrated to the planet Beyond and that there was no one left on Earth. I know that sounds strange, but remember, much of my memory had been erased surgically," said Robert.

"Do you understand now, Robert?" asked Leslie.

"I think I do, and it makes me sick to my stomach. How can I help, Leslie?"

"I have a problem. Aristides, the leader of the Rebellion, is an egomaniac and has lost his moral compass. He is taking the Rebellion to the planet Beyond. He wants all-out war—a war where no one can win. I need your help!" pleaded Leslie.

"What does help look like?" asked Robert.

"Help looks like replacing Aristides with someone who is smart and has a moral compass," replied Leslie.

Leslie became very quiet and just stared into Robert's eyes. Robert became uneasy and wasn't sure what to say. But the words came to him and compelled him to speak.

"Leslie, do you want me to take over the leadership of the Rebellion? Why not you?"

"I could, in a technical sense. But I don't have a moral compass like you do. I don't understand Christianity, but I have watched you. You care about people. You are also very smart. Please say yes!" pleaded Leslie.

Suddenly, the hatch to the Space-Time Lab opened, and in came Aristides. He looked at both Robert and Leslie with suspicious eyes and said, "Just the two I wanted to see. Have you figured out how to operate the Space-Time Lab? We need to capture a new admiral to take Admiral Torres's place."

Chapter 39

The Defeat of Admiral von Spee

I cannot reach Germany. We possess no other secure harbor. I must fight my way through the seas of the world doing as much mischief as I can, until my ammunition is exhausted, or a foe far superior in power succeeds in catching me. But it will cost the wretches dearly before they take me down.

Vice Admiral Maximilian von Spee, 1914

Admiral Maximilian Johannes Maria Hubert Reichgraf von Spee of the German Imperial Fleet had reason to feel elated—and good reason to be concerned. He was elated because his small fleet had just annihilated the British Fourth Cruiser Squadron at Coronel, off the coast of Chile. He was concerned that he had to take his small fleet of cruisers halfway around the world through oceans infested with the British and French Navies, and Germany was at war with both England and France.

His small fleet of two armored cruisers and three light cruisers had broken out of a German harbor in China at the commencement of the Great War. His goal was to return to the German Empire to be united with Germany's High Sea Fleet, located in the North Sea. To remain in the German trading port of Qingdao on the Yangtze River estuary would allow the superior British naval squadrons to sink his small fleet in port in faraway China.

His fleet of cruisers included the *Scharnhorst* and *Gneisenau*, which were adequately armed with eight 21 cm guns, and three light cruisers that were only armed with 10.5 cm guns. Vice Admiral von Spee did not worry too much about any British cruiser that he might encounter; his two armored cruisers were up to the task. What he worried about were two things: how to navigate halfway around the world through oceans patrolled by the British, who possessed the largest navy in the world—and a particular type of British ship, known as Battle Cruisers. These ships were armed with eight 30.5 cm guns that had a much farther range than his 21 cm guns. If he encountered one of these monsters, he would not be able to outrun them, since they clipped along at 25 knots, while the best his cruisers could do was 22 knots. He would be outgunned and outmaneuvered.

Returning to Germany through the shorter Indian Ocean route would be suicide. The British Raj in India lay in his path, as well as the British Indian Ocean Fleet. There would be no way he could pass through the British-controlled Suez Canal. He had decided to sail his fleet across the Pacific Ocean. He had coaling ships along so he could refuel his fleet. He decided to cross over to South America to neutral Chile, where he could refuel and take on provisions.

However, Admiral von Spee was not going to simply elude the British Navy; he was going to harass the British and French colonial islands, and any enemy cruisers he might encounter on his journey. After all, this was war, and the German colonies in the Pacific were threatened by his enemies. At first, he attempted to retake the German colonies in the Pacific but instead decided to save his ammunition for British ships.

He made it all the way to Chile near Coronel, where he spotted a lone British cruiser, the *HMS Glasgow*. He went out to destroy this cruiser and found the entire British Fourth Cruiser Squadron present. He and his small fleet gave battle, sank three British armored cruisers, and scattered the rest of the British squadron like a cat scatters a nest of mice. British Admiral of the squadron, Christopher Craddock, went down with his flagship, *Good Hope*. Two other British cruisers, the *Monmouth* and *Glasgow*, went down, along with 1,660 men. It was the British Navy's first defeat since the time of Napoleon.

Once on shore in Chile, Admiral von Spee was able to communicate with the German Admiralty. The Admiralty's command was simple: break through and return to Germany. Unfortunately, the entire Atlantic Ocean lay between his small fleet and Germany. The only way he could make it back was to make sure he kept his whereabouts hidden from the British.

Once von Spee's squadron cleared Cape Horn, a small chain of islands lay in his path. These were the British Falkland Islands. These islands presented both a risk and an opportunity for the German squadron. It was a major coaling station for the British fleet, which would enable the German squadron to refuel before they made their dash across the Atlantic Ocean. The risk was the presence of a wireless station that could notify the British fleet of the German squadron's whereabouts.

It was a tough decision. Many of the German officers insisted that the squadron bypass and stay out of sight of the Falkland Islands. Admiral von Spee did not agree. His plan was to take the *Scharnhorst* into Stanley Harbor on the Falkland Islands and destroy the wireless station. Then the rest of the German squadron could come in and refuel and restock their provisions.

When the *Scharnhorst* came in, the crew noticed black smoke and assumed the smoke was from the British trying to burn the naval stores of coal. What they encountered was much different. In the harbor was a relic of a British battleship, the *HMS Canopus*. The *Canopus* was grounded by the British because the old battleship was too slow to maneuver in the open sea. But the *Canopus* did have something that caused Admiral von Spee to stop: four 30.5 cm guns. The *Canopus* opened fire on the *Scharnhorst*. The *Scharnhorst* could not get into range to fire her smaller 21 cm guns, so Admiral von Spee broke off his engagement.

As the *Scharnhorst* fled, something came toward the German flagship that struck terror in Admiral von Spee: two British Battle Cruisers—the *HMS Invincible* and the *Inflexible*, commanded by Admiral Doveton Sturdee. Admiral von Spee's worst nightmare was coming true. His fleet tried to outrun the battle cruisers, but the Germans' speed of 22 knots was no match for the British battle cruisers' speed of 25 knots. What was worse was the range of the Battle Cruisers' 30.5 cm guns, which was greater than the range of the German guns.

Admiral von Spee fought bravely and brilliantly. He used the wind to his advantage. The smoke from his guns did not interfere with his gunnery range finders, while the smoke from the British guns practically blinded the British gunnery personnel. Eventually, the *Inflexible* and *Invincible* gunnery crews found their mark, and the *Scharnhorst* and *Gneisenau* were hammered by the 30.5 cm shells. Eventually, both ships sank beneath the waves. The German light cruisers tried to make a run for it, but they too succumbed to the 30.5 cm guns of the battle cruisers.

Later, Admiral Sturdee met with the gunnery officers of both battle cruisers. He was interested in lessons learned from the Battle Cruisers' first engagement with the enemy. Most of the talk was technical. However, at the end of the meeting, Admiral Sturdee asked a simple question: "Did you men see anything through your gunnery range-finding scopes that was strange?"

Two gunnery officers looked nervously at each other. "No, sir!" they both replied.

"You seem to be holding something back. Just tell me. We are all trying to learn about gunnery from this battle."

"Well, sir," one of the gunnery officers started, "I was sighting in to the *Scharnhorst* right before she went down. The ship was suddenly enveloped in a cloud. It could have been a fog bank, or maybe it was from the fires on the *Scharnhorst*. At any rate, I saw this bright light appear in the cloud above the *Scharnhorst*."

"Maybe it was from an explosion on the *Scharnhorst*," replied Admiral Sturdee.

"No, sir. The bright light was above the ship. In the clouds."

"I saw the same thing too, sir," stated another gunnery range finder.

"It's too bad that we didn't pick up any German survivors. Maybe they could have explained the phenomena," Admiral Sturdee mumbled under his breath.

"Yes, sir."

Chapter 40

A Double Capture

"We need you to capture an admiral from the past!" commanded Aristides.

"Well, there is a Red Giant star that will be making a close pass to the black hole in 10 days," answered Robert Hays.

"I want you and Dr. Jones to work up a plan and the calculations necessary to capture this admiral. I want it done right the first time!" exclaimed Aristides.

"We will get to work on this right away, Aristides," responded Robert. "We may need some help to get this done."

"You may have my assistant, Jennifer Bo, help you in this matter. She is the best person to help you, since she did the historical work-up on the admiral that we are interested in," responded Aristides.

Aristides then turned to Leslie Jones and said, "Leslie, I want you to meet me at my cabin in 10 minutes." The look on his face seemed to be one of anger. He turned away and left the Space-Time Lab in a hurry.

"Looks like you and Aristides need to work things out. Is he always angry like this?" asked Robert.

"This is a recent behavioral change in Aristides. He used to be kind and charismatic. Now he is a monster," replied Leslie.

"Maybe I should talk to him," said Robert.

"That would be a really bad idea. I'll talk to him. I know how to handle him when he gets like this. Jennifer is a very bright woman, but she is a bit anxious. Please don't overwhelm her when you meet her," said Leslie.

A few minutes after Leslie left the lab, the hatch to the Space-Time Lab opened and a petite young woman entered.

"Hi! I'm Jennifer Bo. Aristides told me that you needed my assistance with capturing an admiral from the past."

"Pleased to meet you, Jennifer. I understand that you have all the history I need to pinpoint the admiral that we are interested in capturing. Did you bring this information with you?"

"I have it right here on my tablet," responded Jennifer cheerfully.

"Great! Let's get started," answered Robert in a calming but cheerful voice.

***

Meanwhile, Aristides and Leslie were having another argument.

"Are you implying that Dr. Hays and I are having an affair? Come on, Aristides, you have to be joking! He's old enough to be my father!" screamed Leslie.

"Look, if I ever have proof that you two have a thing going on between you, I will have both of you spaced!" screamed Aristides.

Suddenly, it became really quiet in the cabin. Then Aristides spoke quietly, "I'm sorry. The stress is getting to me. Please forgive me."

"I forgive you, Aristides," responded Leslie.

Aristides sat on his bed and began to weep uncontrollably for a few minutes. Leslie really felt sorry for him, so she sat down next to him.

Finally, he stopped crying and regained his composure to the point where he could speak. "I need to tell you I am leaving the space fortress for a while to join Admiral Torres on the 74-gun *Brazil*. I have some business to attend to. I'm not sure how long I will be there."

"What do you want me to do while you are gone?" asked Leslie.

"Make sure the capture of the 20th-century admiral goes without a hitch. And make sure that you keep yourself from becoming emotionally involved with Dr. Hays," pleaded Aristides.

***

Ten days later, the Time-Space Lab was a hive of activity. Robert Hays took his position at the center of the lab. To his right was Dr. Leslie Jones. To his left was Jennifer Bo. The other positions in the lab were taken by rebels who had some scientific backgrounds.

Dr. Hays and Dr. Jones spent most of their waking hours training the rebels on the intricacies of the space-time instrumentation.

He brought up the image of the black hole, Sagittarius A*. The screen came alive with the image of the area around the black hole.

After examining the instrumentation that provided data for the black hole and the red giant star, he said, "Jennifer. Have you ever seen the black hole at the center of our galaxy?"

"I can't see it, Dr. Hays. Where is it?"

"I imagine you can see the impact that the black hole is having on light," answered Robert cheerfully. Robert was having an enjoyable time teaching Jennifer astrophysics.

"Oh, I see a very bright ring, and something that looks like the rings of Saturn circling the bright ring."

"What do you see in the center of the bright ring, Jenn?"

"It's very black… Oh! That must be the black hole!" exclaimed Jennifer.

"Okay, Leslie, now bring up the red giant star on the screen."

The screen refreshed, and a filtered image of the red giant filled most of the screen.

"Why is the star teardrop-shaped?" asked Jennifer.

"The black hole's massive gravitational force is pulling the star's corona and photosphere towards it. In another minute or so, you will see a bright filament of the star get pulled into the black hole. More specifically, you will see the filament flow into the Saturn-like ring. That ring is called the accretion disk," answered Robert.

Suddenly, a filament from the star arched over to the accretion disk. When this contact happened, bright jets shot from the top and bottom of the black hole. This was followed by what looked like whirlpools in the accretion disk.

"Jennifer, do you see the whirlpools? That's where all of the action is."

Suddenly, the whole space fortress started rocking. Robert held onto the instrument panel, righted himself, and said, "Those are gravitational waves impacting the space fortress. The black hole is becoming angry! Leslie, adjust the orbit of the space fortress to keep us at a safe distance from the accretion disk."

"We are acquiring a new orbit as we speak."

Dr. Hays reached out to the virtual screen in front of him and started selecting images of whirlpools in the accretion disk. Then he turned to Jennifer and said, "Jennifer, the lab supercomputer is color-coding these whirlpools per their wormhole destination, from red to blue. The computer is also assigning a number that establishes the time travel destination. Remember that I had you create a time-past and future-number code and a color-location code matrix. I hope you have been studying it well this week."

"I have. The whirlpool over there that is yellow-orange looks like a good primary target," responded Jennifer as she pointed at the computer screen. "Its space-time potential code has good agreement for 1914 in the South Atlantic Ocean."

Robert could sense that Jennifer was starting to become anxious. He turned toward her, placed his right hand on her shoulder, and said in a cheerful voice, "I agree. Let's launch probe number one on my command."

Then Dr. Hays' lips seemed to be mouthing a countdown that only he could hear. Then he said, "Launch the probe!"

The probe appeared on the screen and headed to the accretion disk of the black hole, and was soon out of sight. Robert looked at Jennifer and said, "Good work, Jennifer! I'll make an astrophysicist out of you yet. Dr. Jones, ready probe number two to acquire the secondary target."

A murmur in the lab filled the room. "What secondary target?" asked several of the rebel technicians.

Dr. Hays responded to the murmuring, "We accidentally sent the secondary target into the future by mistake sometime back. He is a good friend of mine, and I want to bring him back." Dr. Hays then gave a look to everyone that froze them all in the Space-Time Lab. They could tell he meant business. Then he selected a bright blue whirlpool on his virtual screen. "Launch probe two to acquire secondary target on my command... Launch probe two now!" shouted Dr. Hays.

***

Probe one came back to the space fortress in about 30 minutes. The probe entered the airlock and settled on the floor. It took about 10 minutes for the airlock to come up to pressure, while Robert, Leslie, Jennifer, and a small detachment of rebel marines waited outside the airlock.

Once the airlock pressure equilibrated, the hatch from the lab to the airlock opened. Then Robert spoke, "Marines, make sure your riot rifles are set to stun. We don't want to injure the captured subject; we just want to render him unconscious if he becomes bellicose."

The hatch on top of the probe opened, revealing a middle-aged man with a goatee, dressed in an early 20th-century naval uniform. He stood straight up and rubbed his lower back, wincing in pain. His uniform was soaking wet. He muttered something in German, which Jennifer translated:

"Where am I? Who are you? What was the strange craft that rescued me from drowning? Oh, my rheumatoid back is killing me! May I have some morphine?"

Jennifer responded in German, "You are on the Space Fortress *Sagittarius A**. I am Jennifer Bo, and with me are Dr. Hays and Dr. Jones. The craft that rescued you from drowning is a Space-Time Continuum Probe, and yes, we can give you some morphine for your rheumatoid arthritis."

When the captured naval man heard this, he simply cocked his head and became speechless. Then Leslie gave the order to the marine detachment, "I sense that our captured admiral is becoming disoriented and may become bellicose. Stun him and render him unconscious, then bring him to sickbay."

That was the last time the three of them saw the captured subject in his right mind.

***

The second capture took a bit longer…

Myron Abbot, who was two years in the future in Jerusalem, was reciting his morning *Shema*:

"Hear O' Israel, the Lord is our God, the Lord is One.

Blessed is the name of His glorious kingdom forever and ever."

As soon as he completed these two verses, a commanding voice spoke to him, "Myron Abbot!"

Myron looked around him but saw no one. Then the voice returned, "Myron Abbot!"

Myron again looked around and saw no one. He thought he was having a delusion associated with his Alzheimer's Disease. Then he heard the voice a third time.

"Myron Abbot!"

This time, Myron responded to the voice, "Yes, Jehovah! This is Myron Abbot. Speak to your servant—your command."

"Go to the Temple Mount to where my two Witnesses are speaking. You will be shown what you must do," said the voice.

In response to this command, Myron ran to the Temple Mount. When he arrived, Elijah and Enoch were speaking to the masses. Myron looked around and saw Elijah and Enoch suddenly look up into the sky. Everyone in the crowd was also looking up. Then Myron looked up. What he saw caused his jaw to drop in amazement.

There above him was a flaming torus of light, and out of the torus flew a black object, which landed between Myron and Elijah.

"Behold, the chariot of God!" cried Elijah.

Myron ran toward the black object. So did Elijah. They came to the black object at the same time.

"No, brother Myron, this chariot of God is for me. Stand back!" screamed Elijah.

Something broke inside of Myron, and something powerful took its place. Myron boldly shouted at Elijah, "No! This chariot of God is for me. God told me…"

"How dare you speak against me. I am a prophet of God!" screamed Elijah.

Elijah tried to push Myron out of the way. But something strange happened. Myron pushed Elijah out of the way—in fact, Myron pushed Elijah back 10 meters. When this happened, Myron simply stared at his own ancient, scrawny arms.

How was I able to do that? Elijah, who had landed on his butt, replied, "Look! The chariot of God is opening, and I think it is going to speak."

"Myron Abbot, get into the probe and return to the space fortress. Now!" ordered the probe.

Myron instantly recognized the recorded voice as that of Robert Hays. After Myron entered the probe, it lifted off and disappeared into the flaming torus of light. Then the torus snapped shut. Elijah, Enoch, and the crowd in the Temple Square stared skyward. Finally, Elijah said, "Myron Abbot is now amongst the Prophets!"

Chapter 41

Assassination of Admiral Torres

The rebel fleet was still stalled at the Beta Wormhole gateway. The Federation light frigate had slipped past the rebel fleet and had returned to the planet Beyond. This being the case, Aristides assumed that the captain of this frigate had reported the disposition of the rebel fleet. This sorry situation was eating a hole in Aristides' stomach. To make matters worse, another light frigate had exited the Beta Wormhole on some sort of secret mission.

However, now Aristides had a plan. He would replace Admiral Torres with Admiral von Spee, after von Spee had recovered from his brain surgery. He still needed to get rid of Admiral Torres as soon as possible, and he had to make it look like an accident.

"Admiral Torres, this is Aristides. Please report to my cabin immediately."

A few minutes later, Admiral Torres entered Aristides' cabin and said, "You wanted to see me, Aristides? You haven't spoken to me in a while."

"Yes, I want you to meet with your commanders as soon as possible to put a plan together for deploying your ships through the Beta Wormhole, and ultimately taking control of the planet Beyond."

"I do not want you to be part of that meeting, Aristides. You know nothing of naval strategies and tactics."

"Admiral Torres, you know you can't keep me out of the meeting."

"Then I will have the meeting on a different ship, Aristides. I will have a detachment of marines guard you to make sure that you don't follow me," responded Admiral Torres with a smug look on his face.

"You know you can't do that. I am the leader of this Rebellion, and you need to submit to my authority!" screamed Aristides.

At this point, the hatch to Aristides' cabin flew open and a detachment of rebel marines entered. As soon as they came in, the cabin became very quiet. Only the sound of the laser rifles' safeties clicking off could be heard.

"Sergeant, take Aristides to the brig and leave him there under guard. Let no one in to see him for any reason. You may release him once I am safely on board the 74-gun *Canada*. Understand?" asked Admiral Torres.

"Yes, sir!" snapped the commanding sergeant.

"Make it so!" responded the admiral.

After Aristides was locked up, Admiral Torres went to the communication officer and said, "Send a message to all commanders in the fleet. They are to meet aboard the ship-of-the-line *Canada* at 1500 for an important meeting. A security clearance code will be issued to all participants."

"Yes, sir!"

***

Admiral Torres, with a detachment of marines, entered the shuttle bay of the *Brazil*. A guard stopped them and asked for the security code.

"57!!5F.1101A," responded Admiral Torres.

"You may pass."

The admiral strapped himself into the shuttlecraft next to the pilot and said, "Set your course for the 74-gun *Canada*. Set your speed to full speed ahead. I don't want to keep my commanders waiting."

Soon the shuttlecraft was on its way. The journey to the 74-gun *Canada* was quite routine, and Admiral Torres was a bit tired, so he decided to take a short nap.

Sometime later, while he was still asleep, the shuttlecraft began to bounce violently. Torres woke up with a start.

"What's going on?" shouted the confused admiral.

"Sir, the helm is not responding," replied the shuttle pilot.

"Override the navigational computer," shouted the admiral.

"I can't, sir. The controls don't respond."

"What is causing all the turbulence?"

"Gravitational waves from the Black Hole Sagittarius A*!" screamed the pilot.

"The black hole? We are too far from the black hole to experience gravitational waves."

"Sir, the navigational computer is taking us directly toward the black hole. Time to impact with the event horizon is two minutes!" screamed the pilot.

"That's impossible! We can't go that fast to cover the distance to the black hole. These shuttlecrafts are only capable of 5,000 kilometers per hour."

"Sir, we are moving at relativistic speed," said the pilot.

"Get on the radio and contact the *Brazil*. See if they can override the navigational computer."

"We're too close to the black hole; the radio waves simply curve into orbit around the black hole," said the perplexed pilot.

Then blinding light entered the shuttlecraft. The left side of the craft entered the event horizon first. The marines closest to the left side became frozen in place, like statues. Admiral Torres was the last to be impaled on the event horizon, becoming a frozen statue forever.

Back on the 74-gun *Brazil*, Aristides was sitting on his bunk in the brig. He had a slight smile and was chuckling to himself. The guard thought that he had lost his mind.

"Sir, what do you find so funny? You know what I've heard? You are going to be spaced when Admiral Torres returns."

"Admiral Torres is not coming back. About now, he is frozen in time. In a practical sense, he is dead. Call the communication officer and see if I am telling you the truth. Go ahead: I dare you," said Aristides in a somewhat patronizing tone.

"Communications, this is Corporal Hing. Has Admiral Torres reached the 74-gun *Canada*?"

"We have lost contact with the craft. The last known position was at the event horizon of the black hole Sagittarius A*," responded the officer on the bridge.

The guard slowly turned around and saw Aristides smiling. Aristides stood up and walked over to the guard and said, "Corporal, you can release me now."

The marine aimed his laser at Aristides. "Give me the security code, or I am under orders to kill you."

"57!!5F.1101A," responded Aristides.

***

Myron, Robert, and Leslie were in the conference room on board the space fortress, drinking what passed as coffee. Robert turned to Myron and said, "Myron, I would like to introduce you to a friend of mine, Dr. Leslie Jones."

"Pleased to meet you," said Myron. "Please forgive me if I don't remember your name. I have a memory problem."

"Myron, would you like to tell us about your trip to Jerusalem?" asked Robert.

"You will never guess who I met there! I ran into Elijah and Enoch. I think you accidentally sent them to the right time and place. They were preaching daily at the Temple Mount in Jerusalem. Thousands of Jews and Muslims were coming every day to hear God speaking through them. I even had a chance to talk with them at their apartment."

"Wow! You are seeing two years into the future. Do tell us more," exclaimed Leslie.

"They told me that Jesus will be coming soon. More importantly, they told me how I could have my sins forgiven, forever. I just need to believe that Jesus Christ was crucified for my sins."

"Myron, do you believe that Jesus was crucified for you?" asked Robert.

"Not yet. There is something inside of me that wants to believe, but I am too immersed in my Jewish faith. I need time to think about it," replied Myron.

Leslie was quietly listening to this conversation. Something inside of her wanted to hear more from Myron about Jesus. She also wanted to understand the friendship between Robert and Myron. They seemed so different from each other, and yet, they seemed to be the best of friends.

"Excuse me," interrupted Leslie, "but how can you be such good friends with each other, even though you have different faiths?"

"That is hard for us to understand too. Myron and I have learned a lot from each other and have helped each other. We both have memory problems. Myron has incipient Alzheimer's disease, and I had most of my memories surgically removed. But when we are together, we both become more than the sum of the whole—we become much more. Myron and I share something else that is precious: we are very fond of each other," answered Robert.

"You know, I think I am starting to understand this thing called friendship," responded Leslie. "I am experiencing the same thing between Robert and me. It's hard to understand," said Leslie.

"Then don't try. Just enjoy what you have now," interjected Myron.

"Myron, I have a question for you. You said that all one needs to do to have God forgive them for their sins is to believe that Jesus was crucified for their sins. I have committed many grievous sins in my life. How can one man's death allow me to be forgiven of so much?" asked Leslie.

"Christians, like my friend Robert, believe that Jesus is the Son of God, and that Jesus' death on the cross is the only way to have their sins forgiven. Isn't that right, Robert?"

"That's correct, Myron, but there is more. Accepting Jesus' death as a payment for my sins also brings something else into play. I now have a personal relationship with God," said Robert.

Leslie thought about this for a while, then responded, "Robert and I are friends, and I really like that. I like being around him, and he has been helping me go through this difficult time with Aristides. I have not studied anything about the God that you two believe in. What do I need to do to have this relationship with God?"

"Accept that Jesus died on the cross for your sins. Then you should get a Bible and read it to learn more about God and His wonderful gift of salvation," responded Robert.

"Okay, I will do that right now," responded Leslie.

Myron and Robert stared at each other in stunned silence for a minute. Then Robert responded, "Excellent! How about you, Myron?"

"I need more time to think about this," responded Myron.

Chapter 42

The FNS *Lockford* Engages the Rebel Flagship *Brazil*

When the *Lockford* exited the Beta Wormhole, the ship was moving at 10% the speed of light. The rebel fleet, which was guarding the exit of the Beta Wormhole, was not prepared to capture or destroy a Federation ship moving at that speed. When the *Lockford* cleared the wormhole gate and the gate snapped shut, the rebel flagship picked up the light frigate on their sensors but was too clumsy to bring its missiles and plasma guns to bear on the target.

So, Admiral Torres ordered Captain Spinelli, commander of the heavy frigate *Farragut*, to give chase and capture the *Lockford*. In the confusion, Admiral Torres ordered Captain Spinelli to override the ship's safety interlocks on the fusion propulsion system to bring the *Farragut* up to speed faster.

This resulted in the fusion engines onboard the *Farragut* going super-critical, and the ship became very supernova-like. All matter on the *Farragut*, along with the rebel sailors and marines, was annihilated in a fraction of a second. This violent explosion rocked the entire rebel fleet.

The ship closest to the explosion was the rebel flagship, *Brazil*. The percussion felt by the *Brazil* rendered most of the crew unconscious for the span of several minutes. By the time the *Brazil*'s crew regained consciousness, the light frigate *Lockford* was way out of range of the rebel fleet's guns and their sensors.

Where did the *Lockford* go?

***

The FNS *Lockford* was on the other side of the black hole, Sagittarius A*, which shielded the light frigate from the rebel fleet near the Beta Wormhole. On the bridge of the *Lockford*, Captain Alvarez was discussing his options with his officers.

"I would like to rearrange orders that I received from the Admiralty. We have given the rebel fleet the slip, but before we attempt to capture the space fortress, we may have an opportunity to capture the rebel flagship and Admiral Torres. If we capture the rebel flagship with the rebel admiral first, we may stand a better chance of capturing the space fortress. We need to develop a plan to capture their flagship. Any ideas?" asked the captain.

The silence that followed was deafening. Captain Alvarez then stared at Lt. Ming Chu. This made Ming very nervous. He wanted to create his own black hole, climb inside, and disappear. This confusion in his mind lasted about a minute, but to Ming, it seemed like a lifetime. Finally, he mustered the courage to speak.

"We could use the gravitational field of the black hole to accelerate the *Lockford* to even greater speeds. We could slingshot around the black hole and surprise the rebel flagship."

"And how do you propose decelerating the *Lockford* once we get to the other side of the black hole?" asked Capt. Alvarez.

"We would need to flip the *Lockford* around 180 degrees and use our fusion engines to slow the ship down to the point where Capt. Jackson could get his company of marines across to the rebel flagship and take her as a prize," responded Lt. Chu.

"One problem with your plan, Lieutenant. When we use the fusion engines to decelerate, we will announce our arrival to the entire rebel fleet. The energy from our fusion engines will become a bullseye for all their ships to fire at."

"I see your point, Captain." Ming went quiet for a minute, then spoke. "Maybe we should not decelerate at all."

"But then we will simply zip past the rebel fleet," said the captain.

"Not exactly. If we are moving fast enough… closer to the speed of light… the *Lockford* will be supermassive and have its own huge gravity well that could be used to pull the rebel flagship away from the rebel fleet."

"I'm not following you. Why would we be supermassive?"

"Because of the laws of relativity, you know, $E=mc^2$. Here, let me show you on my tablet."

Ming wrote out $E=mc^2$ on his tablet, then his fingers danced madly on the screen until he derived the following formula:

$$m = m_0 / \sqrt{(1 - (v^2/c^2))}$$

where:

m is the observed mass,

m_0 is the rest mass,

v is the velocity of the *Lockford*,

c is the speed of light.

"As we approach the speed of light, the *Lockford*'s mass will approach infinity."

Capt. Alvarez pondered this for a moment. "Are you sure about this? What about the crew? Won't they be crushed by the massive gravity of the *Lockford*?"

"No. We will also become massive, so we will not feel the effect of the change in mass of the *Lockford*," replied Lt. Chu.

"Okay, let's assume you are right, Lieutenant. How will we capture the rebel flagship with all this speed?" asked Capt. Alvarez.

Again, Ming became quiet. Captain Alvarez had the good sense to let the wheels turn in Ming's head. Finally, Ming spoke.

"The act of the *Lockford* pulling the flagship away from the rest of the rebel fleet will disorient the rebel crew. It will also slow us down a bit. When we have pulled the rebel flagship sufficiently far from the rest of the fleet, then we flip the *Lockford* 180 degrees and use our fusion engines to decelerate. As we decelerate, we should fire all six of our nuclear missiles near the rebel flagship—not at the flagship, but around it. Then detonate the missile warheads. The shockwave will temporarily trigger the safety interlocks on the *Brazil* so that the fusion engines on the flagship will shut down, which will keep them from escaping. Then Capt. Jackson could take his company on a shuttle and board the flagship, taking her as a prize."

Capt. Alvarez responded, "Make it so, Lieutenant."

Then Lt. Chu turned to the weapons officer, Lt. Opel, and asked, "Lieutenant, can you estimate the trajectories of the missiles to produce this effect? We don't want to destroy the flagship or breach the hull. We just want to give enough of a shockwave to trigger their fusion engine safety interlocks into a safe mode that will shut down their fusion engines, and enough shock to render the flagship's crew unconscious."

"I am working on it now. I have been inputting the data into the ship's computer as you have been talking. Okay, here is the answer: We don't need all our missiles to produce this effect, only three of them. If we detonate them in an equidistant pattern around the flagship at a distance of 10 kilometers, that should trigger the flagship's fusion engine safety interlocks and knock out all her guns and missiles for at least two hours. It may kill some of the flagship crew, and the rest of the crew will be knocked dingy," said Lt. Opel.

***

The FNS *Lockford* changed its course to an oblique angle toward the massive black hole. Most of the crew were given a sedative to render them unconscious. Then the unconscious crew were strapped into their bunks to keep them from flying about due to the extreme acceleration. Critical crew members were administered oxygen mixed with helium instead of nitrogen. This atmospheric blend would keep these crew members from getting decompression sickness from nitrogen and help keep them functional. These remaining functional crew were strapped into their stations to prevent them from flying around during the massive acceleration and deceleration.

"Captain, ship speed is now approaching 30% the speed of light. We are getting multiple warning signals from our safety systems. At our rate of acceleration, the safety interlocks will shut down all power to the *Lockford*'s fusion engines in 10 minutes," declared the navigational officer.

"We are now at 70% the speed of light."

Another message from the Space-Time Deck came to the Bridge. "Captain, our sensors regarding space-time inside and around the ship are going off scale. Can the *Lockford* hold up to the stress being put on the ship?"

Captain Alvarez turned to Lt. Chu and said, "Recommendations, Lieutenant. Now!"

"We are now at 95% the speed of light!" screamed the Navigational Officer.

Ming only paused for a few seconds and responded, "Override all safety interlocks. Our speed has increased our mass and enlarged our physical dimensions significantly. The *Lockford*, in its current enormous state, should be able to withstand the stresses."

"Lt. Chu, how close should we come to the flagship for our increased gravitational field to capture and drag the rebel flagship away from the rest of the rebel fleet?" asked Capt. Alvarez.

"Plot a course to take us within 0.5 kilometers. When we capture the flagship in our gravitational field, expect turbulence and deceleration for a few minutes. The flagship will accelerate and be dragged with us, but it will steadily fall behind. Once the flagship is 1,000 kilometers behind us, flip the *Lockford* 180 degrees and use the fusion engines to slow us down so we can launch our missiles and send our marine transport vessel over to the rebel flagship," responded Lt. Chu.

"Make it so!" responded Capt. Alvarez.

As the *Lockford* made its close approach to the rebel flagship, there was turbulence and deceleration, just as Ming had predicted. The *Lockford*'s helmsman deftly flipped the *Lockford* 180 degrees, and Lt. Opel fired three nuclear missiles that exploded around the rebel flagship.

"How far did we drag the rebel flagship away from the rest of the fleet?" asked Capt. Alvarez.

"The flagship is now 15,000,000 kilometers from the nearest rebel ship," responded the Navigational Officer.

"Sensor Operator, scan the rebel flagship and report on the status of her fusion engines and crew. Also determine if there are any hull breaches," ordered Capt. Alvarez.

"All fusion engines on the rebel flagship are shut down. No hull breaches detected. Estimated 70% casualties on board the flagship," responded the Sensor Operator.

Capt. Alvarez picked up the comm and spoke to Marine Capt. Jackson, "Capt. Jackson, you may deploy the transport and your marine company. Use whatever force is necessary to capture the flagship intact. If possible, take the rebel admiral alive."

There was a pause for less than a minute, and Capt. Alvarez added, "Capt. Jackson, the rebel flagship crew has experienced massive casualties. Ship Surgeon Henderson and her medical team will join you to render medical care to the wounded rebels."

***

When the marine transport reached the rebel flagship and docked, there was an uncanny silence amongst the 120 marines. Some of them tightly gripped their laser rifles and fiddled with the safeties. After a minute or so of this nervous behavior, Capt. Jackson spoke.

"Enough of that, men! Keep your rifle safeties on. I have heard that there are massive casualties on the rebel flagship. Be ready, though—there may be a few rebel hotheads on board. I want Platoon A to make a straight run to the flagship's bridge and secure control. Take naval Lieutenants Chu and Opel with you and assist them in any way you can. Platoons B, C, and D will sweep the other decks for resistance and survivors. Ship Surgeon Henderson and her medical team will join you. Make sure you provide cover for the medical team—we need every one of them."

When the airlock door to the flagship opened, there was a collective gasp.

Throughout the ship, there were bodies strewn everywhere. Some were obviously dead; many were moaning on the decks. A few were able to stand and were rendering aid to their comrades. None of the rebels offered any resistance.

When Marine Platoon A reached the rebel flagship bridge, it was much the same scene. Capt. Jackson walked over to a man who seemed to be wearing an admiral's uniform. He approached him and said, "I am Marine Capt. Jackson of the FNS *Lockford*. And you, sir, are my prisoner."

The rebel admiral looked dazed and confused. He had a large bandage wrapped around his head. The admiral was administering first aid to a man wearing buckskin clothing. After a few moments, the rebel admiral spoke in broken English.

"I am Vice Admiral Maximilian Johannes von Spee. Vaht are your terms of surrender?"

"I am not authorized to give you terms of surrender. That responsibility will belong to the Federation Admiralty or their designee. Who is the man you are tending to?" asked Capt. Jackson.

"This is Aristides, leader of the Rebellion," responded Admiral von Spee.

* * *

Dr. Kat Henderson was feeling overwhelmed by the sheer number of casualties on the *Brazil*. The best her small team could do was perform triage to identify the patients who did not need immediate treatment, those that had a good chance of survival if they received medical care, and those who were moribund. The patients not needing immediate treatment were loaded onto the marine transport shuttle and sent over to the *Lockford*. Patients needing immediate treatment were moved to sickbay on the *Brazil*. The rest were given morphine to ease their suffering.

Unfortunately, there never was much of a medical staff on any of the rebel ships, let alone on the *Brazil*. There were a few First Aiders on the *Brazil* who were not critically wounded. Dr. Henderson was able to put these First Aiders to work under her supervision.

As Dr. Henderson was setting up the *Brazil*'s sickbay, Captain Henry Jackson paid her a visit.

"Kat, is there anything you need from the *Lockford*? I am heading over there with my prisoners and the walking wounded from the *Brazil*."

Dr. Henderson pondered for a moment and said, "Henry, we need all the morphine you can find, bandages of all sizes, cold packs, sterile saline and I.V. kits, antiseptics, antibiotics, and blood of all types. See if you can rustle up all the First Aiders on the *Lockford* and bring them over here. We need all the help we can get."

Suddenly, one of the nurses screamed, "Doctor, we need you right now! This rebel officer is experiencing a massive brain hemorrhage!"

"Prep the surgery table, NOW! Standard surgical equipment, along with a sterile Stryker saw!"

Then Dr. Henderson turned to Henry Jackson and put her hand on top of his and said, "Thank you for all your help, Henry. Could you leave some of your marines here to act as orderlies?"

"Yes. You take care of yourself, Kat," said Henry Jackson, with tears in his eyes.

***

When the Marine Transport Shuttle returned to the *Lockford*, the walking wounded from the *Brazil* were escorted to the cafeteria for interrogation. Capt. Jackson escorted his two prisoners to the bridge to present them to Capt. Alvarez. Aristides, who was unconscious when captured, was now able to walk on his own, albeit with an unsteady gait.

"Captain, I present to you my prisoners: Vice Admiral von Spee, and Aristides, the leader of the Rebellion."

"Captain Jackson: Where is Admiral Torres?" asked Capt. Alvarez.

"We were told that he died in an accident a few days ago," responded Capt. Jackson.

"Captain, you are relieved of your prisoners," said Capt. Alvarez. Then turning to the prisoners, Alvarez said, "You men, follow me to my cabin."

Once Capt. Alvarez reached his cabin with the prisoners, he received a message on his comm from a space-time scientific officer: "Captain, the rebel fleet is now moving in our direction at top flank speed. I have contacted the Engineering Deck and requested bringing the fusion reactor up to full power. We need to get the remaining *Lockford* crew off the *Brazil* now."

"Who is still there?" asked Capt. Alvarez.

"Dr. Henderson and her staff. Lieutenants Chu and Opel, and about 30 marines."

"Send the Marine Transport Shuttle to the *Brazil* NOW!" ordered Capt. Alvarez.

"Yes, sir! We have put the remaining marines and Lt. Opel and Lt. Chu on notice to report to the *Brazil*'s shuttle bay immediately. We have a problem, though. Dr. Henderson and her staff have elected to stay on the *Brazil* so they can continue to treat the critically wounded."

"Put me through to Dr. Henderson, NOW!" ordered Capt. Alvarez.

"She is performing surgery."

"I don't care! Put me through to her, NOW!"

"Yes, sir."

"Dr. Henderson: I order that you and your staff report to the shuttle bay now for transport back to the *Lockford*," commanded Capt. Alvarez.

"Pass me the hemostat. Argh! Apply pressure to the cerebral artery, and someone—please wipe the blood off my face shield. I can't see a thing."

"Did you hear my command, Doctor?" shouted Capt. Alvarez.

"With all due respect, sir: You can go to Hell!" shouted Dr. Henderson.

"This is insubordination!"

"Aspirate the blood from the cranial space. Pass me a 21-gauge suture… Okay, now pass me gauze."

Someone in the operating room said, "Doctor, the patient's blood pressure is dropping rapidly."

"Increase IV drip of blood and saline. Prepare an adrenaline syringe, and make sure the paddles are fully charged. We have stabilized the cerebral hemorrhage; we are not going to lose this patient to cardiac arrest."

"Doctor, we have cardiac arrest!"

"Pass the paddles, NOW! Clear!"

Ka THUMP!

"Clear!"

Ka THUMP!

"Clear!"

Ka THUMP!

"We have a pulse! (Cheering)"

"Blood pressure?"

"90 over 60 and rising."

"Great. Now move this patient out of here. Sally, you keep an eye on this one. I need to operate on the next patient," said Dr. Henderson. Then turning back to her communicator, Dr. Henderson said, "Okay, Capt. Alvarez. I have a minute or two to explain our situation here."

"No need to explain. I fully understand. You know if you and your staff stay on the *Brazil*, you will be captured by the rebels," said Capt. Alvarez, as his voice began to break.

"My staff and I are fully aware. When I became a ship surgeon, I took an oath. I am committed to that oath to heal the wounded, no matter what side they are on. I gave all my staff the choice of staying on the *Brazil*, or leaving. They all elected to stay," explained Dr. Henderson.

"I understand, Doctor. Is there anyone I should notify?"

"My parents on the planet Earth, Lt. Chu, and Lt. Henry Jackson."

"Will do. It may take some time to notify your parents, with the war and everything. Godspeed, Kathryn!" said Capt. Alvarez, with tears choking out his voice.

Chapter 43

Rebellion Against the Rebellion on Space Fortress *Sagittarius A**

Cold-hearted orb that rules the night

Removes the colors from our sight

Red is grey and yellow-white

But we decide which is right

And which is an illusion

Graeme Edge

Moody Blues Band

The entire rebel fleet was chasing the light frigate, FNS *Lockford*. This action moved the rebel fleet away from the gate of the Beta Wormhole. This was a stupendous strategic error on the part of the Rebellion. Without Aristides and Admiral von Spee at the helm, the fleet was headless. When any aggregate of humans loses their leadership and there is no exceptional leadership to replace the head, the surviving aggregate becomes reactive.

This explains why the sound, conservative decision for the rebel fleet to guard the gate to the Beta Wormhole was so quickly abandoned.

The rebel fleet was so reactive that it ignored and left behind their disabled flagship *Brazil*, and put all their effort into pursuing the FNS *Lockford*. This left Dr. Kat Henderson and her medical staff marooned on the disabled *Brazil* to treat 57 critically wounded rebel sailors and marines without adequate supplies.

The space-time sensors orbiting the planet *Beyond* became aware of the rebel fleet's movement away from the Beta Wormhole in a matter of hours. At first, the Admiralty on the planet Beyond hesitated to respond to this new development. Their default assumption was that the Rebellion was laying a trap—a trap which would draw a significant portion of the Federation's 2nd Fleet through the Beta Wormhole, while the rebel fleet waited for them to exit the wormhole from some unseen location. Then the 'hidden' rebel fleet would use their concentrated firepower to destroy each Federation ship as it exited the Beta Wormhole.

The Admiralty debated amongst themselves for two days before they came to a compromise: they would only send out two fast frigates and two 74-gun ships-of-the-line—FNS *India* and FNS *Niger*. The objective of this squadron: recapture the Federation Naval Fortress *Sagittarius A**. If recapture was not possible, the squadron was to destroy the space fortress.

This four-ship squadron was commanded by Commodore Alexei Kirkoff, a seasoned veteran with a reputation for good leadership, risk-taking, and diplomacy. The squadron accelerated to full flank speed upon exiting the Beta Wormhole. They plotted a course for the space fortress, but instead of following the course set by the *Lockford* and the rebel fleet, they set their course around the opposite side of the black hole. This shielded their movements from the rebel fleet.

***

Meanwhile, the *Lockford*, with its vastly superior speed, was leading the entire rebel fleet on a wild goose chase. The fastest that the rebel fleet could muster was 0.1% the speed of light. Because of this relatively slow speed, the fleet could not take advantage of using the *Sagittarius A** black hole for a gravity assist to increase their speed. If they tried to do this, they did not have adequate escape velocity and would simply fall into the black hole's event horizon.

As the *Lockford* extended its lead on the rebel fleet, Captain Alvarez was meeting with his lieutenants on the bridge.

"We can pretty much go wherever we want. It seems a shame to waste an opportunity. I would like to use my discretion given to me in our orders to probe the possibility of taking the *FNF Sagittarius A** as a prize. What are your thoughts on this?" asked Capt. Alvarez.

His lieutenants just looked at each other. The goal that was put before them was simply absurd. Finally, Lt. Chu spoke up, "Sir, FNF *Sagittarius A** has over 100 plasma guns and nuclear missile launchers. We have 22 laser guns, which are much smaller than the fortress's plasma guns. We are clearly outgunned, and the rebels will be reluctant to abandon their prized naval possession."

"True, Lieutenant. However, we have their top admiral and their rebel leader in our possession. Our sensors indicate that the rebel fleet has abandoned their position at the gate of the Beta Wormhole. Connect me to the Space-Time Deck. They should be able to tell us the disposition of the rebel fleet, give or take 10% of their collective mass."

A few minutes later, a reply came from Dr. O'Donoghue on the Space-Time Deck.

"Near as we can tell, the mass equivalent to the entire rebel fleet has moved from the area around the Beta Wormhole to a position in the vicinity of the black hole, and possibly the space fortress."

Capt. Alvarez thought about this for a minute, then said,

"I would imagine that the Admiralty back on the planet *Beyond* is aware of this development. They may be bold and reckless and send the entire 2nd Fleet through the Beta Wormhole. However, the brass in the Admiralty are a conservative lot. I think they will only send a couple of 74-gun ships-of-the-line, and maybe a few frigates. If we assume my conservative estimate, that would be almost 150 large missiles and plasma guns, and a hundred or so lighter missiles and guns. That would even the Federation's chances of capturing— and if necessary, destroying—the FNF *Sagittarius A**. If we get to the station first, we could scout the area and test the will of the rebels to defend the space fortress. Do I have your support?"

All the officers said, "Aye-aye, Captain!"

Then Capt. Alvarez said, "Make it so." Then turning to Marine Capt. Jackson and Lt. Chu, Alvarez said, "Please join me in my cabin."

***

Five minutes later, another explosion was occurring inside Capt. Alvarez's cabin. Lt. Chu and Capt. Alvarez were arguing about the fate of Dr. Henderson on board the rebel flagship *Brazil*. Lt. Jackson looked on, trying not to become collateral damage.

"What do you mean that you had to leave Kat Henderson on the *Brazil*! What's wrong with you?" screamed Lt. Chu.

"She and her medical staff chose to stay and treat the critically wounded rebels. I tried to get her to leave, but her commitment to treat the wounded compelled her to stay," replied Captain Alvarez.

"We have to turn around and rescue them NOW!" screamed Lt. Chu.

"We can't do that, Lieutenant. We would have to plot a course right through the rebel fleet. We would be blasted to atoms before we could reach them. This discussion is academic anyway, since they are most likely prisoners of war by now."

Then there was a deadly silence between them. All three of them wanted to do the right thing for Dr. Henderson and her medical staff—but what?

Capt. Jackson took advantage of the silence to suggest a possible solution.

"Once we have completed our mission to retake the FNF *Sagittarius A**, we can try to locate the *Brazil* and then rescue Dr. Henderson and her staff."

"Capt. Jackson, this is a very large galaxy. It may take a lifetime to find them. We don't even know if they are still on board the *Brazil*," screamed Lt. Chu.

Capt. Alvarez jumped back into the discussion.

"Gentlemen, we are all officers in the Federation Navy. We need to act like officers. We can continue this discussion later after we complete our mission."

All three of them left Capt. Alvarez's cabin feeling ill at ease.

***

Meanwhile, on the FNF *Sagittarius A**, Robert Hays, Leslie Jones, and Myron Abbot plotted how to get rid of Aristides and Admiral von Spee, and how to turn the Rebellion around to get it back to its original intent of saving planet Earth from global climate change.

Robert started the discussion. "Myron, we need your wisdom. Leslie and I need you as a sounding board as well. Here is what has happened: Aristides started this rebellion back on Earth in response to the effects of global climate change. The temperature has been increasing as the result of increased carbon dioxide levels in the atmosphere. This temperature increase has resulted in the expansion of deserts, the loss of ice in the Arctic, Antarctica, and Greenland, along with a rapid rise in ocean levels. These changes have caused about a billion people to be displaced from their homes. Also, these changes have caused massive crop losses, which in turn have caused widespread food shortages to the extent that one-third of the population is undernourished and 15% of the Earth's population is at risk of starving to death."

"At any rate, Aristides, operating from a base along the Big Sur River in the Ventana Wilderness in North America, gathered quite a following of environmentally-thinking people. The Rebellion quickly spread to include hundreds of thousands of followers. Shortly after you were brought to this space fortress, the Rebellion essentially took over planet Earth. They also captured the last teleporter on Earth, and with Leslie's technical expertise, thousands of rebels were able to teleport to the mothballed star fleet. This has resulted in interstellar war between the Federation and the Rebellion."

Robert continued, "Leslie, who knew Aristides intimately, has discovered that Aristides used global climate change as a foil to become the worldwide dictator of planet Earth. He wants to capture the geoengineers and environmental scientists who are currently working to terraform the planet Beyond. Aristides wants all of these scientists to be forced to return to Earth and use their technical skills to reverse global climate change through geoengineering technologies at the expense of ceasing terraforming efforts on the planet Beyond. Aristides is using all of these issues to consolidate power. A better approach is to share these technical resources between Earth and the planet Beyond. Aristides is ruthless and has murdered and sent many to their deaths in order to gain power. Therefore, Leslie and I propose the disposal of Aristides as leader and to forge an alliance between Earth and the planet Beyond to solve the challenges of terraforming an alien planet and reversing global climate change on Earth," concluded Robert.

"How do you propose disposing of Aristides as the leader of the Rebellion?" asked Myron.

Leslie answered, "Aristides is not on the space fortress now. He has left me in command of the space fortress during his absence. Aristides has relocated to the rebel fleet at the gate of the Beta Wormhole. His intention is to use the rebel fleet, under the command of Admiral von Spee, to invade the planet Beyond. As we understand it, a stalemate has developed at the wormhole gate."

Robert was puzzled regarding the replacement of Torres as the admiral of the rebel fleet, so he asked, "What happened to Admiral Torres? I thought he was in charge of the rebel fleet?"

"I heard a rumor that Admiral Torres has been killed by means of the black hole event horizon," replied Leslie.

When she had finished saying this, her communicator beeped.

"Dr. Jones, this is Lt. Williams on the Communication Deck. We have just received a message from the rebel fleet that a Federation light frigate just exited the Beta Wormhole and is heading to the far side of the black hole and may be a threat to the space fortress. I recommend putting the space fortress on high alert."

"I am in consultation with Dr. Hays and Dr. Abbot right now. I will get back to you shortly."

Returning to her conversation with Robert and Myron, Leslie continued, "Okay, now what do I do? If I do nothing, the space fortress crew is likely to space me. If I put the fortress on high alert and we blast the Federation frigate, I am complicit with the state of war that exists between our two planets."

"There is a third way, Dr. Jones—pray for wisdom," answered Myron.

Then Robert spoke up. "May I add Jesus's own words that He used in the Sermon on the Mount: 'Blessed are the peacemakers, for they shall be called the sons of God.'"

The three of them prayed for about 10 minutes. When they had finished, Leslie looked up into Myron and Robert's eyes and said, "The time to start the counter-revolution and start down the road to peace is now. Let's proceed courageously!"

She then unmuted her communicator and said, "Lt. Williams, we will not place this space fortress on high alert, and we will not open fire on the Federation frigate if it approaches the fortress. If the frigate approaches the space fortress, send them this message: 'Dr. Leslie Jones, acting commander of the Rebel Space Fortress *Sagittarius A**, wishes to enter negotiations with representatives of the Federation on sharing technical resources that are being used to terraform the planet Beyond for the purpose of reversing the effects of global climate change on Earth.'"

"Are you crazy?" screamed Lt. Williams. "What would Aristides say to this?" Then there was someone in the background talking to Lt. Williams for a minute or so. Then Lt. Williams returned to the comm.

"We just received another message from the rebel fleet… Understood… Okay… Dr. Jones, we have an update on the Federation frigate. It's no longer in our area of space, but it rapidly swung around the black hole toward the rebel fleet… Please confirm… Understood… This is crazy. The frigate has engaged the rebel fleet flagship *Brazil*. Heavy casualties reported on the flagship. The flagship has been dragged away from the rebel fleet by some unknown force and has been boarded by marines from the Federation frigate… Hold on, there is another message coming through… Aristides and Admiral von Spee have been captured by Federation marines."

"If Federation ships approach this space fortress, send them the message I told you regarding negotiations. Failure to do so could result in the destruction of this space fortress and the entire crew. Understood?" asked Dr. Jones.

After a long pause, the voice on the other end of the communicator said, "Copy that, Dr. Jones."

***

When the FNS *Lockford* returned to the FNF *Sagittarius A**, it was accompanied by two Federation 74-gun ships-of-the-line and three Federation frigates. The five Federation ships had rendezvoused near the space fortress after communication contact was established between the *Lockford* and the Federation squadron.

Far behind this squadron was the entire rebel fleet. Since the rebel ships in this previously mothballed fleet were quite old and obsolete, the rebel fleet was too slow and dropping further behind the Federation squadron. The navigation officer on the *Lockford* estimated that it would take a week for the rebel fleet to catch up with them.

Alexei Kirkoff, Commodore of the Federation Squadron, headed the delegation to the space fortress. Both delegations met in the space fortress conference room. Leslie Jones, Robert Hays, Myron Abbot, and Jennifer Bo came into the room unarmed, while Commodore Kirkoff and his staff came into the room fully armed with laser pistols and were escorted by two marines armed with menacing laser rifles.

Leslie Jones started the meeting. "Commodore Kirkoff, welcome aboard. Jennifer Bo will be keeping the meeting minutes. First, We present to you the Federation Naval Fortress *Sagittarius A**. We request that its rebel crew be given parole with the proviso that they surrender their arms and sign an oath not to rebel against the Federation."

"What do you want in return?" asked the Commodore.

"We request that all resources being used to terraform the planet *Beyond* be shared with the people of planet Earth to reverse the effects of global climate change," answered Dr. Jones.

In response to Dr. Jones, Commodore Kirkoff said, "I am not authorized to agree to these terms. However, you have shown goodwill in surrendering this fortress, so I will parole you, Jennifer Bo, Dr. Hays, and the rebel crew on this space fortress. I will take your request regarding sharing terraforming technologies with planet Earth back to the Federation Admiralty and to President Nelson. You need to remember, however, that there still exists a state of war between Earth and the planet *Beyond*. In fact, the rebel fleet is one week behind us. Even if our ships are faster and more modern than the rebel fleet, the rebel ships outnumber the squadron's guns and missiles by 10 to 1. Having Aristides and

Admiral von Spee in our custody is good, but there can be no peace until the entire rebel fleet surrenders."

Commodore Kirkoff paused for a moment, then added, "One other consideration: We cannot let this space fortress fall back into the hands of the Rebellion again, since it guards both the Alpha and Beta Wormholes and possesses time-travel capabilities."

At this point, Dr. Hays spoke up. "Sir, I have the same concern about this space fortress falling into the hands of the Rebellion. Dr. Jones, Myron Abbot, and I therefore recommend that the FNF *Sagittarius A** be put into a degrading orbit that will ultimately cause the space fortress to cross the black hole's event horizon. I can start this process immediately, at your authorization, and the space fortress will cease to exist in three days."

The Commodore thought about this proposal for a couple of minutes, then said, "The main purpose of this space fortress, along with time-travel capabilities, is to guard the gates to the Alpha and Beta Wormholes. If the entire Federation 2nd Fleet were to deploy through the Beta Wormhole, we could easily destroy the obsolete rebel fleet without the aid of this space fortress. Hmmm. Make it so, Dr. Hays!"

"Thank you, sir. We should begin evacuation of the space fortress immediately," responded Robert Hays.

***

Note from the Oracle of the Federation:

Two days later, gravitational waves from the black hole ripped FNF Sagittarius A to shreds. The next day, 1,000,000 metric tonnes of debris that was once the most powerful weapon ever devised by* *mankind crossed the event horizon of the black hole, Sagittarius A*. It was crushed to a point of singularity. The firepower of this fortress was second to none. However, the power of this space fortress to control time itself was terrible beyond all belief. This terrible technology has now been relegated to a prison where time no longer has any meaning—buried at the heart of our galaxy.*

J. Gerard

Oracle of the Federation

Chapter 44

Federation Squadron Returns to the Planet Beyond, After a Detour

If you smile at me

You know I will understand

'Cause that is something everybody everywhere does

In the same language

Well I can see by your coat, my friend

That you're from the other side

There's just one thing I got to know

Can you tell me please who won?

David Crosby, Paul Kantner, and Stephen Stills

Robert, Myron, Jennifer Bo, and Leslie, as well as prisoners Admiral von Spee and Aristides, boarded the FNS *India*. The paroled rebels were loaded on the FNS *Niger*. Commodore Kirkoff thought it would be wise to keep Aristides and the paroled rebels on separate ships. With their mission fulfilled—which included the destruction of the Federation Naval Fortress, *Sagittarius A**, and the capture of the rebellion's leadership—they started their long trip back.

They encountered a detour on the way, however…

***

Meanwhile, Dr. Henderson and her medical staff were working around the clock on the rebel flagship *Brazil*.

"Dr. Henderson, the patient you operated on last week has regained consciousness," said the surgical nurse.

Dr. Henderson was taking a short nap when the surgical nurse spoke to her. "Which one? I operated on nine patients last week," the doctor responded.

"The officer who had a cerebral hemorrhage."

"Oh, that one," responded Dr. Henderson as she rubbed the sleep from her eyes. "What do his vitals look like?"

"His blood pressure is a little low—105/60. His pulse is a little fast at 90 per minute," answered the surgical nurse.

"Okay, I'll check up on him," responded the bleary-eyed doctor.

Kat Henderson slipped into her lab coat but quickly took it off and sent it down the laundry chute. *Too bloody,* she thought. She quickly replaced the lab coat with a clean one and climbed up the ladder to gain access to the recovery room.

She was surprised to see the recovering officer sitting up in bed reading a book. The book had Chinese characters all over it.

"What are you reading?" asked Dr. Henderson.

"Sayings of Buddha," replied the rebel officer.

"Are you Buddhist?"

"Yes. Are you a Christian?"

"No, but I am open to the teachings of Christ. How are you feeling today, Mr. Ah, ah… I don't know your name," replied Dr. Henderson.

"I am Hung Ching, captain of the 74-gun *Brazil*. Who are you?"

"I am Dr. Henderson, ship surgeon, FNS *Lockford*."

"You are too young to be a doctor…" Capt. Ching paused for a moment, then continued, "Was it the *Lockford* that gave us such a thrashing? How did you get on the *Brazil*?"

"I came over with a company of marines," said Dr. Henderson.

"So, I am now a prisoner of war? I am ashamed that a 74-gun ship-of-the-line was defeated by a mere light frigate."

"No, you are not a prisoner, Capt. Ching. The marines went back to the *Lockford*, which moved off at full speed to evade capture by the rebel fleet."

"Why did you stay on the *Brazil*, Doctor?" asked a puzzled Capt. Ching.

"To provide medical treatment to you and your crew," answered Dr. Henderson.

"That is very altruistic of you. How is my crew doing?"

"About half of them that were not seriously wounded were transported to the *Lockford*. The rest were too seriously wounded for transport. My staff and I elected to stay here to take care of them."

"How many of my crew were killed?" asked Capt. Ching.

"We were able to save most of the crew who remained behind. You need to get some rest," said Dr. Henderson.

"You know, I have been asking for a ship surgeon and nurses ever since I took command of the *Brazil*. Can you imagine that? A 74-gun ship-of-the-line on active duty without a medical staff. That is criminal. I am ashamed that medical treatment had to come from our enemy."

"You take it easy. We almost lost you last week. You went into cardiac arrest…"

"That's why I have these burn marks on my chest! You saved my life, Doctor!" exclaimed Capt. Ching.

There was silence between them for a few minutes as Dr. Henderson checked his vitals. Then Capt. Ching continued, "I was becoming disillusioned with the Rebellion—bad leadership, inadequate crews, and supplies. The rebel fleet was not well-led." Then Captain Ching lowered his head on his pillow and began to weep. "I am ashamed of myself, and I am fighting for the wrong cause."

Suddenly, he raised himself up in his bed, looked straight into the eyes of Dr. Henderson, and said, "Dr. Henderson! I present myself as your prisoner, and my ship, the *Brazil*, as a prize."

"I don't think there has been a time in history when a captain surrendered his ship and crew to a ship's surgeon," said Dr. Henderson, smiling.

They both started to laugh.

***

It was Lt. Chu's turn to have watch on the bridge of the *Lockford*. Things were quiet, with most of the crew asleep. Lt. Chu was daydreaming when his comm broke into his reverie.

"Lieutenant, this is the Space-Time Deck. We are picking up a mass that is identical to a 74-gun ship-of-the-line at coordinates 12.714 - 180.972 - 87.375. It could be the rebel flagship *Brazil*."

"Are you sure?" asked Lt. Chu.

"Quite sure," responded the space-time scientist.

"I will notify the captain at once."

Ming changed channels on the comm to reach Capt. Alvarez. "Captain!"

"Ugh, who's that? Wait a minute… This is the captain. Speak!"

"Sorry to wake you, sir. This is Lt. Chu. Space-Time Deck has picked up the rebel flagship *Brazil*. Should I set a course for her?"

"By all means, but approach the *Brazil* slowly. Remember, she may be slow, but she has over twice our firepower. I will be on the bridge shortly," responded Capt. Alvarez as he slipped into his uniform.

"Aye, aye, sir. Wait a minute, sir. We are receiving a subspace communication… It seems to be a distress signal from the *Brazil*," said Lt. Chu.

"Is the *Brazil* moving?" inquired the captain.

"No, sir. She is just sitting there," responded Lt. Chu.

"Could be a trick. I'm on my way up now."

Capt. Alvarez climbed the ladder from the cabin deck to the bridge. When he opened the hatch, he floated onto the bridge, and Lt. Chu beckoned to him.

"Captain on the Bridge!" shouted Lt. Chu.

"Captain, the *Brazil*'s fusion propulsion system is not operational, but their life support systems are fully functional. Sensors report life on board."

"Lt. Chu, notify Capt. Jackson to mobilize his marine company and order him to man the transport and prepare to board the *Brazil*.

"Communications Officer: Get me on the comm and reach out to the *Brazil* on all hailing frequencies."

"We are connected, sir," replied the Communications Officer.

"This is Capt. Alvarez of the Federation Frigate *Lockford* to the *Brazil*. What are your intentions?"

Buzz crack. "This is Capt. Hung Ching of the 74-gun *Brazil*. Our intentions are to surrender and present the *Brazil* as a prize… *muted voices in the background...* Is Lt. Chu on the bridge?"

"Lt. Chu, you have the comm," said Capt. Alvarez as he turned to Lt. Chu.

Suddenly a familiar female voice came on the comm, "Ming, is that you?"

"Kat, you are alive! Uh… are you okay?" shouted Lt. Chu.

"I'm a little sleep-deprived, but yeah, I'm fine," said Kat Henderson, after a prolonged yawn.

There was an awkward moment. Neither Kat nor Ming knew what to say.

Finally, Ming broke the silence. "Marry me, Kat!"

"What?"

"You know, Capt. Alvarez could marry us right now."

"Ming, don't be absurd! I like you, and you are a fine young man, and I am very fond of you, but I don't love you enough to… marry you!" said Kat Henderson in total amazement.

Captain Alvarez, who was still in the weightless part of the bridge, was laughing and turning somersaults.

"Ming, I order you to go over to the *Brazil* on the marine transport and bring the ship surgeon back to the *Lockford*. Now!"

***

By now, the rebel fleet was almost two weeks behind the Federation squadron when it reached the gate to the Beta Wormhole. Passage through the wormhole was uneventful. They exited the wormhole on the far side of the moon that orbited around the planet Beyond.

In the *Lockford* galley, Dr. Henderson, Lt. Chu, and Capt. Jackson sat around a table enjoying what passed for bad coffee.

"Hey, the two of you have been staring at each other for the last 10 minutes and haven't spoken a word. You look kind of mad to me. Do I need to leave so the two of you can speak in private?" asked Capt. Jackson, who was looking both ways to make sure no one was listening.

"Please leave, and close the hatch behind you," responded Kat Henderson.

When the hatch clinked shut, and Kat and Ming were all alone, Kat spoke first. "Don't look so sad, Ming. I really do like you. You're smart, funny in your own autistic way, and handsome. I would like to get to know you better before I can commit to a relationship with you. Also, we are both in the Federation Navy, and we are still at war with the Rebellion. For now, we are still stationed on the same frigate, but that could change at any time. Let's take advantage of that time and get to know each other better. Does that seem reasonable?"

"It sounds reasonable, but I still don't like it," responded the grumpy lieutenant.

"Let's enjoy a marvelous friendship for now, okay?" pleaded Kat.

"I can agree to that," said Ming as he reached across the table and held Kat's hand.

Just then, Ming's comm interrupted their conversation.

"Lt. Chu, you are to be transported to the planet Beyond. Please report to the shuttle deck… and if Dr. Henderson is with you, bring her along," ordered First Officer Shah.

"Aye, aye, Commander," responded Lt. Chu.

Chapter 45

Rebel leaders are condemned, then befriended

And though this world, with devils filled,

Should threaten to undo us,

We will not fear, for God hath willed

His truth to triumph through us:

The Prince of Darkness grim,

We tremble not for him;

His rage we can endure,

For lo! his doom is sure,

One little word shall fell him

Martin Luther

The courtroom was deathly quiet as the verdicts were given.

"Has the jury reached a verdict?" asked the Judge.

"Yes, Your Honor," replied the Jury Foreman.

"What is your verdict for Aristides?"

"The jury finds him guilty of sedition and leading an armed rebellion against the Federation. The jury also finds him guilty of war crimes against prisoners of war."

"What is your verdict for Admiral von Spee?" asked the Judge.

"Guilty of leading an armed conflict against the Federation, with special circumstances."

"What are those special circumstances?" asked the Judge.

"He was the admiral of the rebel fleet for only a limited time. There is also evidence that his brain may have been altered by the Rebellion, which may have hampered his better judgment," replied the Jury Foreman.

"Thank you for your civic duty, Jury. You are now dismissed." With that, the Judge brought down his gavel.

After the jury had left the courtroom, the Judge asked both prisoners to rise to receive sentencing. The Judge first turned to Aristides and asked, "Aristides, do you have anything to say before you are sentenced?"

Aristides pulled a piece of paper from his pocket and read, "Your Honor, I led the Rebellion against the Federation to acquire the technology and expertise necessary to reverse the effects of global climate change and the effects it has on billions of people on planet Earth. I find it ironic that I am on trial. The leaders of the Federation and preceding governments should be on trial. It is their policies that have brought the Earth to the precipice of destruction. If I am condemned to execution, I will go willingly as a martyr of the cause to restore Earth and save the lives of billions of humans."

"Aristides, I could condemn you to death for your crimes," said the Judge. "However, the court wishes to be merciful. It therefore condemns you to lifelong banishment to the Forbidden Continent.

You will be escorted out of this court and will be transported to the Forbidden Continent forthwith."

Then the Judge turned to Admiral von Spee and asked, "Admiral von Spee, do you have anything to say before you are sentenced?"

"Only vat my good name vould be cleared. I confess… I made some very bad choices… some of the choices vere influenced by ah… alteration of my brain. I throw myself on de mercy of this… court," said von Spee in broken English as he bowed to the Judge.

The Judge thought about this for a minute or so, then pronounced the admiral's sentence.

"I believe you are sincere, Admiral. You too will be banished to the Forbidden Continent forthwith. However, the court will be merciful. Your banishment will be for only a 6-month period. After 6 months, you will be placed on paroled supervision for an additional two years."

"Thank you, Your Honor!" shouted von Spee as he snapped to attention and saluted the Judge.

"Court dismissed!" said the Judge as he brought the gavel down.

Then the prisoners were escorted to the shuttlecraft to be taken to the Forbidden Continent.

***

Once on the shuttle, the two prisoners sat back and relaxed. Von Spee was not in the mood to talk, so Aristides decided to talk to the young lieutenant who was piloting the shuttle to pass the time.

"It looks like the admiral and I will have a whole continent to conquer. Are there any women there?"

The lieutenant simply answered, "No."

"No women?" replied an astonished Aristides.

"There are no human women there."

"What is on the Forbidden Continent?" asked Aristides.

The lieutenant remained silent.

"Do they have wildlife?" asked Aristides.

"All kinds of wildlife. The wildlife makes the Forbidden Continent real interesting," answered the lieutenant.

"Interesting? In what ways?" asked the puzzled Aristides.

"You will have to wait and see. Look out your window, you can see your new home coming up."

"It looks like a tropical rainforest. Are there any dangerous animals there?" asked Aristides.

"Just one species," replied the lieutenant.

"If there is just one dangerous species, we should be able to avoid it, right?"

"Wrong," responded the lieutenant.

"Wrong, what?" asked Aristides.

"You can't avoid it. It will find you," responded the lieutenant in a sarcastic tone.

"Is there a place on the continent, like a fort or blockhouse we can stay in where we will be safe?" asked Aristides.

"There is an underground bunker where we will be landing. However, you will need to go above ground to find food and water. Keep your eyes on the sky above you. This apex predator flies fast and silently. Run like crazy if you see the predator."

"The predator flies? If it flies, it can't be too big, right?" asked Aristides.

"Wrong. It's real big."

"You're just trying to scare us. Come on, level with me!" responded Aristides.

The young lieutenant was silent for a few minutes, then he spoke.

"You are going to be hunted constantly. I have not seen this predator myself, but a friend of mine has. It has a 60-meter wingspan. Its body is 20 meters long from head to tail. It spits sticky fireballs."

"You're making this up to scare us," said Aristides, nervously.

"My friend saw this predator kill a terraforming biologist."

"Are you leaving any weapons for us?" inquired Aristides.

"Yes. Two high-powered laser rifles. We will be dropping power packs to you every week. I suggest you do some target practice first thing. If the predator attacks you, you will only have time for one shot. Watch out, they hunt in packs. As I understand it, they can communicate with each other in their own language."

"Does this predator have a name?"

"Yes. Its name is the Fiery Dragon," responded the lieutenant.

The shuttle reached a clearing in the forest near a wetland. On the ground near where the shuttle landed was a large, heavy hatch that led to a set of stairs. The young lieutenant took them down the stairs and showed them their bunks, a small kitchen and bathroom, a two-way radio, and of course, their two laser rifles.

"Hey! There's no food or water here!" shouted Aristides.

"What did you expect, a five-star hotel? You must go outside to get your food and water. Radio us sometime. We would love to hear how you are doing," said the smiling lieutenant.

"You mentioned that the dragons can communicate with each other. Have humans tried to communicate with the dragons?" asked Aristides.

"Yes. The friend I told you about communicated with the dragons. They can communicate through pictograms. My friend was able to make out a few words that the dragons used. Here, let me write these down for you:

INESTERINE: Human(s)

GOGA: Go

GOG: Stay"

Then the lieutenant said, "I need to go now. Stay in touch."

***

When Myron, Leslie, Jennifer, and Robert returned to the planet Beyond, they were invited to a meeting with President Nelson and his advisors at the Presidential Palace. Also in attendance were the scientists who oversaw the terraforming efforts on the planet Beyond.

The meeting began with the president making an opening statement:

"This meeting is being convened at the request of Dr. Leslie Jones. We continue to be at war with the rebels. Sometimes, in the fog of war, the really important issues are never discussed. People just keep killing each other because they want to win the war.

However, wars that are fought solely just to win produce no winners at all.

"Dr. Jones has clearly stated what the real issue is behind this armed conflict. It's about who gets to use the resources and skills to save their world for future generations. Which world will win the resources and skills? Will it be the planet Earth, or will it be the planet Beyond? I submit to you that these resources and skills can be mutually shared by all parties. Dr. Jones will discuss the strategy to bring this to fruition."

Leslie Jones then stood up and said, "Thank you, Mr. President, advisors, and fellow scientists. As you know, the terraforming effort on the Beyond is progressing rapidly. When humans first came to the Beyond, atmospheric carbon dioxide levels were at 10%. Since terraforming efforts began, current carbon dioxide levels have been reduced to less than one percent. Coinciding with this reduction of carbon dioxide is a reduction of the average temperature from 34 degrees C to 25 degrees C. Last year, for the first time, snow has fallen in the polar regions. Many of the bioengineering technologies could be transferred to planet Earth to reduce atmospheric carbon dioxide and bring about a concurrent reduction in global temperature.

"What I propose is that a scientific task force be formed and composed of terraforming experts. This slide shows the goals of the task force:

Identify and implement terraforming technologies that can be used to reduce atmospheric carbon dioxide and other greenhouse gases on Earth.

Identify and implement technologies that, once and for all, replace the use of fossil fuels.

Identify and implement means by which the cryosphere on Earth can be reconstituted. This would include re-establishment of the ice fields of Antarctica and Greenland, and the re-establishment of the sea ice on the Arctic Ocean.

Identify and implement adaptation strategies, such as seawalls to contain rising sea levels and developing crops that can survive elevated temperatures associated with climate change, that enable people to thrive in the likely event that greenhouse gases cannot be brought back to pre-industrial levels.

The first three goals are to be given the highest priority, since these goals strike at the root causes of global climate change."

After Dr. Jones finished, one of President Nelson's advisors rose to ask a question.

"How can we work with planet Earth if we are still in a state of war with Earth? I understand that Aristides, the rebel leader, and Maximillian von Spee, admiral of the rebel space fleet, are incarcerated on the Forbidden Continent. However, the rebel fleet is still at large in the vicinity of the black hole. Their presence in this area will impact our ability to traverse the space between the Alpha and Beta Wormholes. Will the rebel fleet effectively block the transfer of technologies between the planet Beyond and planet Earth?"

President Nelson rose to answer this concern.

"That is a very good question. There are two strategies that will be used to mitigate the problem of the rebel fleet. First, we are going to reach out to Aristides and Admiral von Spee to seek their cooperation. If they agree to cooperate by having the rebel fleet stand down and have their ships de-weaponized, the rebel fleet will no longer be an issue. This strategy has an obvious risk — that Aristides cannot be trusted.

"Second is to have the Federation 2nd Fleet pursue the rebel fleet until it is destroyed. If we can open the Alpha Wormhole gate, we will be able to bring the Federation 1st Fleet through. The combined fleets could then rapidly destroy the rebel fleet. As you know, the 1st Fleet is currently in the vicinity of Earth and cannot join the battle until the Alpha Wormhole is secured by the Federation."

One of the terraforming scientists then rose to ask another question.

"How soon should this scientific task force meet?"

"As soon as possible!" said Doctors Jones, Abbot, and Hays in unison.

***

"Hey, that was quite a reception that the Admiralty threw for us. I ate so much that I can hardly get into my uniform!" said Lt. Chu, as he pointed at his stomach.

"Yeah, look at you: a fat guy with a Distinguished Naval Cross on his chest!" said Capt. Jackson.

"You should talk. I ate too much and you drank too much. I would rather be fat than drunk in front of Kat."

Capt. Jackson and Lt. Chu were stumbling to their quarters. Dr. Henderson followed them at a distance, making sure they didn't get lost and that they arrived at their quarters in one piece.

When they reached their quarters, Kat said, "I'll see you guys tomorrow at the briefing at 0800. Be there and look sharp!"

Kat then walked to her quarters on the other side of the Admiralty. While she walked, she saw two familiar faces across the quad.

"Mr. President! Heinrich! What are you doing out at this late hour?" shouted Dr. Henderson.

The two familiar faces peered at her in the darkness. She overheard Heinrich say, "That's Kathryn Henderson. She is now the ship surgeon on the frigate *Lockford*."

"We were meeting with Commodore Kirkoff. I hear that congratulations are warranted," the president said while walking toward her. "I hear that the captain of the rebel flagship surrendered to you and presented his ship and crew to you! Is that true?" shouted President Nelson, as he and Heinrich crossed the quad to her.

"Ah… yes, but it's a little more complicated than that," demurred Dr. Henderson.

"Please let Heinrich and me escort you back to your quarters. I have something that I need to discuss with you," said the president in an excited voice.

"Sure! I have never been escorted by a president before."

As they walked, the president said, "I have confirmed that my wife disappeared at the same time that the rest of the Christians disappeared. I have been reading her old Bible and found this passage in 2 Thessalonians, the fourth chapter:

'For this we declare to you by a word from the Lord, that we who are alive, who are left until the coming of the Lord, will not precede those who have fallen asleep. For the Lord himself will descend from heaven with a cry of command, with the voice of an archangel, and with the sound of the trumpet of God. And the dead in Christ will rise first. Then we who are alive, who are left, will be caught up together with them in the clouds to meet the Lord in the air, and so we will always be with the Lord. Therefore encourage one another with these words.'

"It was Jesus who took Marina and the other Christians to be with Him! Pretty exciting! Now that I am a Christian too, I know that I will see her again. Oh, by the way, my friend Heinrich has also placed his trust in Jesus's work on the cross."

Then Heinrich spoke, "We both think highly of you, Dr. Henderson. We would be thrilled if you placed your trust in Jesus!"

"Let me think on it. It's been a long day and I am tired," responded Dr. Henderson. "However, I will give it serious thought. Thank you for walking with me to my quarters. I hope to see you again."

***

The next morning, after a very uncomfortable sleep, Aristides and von Spee looked at each other and realized if they were going to have breakfast, they would need to go above ground and get it themselves.

"Aristides, how you say, propose, ja? To get fud without us becoming fud for ze dragons?" asked von Spee.

"Von Spee, I think we are looking at this the wrong way. Instead of us cowering from the dragons, maybe we should look for an opportunity to communicate with them."

"Okay, vot sounds gut, ja. How do ve initiate this communication?" asked a puzzled von Spee.

"Let's go outside in the meadow and draw a large pictogram. That shuttle lieutenant did tell us that the dragons communicated with humans using pictograms. Maybe we should do the same thing," responded Aristides.

"Great, vot do we do if ze dragons show up before ve complete ze pictur?" asked von Spee, with a worried look on his face.

"We lay down our laser rifles, point to ourselves, and say, 'Inesterine gog,' which means 'humans stay.' Then again, maybe the first pictogram we draw should be of two humans laying their lasers down and draw an unharmed dragon opposite the humans. What do you think, von Spee?"

"Hmm. I do not know if dat vil work. Still, might be vorth a try," replied a reticent von Spee.

"Okay, let's go! We will need to be quick with the pictograms," exclaimed Aristides.

Once outside, Aristides worked quickly to complete the first pictogram. They found a bare patch of ground, and with the butts of their rifles, they drew a pictogram of two humans laying down their weapons before an unharmed dragon. Then they started drawing the second pictogram, which involved two humans in a jail cell, and a dragon freeing the humans. This is as far as they got when the first dragon appeared.

At first, they heard a loud screech. Then they both clearly heard "Inesterine!" They looked in the direction of the sound and saw a dragon approaching from a couple of kilometers away, and approaching rapidly. A second dragon appeared from the opposite direction. It came to roost in a giant tree about one kilometer away.

The first dragon flew silently into the meadow and landed 20 meters away from Aristides and von Spee. At first, the dragon threw its head back to its tail, like it was getting ready to strike and eat the two of them.

Both Aristides and von Spee carefully laid their laser rifles down in front of the dragon. Then Aristides said in a loud voice, "Inesterine gog!"

The dragon just cocked its head. Then slowly, the dragon scanned the ground until its gaze came to the first pictogram. It hopped on its hind legs over to the pictogram and examined it carefully. Then the dragon spoke:

"Inesterine raha?"

Aristides pointed at himself and said, "Inesterine!" and then he said, "Raha?" and shrugged his shoulder and put a quizzical expression on his face.

The dragon found a bare patch of ground and drew with its wing finger two pictograms. The first one was a human standing near a dragon with a line separating the two. When the dragon finished the first pictogram, the dragon said, "Inesterine rog!"

Then the dragon drew a second pictogram of a man and a dragon, with no line separating them. Then the dragon said, "Inesterine raha!"

Aristides looked over at von Spee and said, "I think the dragon is asking us if we are their friends or enemies. Let's tell them, 'Raha,' which is 'friend' in their language."

Aristides and von Spee shouted in unison, "Inesterine raha!"

The dragon in front of them moved back two steps and began to screech, "Inesterine raha, Inesterine raha!" Suddenly, the second dragon began to screech. The sound level of the two dragons was so deafening that Aristides and von Spee had to cover their ears. Then three more dragons flew overhead and landed in trees that ringed the meadow and began to screech, "Inesterine raha!"

This deafening chorus went on for 30 minutes before it ceased. Then the first dragon drew more pictograms on a bare patch of ground. The first one showed a human holding a rifle and a dead dragon on the ground. The second pictogram showed a human with a rifle shooting the human who had killed the dragon. The dragon then said, "Inesterine raha gog!"

Aristides looked over at von Spee and asked, "What do you think the dragon is trying to say?"

"I sink he is asking us to join vith them in killing humans who are killing the dragons," replied von Spee.

Aristides and von Spee shouted in unison, "Inesterine raha gog!"

This set off another deafening dragon chorus that went on for 30 minutes. When this deafening chorus ceased, the first two dragons approached Aristides and von Spee. The dragons then got on their bellies and with one wing finger pointed at their backs.

"I sink they vant us to get on deir backs and take a trip vith them. Do you sink that is a goot idea?" asked von Spee.

"I think it will be impolite if we turned them down. They may be our friends and allies against the Federation," whispered Aristides.

Chapter 46

Rebel Fleet Comes to the Rescue

The meeting was total chaos. It was a conference room full of rebel captains with no leaders. Finally, one of the captains of a 74-gun ship-of-the-line took off one of his shoes and slammed it on the table several times.

"Ladies and gentlemen. We are getting nowhere. We need to find Aristides and Admiral von Spee and bring them back to this fleet. I have a plan that should work," yelled the captain.

The room fell silent. The only sound that could be heard was the ancient fusion engines on the obsolete ship-of-the-line and the breathing of rebel fleet captains.

"What's your plan, Captain DeVolmer?" asked one of the captains.

"The scientists on my Space-Time Deck have informed me that a squadron of Federation ships is just outside the Beta Wormhole gate. Let's select the fastest 74-gun ship-of-the-line and the fastest frigate. This small squadron will move toward the Beta Wormhole gate and stop just short of the gate to show a 'flag of truce.' When we make communication contact with the Federation fleet, we tell them that the two rebel ships would like to discuss terms of surrender.

The commander of the Federation fleet will suspect a trap. So, he or she will deploy a small, fast frigate to investigate. I am sure that any Federation frigate captain would jump at the opportunity to receive the surrender of two rebel ships.

We allow the Federation marines from their frigate to board our 74-gun ship. Once on board our ship, we ambush their marines and neutralize them. Our marines then will put on their uniforms. These 'disguised' marines will escort one of our captains back to the Federation frigate.

Once our marines, disguised as their marines, are on their ship, they will take over the frigate while our captain and their captain are discussing terms of surrender. Our captain will produce a concealed weapon and coerce the Federation captain to tell his fleet that his frigate will be escorting our two ships through the Beta Wormhole gate as prizes of war.

As I understand it, all Federation naval captains have the security codes for passing through the Beta Wormhole gate. Once we are inside the wormhole, we can use our unorthodox interrogation methods on the Federation captain to find the location of Aristides and Admiral von Spee."

"Unorthodox interrogation methods? Do you mean torture?" replied one of the captains in the room.

This reply brought a roar of laughter. After the commotion settled down, all the rebel captains looked at each other. Finally, one of the captains in the room said, "I think Capt. DeVolmer's idea is a good one!"

Everyone in the room yelled a hearty vote of agreement.

"Since this was my idea, I will be the captain of the 74-gun ship-of-the-line," said Capt. DeVolmer.

***

It took some time for the two rebel ships to approach the Beta Wormhole gate. Once they approached the gate, the Federation fleet hailed the rebel ships.

"You are not authorized to be in this area of space. Stop your ships and state your intentions. Any aggressive move on your part will be met with lethal force," commanded the Federation squadron commodore.

When Capt. DeVolmer heard the warning, he whispered to his first officer, "Touchy lot, aren't they?"

Then DeVolmer spoke to the Federation commodore, "I am Capt. DeVolmer of the rebel fleet. I wish to defect to the Federation and seek asylum. I have sensitive information regarding the disposition of the rebel fleet that has high strategic value for the Federation. Please send a platoon of marines over to my flagship, the 74-gun *Peru*, and have them escort me to a ship of your choosing."

There was a 10-minute pause in the Federation response. Then the Federation squadron commodore communicated back, "We are sending the light frigate FNS *Buenos Aires* to your flagship. The detachment of marines should be at your flagship in 20 minutes. You are to report to Capt. Horrocks and turn command of your squadron over to him."

After receiving this invitation to board the FNS *Buenos Aires*, Capt. DeVolmer spoke to his marine commander, "I want you to make sure that you give a warm welcome to our guests. I want you to do the job quickly and do it right. Kill their marine commander first thing so he cannot communicate back to the Federation frigate about the ambush."

The ambush came off just as Capt. DeVolmer had hoped. The uniforms were quickly cleaned of blood and were put on the rebel marines. When they returned to the Federation frigate, no one suspected that anything was amiss. The marines escorted Capt. DeVolmer to the Federation captain's cabin for the negotiations. Then the disguised marines went straight to the FNS *Buenos Aires* bridge and immediately took command of the vessel.

Meanwhile, in Capt. Horrocks' cabin, Capt. DeVolmer was enjoying a drink with the young frigate captain and sharing stories of their exploits in space. Suddenly, Capt. DeVolmer produced a laser pistol from his tunic.

"Hold it right there, Captain Horrocks," said Capt. DeVolmer. "One false move and I will reduce you to atoms. Stand up and hold your hands where I can see them. That's better. Okay, we can make this easy, or we can make this hard: give me the security code for the Beta Wormhole gate."

"They are in the wall safe, behind that picture over there," responded Capt. Horrocks.

"Open it."

When Capt. Horrocks reached the safe, Capt. DeVolmer stood next to him with his pistol pressed against his head. At that moment, the frigate began to move.

"Oh! Your frigate is starting to move," said Capt. DeVolmer in a patronizing voice. "That means that your communication officer has communicated to your fleet commander that this frigate is escorting my two ships through the Beta Wormhole gate as prizes of war. Did you give that command? No. I didn't think so. I suspect that one of my marines has a pistol to your communication officer's head. Oh, I know about the two of you. One of my marines saw a picture of you two at her station. It would be a shame to blow her head off. So, let's make our passage through the Beta Wormhole a pleasant one so no one gets hurt."

***

Aristides and Admiral von Spee spent a week with their new friends learning dragon-speak. Finally, they were allowed to return to their underground bunker.

"It's gute to be back to our bunks! Sleeping on the ground vith all that dragon shouting kept me from sleeping," said Admiral von Spee.

"Hey, von Spee. What do you think of the dragon's leader?" asked Aristides. "You know, the one with seven heads. He kind of creeped me out at first. But the more I talked to him, the more I liked him. He wants to be part of the action when we go back to fighting with the Federation."

"If we get the opportunity to fight da Federation… I do not know… I am, uh, content to, you know, just sit out my, ähm, six-monat banishment, and den go free," responded von Spee.

"Do you actually think that they will let you go free, von Spee?" asked Aristides sarcastically. "Oh sure. They will get you off this continent, but you will never be free. You know too much about the rebellion."

Admiral von Spee pondered what Aristides said for a few minutes, then he replied, "Maybe you is right, ja, Aristides."

"Oh, by the way," said Aristides after he paused for a minute, "I have been thinking about our escape. Do you want to hear my plan?"

"Sure. Vat is it, hm?" responded von Spee.

"When we first came to the Forbidden Continent, I checked out the radio. It seems to work fine and has a good range. Maybe we should use it as a beacon," said Aristides.

"A beacon? I do not verstehen, eh?" asked von Spee.

"I'm sure that the rebel fleet captains know by now that we were taken prisoner. If you were the Federation, where would you keep the two of us?"

"On dis side of da Beta Wormhole, on da planet Beyond. Wait a minute! I would also think dat we would be kept on da Forbidden Continent!" shouted Admiral von Spee.

"Very good, von Spee. It seems reasonable to presume that the rebel fleet would come to the same conclusion and make some attempt to rescue us."

"How can you be sure?" asked von Spee in a skeptical tone of voice.

"Well, none of the captains from the old mothballed fleet excelled in leadership, so there is no one to take our place. I imagine the rebel captains are in panic. They know that if they lose this war, they will be tried as war criminals, since all of them have been complicit in 'spacing' prisoners of war."

"Okay," said von Spee. "Let us say, maybe some rebel ships, they get, uh, through ze Beta Wormhole. How zey will find us, hmmm? Since ze Forbidden Continent is very big place, ja?" asked von Spee.

Aristides pondered a bit, then said, "I noted that the Judge was lenient on you during sentencing. He may even pity you a bit, with your altered brain and all. Let's say that you are starting to lose your mind because of your isolation on the Forbidden Continent. So, you set up daily conversations over the radio with a Naval Psychiatrist on Paradisus continent. During those conversations you can slip in something that identifies who you are. If a rebel ship is on this side of the Beta Wormhole, they would pick up the transmission. They might even recognize your German accent."

"Might work!" said von Spee. "Ich am feeling a little bit crazy, ja? Let us, uh, give it a try, ja!"

***

Buzz, static, whine…

"Hello, Dr. Gorchev, dis is Admiral von Spee."

"How has your day gone so far?"

"I had, um, that same, uh, nightmare again last night, ja? You know, um, de one about my, uh, defeat at de Falkland Islands."

"Did you do the cognitive recognition exercise I taught you?" asked Dr. Gorchev.

"Ja, I sure did, but it, uh, no help it seem," said von Spee in a plaintive tone of voice.

"Keep working at it. Eventually you will not have this nightmare. How about the rest of your day?"

"I can-no stand leben in dis underground bucker, ja, mit Aristides on da Forbidden Continent…"

Buzz, static.

***

Meanwhile, on board the rebel ship-of-the-line *Peru*:

"Captain DeVolmer, did you hear that radio transmission?" asked the Communication Officer.

"No. Play it back to me," replied Capt. DeVolmer.

Buzz, static, whine...

"Hello, Dr. Gorchev, dis is Admiral von Spee."

"How has your day gone so far?"

"I had, um, that same, uh, nightmare again last night, ja? You know, um, de one about my, uh, defeat at de Falkland Islands."

"Did you do the cognitive recognition exercise I taught you?"

"Ja, I sure did, but it, uh, no help it seem."

"Keep working at it. Eventually you will not have this nightmare. How about the rest of your day?"

"I can-no stand leben in dis underground bucker, ja, mit Aristides on da Forbidden Continent..."

Buzz, static.

"We found them!" yelled Capt. DeVolmer. "Can you get a fix on their location?"

"The computer just finished locating the origin of the signal. It is North 12 degrees, 47 minutes, 32 seconds latitude and 124 degrees, 14 minutes, and 48 seconds longitude," replied the Communication Officer.

"Helmsman, set a course for those coordinates! Order the marines to man their transport and to set their landing course to these coordinates!" shouted Capt. DeVolmer.

After the marine transport went to the surface, the captain waited about an hour and heard nothing from the marines. He finally lost patience and contacted them.

"Did you find Aristides and Admiral von Spee yet?"

"We found them 45 minutes ago," answered the young lieutenant.

"Why haven't you returned?"

"We have a problem, or should I say, we have an additional passenger to bring up. Hold on… Let me talk to Aristides. Okay… I'm putting Aristides on the comm now," replied the lieutenant.

"Capt. DeVolmer, this is Aristides. We have a special guest to bring on board. He wants to be our ally. One problem: He is a bit large."

"I have the 74-gun ship-of-the-line at your disposal. We should be able to accommodate your guest… Just how big is he?"

"He has a 60-meter wingspan, and his body is 20 meters long. Oh, by the way: He has seven heads," said Aristides, who could hardly restrain himself from laughing.

"Say again? I don't think I heard you right," responded a puzzled Captain DeVolmer.

"I forgot to tell you. Our guest is a dragon."

"Let me talk to my marine lieutenant again… Lieutenant, confirm what Aristides just told me."

"Well, Sir, our guest is a very large dragon. The dragon seems to be safe and should not be a threat. His name is Abraxas," said the young lieutenant. "I think he would fit quite nicely on the Engineering Deck of the *Peru*. He will have to fold himself up a bit to fit on the Marine Transport, but the dragon seems to be okay with that for the short trip back to the *Peru*."

***

After Aristides, Admiral von Spee, and Abraxas were transported to the 74-gun *Peru*, they and the two escort frigates (one of the frigates was the captured FNS *Buenos Aires*) made their way to the gate of the Beta Wormhole. Capt. DeVolmer was not sure how to gain passage through the wormhole at first, but he developed a plan that he thought had a good chance of succeeding. As he came near to the wormhole gate, on the far side of the planet Beyond's moon, he brought Capt. Horrocks from the brig to the bridge.

"Okay, Capt. Horrocks, you are our one chance for us to get through the Beta Wormhole. Do this right, and you and your crew will go free. Mess this up, and I will see that each of your crew members are 'spaced' in front of your eyes, starting with your girlfriend. Do we have a deal?" whispered Capt. DeVolmer into Capt. Horrocks' ear.

"Yes," whispered Capt. Horrocks.

"Here is what I want you to say when we get to the wormhole gate: 'This is Capt. Horrocks of the FNS *Buenos Aires*. I am escorting these old, obsolete rebel ships out of the Beyond system and onto the Sagittarius A* Black Hole for scrapping out. Request permission to enter the gate.' Do you understand?" said Capt. DeVolmer.

"I can do that," responded Capt. Horrocks, as he looked down in shame.

When they reached the gate to the Beta Wormhole, Capt. Horrocks, with Capt. DeVolmer standing next to him with a pistol to his head, got on the comm and said, "This is Capt. Horrocks of the FNS *Buenos Aires*. I am escorting these old, obsolete rebel ships out of the Beyond system and to the Sagittarius A* Black Hole for scrapping out. Request permission to enter the gate. The security code is bb#964a2"

Then the voice on the other end responded, "Hey Horrocks, this is Ikram! You know, we were bunkmates at the Academy."

Capt. DeVolmer pulled Horrocks closer and whispered, "Go ahead and have a little chat with Ikram, but sound normal."

"Hello, Ikram! I didn't know you were the gatekeeper at the wormhole. Do you like your posting?"

"It is okay, but very boring. I wanted to get on a ship like you when the hostilities broke out, but they say my skills are in critical need, now that the space fortress is gone. Hey, turn on the comm visual scan. I want to see your ugly face," joked Ikram.

Capt. DeVolmer leaned close into Horrocks and whispered, "Tell him the visual scan is broken."

"I'm sorry, Ikram. The visual scan is down for maintenance. You know that frigates get low maintenance priority compared to ships-of-the-line."

"I hear you! Gatekeeping is even a lower priority. Next time you come through and have some time, stop by my cabin so we can talk about old times," said Ikram in a disappointed tone.

"Look forward to it. Signing out," responded Capt. Horrocks.

"Very good, Horrocks. When we get to the other side of the black hole, we will set you, your ship, and your crew free," said Capt. DeVolmer in a patronizing tone.

"But the *Buenos Aires* does not have enough tritium and deuterium fuel for the return trip," responded Horrocks in desperation.

"Well, then. You will need to send out a distress signal to the fleet for them to come and get you. I do hope they can reach you before the black hole swallows you," replied Capt. DeVolmer with a chuckle.

***

Back at the Admiralty, the Naval Psychiatrist Dr. Gorchev was in a tizzy. She finally tracked down a captain that worked with the Joint Chiefs of Staff, and pleaded, "I have been unable to reach the prisoner, Admiral von Spee. I hope he is okay. He was having a tough time psychologically on the Forbidden Continent."

"Don't worry about it, Doctor. We will send a shuttle over to him and Aristides next week to check up on them. Their well-being is not the highest priority right now. We lost one of our frigates near the black hole, and the investigation is taking up all our resources at the Admiralty."

***

Leslie Jones, Myron Abbot, Jennifer Bo, and Robert Hays were sitting at a table in a banquet room in a plush restaurant on the planet Beyond, reminiscing about everything that had taken place. Suddenly, Myron stood up, and holding his glass of wine in the air, he proposed a toast:

"Everyone be quiet! That's better. I would like to propose a toast to my two good friends, Robert and Leslie, who are now 'one flesh' in marriage: 'L'chaim!' which is Hebrew for 'To life.'"

Then Myron carefully set his wine glass on the floor and crushed it with his boot. Everyone in the banquet room shouted either "L'chaim!" or "To life!"

Leslie and Robert simply ignored the crowd and kissed.

The End,

Of the Beginning,

Of the End.

Jack Gerard

Oracle of the Federation

www.ingramcontent.com/pod-product-compliance
Lightning Source LLC
Chambersburg PA
CBHW071218300726
48975CB00002B/266